The Jump Ship

Adventures of a Jump Space Accountant

Book 5

Andrew Moriarty

Andrew Moriarty

This is a work of fiction.

The character of Scott Russell is based, with permission, on my good friend Scott Russell, USMC. Semper Fi Buddy!

The character of Vincent Pletcher is based, with permission, on my good friend Vince Pletcher. If you have some money, need a spaceship, and don't ask too many questions, Vince is your guy.

Admiral Edmunds/Lieutenant Edmunds shares a name with Colonel Bryan Edmunds, USAF, retired. I will leave it up to his former squadron mates which rank from this book properly reflects his competence.

Other names, characters, businesses, places, events and incidents are either the products of the author's imagination or used in a fictitious manner. Any resemblance to actual persons, living or dead, or actual events is purely coincidental.

Special thanks to my dedicated team of beta readers – Michael R, Michael G, Peter B, Greg D, Dave W, Christopher G, Jolane W, Bryan, Scott, Tigui R, Vince, and Alex, and to my editor Samantha Pico.

CONTENTS

CHAPTER 1

The electric ground car skimmed to a stop in front of the Imperial Department of Planetary Agriculture building. Armed Militia surrounded it, facing outward, looking for threats.

An officer stepped up and opened the door. "Let's move along now. There are too many unaccounted-for guns out there."

Jose stepped out and looked around. "It's too far for anybody to hit us with a revolver. We'll be fine."

The guard shrugged. "Your call." He handed Jose a credit chip. "My bet is Vasilly."

Jose nodded, then reached back to help Dashi out of the car.

Dashi's cane clicked as he snapped it onto the stone walkway in front of him, then clicked again as he stepped forward. He stumbled, and only the younger man's swift reaction saved him from falling. The smoke swirling choked him.

"No need to rush, sir," Jose said. "Nothing will start without you. I've already been in contact with everyone and stressed your physical condition."

Dashi gestured to the uniformed group standing at the head of the stairs. "Those people are waiting. For us, Jose. Punctuality is the courtesy of kings."

"Would you like to be a king, sir?"

Dashi turned to Jose and smiled. "Do you think you could arrange that?"

"Yes, sir. I think I could, if you thought it wise."

"The student has become the master, but I will not be a

king." With great care, Dashi levered himself over a single step in the walkway.

"What will you be, then, sir?"

"What I have always been—a loyal servant of the Empire."

"Until it returns, sir?"

"It has never left. It's just been quiet for a time." Dashi paused at the base of a new set of steps. "Ladies and gentlemen, good morning. Admiral, you smell awful."

"A good Imperial welcome to you, too, Dashi," Admiral Edmunds said. "The remaining Growers set fires as we stormed the warehouses. I was on fire for a while."

"Were you able to secure the food stores?"

Edmunds turned to a soot-covered woman with a Major's insignia who was standing behind him. The insignia was shiny as if brand new.

"Not enough," she said. "Not enough."

"The power plant?" Dashi asked.

"It won't explode, but it won't send any power, either," she said. "These lights are coming from local supplies."

"Are you in control of the city?"

"There is no more organized resistance, but lots of unorganized groups are roaming around."

"I see. Any good news?" Dashi asked.

"Reports have arrived that you have somehow acquired a functioning Jump ship," Edmunds said.

"Mr. Jose has been handling that for me." Dashi turned to Jose.

"We have one," Jose said, "and it appears to be working. The crew are on their way here."

"You can't choose a crew without consulting us," Edmunds said.

"Why did you choose the Imperial Department of Agriculture for this meeting without consulting us?"

"Because it was the only Imperial building not actually on fire, and it has computer access and a room big enough to be a council chamber."

The two groups looked at each other, then Edmunds shook his head. "Neither of us have any choice. We need to work together, or we're all going to starve. Let's get to our council chamber and formalize this. Jose, here is one hundred credits, and my bet is Clarence."

Jose nodded and made a notation on his comm. Dashi looked at Jose with his "query" smile, but Jose ignored it.

Edmunds stepped up beside Dashi, and they walked down the hallway, speaking in hushed tones.

Jose and a group of officers followed. Jose seemed to know them all by name and shook each of them by the hand. Each of them chatted with him, then offered him a credit chip and a name. Their guesses included Benjamin, Alesky, Aristride, Zebediah, and many others.

The group approached a set of double doors. A stylized depiction of a group of stars, including Polaris, hovered over the door.

Armed guards slouched in front of the doors, not in Militia uniforms. Rather, they had shoulder badges from the Free Traders' Council.

A woman approached them. "Admiral. Mr. Dashi."

"Ms. Marianne," Dashi said. "Thank you for coming. We welcome your participation in this new endeavor."

"Participate or starve?" she asked.

"Just so you know, I voted 'starve' for you," Edmunds said. "Self-serving treacherous opportunists, the lot of you."

"Bonjour to you, too, Admiral," Marianne said. "The less powerful have to take the hand they are dealt—in particular, if they are caught between two more powerful allies. The question is, can we work together?"

"I've promised to work with you. I keep my promises," the admiral said.

"We can all agree on that, but I rather wish you hadn't promised to destroy the Growers' headquarters."

"I lost a lot of good men and women keeping that promise. I'm not going to betray their trust now,"

Edmunds said. He turned to the officers with him and introduced them.

"You know Mr. Jose, of course," Dashi said when Jose's turn came.

"Good to see you again, Ms. Marianne," Jose said.

"You as well, Mr. Jose. My guess is Pradeep," she said, handing him a credit chip.

Mr. Dashi gave Jose another questioning smile, and Jose, again, ignored it. Dashi frowned. Jose never ignored his questioning smiles.

A commotion rose behind them, then a new voice. "I said we have an invitation to the ceremony, and we're going to go, you Imperial turd, so get out of my way, or I'm going to shoot the lot of you."

"Ms. Nadine is here, sir," Jose said to Dashi.

"So I hear," Dashi said.

The admiral's expression blanked as he heard the voices. He started forward, running toward Nadine. He shoved the arguing guards to one side and grabbed her in a giant bear hug. He twirled her around, tears running down his cheeks, before he finally stopped and put her down.

"Well," he said, pushing away his tears. "Well," he said again. He coughed. "You look okay. Are you okay?"

"I'm fine," Nadine said.

"I heard you rammed that Grower ship."

"I hit it with Jake Stewart's patented starship grabber and food storage hook. Worked great. You should install one on all the Militia ships," Nadine said.

"Maybe I will." The admiral turned to Jake. "You're Dashi's troubleshooter—Stewart?"

"I'm Jake Stewart, yes," Jake said. "I wouldn't call myself his troubleshooter, though. More like his auditor."

"Yet, every time there is some sort of trouble involving Dashi, you seem to be nearby."

"I g-guess so," Jake said.

The admiral crossed his arms and stared at Jake. "I thought you'd be taller."

Not knowing how to respond, Jake blinked.

"Treat her well, or I'll have you killed," Edmunds said.

"Pardon?" Jake said.

"Just kidding," Edmunds said.

Jake exhaled. "Oh. Funny joke."

"Just kidding. I won't have you killed. This is personal. I'll do it myself."

"Good to see you, Mr. Stewart," Dashi said, "and you, Ms. Nadine. Have you learned a lot in the last two weeks together on that Jump ship?"

"Sir?" Jake blushed. He and Nadine had been left alone on the Jump ship for the last two weeks and had done quite a bit of exploring, albeit not always the technical type.

"Jump systems. Propulsion. Interstellar navigation," Dashi said.

"Oh, that. Yes, sir. We've learned a lot and done a lot of system tests."

"What did you think I was referring to, Mr. Stewart?" Dashi asked.

"Uh ..." Jake said.

"I protest again," Ms. Marianne said, "that they will be the crew. We should be providing a Free Trader pilot. They are much more experienced than these two."

"You will get your representatives," Jose said, "as agreed. We also agreed that the most experienced crew should be given priority. Since there have been no functional Jump ships in this system for more than eighty years, Mr. Stewart is currently the most experienced Jump system operator and engineer, so he will be going. Ms. Nadine is an experienced pilot, and they are used to working together, so she will be going as well."

"You manipulated us into this decision," Marianne said.

"Of course," Jose said. "That's my job." He smiled, looking like a younger Dashi. "Right now, it's time for the ceremony. Jake, you and Nadine are upstairs."

"Thanks, Jose," Nadine said. "Oh, and I've got Peter."

"And I'm taking nothing," Jake said.

"Nothing?" Jose asked.

"He doesn't have one. It doesn't exist," Jake replied.

All three of them looked at Dashi.

"I have no idea what you are all talking about," Dashi said. "What is this?"

"See you later, sir," Jake said. "Let's go, Nadine." With that, the two hustled off.

"Jose, I insist you tell me what's going on with these names," Dashi whispered.

Jose smiled and pointed forward. "Showtime, sir. Smile for the cameras."

They turned toward the door and marched into the temporary meeting chamber.

***

Jake and Nadine had reserved seats on a set of bleachers that overlooked the council tables.

"Nothing?" Nadine asked.

"Yes. I don't think he has another name at all."

"He can't be just 'Dashi.' He has to have some other names. A family name. A house name. A corporate extension, if nothing else."

"I have a suspicion. I think he's just 'Dashi.'"

"Why do you think that?" Nadine asked.

"Something I read a few years back. We'll find out shortly."

"Why are those women here?" Nadine pointed. "The skanky looking ones."

"Marianne? She's on the Free Traders' council now. Same with the other two- Yvette and Odette. They represent different groups," Jake said.

"They talk funny," Nadine said.

"Francais accents. Kind of sexy," Jake said.

Nadine narrowed her eyes.

"I mean, sexy, if you like that sort of thing, which I

don't of course."

Nadine glared some more.

As they spoke, the ceremony was going on below them. A master of ceremonies was speaking. "... meeting as the new emergency council of Delta. Until the Empire returns."

"Until the Empire returns," the crowd said back in chorus.

"I'm still not happy leaving that ship up there," Nadine said.

"We need a better name than 'that ship.'"

"Something could happen to it."

"You just want to be up there, playing with the controls."

"There are plenty of things I want to play with. That's just one of them," Nadine said.

Jake blushed again. "We need to test the Jump power system shunts."

"I'm willing, as long as we can do it naked," Nadine said.

Jake blushed even harder. His comm alerted him with a soft bong, and he opened the message.

"State your full legal name and all Imperial titles, for the record," the master of ceremonies said below.

Jake and Nadine listened. The chancellor was just the chancellor, and the corporate and Free Traders had no Imperial titles. Edmunds had missed his cue and was paging through his own comm. He grimaced, then turned and signaled at Jose, who was steps behind Dashi.

Jose was watching his comm as well but caught the admiral's glance and jerked his head toward the spectators' gallery, at Jake.

Jake leaned over and grabbed Nadine's arm. "Nadine, we have to get back to the ship. Now."

"Easy, tiger," she said. "There's plenty more where that came from. We ought to pace ourselves."

"Not that," Jake said. "Sensors on the ship have

detected another ship."

"There are plenty of ships in this system, Jake."

"Another Jump ship. Another Jump ship just arrived. I copied all the alerts to me, Jose, and Dashi. Dashi copied them to the admiral. We have to get up there and get more info. Now."

Nadine nodded. They stood and shoved their way to the door.

The admiral finally stood and did his part. "Bryan Edmunds, Admiral of the Delta Militia, Lieutenant in the Imperial Customs Reserve," he said.

Nadine slowed. "Imperial Customs Reserve?"

"It was the only Imperial department actually present here after the abandonment," Jake said. "At least, the only one that the computers agree there is continuity for. Wait—here's Dashi. We need to see this."

Dashi had climbed up, using his cane, and faced the Imperial seal at the front of the room. "Dashi, president of this council," he said, then sat down.

Silence ensued for a moment, then the master of ceremonies said, "Sir, the computer requires your full legal designation for registration as well as all Imperial titles."

Dashi sighed and looked down at Jose, who gave him a bland smile.

"Fine. I am the Count Von Dashi, Warden of the Marches, Count of the Greater Cluster, Knight of the Realm, and seventh of the house of succession to Pradeep IV. Heir of the Empire."

The council gasped, and murmuring spread across the room.

"Emperor's testicles," Jake said, "do you know what this means?"

"He's claiming to be one of the heirs to the Empire?" Nadine said. "Can that be true?"

"Computer would have rejected it by now if he wasn't. But what's more important than that?"

"What?"

"I just won the bet. He only has one name."

CHAPTER 2

"Let us proceed," Dashi said. The group from the council meeting bunched together as they flowed down the stairs in front of the agriculture building. Everyone had agreed the jump ships could be ignored for the moment while the temporary council got a reading on what was still working on Delta and what wasn't. Jake, Dashi, Jose and Nadine walked together.

"Nadine and I have to get on board our jump ship, sir," Jake said. "As soon as possible."

"For which you'll need either a working shuttle, or a train ride to our lifting body," Dashi said. "We'll try to walk to the shuttle port first. If it cannot be brought into service, then we'll have to get you across town to the monorail station." A shotgun boomed in the distance. "If we can. We may need to wait for an escort."

"I've already got a crew in mind sir," Jake said.

"We will discuss your crew issues later, Mr. Stewart," Dashi said. "We may have to adjust things as circumstances dictate. And we will have to take our allies into account as well."

"And the other Jump ship sir?" Jake asked.

"One problem at a time, Mr. Stewart. Excuse me, I need to speak to Jose for a moment." Jake dropped back next to Nadine as Jose and Dashi muttered together.

Why can't we take ground cars?" Marianne asked, starting across the street. She stopped when gunshots rang out in the distance.

"Are the Free Traders too lazy for a little walking?" Major Shutt asked. "Or scared of guns?"

Marianne made a rude gesture with her finger. "Safer for the Imperial Council."

"Too much debris from the fires in the streets and too many pot shots from the rioters," Shutt said. "We can't risk the few ground cars we have. And they're not an Imperial Council. They're just the temporary working group of the larger Delta committee."

"Walks like an Imperial Council, smells like an Imperial Council. They're a council."

"They're only the Imperial Council if you believe Dashi is the Emperor," Shutt said.

"I notice you didn't vote against it, nor did the admiral."

"Wanting good governance is not the same as accepting that Dashi is the Emperor reincarnated."

The admiral, Marianne, and their personal guards and aides were walking with Dashi's group. Glass and debris crunched underfoot as they walked."Why are there still shootings? Why hasn't the Militia done their job and regained control?" Marianne asked.

"Organized resistance has ended," Shutt said. "But there is a great deal of unorganized resistance still in play. We're working on it."

A fusillade of revolver shots echoed off the buildings. In the distance, the boom of a shotgun answered.

"Seems pretty organized to me," Marianne said. She stopped to climb up over a pile of bricks in the street. "Organized enough to set fire to buildings." She picked up a piece of the debris. "What's made of bricks? I thought the Empire only built using concrete."

"Front of that building fell over," Jose said, pointing to a nearby warehouse. "Building is concrete, but the facade was fake."

"So, who is this 'unorganized resistance?'" Marianne asked. "Rogue Galactic Growing troops?"

"No," Shutt said. "Those mostly got killed when their main station blew up or in the fighting dirtside. The few

11

that were left in orbit were dealt with."

"Dealt with how?" Marianne asked.

"Thrown out of an air lock," Shutt said.

"Your idea of Imperial justice is to throw people out of air locks?"

"Cool your jets," Shutt said. "I didn't throw anybody out of anything. Most of the time, it was their own people or the survivors of an assault."

"So, it's Militia then?" Marianne asked.

Shutt kicked a brick. It bounced off a wall in a cloud of red dust. "Not Militia. There are only a few small groups of troops left unaccounted for."

"Causing problems in orbit?"

"No, the orbital stations are secure. But two cutters and a shuttle escaped with officers from the officers' council."

"Where are they?"

"That's need-to-know information," Edmunds said, hopping down off a pile of bricks behind them. "You don't need to know."

"Use my shoulder, sir," Jose said to Dashi.

Dashi was having problems climbing down the pile. He slipped when he got to the bottom, a firm grip on Jose's shoulder saving him.

"The shuttle crashed on the south continent," Dashi said. He sat, panting. "A dozen members of the former officers' council and thirty-seven rebel troopers are there. That accounts for all of the rebel officers that were on planet. They have food and supplies and can stay there pretty much indefinitely. But they don't have any way to get back north. Not right now."

"Thank you, Mr. Dashi." Marianne turned to the admiral. "I thought if we're together on this council, we're supposed to share information. Why are you keeping secrets?"

Edmunds ignored her. "How do you know this?" he asked Dashi.

"As far as the cutters," Jose said. "One cutter is hiding

in a high orbit. There are thirty-two on board. It has all the former members of the officers' council that escaped the orbital fighting and a few other ranks. They are having supply problems and will have to make a move soon. The other is docked at an abandoned outer rim station. They are awaiting developments. In five days, they have a vote scheduled regarding whether to come back or not. Their vote will go in favor of returning. There is only the crew of four on that one."

"You sound pretty sure of those facts," Admiral Edmunds said. "Again, how do you know all this?"

"It doesn't matter how I know. I do. And before you ask, yes, I'm sure." Jose smiled. "How, well, I guess you would say that's need-to-know. And you don't need to know." He typed on his screen. "In fact, for everybody, here's a list of all the rebel officers and where they are located right now."

"Well," Marianne said, examining the list sent to her comm, "I'm sure the admiral has a plan to deal with these rogue elements. Since he is in charge of security and all?"

Shutt and the admiral exchanged glasses. "I'm already taking care of it, sir."

"You going to toss them out an air lock?" Marianne asked.

"There will be no tossing out of air locks," Edmunds said. "First, we'll give them a decent meal. Second, they get a trial. Third, a verdict."

"That's quite forgiving of you, Admiral," Jose said.

"I'm a forgiving type of guy," the admiral said. "Food, trial, verdict. That's the proper way." He smiled again. "Then we throw them out of the air lock."

***

The group passed another burned-out warehouse. The next street was unmarked by fire, but all the buildings were completely dark until they crossed the perimeter of the fusion plant complex. Militia guards with revolvers guarded the main gate.

"I thought that the fusion plant was running?" Jose pointed toward the plant as they rounded the corner. "At least for lighting. Doesn't that steam mean that the cooling systems are operational?"

One of the far towers arced to the ground with a crackle of blue light.

Dashi leaned against a wall. "It appears to be operational, at least in the sense of providing power."

"Sir," Jose said, "perhaps it's best if you wait here, and I'll see what's happening."

Dashi slumped against the fence. "Perhaps that is best. Please find out what's happening. I will wait here."

"I'll come to keep an eye on you," Shutt said.

"And I'll come to keep an eye on her," Marianne said.

"Sir," Jose said. He, Marianne, and Shutt walked across the yard. Marianne eyed Shutt. Shutt eyed her right back. Jose ignored them.

"Why is nobody trying to fix things?" Marianne asked. "Do you see anybody at work?"

"I see a big yard full of giant metal grid things, lots of wires, and a bunch of twisted metal poles," Jose said, peering around. "And a burning truck with six firemen not trying to put the fire out. That's an electrically powered truck. We could repair it. Shouldn't somebody put that fire out? We could use that truck in the future." He sniffed. "What's that smell?"

Shutt pointed to the firemen in the distance. "Let's go ask them," she said. "What does that smell remind you of?"

"Some sort of fire, I guess."

"Ever overcooked your dinner?"

"No."

"No?" Shutt snickered. "You're a perfect cook?"

"I'm no cook at all," Jose said. "I spend most of my time in orbit. We eat from trays. You put them in the microwave, push a button, and a minute later, they're cooked."

"You never cooked anything on a campfire or something?"

"What's a campfire?"

"You've never been camping?" Shutt said. Jose shook his head. "I'll take you camping someday. Hey, Pat."

"Clarisse, my favorite trained killer. How are you?" a fireman with 'Dunlop' on his uniform said. He stood with his arms crossed, watching the fire.

"Don't be rude, Pat. I haven't killed anybody in, well, hours."

"I'll keep that in mind and give you a call if I see somebody needs killing," Dunlop said. "Doesn't happen often, though. How about if I contact you if we just find somebody who needs beating up?"

"Beat 'em up yourself. I only do the hard stuff. What's going on? Is the reactor shut down?"

"For now. We could probably get it back online soon, but we don't need the power right now."

"Because we think that giving people lights to read or work by is a bad thing?" Jose asked.

"And who might you be, my good friend?" Dunlop asked.

"My name is Jose, and I work for the council." Jose pointed his thumb over his shoulder. The admiral and Dashi had remained by the entrance, conversing with each other.

"The council? Wow, that must be exciting. Come down to give us advice on how to do things, have you?"

Jose smiled at him. He was trying for Dashi's number five smile. Interested but nonthreatening. "No, sir. I don't know much about electrical power. I'm here to learn. I'm just interested in what you're waiting for." He sniffed. "There's that smell again. Major Shutt said it was like something that I would get at a campfire?"

Shutt smirked at Dunlop. "Mr. Jose has never been camping. He's never seen a campfire. Nor smelled one."

"If that's a campfire, it smells horrible. Why would you camp with that?" Jose asked.

"I don't," Dunlop said. "Unless I'm really unlucky."

Jose sniffed again. "The council has tasked me with collecting information. Can I walk over to that truck and check its registration for our records?"

"You want to walk over there?" Dunlop asked. "To the truck? And check the registration?"

"Yes, please. Would it be too much trouble?"

Dunlop laughed. "Funny." Jose kept smiling. "You're serious?"

"Only if it doesn't cause difficulties."

"For me. Not at all. You three"—Dunlop pointed at three firemen loitering beside them—"one of you suit up and go with him."

"Who?" one asked.

"You decide," Dunlop said.

The three did a quick round of rock-paper-scissors, and the tallest, a man with 'Evay' on his uniform, lost. He turned to Jose. "Follow me." Evay donned insulated rubber boots over his heavy jacket, a thick ceramic helmet, then heavy rubber gloves. He picked up a ceramic pole with a hook on the end and waddled toward the truck.

Jose matched him step-for-step and analyzed his gloves. "Do you have to wear that outfit all the time?"

Evay made a muffled sound, which Jose interpreted as 'no.' "But, then why are you wearing it now?" Jose asked. He looked at the rest of Evay's uniform. It was akin to a hard-sided space suit, mostly made of rubber and ceramics.

A light snowfall had occurred the night before, just enough to cover the ground. The area adjacent to Evay was wet, and the snow had been walked over, but the white blanket was pristine around the truck and all the twisted metal beams ahead.

Jose stopped. Evay stopped as well. Jose looked at the burning truck, the giant yard, the twisted pieces of metal. He turned and looked back at all the fireman, who were standing back. He examined the unmarked snow in front of him, frowned at Evay, then glanced down at his feet. He selected a metal bar from the debris and flung it as far as he could, aiming for the front of the truck. It got close, followed by cracking and a blue flash. Electricity arced from several of the vertical metal poles and snapped into the thrown metal. The metal exploded, and pieces of red-hot shrapnel flew off.

One of them impacted Jose's arm. He yelled and waved his arm. The fireman waddled to him, grabbed his arm, and used his rubber gloves to knock the red-hot metal to the ground.

Jose watched it drop in place. It smoldered on the ground and appeared to have melted. He turned to Evay, nodded, and walked back, flexing his arm and shaking his hand.

Shutt was waiting for him. "Having fun?"

"This suit is ruined," Jose said. "I just bought it."

"To celebrate you joining the council."

"Council members should dress in a certain style," Jose said, "as befits the position."

"The position of electric lineman befits heavy non-conductive clothing," Shutt said. "You should perhaps pay more attention to that."

"This is an electric power-switching station," Jose said.

"It's not an electric power-switching station, it's *the* electric power-switching station," Shutt said. "Only one connected directly to the fusion plants."

"And it's heavily damaged," Jose agreed. "Can it be repaired?"

"Maybe," Dunlop said.

"Maybe?" Jose said.

"According to the power guys," Dunlop said, "they don't have all the parts for it. They need some computer modules and some big switching bars. The bars could be fabricated. Somewhere. Where to get the other parts, we have no idea. Doesn't matter yet cause we need the bars done first."

"So fabricate them. Wait. Fabricator needs power, doesn't it?" Jose said.

"Glad we have council-trained guys like you around to help us with those hard questions," Dunlop said. "But yeah, first, they're trying to cut this station out of the circuit, so they can send power direct to the city, where the fabricator is. They're going to bypass this mess and get the big printers at the university enough electricity so they can be up and running. Then they'll fabricate the parts, bring 'em here, somehow, and replace 'em, and bring it back online. Once it's online, they can spin the second reactor up. And then deal with the other systems."

"But they can't turn the main reactor off because they need power to start it back up," Jose guessed.

"Right," Dunlop said. "They think they can do something with batteries or something like that. I don't understand that part. You'll have to talk to them."

"Can't we fabricate these parts in space? There's printers and foundries up there, and they have their own fusion plants."

"I don't know anything about that," Dunlop said. "But how would we get the fixed parts here? We can't exactly carry them."

"How indeed," Jose said. "I'll work on that. Have the people who did this been identified?"

"Yes," Shutt said. "We know their names."

"Well, they need to be punished."

The flames on the truck popped and roared. Smoke drifted toward Jose. It smelled like ... like pork that he'd had once at a restaurant.

"Punished?" Shutt turned to the truck. "That part's already been taken care of."

CHAPTER 3

The Militia ship's control room was crowded. All four consoles were occupied, and about twenty officers and a dozen enlisted ranks occupied the back, on a ship whose life support was rated for half that many.

"We're short on fuel, food, medicine, everything. We can't stay in this orbit forever," Jammy said. On paper, he was the chief pilot, but that was because of rank, not experience. The screen in front of him flickered. "And that voltage regulator isn't working."

"We're a long way out here," Daav said. He wasn't the most senior of the four pilots in the control room, but he was driving because he had the most hours on cutters. "And this ship is hard used. We should expect some issues."

"If we over-voltage the environmental controls, we'll suffocate," Jammy said.

"Hasn't happened yet," Daav said.

"Look at that Jump ship. See? That burn will put him around the Dragon, high around the Dragon. And then, at the top of that orbit, he'll fire again and head out into space." Jammy sniffed. "You stink."

"You think you smell like oranges? I've never seen this type of orbit before." Daav's fingers made a tapping sound as he changed screens.

"Of course not. None of our ships could leave the rings. We didn't have the fuel or provision for it."

"And we do now?"

Jammy turned to the two Militia behind him. "Close the hatch."

Perlins, a shuttle pilot, was closest to the hatch. She leaned back and shut it.

Jammy continued. "If we follow them into that orbit, we have to somehow take that Jump ship intact. Otherwise, we can't get back to Delta. Not in this crate. Once we're out of the Dragon's orbit, we'll have an Imperial anus of a time coming back, if it's even possible."

"What happens if we can't come back?" Perlins said.

"I don't care if we can come back. We're taking that ship, jumping to the next system, and starting life over. This war thing didn't work out. The officers' council was a bunch of Imperial turds."

"Don't let them hear you say that," Perlins said, looking up from her console.

"That's why they're back there, and we're up here. We've got to take control of things. We need to set up a boarding party and suit up to go get that Jump ship. How many people do we have on board?"

"Not including us? Thirty-two."

"How many would we normally have life support for?"

"Ten. Twelve?"

Jammy raised his eyebrows.

"Six," Perlins said. "Normally." The lights in the control room flickered again. "Zero if the power fails."

"So." Jammy spread his hand. "You folks may not have figured it out, but we're all dead if we don't turn around and head back to a station right now."

"We could find a small station, go hang out there," Daav said.

"Go ahead. Let me know what you find. By now, Dashi and company has warned every station in the rings that there are rogue Militia elements out there. We could storm a station, not dock with one. And if we storm it and damage anything, then we'll die along with the station people."

"We should never have left Landing," Perlins said.

"Have you seen what's going on there? The whole

place is burning," Jammy said.

"They burned the food stores. Why burn those?"

"Because they're dumb. Dumb like those officers back there who started this war."

"You didn't have to follow them."

"Neither did you. But we did."

Krikweigh, a tug pilot in the back seat, spoke up. "I'm watching that course. We can catch that ship. Not come to zero-zero rest, but pretty close. Put a bunch of us out on the hull with suits, hop over. If we can board, we stand a good chance. I've got a course here."

"Never work," Jammy said. "Jump from ship to ship?"

"Did it all the time in tugs," Krikweigh said. "None of you hotshot pilots could dock worth an Imperial anus. I was always having to jump with a line, then get a chain to crank you in."

"Clearly, none of these pilots were as skilled as me," Daav said. "My dockings are always as soft as a tabbo's fur."

"I watched you crack a magnetic grabber at drop seventeen before," Jammy said. "And I recall you actually having to be winched in at Ring-230 once."

"That's because they didn't load enough fuel for my approach," Daav said.

"No, it was because you made seventeen approaches, without getting even close to that station, and burned through all the reserves."

"Shut up, you two," Perlins said. "If I understand this course plot correctly, we have to decide what to do now."

The other three officers peered at their consoles. "Anyone have anything else to say about this?" Daav asked.

"Yeah, it's weird having four pilots on the same ship," Perlins said.

"The last four rebel pilots," Jammy said.

"I think the word they will use is 'mutineer,'" Daav said.

"Looks good to me," Perlins said. "Everybody?" The other three nodded. "Setting it up, then."

"Okay, we chase them. No shooting," Jammy said. "Then we get out on the hull in suits, power across, and try to board. Let's assume we take them. Won't we have the same problems with provisions that we have now?"

"It's a bigger ship," Perlins said, "and I assume designed for longer voyages."

"Will they have enough food for all of us?" Jammy asked.

"Enough for the four of us," Perlins said. "I'll bet they do."

"What about the thirty-two on board back there?"

"I have a plan to reduce those numbers."

CHAPTER 4

"So, your Imperial majesty," Admiral Edmunds said. He and Dashi, accompanied by the others, lounged near the power-switching station gate. None of the occasional electric arcs went that far. "We're in control of the city. The rebels are vanquished, and the emergency is over. We are triumphant. What are your decrees, Emperor designate?"

"There is the small matter of fires burning out of control," Dashi said, "senior elements of the rebels unaccounted for, and whatever problems Marianne, Shutt, and Jose report to us. All of which were the responsibility of the Militia. The remaining Militia, at least." Dashi tapped his fingers as he listed each of the Militia's sins.

"We're looking into those," Edmunds said. "Major Shutt has a line on the missing rebels, and we're putting out the fires."

Dashi pointed at the approaching group. "From the look on Jose's face, we are overcome by other issues."

"Pessimistic guy, your Mr. Jose, isn't he, your Imperial majesty," Edmunds said.

"It's just Dashi, Admiral," Dashi said. "I'm not an Imperial majesty."

"Computer says otherwise."

"It just verified my identity."

"Now you're claiming that you're not in line to the throne?"

Dashi gave up leaning against the fence and sat on the ground. "I was when I was born, according to my father, but things have certainly changed in the last eighty years since he was born. If any of the Imperial princes succeeded, then their descendants will automatically supersede me."

"Never met your father," Edmunds said. "Was he Emperor, too?"

"No."

"And yet, that's how you introduced yourself to the meeting."

"It's my only title of merit," Dashi said. "I said I was one of the heirs, and I am. We need some unity to bring things together at the meeting. Your officers will only follow orders from Imperial officials, for example."

"I'm an Imperial official," Edmunds said. "They can follow my orders instead. If you're not the Emperor, then I don't owe any loyalty to you. Claiming to be the Emperor without justification makes you a traitor."

"I am not a traitor," Dashi said. "If the Emperor is still alive, if an Emperor is still alive, that would be treason, yes. But I'm just pointing out my potential position in the hierarchy."

"We have no indication that there is not a legitimate Emperor out there." Edmunds stood and paced back and forth.

"We have no indication there is, either." Dashi said. "The council has elected me its leader, Emperor or no Emperor. I currently make no claim to being any sort of Imperial personage. Let's move on. We should look at our present problems."

"Well, if you're not an Emperor, I don't work for you," Edmunds said. "Nor do I work for the council. As leader of the Militia, I report to the senior Imperial official in-system. And if you're not an Imperial official, you don't have any Imperium, so I don't have to listen to you at all."

A murmur swept through the group surrounding Dashi and Edmunds. Jake and Nadine leaned against the fence, along with all the other minions, watching the proceedings.

Nadine leaned over to Jake and whispered, "What's this

Imperium thing?"

"Executive power granted by the Senate," Jake whispered back. "Let's someone act in the name of the Emperor. There's two types, limited, such as was granted to a general or admiral which allowed them to command troops, or unlimited, which was granted to a sector governor or official, which allowed them to be both the military and civil head. But there were different types of limited ones as well, for example, the Imperial rescript of 237—"

"Holy boring Imperial history, Jakey," Nadine said. "Is there no topic that you can't totally beat to death with useless information?"

Jake contemplated. "No, I don't think so."

Dashi was still talking. "…for the good of the Delta Corporation," he said.

"No Imperium, no command," Edmunds said. "If you're not the Emperor, if you're not claiming to be the Emperor, then I'm the senior official in-system. I'm calling the shots from now on, regardless of your many theoretical titles," Edmunds said.

Jose, and the others arrived. Jose bent over Dashi and helped him stand. Dashi murmured a few words to him. Jose turned and faced off against Edmunds. "If there are questions of authority, then there is some change in the status of Mr. Dashi's many titles that is relevant, Admiral."

"What change would that be, young Mr. Jose?" Edmunds asked.

"Well, firstly, Mr. Dashi has been appointed the Chairman of the TGI Corporation."

"Who appointed him?" Edmunds asked.

"I did, sir."

Jake and the others leaning against the fence stood to look at Jose. Edmunds stepped forward until he was in Jose's space.

Jose didn't back off, so the admiral leaned in. "You don't have authority to appoint the chairman of the volunteer library, never mind the chair of the board of TGI."

Jose didn't move. "He was elected at the last general meeting. Well, not exactly, I was elected as the head of the exploratory committee to handle emergency appointments, and I elected him."

"I attended no such meeting," Dashi said.

"Of course not, sir," Jose said. He kept his eyes on the admiral. "This was during the—er, attempted occupation of TGI Main station by rogue Militia elements. As they approached, the board of directors fled the station. The board enacted certain emergency protocols, some regarding continuity of management. They also transferred their proxies to me at that time."

Edmunds glared at him. "You expect me to believe you had a board meeting in the middle of a battle?"

"A short one."

"Who attended?"

"I did."

"Just you, youngster? So, no proof of anything?"

"Our vice president of security, Mr. Singh, also attended, but as he had no proxies and could cast no votes, it's hardly relevant that he was there. We recorded the entire event, however."

"Jose," Dashi said. "What was the result of the meeting?"

"Given the current emergency and the failure of the existing chairman to answer repeated comm calls and his departure from our headquarters, the attending shareholders voted to appoint an emergency search committee to locate a new chairman."

"Who was on this committee?" Dashi asked.

"Myself."

"Just you."

"Yes."

"And then?"

Jose finally broke eye contact with the admiral and

surveyed the entire council. "The committee met, and after an exhaustive search, recommended Mr. Dashi as the new chairman of TGI."

"You can't have a meeting with just yourself," Edmunds said. "There has to be a quorum of votes."

"There was. I had, uh, extracted proxies from council members and others as they fled the station. Since I had the use of those proxies, there was a sufficient quorum of voters. I proposed myself for the committee and voted for myself, then conducted the search and gave a recommended list to the stockholders. Who, Whom? Were also myself. Myselves?"

"How many people on the list?" Edmunds asked.

"Just Mr. Dashi, Admiral," Jose said.

"You can't have a list with just one person," Marianne said.

Jose smiled at her. Marianne smiled back. Jose continued. "The corporate articles require a list be submitted. They do not specify a minimum number of candidates. The list was presented to the stockholders present, who was also me, who voted, and chose Mr. Dashi as the new chairman of TGI. Quod erat demonstrandum."

"Well, congrats to Dashi, then," Edmunds said. "Why do we care?"

"Because the Delta charter parcels out certain honorary Imperial offices to the chair of the boards of the original founding companies. Mostly for administrative reasons, relating to their original contributions, of course. For example, the chairman of Tri-System medical, if they were alive, would automatically be appointed a lieutenant in the public health corps."

Edmunds rubbed his forehead. "Wait for it," he said to Shutt, who had come to stand beside him. "Just wait for it. What's next, Jose?"

"Well, the chairman of TGI is appointed a senior inspector in the customs reserve, and since you claim that your authority over the Militia comes from your Imperium as the senior officer in a line formation, and you are simply a junior customs inspector, Dashi being a senior customs inspector ..."

"He's my boss. You made him my boss," Edmunds said. "Even if he isn't an Emperor—the Emperor, whatever, I have to listen to him.

"That's screwed up," Nadine whispered to Jake.

"The man is a genius," Jake whispered back. "I stand in the presence of a master."

"All right," Edmunds said. "It was a fantasy to think I could outmaneuver you, anyway. And truthfully, the Militia haven't done so well running things. Time to give somebody else a try. You think you can run things, youngster? Go ahead." Edmunds turned. "What do we do first, Dashi?"

"We must get the main part of our infrastructure working," Dashi said. "That is our first priority."

"What about your lifting-body thing you have hidden away at the end of the monorail line?" Shutt asked.

"We need heavy-lift to orbit," Dashi said. "Our lifting body is very small, and there is only room for a small amount of cargo. Even the shuttles here in Landing mostly moved limited amounts of personnel. We need the high capacity of the mass drivers to keep all our orbital citizens supplied."

"What about this other Jump ship?" Marianne asked. "That is a surprise. We had no Jump ships in-system for eighty years, and now, we have two."

"The new Jump ship is not answering comms," Jose said. "It looks to be conducting some sort of reconnaissance. It's not in the way, so we can ignore it for now. We need to concentrate on how to get our infrastructure back up. We can worry about visitors later. There is a working console in the shuttle control room. Give me a few minutes there to check some numbers, and I'll have a proposal."

"And our Jump ship?" Marianne asked.

"As promised, you'll get your representatives on it. As will the admiral. Once we have a crew on it, they can see if it's operational, and we'll decide what to do."

"Who put you in charge?" Edmunds asked.

"I did," Dashi said. "I'm the head of the council. Everyone, including you, has agreed to this. I think Mr. Jose's plan is the best for now, so let's get out of this cold and smoke and see what he has to say."

"One other thing," Jose said.

"Yes, Jose?" Dashi said.

"The admiral expressed interest in some other topics."

"What topics?" Edmunds said.

"The admiral had inquired about the local volunteer library. As your assistant, with your current position, I have certain appointments in my gift. I'm pleased to announce that Admiral Edmunds is the new chairman of the volunteer library lending committee. Next meeting is tomorrow at 08:00."

"You've put me in charge of library books?" the admiral asked.

"Only overdue ones," Jose said. "But there are a lot. It's a position of great responsibility. I hope you're up to it."

CHAPTER 5

"Where are we going sergeant?" Chaudhari said. The squad of Militia troopers was marching through Landing, dragging two men along.

"Shut up," Sergeant Russell said. He sniffed the air and turned down a side street. "This way."

"Are we going to Militia headquarters?"

"I said shut up," Russell said. "We're marching. That's all you needed to know."

"March or die, that's the spirit," the first prisoner said. His name was Molina, and he had sold weapons.

"You shut up, too, or else," Russell said.

"Or else? That's a pretty scary threat. But kind of nonspecific, don't you think?"

Russell stopped and surveyed his squad. Eight troopers, including him, wore soiled Militia overalls over standard Militia skin suits. It was cold enough that they were glad for the skin suits. Four of them had standard Militia belt holsters with revolvers in them. The other four had odd, mismatched outfits. Two had revolvers stuck in them, one had a thigh holster, and the other had some sort of cross chest thing.

"Kim Two, put that one, Molina, on the ground," Russell said, gesturing at the first prisoner.

"Yes, Sergeant," Kim Two said. Two Kims had joined the squad, both female, and she was the second Kim to have joined, so she was Kim Two. She pushed Molina to his knees.

"All the way, flat," Russell said. Kim Two complied and rolled Molina onto his back.

"You want specificity?" Russell said. "I'll give you specificity. You should shut up. Otherwise, I'm going to have Kim here kick you in the ribs until one breaks. Then you can march or die yourself, see how it feels."

"You're bluffing," Molina said.

"In the name of the Emperor's twin testicles, why would I bluff? We're in enough trouble for having taken orders from those clowns on the officers' council. Nobody in the Militia trusts us, the TGI people would probably shoot us—if they could do it quietly—and the Free Traders have always thought we're goons, anyway. In fact"—Russell paused—"in fact, beating a former Galactic Growing operative to death might enhance our standing with them."

"I don't think you'll just kick me to death," Molina said.

Russell laughed. "You're right. I won't." He grinned. "I'm a sergeant. I have people for that. Kim One, front and center."

One of the other troopers jogged forward. "Yes, Sergeant?"

"I want you and your sister here, to kick this man to death."

"We're not actually sisters, Sergeant," Kim One said.

"You both have the same name."

"Lots of people are called Kim, Sergeant."

"You're the only two Kims I know. Stands to reason that you're related."

"We're not, Sergeant."

"Have you ever asked? You know, checked if you are cousins or something?"

"Are you related to every Russell in the Empire, Sergeant?"

"Don't know. I haven't met every Russell in the Empire. Right, you two, kick this guy to death."

"Sergeant? How do we do that?"

"It's a straightforward request, Private. You need a

man, like this one here. He needs to be alive. Start kicking. When he dies, stop."

"Uh, Sergeant," Chaudhari said. "May I have a word in private with you?"

"Of course, Chaudhari. You two, carry on," Russell said. He walked away from the squad, close enough to hear things but far enough to talk with Chaudhari in private. He stared into the distance. The city was darker than he was used to.

Chaudhari stopped next to him and spoke quietly. "Scott, this is a bad idea. We can't just kick him to death."

"Don't worry, we won't. Those two don't weigh two hundred pounds between them, and they've got those soft shoes. Even trying really hard, they won't have any effect."

"Why do it?"

"He doesn't know how much they weigh, and I'm a little concerned about his attitude. I don't want him talking to the squad. Stirring things up."

"Maybe coming down here was a mistake," Chaudhari said.

"Can't stay up in orbit. Too many ways for 'accidents' to happen."

Molina yipped behind them.

"What happened?" Russell asked. He didn't look back.

"They kicked him."

"And?"

"He said 'ouch.' I think you're right. They won't make much progress."

"Good." Sergeant Russell dug into a pocket and produced a cigarette and a lighter.

"I thought you quit those?"

"Tried to. It's hard."

"They must cost a fortune now."

"Are you my banker? Buzz off."

"They're going to kill you."

"Your concern is noted, but I think lots of other things, lots of other people, are going to kill me first."

In the background, Molina laughed and said something like, "Is that all you got?"

Russell flicked his lighter, lit the cigarette, and inhaled deeply. He stared at a warehouse at the end of the street. The door had been broken open but was nailed shut.

"The Kims seem to be the least effective brawlers we have," Chaudhari said.

"That's why I got them to do this—they need the experience. Besides, they both worked in an office before. They're smart. But they need to toughen up. They'll figure something out."

"If you want him beaten up, why not get me to do it?"

"I needed time to think. I'm not sure we should go back to Militia headquarters. Our reception there might be ... frosty."

"Where else would we go? TGI?"

"I'm thinking about Roi." They both turned left. A tattered Militia officer stood under guard to the side. He had a commander's insignia and a defeated expression.

"He's an idiot."

"Yes, but he was in touch with that officers' council, and I know they didn't get all of them, so he might have some friends around."

"If they're his friends, they probably aren't our friends."

"They would be if we let him go."

"You remember the idiot part, right?"

"He can be managed."

A thump, then a scream came from behind them.

"Status change," Chaudhari said.

"The Empress's vagina, can't a man even try to kill himself slowly with cancer in peace?" Sergeant Russell said. He flicked his cigarette away, reconsidered, pinched it out, then put it back in his pocket. He walked back.

"Is this man dead yet?" Russell asked the Kims.

"No, Sergeant," Kim One said. "Sorry, Sergeant."

"What was that noise I heard?"

"Kicking him in the ribs wasn't working, Sergeant, so Kim suggested we start kicking him in the testicles. It seems to give a better result."

"I don't recall saying you could kick him in the testicles."

"You just said to kick him, Sergeant. You didn't specify where."

"Huh. So, I did. Well, hang up for now. You understand that no-talking thing now, Molina?"

Molina nodded.

"Let's go," Russell said. His comm bonged. "Russell."

"Sergent Russell, Shutt here," a familiar voice said.

"How can I help you, Lieutenant—wait, it's Major now. How can I help you, Major?"

"You have Roi and that Molina fellow with you, Sergeant?"

"We do, ma'am."

"Bring them to the power plant."

"Ma'am, I was supposed to drop these two at Militia HQ"

"Change of plans, bring them there. Shutt, out."

Russell looked at Chaudhari. "Change of plans. The power plant now."

"Does that make any difference to us?"

"Us and them," Russell said. He looked at the prisoners. "Might make a fatal one to them. Maybe us, too."

CHAPTER 6

"How badly is the mass driver damaged?" Dashi asked. The council had walked through the switching yard, past the burning truck, and to the front of the stairs leading to the mass driver control room. He sniffed the smoke. "And what is that smell?"

"Former Militia supporters," Marianne said, mounting the stairs. Yvette and Odette laughed. The admiral, Shutt, and their guards stopped at the top and glared at the Free Traders. The Free Traders glared right back.

"I didn't see you down here helping during the revolt," Shutt said.

"The revolt you started," Marianne said. "Your people, in any event. And we were too busy up-orbit trying to regain control of our own ships and stations, control seized by your former colleagues."

"To the matter at hand," Jose said. He had been tapping his console the whole walk from the power plant. He gestured to the lines of containers stacked up in the marshaling yard. "Most of those containers there are full of food. We'll have plenty to eat here. But without a working shuttle, we will eventually have shortages in industrial items. That comes from orbit."

"What's wrong with the shuttles?" Edmunds asked. He pointed. "They're right over there. They look fine."

Everyone glanced across the river. Two shuttles sat on cradles, undamaged.

"The shuttles are fine," Jose said. "Their launch systems, the power for it, is the problem. The mass driver has no power. No mass driver, no shuttle launch—"

"You said, 'here,' we will survive. Where will we not survive?" Marianne said.

"Everyone in orbit has a problem," Jose said.

"What's in orbit causing problems?"

"It's not what's in orbit. It's what's not in orbit. Food."

"There's plenty of food in orbit," Marianne said. "All the ships carry weeks of food. We carried two weeks on my ship."

"They do. Weeks. Not months. Same with the stations. And those places were resupplied by regular shuttle runs, really mostly mass driver lifts, carrying containers of food."

"They can resupply. At the stations."

"Let's discuss this inside," Jose said. He put his hand on Dashi's arm and helped him climb the stairs. "Less smoke there."

"And we don't have to smell the former Militia people," Marianne said. Shutt glared at her, opened the door to the control room, and entered.

The group collected in the middle of the control room. The consoles were unmanned, with blank display boards.

"Ms. Marianne, you said you carried two week's worth of food," Jose said. "On your ship. What happened when you ran low?"

"Ducked into the nearest station ... tabernac. I see now."

"Right," Jose said. "Without the mass driver running, we can't lift food to replenish stocks. Or anything else, for that matter. But food is the biggest problem."

"Didn't you plan for this?" Marianne asked. "How much is up there?"

"We planned for disruptions. TGI loaded and stored as much food as possible before the current unpleasantness. Remember, the mutineers' opening move was to covertly slow our lifts of critical items, including food."

"You didn't answer my question," Marianne said. "How much food is there up there?"

Jose walked over to a console and typed on it. One of

the wall displays lit, with lists of types of food trays and locations.

"TGI has enough stored for its own people for about six months. The other corps and stations didn't plan as well. They usually had less than two weeks' worth, and that was damaged in the fighting. Full deliveries were interrupted before that, so some are down to almost nothing. They will go hungry soon."

"What if they go to half rations?" Marianne asked.

"Actually, that's with one-third rations," Jose said. "I already calculated that in."

"Can they drink basic?"

"For a while. It gives some calories, but not enough. And supplies of that are limited as well."

Dashi sat in the console chair and steepled his fingers. "Jose, what is the bottom line?"

Jose bit his lip. "TGI has enough food to feed all of its orbital workers for about six months. But we could share with everybody. Feed everybody."

"For how long?"

"Best guess? Six weeks."

"There's only six weeks' worth of food in orbit?" Marianne asked. "But we have months down here."

"We have years down here," Jose said, "and the ability to keep producing more. But we don't have the capacity to lift it in bulk."

Shutt walked closer to the screen and took out her own comm. She did her own calculations. "We shouldn't be sharing with everybody. Just the Militia up-orbit. And TGI staff, of course."

"What about the Free Traders?" Marianne asked. "You think we will stand by while you starve our friends."

"And what about us? What about our people?" the unaligned corps representative asked. "They deserve the food more than the Militia. We didn't go around blowing up stations and starting a war."

"Yes, perhaps we should take the Militia out of the

equation," Marianne said. "They have proven to be untrustworthy. Perhaps we should take them into custody."

"I'd like to see you try," Shutt said. "We'd cut you down before you could say 'Imperial Succession.' You're just merchants, not Militia."

"Merchants with weapons," Marianne said. "We collected quite a few abandoned items during the 'current unpleasantness,' and we don't trust you. We have friends in orbit. Lots of friends. We'd swarm you over on day one."

"You have no training and no organization. You don't know what you're doing. We'd kick you in your Imperial behinds." Shutt stepped forward and put her hand on her belt holster.

Marianne did the same. "We don't know what we're doing? You Militia are the ones who started a war and then lost it. And you're still fighting each other in Landing, if the reports are true."

"Rogue elements that need to be suppressed—" Shutt said.

"Maybe you're the rogue elements, and maybe we should suppress you." Marianne drew her revolver and pointed it at Shutt. "Perhaps you are just useless mouths?" Shutt and the other Militia pulled their weapons. Yvette and Odette followed, pointing their revolvers at Shutt.

Jake and Nadine backed against the wall. Dashi remained seated with Jose next to him. Edmunds scowled and shook his head.

A boom shook the room. Everyone looked out the window—a pall of smoke was rising from a neighborhood across the river.

Dashi tapped his cane on the console. All heads turned to him. "A timely reminder that we have other problems. If we do not all hang together, we shall surely hang separately. Gentleman and ladies, you are interrupting Mr. Jose's report. If we could continue."

The admiral nodded. "Carry on, please, Mr. Jose. Shutt?" He gave her a look. She holstered her weapon, and the other Militia followed suit.

Marianne did the same. Yvette leaned over to her and whispered. Marianne listened, then smiled at Shutt. "Thank you for the suggestion."

"I didn't suggest anything to you, at least not what I was really thinking. Want to know what I really think about you?"

"Thank you for suggesting we need training. And organization." She looked at Dashi. "I have been named to this council. Does that not automatically give me some sort of acting Imperial rank?" She looked at the others.

Jake spoke from the wall. "You and the others are tribunes. Jose would be a legate because Dashi has named him deputy."

"More useless Imperial history, Jake," Nadine said. "Anything else?"

"Tribunes and Legates are granted certain privileges," Jake said. "But I think Ms. Marianne already knows that."

"Thank you, Mr. Stewart," Marianne said. She looked at Shutt. "The next time we have this discussion, things will be different. Mr. Jose, please tell us how you are going to fix your mess."

"It's my mess now?" Jose asked.

"You created all this." Marianne swept her hands across the view outside. "You and these Militia people. You should fix it."

"TGI did not start anything," Jose said. "We just responded to events."

"Events that you triggered," Marianne said. "But it doesn't matter. You are in charge now. Show us your organizational brilliance."

The Militia laughed at that.

Dashi cleared his throat. "The past is not a productive point of discussion right now. We need to look to the future. Jose, how will this food distribution work?"

"Sir," Jose said, displaying items on the screen. "My plan is to disburse the TGI stored shipments to a variety of stations, about two dozen or so, based on their populations, and have them hand out the trays to the inhabitants using their own facilities. We'd freeze ship traffic. If you want to eat, dock at a station. The stations will feed the crews of any ships that arrive. We'll vector all the Free Traders, the remaining Militia, and all corporate ships to specific stations. Anybody who stays at a station will be fed. If you stay, you give up your food and share. If you leave, you leave without food."

"There are hundreds of smaller stations out there," the unaligned rep said. "Family stations, small corps. What happens to them?"

"They come into the big stations to be fed, or they rely on their own resources," Jose said. "If they think they can tough it out, they're welcome to try. Some will think they can ride it out without help. They may be right. We'll give everybody the option at the start."

"Some of them are too far out to make it to close orbit in a reasonable length of time," the rep said. "If they are low on supplies to start with, orbital geometry is going to mean that some will starve before they get in, if we don't go out and meet them."

"No plan is perfect," Jose said.

"That's a pretty blasé attitude," the rep said. "Not caring about people starving to death."

"Yelling doesn't change math. Orbits are orbits. Supplies are supplies."

"Some of the Free Traders won't come in," Marianne said. "Not under any circumstances. They don't trust the big corps, like TGI. And they certainly don't trust the Militia. Why not give the food to the Free Traders to distribute?"

"We need some sort of central control."

"We don't like centralization. Give us food to distribute ourselves. We just want to be left alone."

"If you want to be left alone, you'll starve," Jose said.

The rep pointed at the Free Traders. "The other option that these two started with, about prioritizing certain groups. What about that?"

Jose shook his head. "It's a bad idea. Firstly, whoever got locked out would fight. They'd have nothing to lose. And they wouldn't care about damage, either. And second, we're too incestuous here."

Marianne typed the word into her comm. "Incestuous?" She looked at the screen. "We have sexual relationships with our siblings? I only have one brother, and he's not attractive. We do not do this thing." She looked at the others. "Is this common among the rest of you? This brother-sister lover thing?"

The room erupted in laughter. Even the admiral smiled.

"I didn't mean it literally," Jose said. "What I meant was, we're a very small colony. The different groups are too intertwined. We ran some numbers. Lots of Free Traders and corps have family in the Militia. TGI staff come from all over. The corps are all mixed up. If we took TGI staff only, we'd exclude a huge number of their immediate family. If we included immediate family, then we extend out to every organization. If we include the Militia and the Free Traders family connections as well, we're up about seventy percent of the orbital population, and there will be some we missed, and cousins, and best friends as well. We can't exclude anybody, or we'll have riots."

The room lights failed. They stayed dark for a second before flickering back on.

"It's quiet," Yvette said.

"Fans are out," Jose said.

They listened for another moment, then the fans fired up. The group exchanged glances. And frowns.

"Can we lift more basic? That's caloric dense."

"We're already doing that," Jose said. "We take as much as we can with the lifter—the TGI lifting body—but we're constrained by weight. And volume. There isn't much to lift, either. There is exactly one factory on Delta that makes basic. It's shut down right now."

"Why?" Yvette asked.

"No power."

"So, get power to it."

"It's not that simple. It's on the east side of Landing. The side with the damaged monorail and no hydro plant to power it."

"Regardless," the admiral said. "I think we should limit the people who get the food."

"I agree," Marianne said. "But we must come to some agreement on the groups."

"No, we will not do that," Dashi said. "We will share equally with all. This is a new council, and we cannot start governing Delta by starving people."

"Better to starve some than starve all," Edmunds said.

"If it comes to that," Dashi said, "it's TGI food. We will control its disbursement. And I say we will be catholic with our distribution."

Edmunds looked at Shutt and mouthed "catholic" to her. Shutt shrugged.

"Catholic means 'universal' in this context," Jose said, catching the look.

"Why can't you speak standard, Dashi?" Edmunds asked.

"I do," Dashi said. "Lack of education in others is not my concern."

"Lack of education? Well, let's educate this," Edmunds said. "There are two groups we can exclude, first, former Galactic Growing security who participated in the rebellion."

"Not relevant," Jose said. "There aren't any of those left. Not in orbit."

"Second, those rebel Militia. They come in and surrender, or they starve."

"You'd starve your own people, Admiral?" Dashi

42

asked.

"They're not my own people," Edmunds said. "Not anymore. But the more important question is, what happens next? What's our long-term solution?"

"Fix the fusion plant, electrical distribution, and mass driver."

"And we can do this? Do this with parts and people on hand?" Edmunds asked.

"No. We can't fix it."

"But if we don't ship food to orbit, what will they eat?

"Probably each other," Jose said.

CHAPTER 7

Sergeant Russell banged on the mass driver control room's door. A Free Trader guard opened the door.

"What?" the guard said.

"Sergeant Russell and squad with prisoners, reporting to Major Shutt."

"You're bleeding," the guard said.

"Brilliant observation," Russell said. He rubbed his face. A potshot en route had smashed a brick near his head, and the fragments had cut his scalp. "The major, please."

"Wait here." The door slammed shut.

"Sure we're in the right place, Sergeant?" Chaudhari asked. "Not very friendly, are they?"

"No," Russell said. He pulled the stub of a cigarette out and lit it.

"You're doing that now? Here?"

"I bet they won't let me smoke inside. And it's the surest way to hurry something up. Light a cigarette, and they appear." The door opened, and the guard reappeared. "See?"

"Just you," the guard said.

Russell and Chaudhari exchanged a look. Russell pinched out his cigarette.

"If you are killed, I'll avenge your death," Chaudhari said.

"Like it better if you actually prevented it," Russell said, stepping inside. He walked over to the central part of the control room, faced the group, and braced.

"Hello, Sergeant Russell," Shutt said.

"Hello, ma'am." Sergeant Russell said. "And hello ma'am's friends."

"You're bleeding."

"Snipers. A scratch. I'm here to drop off some packages. Two, in fact."

"The Grower agent?"

"And the, uh, former commander."

"Russell, Russell," Marianne said. "I have heard that name before. Perhaps on one of our lists." She and Yvette pulled out their comms.

"Sergeant Russell was co-opted during the initial events of the current unpleasantness," Shutt said, "but quickly returned to duty when the situation was explained to him. I believe he surrendered to Mr. Jose here, and offered his services in securing the station."

The Free Traders looked at Jose, who nodded. "That is substantially correct."

"I thought we executed all the officers and senior non-coms who rebelled," the admiral said, "and that we—"

"Not a senior NCO, sir," Russell said.

Edmunds frowned. "Do you normally interrupt your superiors, Sergeant?"

"Actually, Admiral," Major Shutt said, "That's kind of his thing. Got him in this mess to start with."

"Did it really?" Edmunds snapped his fingers.

"I remember now. A few years back. Busted down the ranks?" the admiral said.

"He had a few choice words to say to a major one day," Shutt said.

"He was an orbital force idiot, sir," Sergeant Russell said. "He didn't know what he was talking about."

"I'm in the orbital force, Sergeant," Edmunds said. "Have problems taking orders from orbital people?"

"Yeah, sometimes," Sergeant Russell said.

Edmunds laughed. "That's why you're a sergeant."

"True," Sergeant Russell said, "senior officers don't like it when you point out how wrong they are about things, especially if those things are going to get your troops killed."

"You think I'll get your troops killed, Sergeant?" Major Shutt said. "Or the admiral?" She looked at the admiral. "May I have a short moment alone with the sergeant, sir?"

"I need to speak to Ms. Nadine, anyway. Nadine?" Nadine sauntered over from down across the room. She and the admiral stepped away for privacy.

"With me, Sergeant," Major Shutt said.

The two walked over to the corner. Shutt's cane clacked on the floor. Sergeant Rusell turned to her.

"What?"

She snatched his earlobe and pulled it next to her mouth. "Scott, you Imperial turd. Are you entirely out of your mind?"

"That hurts."

"Why don't you just demand that he lock you up?"

"That hurts a lot, Clarisse."

"Don't you 'that hurts a lot, Clarisse' me. You're just avoiding the subject. Do you want him to bust you down again? Lose your rank. Again. Or would you prefer he have you shot for treason? Your joining up with the rebels is a serious problem."

"Can you let go of my ear, please, Clarisse?" Sergeant Russell said.

She let his ear go, then put her hand on her hip and glared at him. "You have only one friend here. Stop telling him he's some stupid orbital guy."

"That's a pretty effective way to immobilize a man," Sergeant Russell said. He rubbed his ear. "He is a stupid orbital guy."

"I trust him. He did the right thing. He stopped that Empire-dammed coup."

"I notice he's not giving me my original rank back."

"He had nothing to do with taking it away. He was retired by then. And what do you think those TGI people are going to say to him if he does something like that? We barely kept you off the proscribed list?"

"We?"

"I barely kept you off the proscribed list. But he didn't interfere. You know what the Free Traders said?"

"I think you're going to tell me, whether I want to hear it or not."

"That they can only hunt down so many people at once, so we'll find all the people on the first list and shoot them. Then we can make a new list and start fresh with your name on the top."

"I'll be number one? I knew people would recognize my talents, eventually."

"Empress's vagina. I don't know why I bother." She tapped her cane on the floor. "Think of your squad. If you go down for treason, so will they."

"They had nothing to do with it."

"I can only do so much. Next meeting of that council is in a couple of days. It's scheduled to address that topic. If your name comes up, then your squad's will, too."

"They didn't do anything. They were just following orders. My orders."

"Then they'll end up in jail, right next to you. For following orders."

"It was that Imperial turd Roi's, fault. Why didn't you just shove him out an air lock?"

"Why didn't you just shove him out an air lock? You had him up at TGI Main."

"I thought he should get, you know, due process, some sort of trial."

"Why wouldn't he?"

"That Jose guy is too sneaky. He'd set something up that would take him out. Take out the troops, too—no witnesses. That's why I didn't stuff him out an air lock. As long as I had Roi, he couldn't do anything."

"Well, that won't be the case now. Bring Roi over to Militia HQ and then go hide somewhere."

"Hide for how long?"

"Till this thing blows over."

"This thing will never blow over."

"I don't like it, either."

"Why don't you just shoot Roi?" Sergeant Russell said.

Major Shutt stared at the wall. "Most of the senior officers involved in the coup are dead. The explosion on GG Main got them. Others were killed in the fighting. One was killed by his own troops."

"I sympathize," Sergeant Russell said.

"We're missing eleven. We think they went south."

"South? South continent?"

"Yes. There's a shuttle unaccounted for. Went up and disappeared. Don't know where it went down exactly. Dashi says he knows it's down there, but the only location he gave was south."

"What's on south continent."

"Nothing that I know of. Criminals."

"Roi knows where they are?"

"Maybe. He's the most senior we have left. He's not that senior, but he was that colonel's aide before the fighting and just got over promoted. But ..."

"But what?"

"He was one of the first to join that Empire-rising thing. He might know something. Militia HQ wants to talk to him."

"They want to ask for information on where those officers are?"

"Something like that."

"Maybe I should interrogate him myself."

"Maybe you should. But you need to get away from all these people with guns who know who you are. Go home."

"Home may have burned down."

"Not my problem."

"What's this Nadine girl's story?"

"Like her, do you?"

"She looks good in that suit."

Major Shutt turned toward Nadine, who was talking to the admiral. "She cleans up well. She's been one of the admiral's operatives for years. He trusts her. Be careful, she's tricky, sometimes violent, and has a mercenary's sense of self preservation."

"Sounds like fun. Look, how do I go about not getting killed out of this?"

"If you bring something of value to the admiral, he might look more favorably on you."

"What type of things?"

"I have a few suggestions," Shutt said, leaning in. "There's an ocean water ship we want you to go see."

***

"These apples are great," Nadine said. The admiral had collected a pile from a vendor on the way to the shuttle port. "You know, I don't like any of the A trays - with the mushed apples, but fresh they're a totally different experience." She faced the admiral and took another long, slow bite.

"I'm glad you like them," Edmunds said.

"Now more than ever." She leaned in and gave him a big hug. "That's a great present."

"Can you stop pawing me in public? People know that you work for me."

"Are you kidding?" Nadine looked at him but didn't release him. "Now that they know, it will be even more effective. They'll think we're degenerates with all sorts of issues they can exploit."

"Fine, we're degenerates. What will your new boyfriend think of this?"

Nadine bit into her apple again. "He's not the jealous type."

"All men are the jealous type."

"Don't worry, I have ways of bringing him around." She looked at the admiral. "What I mean is—"

"I know what you mean, I was young once, too."

"Now, about Major Shutt." Nadine looked across. "She's a pretty woman. Are you-—"

"First, none of your business. Second, No. Third, she's just about half my age."

"Is she half your age plus seven? Because you know, some women think that's the perfect age difference."

"You just can't help your mind going right to the gutter, can you?" Nadine grinned and shook her head. The admiral looked toward Sergeant Russell and Major Shutt. "Is she pulling him down by the ear?"

Nadine looked over and shrugged. "Some guys like that. She looks mad. Some guys like that, too."

He looked to make sure nobody could overhear them. "Do you remember all your code phrases? The list I gave you about a year or so ago."

"The duress codes and the others? Of course. In addition to being beautiful, articulate, and having a great fashion sense, I have an excellent memory as well."

"But somewhat lacking in the modesty department."

"Modesty never did anything for me."

"I'd like you to go with Sergeant Russell there. It's Shutt's suggestion. We've got a ship under guard, an ocean water-type ship. We think it smuggled the guns into the city."

"Think?"

"You're a smuggler of sorts. Why don't you take a look at the ship, see what you can see? You might see more than some others."

"Meaning your officers are all boring, straight-arrow people who have no imagination and won't see a shipload of smuggled goods if it blew up overhead."

"That's how I would have characterized that Jake Stewart guy, and yet he's been useful to Dashi. Beat you out a few times, I understand."

"He did."

The admiral raised his eyebrows. "I'm surprised you agree."

"I'm just lazy and violent, not stupid. He's got some sort of planning mojo thing. I want to learn it."

"So, you'll stop being violent?"

"Oh, no, no," Nadine said. "The violence is a lot of fun."

CHAPTER 8

"Who is going to crew the Jump ship?" Marianne asked.

"I thought we said we would discuss that once we returned to the HQ," Jose said. After their depressing inspection of the mass driver, the council was returning to the agriculture building.

"Why not now? It's hardly a real headquarters," Shutt said. "We might as well have a meeting in the street."

"It does have access to the main colony computer systems," Jose said. "And plenty of meeting rooms and offices."

"The Militia needs access to better comms," Shutt said.

"We have more than adequate facilities for our communications," Dashi said. "We continue to utilize the TGI comms. I assume the Militia would be using their own systems."

"Militia HQ was sabotaged during the recent unpleasantness, sir," Jose said. "They rely on field radios now."

"How unfortunate," Marianne said. Yvette, Odette, and her shared grins.

"I will, of course, be assigning Militia officers to the Jump ship," Admiral Edmunds said. His feet crunched something. "Watch out for the glass. Do we make glass here on Delta?"

"Not in quantity," Jose said. "We can't replace it for the moment. Which officers?"

"No," Jake said.

"No?" Edmunds said. "No what?"

"No. We don't need Militia officers."

"Of course you do. Somebody has to crew it. Now, I propose that we send a group of four—"

Jake kicked a stray piece of plastic with his feet. "No group of four. No Militia crew. We don't need them. I've already picked out a crew," he said.

"You picked out a crew? You little scamp. Look, youngster, you have no experience in crews. The Militia has been putting crews on ships since the abandonment."

"And look where that got us," Jake said. He gestured at the buildings. "Standing in the smoke climbing over broken bricks while we try to hunt down rebel Militia officers who are burning down the city." Jake looked around. "At least I've never set a warehouse on fire."

"He has a point there, Admiral," Jose said.

"Point or not, he can't just take control of a Militia asset," Edmunds said.

"It's not a Militia asset," Jake said. "It's my asset. It's my ship, and I'm going to decide what's done with it."

Nadine turned and grabbed Jake's arm. "Jake, you're so ... decisive. It's making me hot."

Jake grinned. "It is?"

"Sure. Is there a closet or something around here?"

"You shut up, missy," Edmunds said. "This is serious business here."

"Pretty serious for me, too," Nadine said. "When I feel like this, I usually want to take care of it pretty quick."

"In the name of the Emperor," Jose said. "Right now? Really? Are you afraid your head is going to explode?"

"Should I take that chance?" Nadine said. She grabbed Jake's arm. "This will only take a minute, I promise."

"But you told me before that a minute—"

"That was different. Don't worry, this is more of a show thing than a tell thing."

"Nadine," Edmunds said, "try to control yourself for a few minutes while we get this crew sorted out."

"Spoilsport," Nadine said. She stuck her tongue out.

"In so many ways," Jake said.

Boom. A cloud of dust billowed out from a side street.

"Emperor's testicles," Shutt said. "Sergeant Russell, get a squad over there and take a look."

Russell gestured, and half of his squad ran forward with him. They disappeared into the dust cloud.

Edmunds rubbed his forehead. "We should stop here for a moment while this is sorted out." He looked at Dashi. "I'm willing to discuss your representation, but we need some Militia people on that ship."

"Why?" Marianne asked. "So that your goons can beat the rest of us up, shove us out an air lock, and steal the ship?"

"I, or we, are not like that," Edmunds said. "We are not going to steal the ship. We are not going to throw anybody out an air lock."

"D'accord," Marianne said. "Because we will not give you the chance. We will have a Free Trader crew on the ship. We are all experienced spacers, so we are the logical people to crew the ship. Is that not so, Mr. Dashi?"

Dashi sat on a piece of broken furniture. "I am more interested in why Mr. Stewart called it 'his ship.' Do you claim ownership of it, Mr. Stewart?"

"I do, sir," Jake said. "Both de jure and de facto."

Nadine picked up a broken brick from the ground. "There's those funny words again," she said.

"They are Latin, illiterate girl," Marianne said. "A beautiful old Empire language. It sounds a lot like Francais, actually."

"Francais sounds like two raccoons copulating," Nadine said.

"Your lack of schooling is showing," Marianne said.

"Come over here." Nadine dropped the brick and held up her fist. "I'll teach you something you won't forget."

The dust cloud dissipated. Another boom and a second, smaller cloud puffed out of the side street. Shutt answered a radio call from Russell's squad. "That one was our people. They say there is some sort of riot going on, and they are firing into the air to keep the crowds back. They hit a building. The crowds are between us and the headquarters."

"It is important that we do not harm any citizens of Delta." Dashi frowned. "Or harm any more citizens. Please continue, Mr. Stewart. The basis for your claim?"

"Sir," Jake said. "Utilizing certain personal and private information, I acquired the course parameters for a ship currently circling Delta, henceforth known as 'the ship.' I located and boarded it without using any corporate or Militia resources. Once on board, I determined it was space-worthy, made minor repairs, satisfied myself that the systems were operating correctly, and piloted it into close orbit. It's currently in a parking orbit not far from TGI Main. The former owners being unknown and having clearly abandoned it, I claim salvage rights."

"Mr. Stewart, I believe," Dashi said, "that you were onboard a TGI-owned ship when you boarded."

"Not true. The ship was owned by 247312 Delta Corporation, doing business as 'Jake Stewart and Associates.'"

Dashi turned to Jose and raised his eyebrows. Jose was already searching. "Jake Stewart and Associates," he read, "um ... chartered in the outer belt. Majority Stockholder, J. Stewart Esquire, Minor Stockholder, twenty percent, Vincent Pletcher DBA Owl Ship Sales, minority ownership by right of a vendor takeback mortgage."

"What's a vendor takeback mortgage?" Edmunds asked.

"That's where a financial institution lets you take an asset without paying full price," Nadine said. "They convert the remainder into a first mortgage, with a lien on the whole value of the ship. You make regular payments until the mortgage is cleared. But in this case, the mortgage was tied to a special category of corporate shares, with an agreement to sell the shares at no cost once the mortgage was cleared."

Edmunds spoke. "How in the Emperor's name do you know what a vendor takeback mortgage is? You can't even add up a bar tab correctly." He sat down on a curb and surveyed the dust around him. "What's taking Russell and his squad so long?

"I helped negotiate the payback schedule," Nadine said. "Including the financial calendar to use and the amortization schedule."

Major Shutt shook her head. "It's like watching a dog talk, isn't it? On a certain level, it makes sense, but only if you take the whole ridiculous premise of her having two brain cells at face value."

Nadine glared at her. "I don't think we've formally met."

"I'm Clarisse Shutt. Major Shutt to you."

"I'm Nadine."

"I know. You're the admiral's bimbo."

"Bimbo? Bimbo?" Nadine narrowed her eyes. "We're busy now, and people are shooting at us. But we'll talk later. A personal talk."

"Looking forward to it," Major Shutt said. She cocked her head to listen to the radio. "Sir, Russell says that it's too dangerous to continue that way. He suggests cutting back toward the monorail station and continuing from there."

"Very well," Edmunds said, getting up. "Get another squad over there to support him."

Shutt didn't say anything, but flicked her eyes to the waiting council, then back to Edmunds.

Jose caught the look. "There aren't any more squads available, are there? The city isn't nearly as secure as we were told."

"Rogue elements—" Shutt began.

"Enough with your rogue elements," Jose said. He bent over to help Dashi up. "We need to take Mr. Dashi somewhere safe. Back to the monorail."

"From the monorail station, we can collect some more troops and proceed to Militia headquarters. Mr. Dashi will be safe there," Edmunds said. "The council can meet then."

"Or we can take him to the Free Traders' headquarters. We can protect him there. Without the Militia," Marianne said. "And there is plenty of room for the council." She smiled at Dashi. "We have fresh food."

"Or simply take the train to our western headquarters at point-37," Jose said. "Where our ground operations are located, including this moon's only functioning orbital launch site." He smiled at Marianne. "We have wine."

Dashi smiled. "And all of those options require us to proceed to the monorail station. We can defer discussion of those options to there. Lead on, Admiral. Mr. Stewart?"

"Sir?" Jake said.

"I believe you purchased that ship with money we gave you, Mr. Stewart. And I believe you turn left here, after this fire." Dashi pointed to a burning trash can.

"I did, sir."

"And?"

"Thank you for the money, sir," Jake said. "It was most useful."

The silence stretched. Dashi laughed. "We didn't put any conditions on it, did we?"

"No, sir."

"Well, perhaps this Mr. Pletcher will want a share of your claim as well." The crowd turned and walked single file down the alley.

"I don't think he has a claim anymore, sir."

"Jose?" Dashi said.

Jose leaned against a wall and searched. "Mortgage was retired, sir. Mr. Pletcher sold his interest to a"—Jose looked up—"sold his interest to a Ms. Nadine, for the sum of one credit, two cases of wine to be delivered later, and certain personal services."

Everybody turned to look at Nadine. She gave a 'who

me' shrug.

"It appears Ms. Nadine owns one-fifth of a Jump ship," Jose said.

"What's this personal service thing?" Jake asked.

Nadine shrugged again. "Not your concern, Jake. We weren't together then. Besides, his wine was really, really good."

"What I'd expect from the likes of her," Shutt said.

"There is a list here outlining the personal services. And a diagram," Jose said. "Demonstrating them. Huh." He tilted his head. "That's an odd position." He tilted his head farther. "I don't think Ms. Nadine is that flexible. I don't think anyone is that flexible."

Marianne reached across and pulled at Jose's comm to look at the screen. "Oh, no, that's possible. I can do that myself."

Jose looked at her. "Really, you can—er, bend like that?"

"Farther if I put my mind to it," Marianne said. "Want me to show you?"

"Not right now," Jose said. He thought for a moment. "Perhaps later?"

"D'accord," Marianne said. "When I visit your point west, you can show me your wine."

"May I see this list, please?" Jake said. "And the diagram as well."

"You don't really need to see that, Jake," Nadine said. She stepped between him and the others.

"Why not?"

"Well, if you want, I can show you later. Privately."

"We should carry on," Jake said. The crowd resumed their trek down the alley.

Marianne spoke. "Mr. Stewart. You stole this ship from Dashi? Using his own money?"

Jake nodded. Marianne looked at her two colleagues, Yvette and Odette. They raised their eyebrows.

"Formidable," Yvette said. "That is impressive."

"D'accord," Odette agreed. She turned to Jake. "So, it is true, you always win." She threw him a mock salute. "Ready to serve, mon capitan. You do this mortgage thing, and we will handle the rest of the ship's tasks." She turned to Nadine. "You know, I think I realize what you see in this boy. He is one to watch."

"Watch from a distance," Nadine said.

"Why? Does he bite?" Odette asked.

"No. I do," Nadine said.

Dashi leaned against a wall and smiled. "So, it seems you have de jure control of the ship, Mr. Stewart, but the council is the law on Delta. We may adjudicate this matter differently."

"Regardless of ownership, I'm the best choice to command this mission," Jake said. "I located this ship, retrieved it, studied it, and now operate it. Plus, it's clear that it is my personal property."

"Everybody on the wall, please," Shutt said. "Troops coming through." Russell's squad ran past, fanning out as they maneuvered around side streets toward the monorail station.

"Not bad troops for former rebels," Jose said.

"We should shoot them anyway," Marianne said. "Once a rebel, always a rebel. Don't you agree, Admiral?"

"If any Militia need to be shot, I'll be the one doing the shooting, not you," Edmunds said. He looked at the running troops. "But I'll bear your thoughts in mind."

"So, you're not going to shoot them?"

"I didn't say that," Edmunds said. He turned to Jake. "We can just take it," Edmunds said. "The ship. You can't stop us."

"Does the Empire not respect private property now? Regular historical and customary business practices as set forth in the Imperial code?" Yvette said. "Then again, that is what I would have expected from the Militia. Ignoring the law unless it suits them. Rights of mortgage holders are important legal precedents."

"I am in administrative Hades," the admiral said. "All I did was escape from jail and defeat the rebels trying to burn down the town, and now I'm arguing about second mortgages?"

"It's a first mortgage, sir," Jake said. "If it was a second mortgage, it wouldn't even be open for discussion."

"Completely different type of financial transaction," Nadine said.

"You don't know a financial transaction from a superpotato," Edmunds said.

"Far be it for me to overturn historical and customary business practices," Dashi said. "But even both 'de facto' and 'de jure' control of the ship, is not, in itself, proof of competence to command."

"I've been aboard that ship for several weeks, sir," Jake said. "I've been able to configure many of the systems and program the necessary changes to customize it for myself and my operations."

"Well, uncustomize it, then," Edmunds said.

"Sir," Shutt said. "The squad has deployed on the next main street over. It's clear right now. We should hustle." Everyone hurried out of the alley and turned left. The squad occupied the empty street, and the monorail station could be seen in the distance.

"How would you know?" Jake asked.

"Know what?"

"Whether I customized it or not," Jake said. "You don't have any people with experience in Jump ships. In this entire system, I'm the only person who's worked on a Jump ship for eighty years. I am the expert." He turned to Dashi. "Sir, I've been researching and experimenting with the system on that ship every waking moment for the last two weeks."

"Not every moment." Nadine stretched and smiled. "Not every."

Jake grinned at her, then turned back to Dashi. "I know the systems, I know the configurations, I know the demands. I know what type of crew that ship needs."

"Which would be who?" Dashi asked.

"First, myself. I'll handle the Jump systems and the main computer. It's different from anything that I've ever seen on Delta or in the rings. Nadine can be the pilot. She's already had experience with this ship, and we're used to working together. Ms. Yvette has a point—her people are Free Traders and are experienced spacers. They certainly have much more ship time than anybody in the Militia, especially time in the outer rings. Running this Jump ship is going to be much more like running a long-haul ore barge than driving a drop ship. Maintenance, fuel consumption, and the ability to make repairs in situ will be much more important than flashy maneuvers and shiny uniforms."

"All good reasons, Mr. Stewart," Dashi said. A brick slid fell off the second story of a nearby building and thumped into the ground. Everyone froze.

"And also, sir."

"Yes?"

"I've encrypted the main computer programs and locked the board with my own codes. The computer there is amazing. I don't think any effort will be able to unlock them without my codes."

Dashi began to walk again, and the others followed.

"We could assign substantial computer assets to this," Edmunds said. "The main computer at Militia HQ should be able to decrypt anything."

"Or if you just give me a wrench and five minutes with Mr. Stewart's kneecaps, Admiral," Shutt said. "I'm sure I could provide you with the code phrases."

"Better bring two wrenches," Nadine advised.

"Why is that?"

"Because I might break the first one, taking it away from you, and I'll want the second one to work on your kneecaps."

"An interesting discussion," Dashi said. "You think

you can be a starship captain, Mr. Stewart?"

"I can do this, sir. I've never let you down before, have I?"

Dashi nodded. "That is true. Very well. You can be the Jump and computer specialist. Ms. Nadine could be the pilot. Ms. Marianne could put a few of her own people onboard—specialists in ship systems. And a backup pilot."

"I don't like it," Edmunds said. "We need some Militia representation onboard. Shutt, at least. Perhaps more."

"We'll have your bimbo on board, sir," Shutt said. "She should be on our side, at least."

"My bimbo?"

Major Shutt gestured at Nadine.

Nadine turned to Shutt and put her hands on her hips. "You should stop calling me that. I'm here because I'm one of the best pilots there is. Why are you here?"

"You're here because you were sleeping with the admiral," Shutt said.

Nadine giggled. "Is that the reason?"

The admiral massaged his forehead. "Major Shutt, I am not sleeping with Ms. Nadine." He looked up. "Why are we even talking about this?"

"Sir," Major Shutt said. She braced. "I will admit to everyone here that you saved the day during the coup. You fought off the Growers, you regained control from those so-called Empire-first people, you suppressed the rioting, you recaptured the city. Frankly, you saved us all. Me, the Militia, we're all ready to follow you anywhere. But let's call a spade a spade, sir. We've seen you with this woman for years. You are always in public with her. Dinner. And she's very affectionate with you. We know she's your lover."

"Ms. Nadine is not my lover and never has been," the admiral said.

"All evidence to the contrary," Jose said. "We had her listed as such in our files. Or at least the highest probability was you two were lovers."

"Indeed," Dashi said. He reached into his pocket and produced a credit chip. "Jose, you remember our discussion on this matter?"

"Sir," Jose said. "I do." He took out his own credit chip.

Edmunds looked at Nadine. "This is all your fault. Another of your stupid twisted schemes just to torment me."

Nadine stuck her tongue out. "And it appears to have worked wonderfully. Everybody thinks we're sleeping together."

"Fine," the admiral said. "If we're going to be talking about people's sex lives, then let's bring things up to date across the board." He turned to Jake. "You, Stewart. What are your intentions?"

"My intentions?" Jake asked. "What intentions?"

"With Nadine here. Just a little fun, friends with benefits? Going to go see the registrar and pick out matching skin suits?"

"I, uh, what?" Jake said. "Why is that relevant to anything? We haven't talked about it." He looked at Nadine, then back at the admiral. "And why do you care? It's none of your business."

"Oh, it's very much my business," the admiral said. "I'd like an answer."

"I'm not going to give you one."

"I have to insist."

"Why do we care about who is sleeping with who?" Yvette asked.

"Perhaps I can help out," Nadine said. "I guess it's time for some proper introductions." She gestured toward Jake. "Admiral, this is Jake Stewart, formerly of RIM-37 station, TGI operative, mediocre pilot, and hopeless marksman. But a whizz with mortgages and king of the rule books." She pointed at the admiral. "Jake, this is Admiral Bryan Edmunds, Delta Militia, retired, member of the emergency committee doing business as the Delta

Corporation, and sublieutenant in the Imperial Customs Reserve." Nadine took a breath. "And also my grandfather."

The room gasped. Jose handed his credit chip to Dashi. "You win, sir."

CHAPTER 9

"I'm sorry I called you a bimbo," Major Shutt said. They were standing in line to get food at the improvised caf at the monorail station. After a circuitous route, they had arrived in the center of town. On the way, the council had hashed out who was to be on the Jump ship. The crew had assembled and were taking a break before the west train rolled in.

"No, you're not," Nadine said.

"No, I'm not," Shutt agreed. "But the admiral made me come over and apologize, so here I am."

"Had you fooled, didn't I?" Nadine said.

"Yep," Shutt said.

"Maybe I'm not as much of a bimbo as you think," Nadine said.

"That remains to be seen. But it's not the way I'm going to bet."

"Worse for you. When I'm piloting, you can watch and learn."

"Hello, Sergeant Russell," Shutt said, looking over Nadine's shoulder.

"Hello, ma'am. And ma'am's friend," Sergeant Russell said.

"I'm Nadine, and I'm not her friend."

"Why not?"

"I've already got enough friends," Nadine said. "I don't need her."

"What about me?" Sergeant Russell said. "Could we be friends?"

Nadine slowly scanned him from head to toe, then

smiled. "Maybe we could. What kind of friend are you?"

"She's got a boyfriend, Sergeant," Shutt said. "One of those TGI paper pushers."

"No problem breaking that up, then," Russell said.

"You'd be surprised," Shutt said. "But you won't have much time. Ms. Nadine is going to be the pilot of the Jump ship they found, and she's heading up there later today."

"Have to work fast, then," Sergeant Russell said. "In fact, I understand Ms. Nadine, and I will be spending some time together."

"And why is that?" Nadine asked.

"I'm supposed to escort you to see some water ocean ship. It's on the way to headquarters."

"That's right. I'm supposed to look into that. What makes you think I need an escort?"

A revolver fired from outside, six evenly spaced shots. Everyone froze, then relaxed when the shots stopped. "No reason," Russell said.

"How much more of that do we have to put up with?" Nadine asked.

Russell shrugged. "They'll run out of ammunition, eventually. There's a lot of guns out there but not many bullets. And they are truly horrible shots."

"Need to practice more," Nadine said.

Six more shots rang out. "Sounds like they're doing that now," Russell said.

"Let me get some more of those apples, and I'll be right with you." Nadine walked across the plaza toward a fruit stand.

Shutt looked at Russell. He looked back. "What?"

"The admiral. She's his granddaughter. He trusts her. He also won't do anything that might hurt her."

"Understood," Russell said.

"But if you hurt her, that's a different story."

***

"So, Jake, are you ready to help me get this Jump ship going?" Jake turned and was confronted with Major Shutt. After much wrangling, he had managed to get his semi-hard suit back from the TGI stores. He felt much better, much more himself suited up, ready for anything. As a belter, he was used to shipping out with just the personal items he could carry in his suit pockets and a single duffel bag so he could go at any moment.

Ship supplies were another story. He had checked what was available at point-37 and arranged to have the rest loaded onto the west train. He was double-checking his loading as Shutt arrived.

"I've already got it going once by myself," Jake said. "But more hands will make it faster."

"Well, we'll do it right this time. The Militia way."

Jake surveyed her. She reminded him of Nadine, even though she was physically the opposite—brunette, where Nadine's was blond. Brown eyes where Nadine's was blue. Nadine always crackled with energy, like she was going to explode. Major Shutt seemed to embody strength. Nadine would knock you over and leave you bleeding as she raced by. Major Shutt seemed more likely to crush you slowly.

"I did it right the first time. She's in orbit right now. The correct orbit. But I've been reading some of the maintenance manuals. I want to change the hydrogen/oxygen mix slightly. That should give us a longer range and better fuel efficiency. But it seems like the best way is to stop the engines, purge the lines, and restart everything. I'll be running things from the bridge. But I need a skilled engineer to watch the gauges in on the engines."

"Call me Clarisse," she said.

"I don't think that would be proper. I'm going to be the captain. I think I'll call you Major Shutt. You can call me captain."

Major Shutt laughed. "Think you can keep that attitude up for the whole trip, el capitan?"

Jake shouldered his bag. "Yes. Yes, I do."

"Well, it's not like you are a real captain."

"I'm not in the Militia. But you've been ordered to take my orders. And I can make it difficult for you."

Major Shutt threw him a salute. "You can't do anything to me. You're not in the Militia, remember?"

"Dashi can. The admiral listens to him."

"Keep hiding behind Dashi while you can, Jake. But Dashi won't be up there with us. I will. And I'll be watching." Her comm buzzed. "Excuse me, that's the admiral calling." She stepped away from Jake and walked to the platform's edge.

"On the train yet?" Admiral Edmunds asked over the comm.

"Any minute, sir."

"Any issues with Jake?"

"Funny you should ask, sir. He mentioned that Dashi could make trouble for me."

"Dashi can't make trouble for you. I'm the only one who can make trouble for you. You have your orders from the council?"

"Assist Mr. Stewart. Kind of broad and unspecific, sir."

"That was deliberate."

"Miss Nadine is still to be the pilot, sir?"

"Yes. She'll be delayed looking at that water ocean ship."

"I should be the pilot, sir, not her."

"Why don't you two get along? It's not like you're competing for rank or anything."

Shutt looked over at Nadine, who was schmoozing with Russell. "Everyone is allowed one unreasonable dislike, sir."

"Don't let it get in the way of accomplishing your mission."

"I never do, sir. Any verbal addendum to the written orders?"

"That ship should be under the Militia's control. I want

you to take care of that."

"Seize the ship?"

"No violence. But get in control."

"It already has a commander, sir. Mr. Stewart. Appointed by the council, no less. And those Free Traders."

"All sorts of things can happen in orbit, Major. Accidents. Those Free Traders are sloppy. They don't understand discipline. They're bound to mess something up."

"Should I help them mess something up?"

"Use your discretion, Major. But remember, I want the Militia firmly in control when you come back. Accidents or not."

"Understood, sir."

"And Major?"

"Sir?"

"Accidents can happen to captains, too. Even temporary corporate ones."

***

Jake walked over to where the Free Traders were talking. "Marianne. Yvette. Odette."

"Jake," Marianne said. "Here's the crew for the Jump ship. Yvette and Odette. I think you've already met."

"Yes."

"We were discussing chain of command," Yvette said.

"I'm to be captain."

"You're sure of that?" Yvette said. "Shutt seems to think otherwise."

"Indubitably," Jake said.

The women looked at each other. "What?"

"Look it up," Jake said. "I don't have time to explain. Are you ready to do your part?"

"Always. Are you?"

"Always. Ms. Nadine will be delayed while she takes care of some private business for the admiral."

"Is that what they call it these days?" Odette asked. "Private business?"

"It's not like that. She's his granddaughter."

"And that means nothing can happen? Well, it's none of our business. But Marianne showed me that display. Ms. Nadine must be very flexible." She smiled at Jake. "I'm quite flexible, too."

Jake blushed. "Major Shutt will be our engineering officer."

"I heard that. I don't trust her."

"She's very experienced," Jake said.

Marianne looked at her people. "You two might find her a convenient air lock."

"We all have to get along," Jake said. "We don't need to use air locks."

"Whatever you say," Marianne said. "Captain."

"Why didn't you come along on this trip?" Jake asked. "I heard that you turned down a spot."

"I need to keep an eye on the admiral and Jose down here."

"And Dashi."

"Dashi has been a friend. Everything he's done has benefited the Free Traders up 'til now. Benefited him too of course."

"We need to think win-win. Everybody should win something," Jake said.

"Everybody can't," Marianne said. "But Dashi always does. It's best to be on his side. Is there anything specific you need from me? I need to brief the crew."

Jake checked his comm. "I have to go see Dashi out front. We're boarding in a few minutes."

Marianne watched him go, then turned to Yvette and Odette. "This Militia major. Shutt."

"Air lock?" Odette asked.

"No. We have to be subtle," Marianne said. "You can't just toss her out."

"Too bad," Odette said. "I was looking forward to

that."

"Keep her on a leash," Marianne said to Yvette. "Don't let her be so brazen."

"Odette gets excited," Yvette said. "We need her enthusiasm. But no throwing Shutt into an air lock, d'accord."

"No throwing her," Marianne said. "But if she happens to fall into one by herself, that's a different matter."

"D'accord," Yvette said. "What about that Nadine girl?"

"Shutt doesn't like her."

"Why not?"

"I think she wants to be something other than the admiral's subordinate."

"Oh. Oooooohhhhh." Odette said. "I can make something of that. What about Stewart?"

"He's smart. He thinks things through. Watch and learn. And he's Dashi's man."

"Dashi has always been a friend to the Free Traders," Yvette said.

"He has always looked out for us in the past. It suited his plans. And I think he will continue to do so. Until he doesn't."

"What about Stewart then?"

"Whatever happens, when you get back, I want you two in charge of that ship. Don't hurt Stewart."

"And the Militia major?"

Marianne shrugged.

Odette smiled and pumped her hand. "Air lock."

***

"Are you ready to do your duty, Mr. Stewart," Dashi said. He climbed the stairs in front of the monorail station, leaning on his cane.

"Duty, sir?" Jake said. "I'll do my job."

"Is there a difference?" Dashi asked.

Jake thought for a moment. "Duty implies adherence

to some external belief system, or loyalty to some organization. Like the Empire."

"Are you loyal to the Empire."

"Well, I." Jake stopped. "What does that mean, sir? There's been no Empire here for years. Longer than I've been alive. How can I be loyal to something that doesn't exist?"

"Just because we have lost contact is not the same as it not existing." Dashi stopped and regarded more stairs ahead of him.

"Just lean on my shoulder, sir. I'll help you up. The Empire could exist, but it seems like a ... remote thing."

"You said you will do your job, didn't you?"

"To the best of my ability, sir."

"Which is a totally artificial, arbitrary, and unaccountable promise." Dashi grunted as he stepped up one more step. "And really reliant on your personal interpretation. But the more important question is why - why do your best job? Why your best efforts?"

"Sir?"

"Why bother. Why not do a bad job instead?" Dashi reached the top of the stairs and leaned against the wall. He wasn't quite gasping for breath. Not quite.

Jake struggled to answer. Talking to Dashi always messed with his head. "Because, because, well, that's what people do, sir. You do your job. Sir." Jake paused. "What do I call you now? Emperor?"

"The admiral struggled with what to call me. In his case he doesn't want to grant me any extra authority. Is that the case with you?"

"I respect you, sir. Should I call you your majesty?"

"That would be for a king. Emperors are called 'Imperial majesty.'"

"Is that a yes, your Imperial majesty?"

"It is not. I don't even rule a planet, never mind an Empire. Not right now. My name is Dashi, and Mr. Dashi is fine. But back to the topic. Are you up for this? Being captain of this Jump ship?"

"I can do this," Jake said.

"The Free Traders are experienced with trading and maintenance. The Militia are experienced with violence. What do you bring to the table?"

"Reason," Jake said.

"Reason?"

"Reason over passion, sir. The universe favors a prepared mind. I think before I do. Long before I do. This Jump ship is a complicated thing. You need a thinker. Someone to play the long game." Jake looked at Dashi. "Like you do, with the planet."

Dashi smiled his enigmatic smile. "The Militia, in the person of the admiral, thinks the planet should be under military control."

"That didn't work so well before," Jake said.

"They will claim that is because 'other' Militia were in charge, and things will be different now. Other members of the council want a return to the pre-mutiny corporate governorship." Dashi took a deep breath and pushed himself up another step. "My position as leader of the council is not as secure as it looks. The Free Traders support me, but only as long as my interests run with theirs. Long-term, they want to be left alone. Other factions are watching and waiting for my first slip."

"What do you want from me, sir?" Jake said, helping Dashi up the last few steps.

Dashi levered himself to the top and paused to catch his breath. "I have invested a great deal of my prestige in assigning you to this Jump ship. You will have to deal with the other competing factions on this. You will be alone up there, without allies."

"Ms. Nadine will be with me, sir."

"She may not be available. I think her current task may take her longer than anticipated. If she does not make your orbital rendezvous, you must proceed without her."

"Understood, sir."

"Take command of that Jump ship. Bring it up to full operational status. Follow that other Jump ship, if possible. Your first Jump should be to somewhere close. I will send you details. I am quite worried about the lack of replacement parts for the power plant. I may have to divert you to 61 Cygni to pick some up.

"61 Cygni? How do you know the parts will be there, sir?"

"I know many things, Mr. Stewart. I will share the details as appropriate. Is there anything else?" Dashi asked.

Jake hesitated. "There seems to be some ambiguity on who is in command.

"Not for me," Dashi said. "I'm the Emperor—at least, that's what they tell me. I've put you in command. Our discussion on that matter is complete."

"There seems to be some disagreement from the other ... factions, sir." He held a door for Dashi as he stumped down a hall toward the platform.

"I'm counting on you to disabuse them," Dashi said. "You have your instructions. For now. I may send you more detailed needs later." Dashi looked around. "Excuse me, I need to speak to some others." He walked away.

Jake watched him go. Jose walked over and extended his hand. "Good luck, Jake. You know, seeing you here, getting ready to take command of that Jump ship, it's hard to square that with the belter boy who came into my office years ago to see Dashi. You've turned out to be much smarter than I would have thought at the time."

Jake shook. "Thanks, Jose."

"And more ruthless, too."

Jake held the handshake. "Well, you are one of the smartest men I've ever met, and the second most ruthless, much more so than I thought all those years ago, so I guess we both misjudged the other."

"I guess we did," Jose said. "Good thing we both work for Dashi, and don't have to compete with each other. You'd give me a run for my money."

"Or you'd give me one for mine," Jake said. Jake looked up as the western monorail glided in. "Free Trades, Jose, I have a train to catch."

Jose stepped back as Jake shouldered his bag.

"Pompous ass," Marianne said. She had snuck up behind Jose.

Jose crossed his arms. "Maybe. But there has been, effectively, a three- or four-sided civil war over the last few days. By dint of planning, effort, and action, Jake Stewart has helped Mr. Dashi come out on top. His reward is to be in charge of the single most valuable space-based asset this colony has left. He may be pompous, but don't underestimate his ability."

"You think he'll stay in charge? Of that ship? Once they're in the rings."

"Yes."

"I think the admiral's people will take it from him."

"I don't think so. The admiral can't even get all his own people appointed to it. He lacks credibility."

"The admiral says the Militia won the war."

"The Militia started the war, lost the war, almost destroyed the city, albeit the admiral kept them from destroying more. So, if you define 'winning the war' as 'keeping us from descending into total chaos,' then, sure, he won the war."

Marianne smiled. "I agree the Militia didn't come out looking very good here. But can you blame them for what that officers' council did?"

"Odd to hear you arguing their side."

"I'm interested in what you think about them."

Jose watched Jake argue with the train's loadmaster. "I don't blame the Militia for what the officers' council did. You can't stop others from acting. I blame them for not stopping the officers' council from starting it. And not taking extraordinary measures once it started. Had I been in charge, I would have dealt with things differently."

"Jake said you were smart and ruthless."

"He specifically said one of the smartest and one of the most ruthless."

"Who's smarter than you?"

"Jake is. He's smarter than me. One of the smartest men I know."

"You believe that?"

"Of course."

"What about ruthless?"

"There are hundreds of people who are dead, stations that are destroyed, lives that are forever changed, all because of decisions that Jake Stewart made. He's an agent of change and not always positive for the people changed. He's ruthless. But not the most ruthless."

"You're more ruthless?"

"Than him, yes."

"So, this is a battle between smart and ruthless? Which one of you is going to win?"

"Uncertain. Right now, we've got a guarded neutrality."

"You don't think you will win?"

"Not right now, no."

"Jake will."

"Nope."

"I don't understand."

"Jake said I'm one of the most ruthless, and I said he's one of the smartest."

"Who else is there?"

"Dashi, of course. He's smarter than us both. And more ruthless than us both."

"What's he doing, then?"

"Dashi? He's planning how to run an Empire."

CHAPTER 10

The ship was named Gaspar and was tied up to a dock not far from the shuttle port. Sergeant Russell, and his crew could see it from three hundred meters away as they walked down the street. Russell slowed to speak with Chaudhari, then sped up to walk in front with Nadine. Chaudhari walked beside each squad member in turn, speaking to them.

Nadine was crunching into a second apple, holding a sack of them in one hand. "Shouldn't your squad be doing one of those marching things? You know, left, right, up, down, whatever."

"We could," Sergeant Russell said, "but that's not really my thing. These guys can't do it, anyway."

"Bad soldiers, huh?"

"There are lots of Militia people who can march but not many who can keep their heads when things go sideways. I prefer smart, tough, innovative troopers to marching zombies."

"They don't look like much. Those two girls are really small. They can't be much of a threat."

"One's a lawyer, the other is a computer expert. I've got two medics on the squad. I picked this group myself so that I'd have mixed skill sets. Everybody got shot at during the riot and shot back. And they didn't panic. Well, not much."

"You don't look like a fellow who panics." She took another bite. "I'll bet you're always cool."

"Looks can be deceiving. I have a bit of a temper."

"Apple?" Nadine offered one from her sack.

"No thanks." He tapped his mouth. "I've got bad teeth. Might hurt them."

"How'd your teeth go bad?"

"Smoking."

"I hear you used to be a senior master sergeant."

"I'm just a sergeant now."

"What happened?"

"I insulted a useless orbital forces officer."

"How did you insult him?"

"I called him a useless orbital forces officer."

"Creative. They busted you down for that?"

"No. They busted me for ramming him into a trash can headfirst, hitting him with a stick and then pushing the trash can down a hill with him inside it."

Nadine chewed her apple a bit more. "Big hill?"

"Pretty big. With a lake at the bottom."

They arrived at the gangplank where the ship was tied up. A guard sat in a lawn chair at the foot of it. Sergeant Russell addressed the Militia guard. "We're your relief."

"It's about time," the guard said. He drank from a bottle that smelled of whiskey. "We've been here all day."

Sergeant Russell visibly reined his anger in, then looked up at the boat. Three other Militia guards were on the deck. Two were asleep. The third was sitting, whittling something by the rail. A hatch was propped open on the front deck, and two figures bent over something.

"Tough duty," Sergeant Russell said. "They want you back at Militia HQ. Shamus, take this guy's place."

Shamus stepped over as the other struggled up. He made to hand the bottle to Shamus, who glanced at Sergeant Russell. Sergeant Russell nodded, and Shamus took the bottle.

The rest of the squad traipsed up the gangplank, escorting a subdued Commander Roi.

"You guys are done," Sergeant Russell said, kicking the sleeping Militia's feet on deck. "If you can be back at Militia HQ in the next fifteen minutes, say you're with

Sergeant Russell, you'll be dismissed to quarters. But you have to get there right away."

The four guards didn't need any urging. They collected their gear and stumbled off the boat. Russell leaned over to Chaudhari and muttered in his ear. Chaudhari nodded and dispersed the squad around the boat.

"Let's go see the sailors," Russell said. He and Nadine walked up to the front of the boat and looked into the open hatch. Two men, who looked like brothers, were laboring on a rusty metal object. A chain came out of a hole in the front of the boat, wound around a gear, and dropped into a big pit below.

"Hello, sailors," Russell said.

The two men looked up. "Hello, Militia," one said.

"I'm Sergeant Russell." He consulted his comm. "Which one of you is Balthazar?"

"Me," one said. "This is my brother, Melchior."

"You're the owner?"

"Family ship," Balthazar said. "We all own jointly."

"What are you doing?"

"We're greasing the windlass," Balthazar said.

Sergeant Russell and Nadine looked at each other. "Ever greased a windlass, Ms. Nadine?" Sergeant Russell asked.

"Is that what it's called?" Nadine grinned. "I've greased a lot of things."

"It sounds like something I'd want some privacy for," Sergeant Russell said. He peered into the chain locker. "How come you're doing it?"

"If we don't grease the chain regularly," Balthazar said, "the chain gets rusty, and it can get stuck."

"You wouldn't want a rusty chain, would you, Sergeant?" Nadine asked.

"I wouldn't want it to get stuck, either," Sergeant Russell said. He looked at the two men. "Aren't you supposed to be locked up so you don't escape?"

"Escape where?" Balthazar said. "This is our family's

ship, our livelihood, all our money is here. If we 'escape,' you Imperial anuses surely aren't going to clean it or scrape the barnacles off."

"And you wouldn't want too many barnacles, would you, Sergeant?" Nadine asked.

Sergeant Russell shook his head. "I'm not sure how much is innuendo and how much is boat-talk. What's in that bag?" He pointed.

"That's the foresail," Melchior said.

"I've never been on a sailboat before," Sergeant Russell said. "You hoist those sails up, and the boat moves, right."

"That's the gist of it, yes," Melchior said. "There are some other details. You have to not be tied to something, and having the anchor out like we do, will cause problems."

"How far can we go?"

"As far as you want. Could sail around the world's water ocean in this boat, provided the wind lasts."

"How much food you got?"

"Lots. We had just loaded a 90-day supply for us when your people came down and threatened to shoot us all. Kind of harsh for honest merchants, don't you think?"

"I hear you were smuggling guns," Nadine said.

"And yet, no guns were found," Melchior said.

"They probably didn't look right. I'm here to help with that."

"Great," Melchior said.

"Okay, let me understand this," Sergeant Russell said. "You untie those rope things."

"Let go the dock lines, yes," Melchior said.

"Pick up that anchor."

"Hoist the anchor."

"And then tie the far sail up."

"Hoist the sails. Foresail and mainsail."

"Right. Then we're good for sailing for a month or so. Can sail around the world?"

"Not in a month, but we could go a fair distance."

"Could we go to the south continent?"

"Why would you want to do that, Sergeant?" Melchior said.

"Just getting an idea of possibilities. Chaudhari?" Sergeant Russell yelled to the back of the boat. Chaudhari came up front, followed by two troopers. "We're on. Check out that bag there."

Chaudhari went over to the foresail in the sail bag. He pulled the sail out 'til the bag was completely empty. "What do you think? It big enough?" Russell asked.

Chaudhari shook the bag loose from the sail. The sail billowed along the deck. "I think it's big enough." He gestured to two other troopers who closed him, and they walked it over to Sergeant Russell and Nadine.

"That's a big sail," Nadine said. "Too big for one person to handle."

"It's not the sail. My question—is the bag big enough?" Sergeant Russell asked.

Chaudhari held the neck of the bag wide open and brought it over to Nadine.

"Big enough for what?" she asked. She peered into the bag.

Sergeant Russell nodded, and the two troopers grabbed Nadine's waist, pinned her arms to her side, and slid her into the open bag with one smooth motion. It happened so quickly Nadine couldn't resist. Chaudhari managed to get the bag down to her legs as she started kicking. Then the two troopers pinned her legs together. Chaudhari was able to pull the bag over her feet and pull the drawstring tight and tie it off. He set her down on the deck. Nadine yelled as the bag twitched.

"Perfect size," Sergeant Russell said. He turned to the bemused men standing in the anchor locker. "Right. Hoist the dock lines and let go of the bow or whatever you're supposed to do. Let's get this show on the road." He looked around the quiet river. "We're going sailing!"

***

81

The Gaspar slid down the river and picked up speed. The two brothers had been stunned for a moment, but after Sergeant Russell confirmed he was serious about an escape, they had broken out in a flurry of motion. They grabbed the third brother and began a complex series of maneuvers to bring the boat into the center of the river. One of the dock lines yielded some sort of problem, but they tied a second line back to the dock and spun sideways, which fixed the problem, and they were off.

"Chaudhari, take Ms. Nadine below and lock her bag in one of the cabins. Then let Commander Roi loose and ask him to step up here."

"He's not going to be happy," Chaudhari said.

"It was a necessary sacrifice for the Empire," Sergeant Russell said.

"Really?"

"Just go get him. Bring that basic. And follow my lead." Chaudhari and one of the others manhandled a struggling bag down below. Sergeant Russell turned to Balthazar, who was manning the wheel next to him.

"We're happy to be away from that dock, but do you want to tell me why you did this?" Balthazar said.

"Your agent, Molina, talked."

"I don't know a Molina."

"Whatever you say. He spilled his guts at the temporary Council HQ. They know that you brought the guns in for the Growers. I've got a warrant of execution on my comm. I was to tie up the three of you and take you into town for imprisonment and trial."

"Trial?"

"When I say trial, I mean death. They were going to hang you for your part in the rebellion."

"And you're fundamentally opposed to violence?"

"That's why I joined the Militia, to keep the peace. Sure." Sergeant Russell looked around. "I've never been on a sailing ship before. We're moving pretty fast."

"It's a sailboat, not a sailing ship, and that's the river

current and the tide running out."

"Is that good?"

"It makes us go fast. Why did you rescue us?"

Chaudhari interrupted them by escorting a snarling Commander Roi.

"Sergeant Russell, you despicable, groveling traitor," Commander Roi said.

"Good morning, sir," Sergeant Russell said. He took the cup from Chaudhari. "Here's some basic, sir. You must be famished. And things are not as they seem, sir."

"Explain yourself, Sergeant," Roi said.

"Sir," Sergeant Russell said, saluting. "In accordance with directive forty-two, issued by the officers' council and approved by the late Colonel Savard, I inform you that the leadership of the officers' council has devolved to you, Colonel Savard having been killed in the fighting. Pursuant to secret verbal orders issued to me by Colonel Savard before his demise, in the event of his death, I was to secure your person and remove you from enemy proximity to facilitate your taking command of remaining forces. Which I have done so."

"Colonel Savard told you to do this?"

"Indeed, sir."

"You slugged me in the head. Did he tell you to do that?"

"Not precisely, sir. Regrettable, but it had to be done. Our tactical position was untenable at the time, and we needed to effect a ruse-de-guerre to ensure your survival and later removal to a secure area."

"Then you locked me up and gagged me."

"Absolutely, sir. Where would be more secure than the enemy's own cells? You were totally safe, sir."

"The troops abused me."

"As they were instructed, sir. It was necessary to retain a combat capability, and we could only do so by preserving my squad."

"They hit me and shocked me."

"Yes, sir, they thought that part up themselves. I'm quite proud of them. I'm going to recommend them for a decoration when we have time."

"You want them to be decorated for beating an officer with their shoes?"

"Improvise, adapt, and overcome, sir. Just look at the verisimilitude it added to the whole thing. Outstanding work. Don't you agree Chaudhari?"

"Outstanding verisimilitude, Sergeant. Why, I've never seen verisimilitude like it."

"Chaudhari agrees, sir," Sergeant Russell said. "And I will say, he knows verisimilitude when he sees it."

Roi rubbed his chin. "So, this whole thing was a fraud? The capture, the arrest, all of that."

"Yes, sir. It was necessary for the TGI people to believe I was on their side, otherwise I would never get the chance to do what is necessary."

"Lee spat on me."

"It broke her heart, sir. She came to me later and cried. Very sad, sir. I think she has post-traumatic stress disorder. You should go see her, sir, and apologize to her for making her spit on you."

"You want me to apologize to her because she spat on me?"

"Would you, sir? Outstanding. I knew Colonel Savard, the Empire honor his memory, made the right choice." He smiled at everyone within hearing. "Three cheers for the commander! Hip Hip, Hooray."

All the troops cheered and waved their hats in the air. Commander Roi looked even more confused.

"We just need the directions, sir."

"Directions?" Colonel Roi asked.

"To the secret base on the south continent, sir, where you will go to take command of the remainder of the real Empire forces."

Commander Roi's eyes widened, then he stumbled over as the boat rocked. "Colonel Savard told you of this?"

"He did," Sergeant Russell said. "Before he died. Oh, not the secret details, just that I was to spirit you away from captivity and take you to the base."

"Didn't you put me in captivity to start with, Sergeant?"

"You do know the location, do you not, sir?"

"I do," Commander Roi said. "All of the original members of the officers' council did."

"We got this sailship thingy with all these sail for you to take us there, sir," Sergeant Russell said.

"It's not called a sailship, Sergeant" Roi said. "Technically, it's a sloop rigged fourteen- meter sailboat with jib and mainsail. How much do we draw?"

"Sir?"

Roi leaned over the rail and peered at the water. "What's our draft? What type of keel?"

"I don't know those terms sir."

Balthazar spoke up. "Bulb keel. Draws less than two meters."

"How much ballast?" Roi asked.

"Two thousand kilos," Balthazar said.

"Good enough then. We can work with this," Roi said. He and Balthazar began to discuss the technical details of the sailboat.

Chaudhari leaned close to Sergeant Russell. "He sounds almost competent there. Have I been drinking?"

Sergeant Russell shrugged. "He can't be bad at everything he does."

"All evidence to the contrary," Chaudhari said.

Blond hair streaked by as Nadine thumped out from the cabin hatch, leaped up on the rail, yelled, and dove into the water.

"What was that?" Commander Roi said.

"That would be a Militia agent, sir. Also, the admiral's granddaughter."

"What is she doing here?"

"Drowning," Balthazar said from the helm. "Unless

you get her back on board in the next five minutes."

CHAPTER 11

"I understand now what the term 'herding cats' means," Jake said. He was at the pilot's board of the yet-to-be-named Jump ship, attempting an engine restart with his crew.

"What do cats have to do with her unwillingness to do a proper professional launch sequence?" Major Shutt asked from the adjacent console.

"Do cats do a lot of unnecessary talking and perform useless checks? Because that is what we are doing here," Yvette said from the console behind Jake.

"This is a proper launch sequence."

"It's a waste of time. It's designed for idiots in the Militia who know nothing about ships. We waste time checking things three times."

"We need to cross-check our settings."

"Militia draftees need to cross-check their settings because they don't know what any of those numbers mean. We Free Traders are smarter, and we understand what we're doing, unlike you."

"Watch it, merchie, or I'll show you what I know," Shutt said.

"Try me. I'll show you what I've learned." Yvette glared at her. "Let's see who's the better educated."

Shutt stood and turned to face Yvette. "If you want to fight, we need more space. Hab module." The two women moved down the corridor.

Jake took a deep breath. This is important. Don't let Dashi down. Don't screw up, he thought. "No, we don't need more space. We don't need the hab module. We need to get this engine started at a higher flow rate, and I need both of you to watch your boards while I crank up the flow." He looked at them. "And the last thing we need is the two of you to start punching on each other in the lounge." Jake tried to look Yvette in the eye, but he couldn't help shifting his eyeshot between the two. Skin suits weren't designed to conceal, and they were angry, flushed, and fit.

Yvette watched Jake's eyes flicker up and down, then laughed and turned to Major Shutt. "His mouth says no, no, but his eyes say yes, yes. Should we strip down to our underwear and find pillows and hit each other with them?"

Major Shutt looked confused for a moment but then glanced at Jake and smirked. "I'll bet our commander wouldn't stop us then." Her smile grew wider. "We can leave the punching for now. Know that I'm not happy with this."

"Then I have achieved my objective," Yvette said. She looked at Jake. "Any word from your girlfriend?"

"No. She disappeared with a squad escorting some prisoners, according to Dashi."

"I don't trust that girl," Yvette said.

"Me neither," Major Shutt said.

"Strange, us agreeing on that one thing," Yvette said.

"Why don't you like her?" Jake asked.

"I don't think she's a very good pilot. Not good enough for a Jump ship, anyway. I think she slept her way into the job."

Jake blushed.

"I thought so," Yvette said. "Well, if she's not here, then I will take over as first pilot."

"No," Major Shutt said. "I'll take over as first pilot if she's not here."

The women squared off again. Jake sighed and rubbed his head. It was going to be a long shift.

***

They managed to get the engines going at the highest possible flow rate without anybody stripping to their underwear, and they needed no pillows. Yvette ended up flying because Shutt trusted her as an engineer even less than as a pilot, and Shutt couldn't do two things at once. She checked on what they had done to the engines.

"This is amazing technology," Yvette said. "Even at the higher flow rate, there is no loss of efficiency like we would have on our ships. Normally, the faster we go, the worse the fuel efficiency, but here, it stays the same."

"Yes, these Imperials knew how to build a ship," Jake said. "I've never seen anything like it."

"Do we have a course?"

"Just test orbits to make sure everything is working properly at the higher velocities and that all the other sub-systems work. Then we need to get out and track that other Jump ship."

"What's it doing?"

"It's on a least fuel cost course from a point in the rings to the jump limit. It's on target to jump out of the system. If it does, we'll go after it and test our Jump drive."

"I am excited for that. What is necessary for a jump? Operations-wise."

"Just get away from the Dragon's area of gravitational control—one hundred twenty-eight planetary diameters, according to the book, pick a destination, run the computer, wait, then we can jump."

"Where are we going?"

"It depends on that other Jump ship. If it jumps, we should follow it. Right now, it could be going to several places. If it doesn't jump, I'm still discussing options with Dashi. I say we should go here"—Jake pulled up a chart— "this is the local systems. See this one off on the side here? It's kind of a dead-end, but it's close, a very short distance. Traffic there would have come through our system first, and according to the records, it had low population."

"Breathable atmosphere, some water, reasonable

temperature. Sounds like paradise. Why isn't it settled?"

"It was settled—sort of. According to records, it was an Imperial hunting reserve. Members of the Imperial family could go there to hunt, but Dashi said they never did. The big thing is that it's way off the shipping lanes, and it has no substantial mineral resources."

"Why not go there?"

"Because it won't reconnect us to the Empire. It's a dead-end. They would have to come through us to go anywhere. We could go this way." Jake pointed at another spot on the chart.

"That is farther?" Yvette asked.

"Yes, it's at the limit of our jump capacity. If we jumped there, we'd need to refuel, and reprovision before we moved on."

"And you don't know if there will be either fuel or provisions if we go there."

"I believe it is safer to test things by the shorter jump first."

"Well, as soon as your girlfriend gets on board, we can go."

"As soon as Dashi gives us the OK, we can go," Jake said.

"Even without that annoying Ms. Nadine?"

"She's not annoying."

"Not to you, no." Jake's console beeped.

"And there's an incoming from Dashi. Or Jose, in this case. Let me decrypt it," Jake said. He took a few seconds to decrypt it and read it. "Well, can you call everyone up to the bridge?"

"There's a problem."

"You could say that, yes. They've detected the rogue Militia cutter. It's following that other Jump ship, on a converging course. It looks like they mean to board it."

CHAPTER 12

"That's something I never expected to see," Jake said. He gestured to the display. The Dragon, Sigma Draconis IV, filled the display, the rings, their moons clearly visible.

"I've never been this far above the rings," Yvette said. "We normally see them edge on or just a bit above. Why don't we do this more often?"

"It's not worth the fuel to change our inclination," Jake said. "Since we're going from one station to the other, and they're almost all in the plane of the ecliptic."

"Or just orbiting Delta." Yvette pointed. "It looks small from here."

"There's Alpha and Bravo moons, where's Charlie?" Odette asked.

"Behind the Dragon," Jake said. "You can't see it from here."

"It's beautiful, seen from above," Major Shutt said.

"Technically, we're seeing it from below," Jake said. "From this angle, the Dragon is rotating counterclockwise, so that makes us below the ecliptic."

"Had to ruin the moment, didn't you, Stewart? Just have to ruin beauty with facts."

"Beauty and facts are the same thing. The beauty of the universe is seen in how it is, not as you want it to be."

All three women looked at Jake.

"That is remarkably profound," Yvette said.

"Also useless to help us calculate our next course. Stewart, why are you flipping from cynical observation to waxing poetic?" Shutt said.

"I'm not a poet," Jake said.

"Not a good one, that's for sure. What's our new orbit look like?"

"We've changed our inclination. Now we just need to wait 'til we're at the apocenter. Then we fire again and get as far out as we need to for the jump."

"And we're doing this, why?" Shutt said.

"Shouldn't you call me captain?"

"Shouldn't you answer the question?"

Jake shook his head. "Jose has reported that the other Jump ship has settled on a course that will take it above the rings, out of the Dragon's orbit, and in a position to make a jump to an adjacent system."

"Follow that Jump ship, then," Shutt said.

"Jose has also reported that the rogue Militia cutter they were monitoring has changed course and is trying to catch up to that Jump ship."

"Will they catch it?"

"Maybe. But if we have to follow Jump ship number one, and they are also following Jump ship number one ..."

Yvette nodded. "They are closing us as well. We will be close."

"We have to stop them from getting that other Jump ship," Shutt said.

"We have to stop them from harming us," Yvette said.

"I've got a course input," Jake said. "Keep us as far from that other ship but still follow Jump ship number one."

"How long will that take?"

"Long thrust, then a longer coast. At least a shift and a half."

"And what about those guys chasing us?"

"If they're smart, they'll stop following us."

"Why?"

"The weather's going to get worse."

"We're in space, Stewart, we don't have weather," Major Shutt said.

"Not close to Delta, no. But we will," Jake said.

***

"There they go," Daav said. "Starting a really long burn out to beyond the rings."

"You should say the Dragon's rings," Jammy said.

"Thank you, Mr. Obvious Navigator. What other rings are there?"

"That's commander navigator to you. Sigma Draconis III and V both have rings."

"You navigate, I'll fly. And we're not going to a different planet."

"We will if I say so. With this orbit, we're halfway to anywhere in the system." Jammy played with his console. "Only some minor changes to our orbit, and we could hit one of the other planets. More than one."

"Children, stop fighting," Perlins said. "Or the adults will have to get involved. How long to get to another planet?"

"Four months ..." Jammy said.

"We're not going there alive," Daav said.

"We heard you about supplies. No need to belabor it," Perlins said.

"I'm not talking about supplies." Daav brought up a screen. It showed the primary.

"Wow, bright red star, very far away," Perlins said. "Exciting, but I'm going back to my bunk. I'm going to enjoy the solitude of three fat, old majors snoring their boozing off."

"I wouldn't do that if I were you," Daav said. "There's no shielding back there."

"Shielding from what?" Perlins said.

"Heavy radiation shielding," Daav said.

"Where are we going to get heavy radiation?" Jammy said. Then he looked at the course plot. "Imperial anus. We're going outside the magnetosphere?"

***

"So, this solar weather forecast? It is bad?" Yvette asked.

"Very bad," Jake said. "Lots of energetic particles. There's been solar flares these last few weeks. It's a big deal."

"How can it be a big deal? We never even talk about this in the Militia," Major Shutt said. "We never checked solar weather."

"You never went outside the Dragon's humongous magnetosphere, either," Jake said. "We're all protected here by this massive magnetic field. It diverts all the bad stuff away from Delta and the rings. That's why the colony is here, on Sigma Draconis IV, and not closer in. That means that we don't need shielding. When we're in close to the Dragon."

"So, up 'til now, we've been covered by the Dragon's magnetic field."

"Right."

"But we're going outside the magnetic field. What's covering us, then?"

"This ship is heavier and designed for interplanetary orbits. It's shielded. And the room with the Jump computer is even better protected. If there's a storm coming, we can stay there for as long as we need."

"We hide in the Jump room, and we'll be fine," Yvette said. "D'accord. What about that ship chasing us?"

"Delta ships are all short-ranged and not designed to go outside of the rings."

"What's going to happen to them?"

"Nothing good," Jake said.

***

"They're all going to die?" Perlins asked. Her console screen had a red-bordered warning on it. The others were looking at similar ones.

"Not all of them. Well, not quickly, but yes, all of them," Daav said.

"Oh, good, a slow death is much preferable," Perlins said. "Glad you're on side. I'll sleep better now."

"I don't make the rules for how the universe works. I just fly in 'em," Daav said.

"Should we tell them?" Jammy said.

"The whole point of keeping quiet about it is so that it will be a surprise. They're too stupid to figure out that something bad might happen," Perlins said.

"I was too stupid to figure this out until you told me," Krikweigh said.

"Maybe you should be back there," Daav said.

"Maybe you should shut up before I rip your arm off and beat you with it," Krikweigh said.

"You'd like that, wouldn't you?" Daav said.

"Well, yes. Sure, I would." Krikweigh cracked his knuckles. He was at least a head taller than Daav, with big knuckles. "I worked a tug on the docks. I like fights."

"Not your best insult," Jammy said to Daav.

Perlins smacked the back of Daav's head. "Stop being dumb. I'm almost on team Krikweigh. Have you beaten just for being lame."

"Does all this violence make you hot?" Daav asked. "You know, aroused?"

"Says he, asking just in the interests of science," Jammy said.

"It does. Every time," Perlins said. "But then I look at either of the two of you, and the feeling goes away instantly."

"I'm wounded." Daav grasped his heart. "An arrow through the heart."

"Better than a bucket full of high-energy particles through your brain," Perlins said. "Now, curb your libido and think for a moment."

"Yes, Mother," Daav said.

Perlins smacked him again. "Keep still, boy. Jammy, can we change the course so that we stay in the magnetosphere?"

"Not and catch that Jump ship."

"Plus," Daav said, "This way we fix the problem of supplies without us actually having to shoot anyone or eat their corpses."

"I vote we eat Krikweigh first," Daav said. "He has the most meat on his bones."

"You want to try?" Krikweigh said. "And speaking of bones, maybe I'll use yours to pick my teeth with."

Perlins slapped Krikweigh upside his head. "Focus. Don't be gruesome. And no eating the other pilots."

"Would that be wrong?" Krikweigh asked.

"Not wrong. Pilots are just too stringy. We'll find somebody fatter if we need to."

"I'm not stringy," Jammy said. "I'm attractively svelte."

Perlins slapped Jammy's head. "Don't use words you don't understand. Look at this course. Figure out a way to keep us in the magnetosphere as long as you can. I'm getting tired of slapping people."

"Because it's bad for discipline?"

"Because my hands hurt."

"Why should we worry about staying in the magnetosphere?" Jammy asked. "We'll be fine if we shield ourselves from these flares."

"And where in the ship will we do that, master navigator?"

"Well, the main computer is back in engineering. Oh."

"On the other side of twenty-eight people that we're discussing which one to eat. Not a solution." She looked at her screen. "What stops energetic particles?"

"Metal," Jammy said.

"More metal," Daav said.

"Water," Krikweigh said. "Lots and lots of water."

The circulating fans whirred in the background as they considered this. "So," Perlins said, "we need somewhere surrounded by metal that we can fill with water. Got it. Krikweigh, you're with me."

"You know, you're not exactly senior here," Jammy

said. "Who said you could make all the decisions?"

"First, our so-called revolution, aka a coup, failed, so we're really mutineers, which sort of means that our ranks don't matter at all anymore. Second, if they did, some of those ground force doofus Empire-rising types back there outrank you, and we don't want them running things again 'cause they didn't do a great job before."

"Good points," Jammy said.

"And third, none of my plans involve eating putrefying corpses."

"Also a good point," Daav said.

Perlins hit him on the back of the head.

"Ow. What was that for this time?"

"Doesn't matter. You know you deserve it," Perlins said.

Daav nodded. "Yeah, that's true."

"Krikweigh, let's go." Perlins and Krikweigh unbelted and clambered out of the control room.

It was third shift, so most passengers were asleep, except for a group playing cards, so they were able to go outside without any comments. The changes didn't take long. One of the water intake port containers near the control cabin had a water bladder, complete with hoses and pumps. A quick EVA, and everything was connected. Perlins and Krikweigh reentered the main air lock and checked if all the hatches were closed.

"Now we need a sledgehammer and a pipe wrench," Perlins said.

"This is an advanced interplanetary Militia cutter," Jammy called from the bridge, "composed of the latest in locally built fusion drive elements, priceless pre-abandonment electronics, and a complete suite of software-configured sensors. We are highly trained orbital pilots, who have taken years of training to operate sophisticated systems, including old Empire, radar, lidar, optical and fire control systems. We do not use hammers."

"Right." Perlins snapped her fingers. "Fires. Krikweigh,

check the locker there. See if there's an ax."

Krikweigh unlatched the door and reached inside. He hefted a large ax. "Fire suppression 101, right here."

Perlins floated forward and leaned into the bridge hatch. "Jammy, how long 'til the hard radiation?"

"Already starting to climb. Course plot says we'll start hitting serious levels in about twenty minutes."

"Right. There's room for a few more. Should we pull anybody from back there before we start?"

"More people, less food," Krikweigh said.

"You can stand to lose a few pounds. Anybody?"

"There was a corporal," Daav said. "Dalon. He's all right. Not too up in this Empire-rising thing. He's a medic, and he came with one of his squad. Another medic. We should have them up here."

"I agree a medic, but why that medic?" Perlins asked.

"Well, he, I mean," Daav said. "Well, I know him. I talked to him on my last ship. He seemed like a good guy. Liked netball. We made a few bets."

"An incipient gambling problem is not a good reason to take somebody onto an opposed boarding," Perlins said.

"Is not having a gambling problem a good reason to kill him, then?" Krikweigh asked.

"What?" Perlins said.

"Let's be clear what we're doing," Krikweigh said. "We're going to kill twenty-eight or twenty-six people. A bunch. Slowly, without them having a chance to defend themselves. We're just going to let them fry while they sleep. They won't know what hit them. When they wake up, they'll already be dead, they just won't know it. Four hours—tops, that's all it will take to fry them up."

"It's them or us," Daav said. "You volunteering to change places?"

"I'm not. And don't think of trying to make me." Krikweigh held up his fist. "Still time to teach you your manners. But this isn't exactly honorable Militia work."

"I didn't join the Militia for this," Daav said.

"No, you joined the Militia to fly and chase girls," Jammy said. "That's why I like you. You're simple."

Daav stared at his board. "I just wanted to fly. I didn't care about much else."

"Why did you listen to those Empire-rising idiots, then?" Perlins asked. "What does that have to do with flying?"

"They sounded … certain. And that's what I wanted, right? To be the hero? Sally forth and strike the forces of darkness, the forces that would threaten the Empire."

"You really believed that?" Perlins asked.

"The alternative was to take retirement and drive an ore barge to the rings. Or just drink myself to death in an old pilots bar. When that's your future, you can convince yourself of anything."

"That's something we'll never see on a recruiting poster," Perlins said. "'Escape your upcoming misery by joining the Militia.' Why are you telling us this?"

"Cause a lot of people are going to die in the next few hours. Might even be us. Be me."

The ceiling's heating fan burped once, then resumed humming.

"I wanted to be an admiral," Jammy said, looking at the fan. "Or maybe a general."

"An admiral?" Daav shrugged. "You were probably going to be one, anyway."

"Not likely. I wasn't political enough, and the admiral's people didn't like me. These Empire-rising guys were ground forces, they didn't have enough orbital people. If I stuck with them, I'd be the senior orbital guy on board. They'd have to make me a general. I wanted to be a general."

"How about you, boss lady? Since we're confessing our sins, what are yours?"

"Greed. Money." Perlins turned and focused on a screen. "It started years ago. A little surplus equipment I sold on the side. It was going to be scrapped. Who could get hurt? Then the buyers came back. Wanted some cutter parts. Some sensors. Then a computer. Eventually, I was falsifying invoices and shipping paperwork, and one day, these Empire-rising guys came by and asked for weapons. The money was good, and they said they'd expose me if I didn't help. So, I became their main weapons supplier. I didn't like 'em, but they paid on time. Then the inspector general started sniffing around. I thought a good revolution would be a good opportunity to lose some records."

"So, here we are," Jammy said. "A clueless, washed-up retiree, a scheming opportunist, and a career thief who guessed wrong."

"No wonder the Empire abandoned us. I would have, too, if I could have," Perlins said. She looked at Krikweigh. "You've been quiet, big guy. Why did you buy what those Empire-rising people were selling?"

"I didn't," Krikweigh said. "I was a tug pilot. They needed one, so they brought a squad on and took it at gunpoint. I had to ferry them all around the system. At first, they kept a weapon on me, but after a while, they kind of forgot. I was waiting to find a way to get away. Then GG Main blew up."

"So, GG Main blew up. And you used that to get away."

"Nope, I hung around, you see, GG Main ... that was where my family was."

"You had family on GG Main?" Jammy asked. "But GG Main exploded."

"What happened to your family? Are they okay?" Daav asked.

"No."

The fans hummed in the silence.

"All dead. My wife. Two kids."

The heating fan whirred some more.

"I'm so sorry," Perlins said.

"Doesn't bring them back."

"But I—"

"Am not helping, skipper," Jammy said. "Sorry about your family, Krik, but we've got some decisions to make here. You've got some decisions to make here."

Krikweigh frowned. "You didn't do it. Besides, you're helping me out."

"Helping you out?"

"Sure. After the family died, I just gave up. Drove my tug. Followed these Empire-rising guys. After they took off, I had to give up the tug. I just followed along. They figured I had been with them all along."

"But you hadn't? Or weren't?"

"Return of the Empire? Stupid idea. And it will happen when the Empire decides it will. Nothing to be done here."

"So, you don't support them?"

"Don't care."

"So, why are you here?"

"No real reason. Habit. Maybe revenge," Krikweigh said. "GG were the people who killed my family. But it was these guys"—he jerked his hands behind him and pointed to the back of the ship—"who set it up. I want them to die." He turned to Perlins. "I like your plan. Go out and set up some radiation. Zap them all." He spun the ax in his hands. "Let's call that medic and his friend you wanted up here. Then we'll seal the hatch and flood the air lock. We'll all be safe here." He smiled at Perlins. "Then I can kill all the rest of them."

***

Daav had to go back and get Corporal Dalon and his medic friend. They arrived, cradling their helmets.

"What's up?" Dalon asked.

Perlins produced a revolver and pointed it at them. "Don't panic, but we need you to suit up in your skin suits, go to internal air, and hang out in the air lock here."

101

Dalon looked at Krikweigh, who was methodically jamming the hatches by bending the clips shut. They were in the main air lock, just behind the control room. It had dorsal, ventral, side, front, and rear hatches. The side hatch had a second door to make an air lock when the rest were closed, but in a pinch, the single room functioned as a generic air lock in five directions.

"Okay ... we can do that. We just need to put the helmets on and seal up. And I'm not sure how much free air is left in my bottle."

"We'll give you ship air to fill up," Perlins said. "As much as you need." She pointed at a refill port on the wall. "Do it quick, fill two bottles each. We're going to be in this lock for a while."

"We're going to be in the lock for a while? On internal air? Or are we going outside."

"Nope, we're staying in here. All six of us will lock in, then we'll jam the doors and fill this with water."

"I don't really need swimming lessons," Dalon said. "I actually learned at my ranch before I went orbital. I wasn't very good, but I can stay afloat."

"You won't be swimming or floating," Perlins said. "We're just immersing everybody in water."

"Then this is just a fun way to pass third shift?" Dalon asked. "Some sort of aquatic exercise program?"

"Radiation," the medic said. "Are we going to hit hard radiation?"

"Lots of it," Daav said. "Big solar flares coming up. And we're already outside the magnetosphere."

Dalon wagged his arms over his head. "Do I have time to work on my backstroke? Because—"

"Shut up," the medic said. "Suit up, air up, and help them jam those doors. We need to get this room full of water as soon as possible."

They closed and locked all the doors. Krikweigh stepped forward and hammered on the water pipe. Three hits with the ax, and it leaked. A fourth, and it broke, causing the water to gush out.

"Don't know how long it will take this compartment to fill up, and there might be some leakage into the main compartments," Perlins said.

"No," Krikweigh said. "If it's airtight, it's watertight, too. We just have to wait."

"This will stop most radiation," the medic said. "Um, but when we're past it, you do have a plan to drain the compartment, right? Before it freezes solid?"

The water reached the fan on the wall, and it shorted out with a popping sound.

"Well," Jammy said, "we should have considered that, shouldn't we?"

CHAPTER 13

"Push down, D," the therapist said. "It's all about the core."

Dashi grunted in pain as he pressed his leg forward. "Make sure not to break your leg, Jose. It's not the pain of the breaking that is the worst; it's the inevitable and continuous torture afterwards, disguised as medical therapy." He was sitting on a bench in the gym, with his physiotherapist supervising. Jose was standing nearby.

"You think I do this because I like making people yell?" the therapist asked. She was a thin, serious woman with "Doc Holly" embroidered on her yoga shirt. "That I'm some sort of freaky, pain-loving weirdo?"

"It does strain the bounds of credulity, Doctor Holly." Dashi said. "If that was the case, I would expect you to find you ensconced in some other profession, perhaps something in the combat arms."

Doc Holly formed 'ensconced' with her lips, then frowned. "Push," she said. She put her hands on Dashi's leg. "I want to feel your glutes and your hamstrings fighting each other."

Jose examined the gym. There were weight benches and free weights against one corner, a wide area with a rubber mat for stretches and exercises, and some sort of metal frame that looked like it was used for pull-ups. Or perhaps whippings. "Should I come back later, sir?"

"No." Dashi gasped for breath, then gritted his teeth and flexed his leg. "No. I'm unhappy now. Give me the worst."

"Still no power distribution. The crews can fix some

minor things, but they need parts, and we can't give them any dirtside. We need power to make the parts and parts to make the power. The replacements will have to come from orbit. "

"This is unfortunate."

"There's another problem."

"We're beset by problems. What is this particular one?"

"We can get them made in orbit. And get them down. The problem is securing them when they're down."

"Securing them?" Dashi asked. Shots rang out in the background. "Securing them from those people out there."

"Yes, the Militia is having some difficulty maintaining order. They told me that 'things are not going as expected.'"

"Things are not going as expected for me as well. A number of people have not lived up to my expectations," Dashi said.

"That's completely unfair," Doc Holly said. "This has nothing to do with me. It's all on you. If you did your exercises every day, like I told you, you wouldn't be nearly as stiff, and you would have much more flexibility."

"I am not referring to you, Dr. Holly, but to a colleague of ours, specifically the admiral. He promised to extend control over Landing and the surrounding area but has been unable to do so."

"Just so long as you recognize this is your fault, D. I can't do this for you. You have to do it yourself."

"Yes, Doctor," Dashi said.

"And perhaps the problem is you, not this other person," Doc Holly said. "Maybe you didn't pick the right professional or didn't find somebody in the right field. I can only help you with what I'm trained for, and it's your fault if you picked somebody to work for you but give them the wrong job."

"Indeed." Dashi looked at Jose, who was nodding. "Perhaps you are right, Doctor Holly. The fault is not in our stars, but in ourselves, that we are lesser men. Jose, the good doctor has a point. Perhaps we have chosen the wrong person to maintain order in Landing. Should we do something about the admiral?"

"I wouldn't want to launch a coup, sir. Or another coup. Or a counter coup."

"The correct term would be pronunciamiento, I think."

"I don't know what that word means, sir. And you're just speaking that way to throw me off my stride, to make me feel inadequate. It doesn't work anymore."

Dashi stretched his legs and inhaled. "When did you finally ascertain that?"

"It really just hit me just now, sir. I'm impressed with your vocabulary, but it doesn't work on me anymore."

"The effect is sometimes temporary," Dashi said. "But with some people, it has extended effects. I will endeavor to elucidate my thoughts to you with more detailed expressions from now on."

"Endeavor to elucidate?" Jose said. "Really, sir?"

"It's a hard habit to break, Jose. You will have to be patient with me."

"What does it mean, this pronunciamiento?"

"It's a bloodless coup. Rather than a rebel military group starting a fight, a loyal group publicly states their opposition to government policies, hoping for changes."

"Either way, I'd rather you didn't ask me to do that, sir. We haven't planned for it."

"I will have to think on it," Dashi said.

"And I say less thinking, more pushing," Doc Holly said. "Give me another set of ten. Push." Dashi lay on his back and raised his legs up one at a time.

"I don't believe we've met," Jose said to Doc Holly. "I'm Jose."

"You can call me Doc Holly."

"Pleased to meet you, Doctor Holly. What is Mr. Dashi's prognosis?"

"It's just 'Doc.' Prognosis? Did you know that the two of you talk funny? Very stiff."

"You're not the only one to have noticed it."

"Doesn't seem very friendly," Doc Holly said.

"We're not really friendly people," Jose said.

Dashi paused and wheezed for a moment. Doc Holly glared at him. "Nobody said stop moving. Give me ten more." She turned to Jose. "You don't want to be friendly?"

"We value competency and brevity. There is a great deal going on, and Mr. Dashi and I have to make many difficult decisions. You didn't tell me his prognosis."

"He'll be fine, as long as he does his exercises." Doc Holly looked at Dashi sweating on the table. "Take a short break, then another set." She walked across the gym to the water fountain.

"Jose, you mentioned other problems," Dashi gasped.

"Yes, sir. It's not just repair parts for the switching station. We need some repair parts for the reactor itself."

"There are fusion reactors on every station, in every ship. There should be spares up there."

"Plenty of odd things in orbit. Somebody actually offered me a ton of selenium, of all things. Who needs a ton of selenium?" Jose looked at his list. "We've checked with the stations for exactly what we need, no luck. But I've expanded my search."

"To where?"

"There's a lot of wreckage from GG Main. The former GG Main. When it exploded, it sent pieces everywhere. The Free Traders are hunting it down, both for salvage and to prevent it from impacting other stations."

"That's a problem for later. Well, we need to fix things here first. Who is taking charge of this task for you?"

"I've got several people. Normally, I'd ask Mr. Stewart to take on this, but he's occupied with the Jump ship right now. He did pass me on to a Mr. Pletcher, who shows promise in being able to source unusual items. He's not answering his comm right now, though."

Doc Holly walked back. "Next three sets. Off we go,

D."

Dashi sat and grunted his way through more leg lifts.

"I'll have an update tomorrow. The other issue is the Jump ship."

"Have we named it yet?" Dashi grimaced as he pushed another leg lift.

"The Militia wanted to call it Empire Revival. It got voted down. The Free Traders wanted to call it Fraternity. That got voted down as well."

Dashi grunted again, then paused. "What was it called before?"

"Don't know. But right now, we should call it Jake Stewart's theft."

"I assume he's abandoned his test orbits and is now striking out for a jump capable orbit, behind the other Jump ship?"

"As you suspected, sir. But that rogue Militia cutter is closing with him as well. This is all supposition, because he's not answering his comm right now."

"Perhaps the Free Trader crew has overwhelmed him and seized it for their own?"

"Perhaps. But there is a lot of solar activity out there that could be affecting his transmissions. I think he's getting my messages, but I'm not getting his responses," Jose said. "I assume this is part of a plan you haven't shared with me?"

"I share everything important with you, Jose," Dashi said.

"What's important," Doc Holly said, arriving next to them, "is that you finish this set." She waited for Dashi to start pushing again. "Keep it up, D. It's all about the core—that's what's important." She turned to Jose. "What's a Jump ship?"

"A ship that can go to another star system, like we could before the abandonment," Jose said.

"We have one of those? Is that why the power is out across town."

"No, that's from the revolt," Jose said. He looked at Dashi, who was grunting as he finished his leg lifts. "But the Jump ship will reconnect us to the Empire."

"Is that a good thing?"

"Well, we can trade for the things we need."

"If we haven't needed them for eighty years, why do we need them now?" Doc Holly asked.

"We didn't try to burn down our only city before now."

"True. So, this Jake guy is going to go visit the Empire and bring back stuff?"

"Garrup," Dashi gasped. "Yes, after he seizes control back from the people who have stolen this ship from him."

"Seize control? He's a tough guy?"

"Not at all," Dashi said. "He's very intellectual. Quiet. Thoughtful. Not violent at all."

"Doesn't sound like somebody who can seize a ship," Doc Holly said. "We're done here. Let me help you get up."

Dashi stood and took a few small steps. He collected his cane. "Better. Much better."

"Same time tomorrow, D," Doc Holly said. She went back into her office, and Jose and Dashi walked toward the door.

"She's right," Jose admitted. "Jake isn't the type to seize a ship by himself."

"He's a man of thought, not a man of action. But he has that Militia major with him, and, of course, Ms. Nadine is violence personified."

"She's not there. She disappeared."

"She did?" Dashi stopped and leaned on his cane. "How? When?"

"Last heard of when she left the temporary Planetary HQ with a squad of Militia troopers."

"Which squad?"

"A squad that might have been 'shot while escaping' if they hadn't made sure to stage a very public surrender to me," Jose said. "And there is also a sailboat missing."

Dashi stared off into space. "Would this be a sailboat that could sail down to south continent?" he asked.

"Yes. What's on south continent?" Jose asked.

"Mysteries, Jose, mysteries."

CHAPTER 14

Nadine's stomach and legs ached as she thrashed up for the light above her. She'd hit the water hard, and though she could kind of swim, she didn't know anything about diving. Hitting the water had hurt. She surfaced and gasped for air. A glance showed that she was floating in some sort of rocky canyon. The river had narrowed, and the city was invisible behind her. Or was she already into the world ocean? She licked her lips. Still tasted fresh. She lifted her head, kicked her feet, and paddled with her arms. The shore looked far away.

Something loomed over her. It was the ship. She stretched her arms out and paddled as hard as she could.

A rope dropped in front of her. "Grab on, miss, we'll haul you in," a voice said.

"Bite me," she yelled, windmilling her arms.

"You can't dog paddle away from us, miss," the voice said. "The ship's faster."

Nadine ducked under the water and pulled hard. She kept pulling and held her breath until her lungs burned, then pushed to the surface and gulped in another breath. She shook the water from her eyes.

The rope splashed in front of her again. She looked behind her. The boat was four feet away.

"Diving won't work, either, miss," the voice said. "We're all in the current here, moving at the same speed."

"Die, all of you," she yelled.

"Bal, just tap her slightly," the voice said.

"Say when, Estephan," another voice said.

"Over, over ... bit more. Bear away."

Nadine's rhythm stumbled as the side of the boat pecked her shoulder, then eased away, the rope still hanging in front of her.

"Miss," Estephan said, "if you want to die, that's fine, but you can't escape this way. The current's too fast, the shore's sheer cliffs here, and Bal is too good a helmsman."

Nadine stretched out again, going for maximum effort. She managed to pull four feet away from the boat.

"And frankly, miss," Estephan said, "you're a pretty lousy swimmer. You're not making any headway at all."

Sergeant Russell's head appeared over the rail. "No sense running. You'll just die tired."

"Die, traitor," she yelled. "Die, die, die."

"I don't think she likes you," Estephan said.

"Can't really blame her, can we?" Russell said.

"Sheer off, Bal," Estephan said. The boat moved away about forty feet. The three brothers in the crew and Sergeant Russell's squad lined the rail, watching. She struggled forward, managing to gain ten feet. Balthazar and Estephan exchanged words, and Estephan pulled one of the ropes a little tighter. The boat sped up 'til it was level with her. Then Estephan loosened it, making them parallel again.

"You'll never take me alive," she yelled.

"Not at this rate, no," Sergeant Russell said.

"That's hardly our fault," Estephan said.

Nadine gave another heave and realized she couldn't make any headway against the boat. She stopped struggling and floated. At first, the boat sped forward, passing her. Then Estephan adjusted another rope, and the boat slowed down, edging back to rest parallel to her again.

"Emperor's scrotum," she said. "Leave me alone. Let me go."

"Go where?" Estephan said. "You can't get out of the river here. The banks are too steep. The only thing you can do is stay in the middle and go over the waterfall up ahead."

"Waterfall?" Nadine yelled. Estephan pointed ahead. Mist rose from the surface, and the water seemed to end.

"Imperial vagina," she sputtered. She turned toward the boat and paddled furiously. "The rope. Throw the rope."

"Oh, now you want to get on board," Estephan said.

Sergeant Russell laughed. "I don't need a rope, she said. I'm fine by myself, she said."

"Bal, close her," Estephan said.

His brother spun the helm, and the boat slid over 'til she could touch it—more importantly, touch the rope in front of her. She grabbed on, and hands swung it toward the stern, next to a ladder. She grabbed the ladder and climbed out. Strong hands grabbed her and pulled her out but also pinned her arms to her sides.

"How did she get out of the bag?" Sergeant Russell said.

"Sliced it open," Chaudhari said.

"Search her," Sergeant Russell said. Two beefier troopers lifted her off the deck, while Kim One checked her arms, legs, and pockets.

"Knife in an arm sheath," Kim said. She handed the knife to Sergeant Russell. "Not concealed but not obvious."

Sergeant Russell weighed the knife in his hand. "Big knife for a little girl."

"Die, traitor," she said.

"Traitor is what the losing side calls the winning side. Isn't that true, sir?"

"Indeed," Commander Roi said. He looked a little sleepy or perhaps just confused. "You say this is the admiral's granddaughter?"

"I do, sir."

"Good job capturing her, then. And you, sailor man, good job making up that lie about a waterfall."

"I didn't make it up, sir. There is a big rapids on this river, but at high tide, it's not much at all."

"Well, done, then, sailorman," Roi said.

Estephan came up on deck, wearing a bright red life jacket with a long rope attached. It had a carabiner, which he clipped to a ring next to the wheel, then took over control from his brother. Balthazar disappeared below.

"Thank you, uh, your Imperial graciousness," Estephan said. "Unfortunately, high tide was about three hours ago, so now it's a twenty-foot drop with the current raging over it and rocks at the bottom. We're going to go over it in about a minute. You might want to tie yourself to something or go below."

The troops looked at Sergeant Russel. "We should go below?" he asked.

"Yes," Estephan said. "Otherwise, you'll get washed off into the rapids, get pinned under one of the waves, and suffocate under a rock."

"Right, everybody below, then," Sergeant Russell ordered. "Commander, we need a location to sail to."

"Just sail south," Commander Roi said.

"Do we have a destination, sir?"

"Just head south. My, I am sleepy. I think I will go below and lie down as well." Commander Roi stumbled down below. A trooper had to catch him and slide him into a bunk.

Chaudhari looked at Sergeant Russell. "What did you give him?"

"Strong sedative in the basic."

"You doused your own boss?" Balthazar asked.

"His commands can be a little ... erratic," Sergeant Russell said. "What happens if we hit those rocks at the bottom of the waterfall you talked about?"

"Well, the keel of the boat will crack, smash open the bottom, water will rush in, and we'll sink to the bottom of the river to be consigned to a watery grave," Balthazar said.

Sergeant Russell and Chaudhari looked at each other. "Really?" Sergeant Russell said.

Balthazar laughed. "No, not really."

"Oh, good."

"Much more likely," Balthazar said, "and much better, is that we'll smash into pieces when we hit, and all be blown overboard and pushed down the rapids. If we're lucky, those of us who aren't crushed by the crash will be able to grab onto a few splinters of wood, and hold on to them as we are swept out to sea."

"That's better?"

"Sure," Estephan said, "because after hanging on for days in the pounding surf, most of us will die horribly of thirst, but as many as one or maybe two of us might be washed ashore nearly dead." He turned the wheel to bring the boat back into the center of the river. "Provided, of course, we drink our own urine to survive."

"You view saving yourself from dying of dehydration by drinking our own urine as good?" Chaudhari asked.

"You asked. But as long as we get over this thing in one piece, and don't smash on anything, the main thing is to keep going forward at full speed so we don't hang up on any of the snags farther down."

"Good. Shouldn't you start the engines, then?" Sergeant Russell asked.

"We would. Hey, have you met our brother, Melchior?" Balthazar asked.

"No."

"Mel, get up here. Meet the rebel Militia."

"We're not rebels," Chaudhari said.

"Matter of opinion, isn't it?" Balthazar said. "Don't you think?" He spun the wheel. "Hi, Mel."

The third brother arrived on deck. He looked at the two Militia guys. "I'm busy, brother. What do you want?"

"Waterfall in sixty seconds. Will you be ready?"

"Not at all. But I can put some tools and suchlike away. Who are these guys?"

"These are the Militia who hijacked us."

"I wondered why we were heading down river."

"Are you going to start the engine?" Sergeant Russell

asked.

"Of course not."

"Why not?"

"I stripped it down for maintenance. I've got it mostly put back together, but I need to tighten things. Won't be ready for an hour, at least."

Sergeant Russell turned to Balthazar. "You took us down this killer river over a killer waterfall with a dud engine?"

"You had guns. You told us to get moving. We got moving. So, actually you took us down the river. And it didn't seem like a good time to ask too many questions."

The waterfall's roar built in the distance. "You've done this before, right? Sailed over this thing, without an engine?"

"Oh, yeah, lots, lots of times. No problem," Balthazar said.

"Once," Estephan said.

"And it was much closer to high tide, so it was about a quarter as big," Melchior said.

"And I was drunk at the time," Balthazar said. "But, hey, a first time for everything."

***

The waterfall was everything that it was promised to be. As they closed on it, the land on either side opened up, and they could see the ocean in the distance. Steam and spray roiled up as the boat headed toward the drop. The water rumbled and roared.

Balthazar, Estephan, and Melchior tied or clipped themselves to something, then double-checked their knots. Melchior whipped a rope around each of the Militiaman's waist, looped and pulled a sturdy knot, and tied the other end of the line down to a ring. It took him less than five seconds to tie each line.

"That's amazing, that knot," Sergeant Russell said. "You sailpeople have skills."

"Learned it in space scouts," Melchior said. "Called a bowline. Thank Akela Senz. He taught me that when I was eight. Hang on."

The boat's bow slipped easily over the edge of the falls, then tilted forward and raced down. Sergeant Russell glimpsed the white roiling water twenty feet in front of him, then the bow impacted with a giant splash. The boat staggered a bit but didn't slow much. They were knocked off their feet. The boat continued under the water, and a gush flowed backward from the bow over the decks. It covered everything as it roared back, pressing them under the water. But the boat recovered its buoyancy, and the bow rode up. The wave crested over the back, and Sergeant Russell floated for a moment—the water was perhaps four feet deep over the deck. Air bubbled around him as it leaked out of hatches and pipes. The sailboat stabilized, floating under the white water.

Sergeant Russell kicked, but the deck below him rose, then he could stand. It continued to rise and shoulder the water off to either side. The floating water knocked him over again. But the boat's sides were above sea level, and the water flowed over the sides, so he found himself laying on a wet deck that was no longer awash.

"Whooop! Whoop!" Balthazar yelled. He'd stayed strapped into the chair by the wheel the whole time. He spun it to one side. "She answers."

Estephan stared upward. "Mast looks good. Sails are drawing."

Melchior waited for the water to finish flowing off a hatch, then dove below. "About a foot of water in the well, but the pumps will handle it."

The brothers cheered, and Sergeant Russell and Chaudhari hauled themselves upright and looked around. The river had widened and slowed, and the shore was lower.

"Do we have any more of that?" Sergeant Russell asked.

"Nope. That's the ocean out there. We're on our way. You have a course for us."

"Can we just go south, like the commander wanted?"

"What if we don't want to go south?" Balthazar said.

"First, you probably have some friends down there waiting for you. Second, you can't go back to Landing. Some folks will want to talk to you there, and third"—he patted his holster—"we've still got the guns."

"Point," Balthazar agreed. "We'll sail south."

"You do that," Sergeant Russell said. "Chaudhari and I will sit here. Shut up," he yelled down the hatchway. The troopers there were causing a commotion. "Just a little bumpy. Shut up."

He looked at the sun setting on the horizon. "How long to the south continent?"

"Couple of days. Straightforward sailing. We've got a compass, and there's no land 'til we're nearly there. Lots of shallows close by, though, and big, big tides."

"We'll deal with that when we get there," Sergeant Russell said. "The commander will give us better directions. You sure we've got enough food and water?"

"Food? Weeks, even for this many people. Water, we will have to be careful, but we should have enough for a week. We'll get you where you want to go down south, and then we'll be on our way—agreed?"

"And take us back up north," Chaudhari said. "I don't want to be stuck down there."

Balthazar nodded. "Down and back, then."

"Works for me," Sergeant Russell said. "As far as I'm concerned, you're just a taxi." He turned to Chaudhari. "Does that cover everything?"

"I think so," Chaudhari said. "You've covered everything."

A bang, a shout, and a blond-haired streak screamed out of the hatch, up onto the rail and over the side.

"Or," Chaudhari said. "You may have forgotten one thing."

***

Nadine leaned over the rail and vomited the little water she'd been able to drink.

"How do you feel?" Sergeant Russell asked.

"Like I'm dying. And like I'm not dying fast enough," Nadine said. "Are we there yet?"

"Well, according to our great leader, we need to sail 'south by west,' whatever that means, and then we'll be close tomorrow morning."

"I have another day of this?" Nadine retched again. Sergeant Russell had to turn away to prevent from heaving his guts out. "Sorry we picked you up?"

"I would have been fine."

"You swam around in a circle for thirty minutes, and you'd swallowed so much water you probably gained twenty pounds."

"I was fine."

"Mel had to go in the water and tie a rope to your shoulders. You were so tired you couldn't climb up the ladder."

"Stupid rivers," Nadine muttered. "They didn't teach me about currents when I learned to swim."

"Why did you bother to learn how to swim?"

"Are you kidding? Have you seen those lifeguard dudes? And the shorts they wear ..."

"Didn't help you, though."

"We'll see. Are you going to lock me up again?"

"Nope. You can jump off here if you want to."

Nadine surveyed the water. The ocean heaved with large swells from horizon to horizon. The period was long, about ten seconds, and the boat swarmed up, up, up, hung for a moment, then down, down, down. "That doesn't sound like such a bad idea."

"We won't go after you this time."

"You mean can't? All your troops are as sick as me." Nadine pointed. Sergeant Russell's entire squad was lined up at the rail, either heaving or waiting their turn to heave. "You could send your boss after me."

Sergeant Russell looked up. Commander Roi was sitting at the helm, turning the boat from time to time to catch the wind. Sergeant Russell was watching him, so Commander Roi motioned him over. Sergeant Russell carefully climbed from his position at the rail along the side of the boat. He didn't time his crawl into the cockpit with the roll of the boat, so he slammed shoulder-first into the bottom. He got up, cursing, and used his hands to lever himself up to the wheel.

"Glorious day, isn't it Sergeant?" Commander Roi said.

"I really don't agree, sir. I think it's pretty rough," Sergeant Russell said.

"Rough? This is just brisk. A fine wind and an easy swell."

"If this is an easy swell, I'd hate to see an uneasy one, sir."

"You will get your wish, Sergeant. The wind is backing, and the sea state will increase over night, I'm sure of it."

"I don't know what any of that means, sir. Is it good?"

"The good news is that we'll go faster."

"So, we can get to the base before tomorrow?"

"We could, but we won't. There are too many reefs and shoals near it. We'll have to come into it during daylight. So, we'll just slow down."

"That's the good news? What's the bad news. The state of the sea?"

"The sea state-no, wait," Roi pointed to the side. "Feel the wind? Okay, the wind is changing direction. Right now, the waves come from the west, the right side of the boat. We're going south. So, the waves are on the side. The wind is to our right as well. But there's a storm coming, the wind is changing direction, it will come from more ahead of us. We'll have to turn more to the right, more into the waves to keep using the wind. So, we'll be banging into the waves rather than riding over them."

"Wonderful," Sergeant Russell said. "So, the motion will be worse?"

"Much, much worse." Commander Roi agreed. "And the wind will strengthen, too, if the barometer is to be believed. And the change of direction of the wind will put it in opposition to the waves, which will make them very steep and confused. We'll be tossed around all night."

Sergeant Russell sighed. "I joined the Militia to get away from this stupid planetary stuff." He looked at Commander Roi. "You don't look upset, sir. You look happy."

"I am happy, Sergeant. This will be great fun. This is a well-found boat. These three brothers know how to sail, and they know how to keep a boat. This will be an exhilarating run. Why, I think we'll make over two hundred miles in a day!"

Commander Roi peered at the compass, looked up at the sails, then adjusted the helm.

"Pardon me for asking, sir," Russell said, "but you seem, well, you seem much more relaxed and happier as a sea captain than you ever did as a Militia officer."

"The sea was my first love, Sergeant. When I was young, my family lived on a farm down the coast. We had to hike quite a distance to the monorail. But there was a big lake on the river near us. We kept a small boat there for fishing, and there were some commercial traffic as well. When the tide was right, we could ride out the bores and into the ocean. I sailed along the coast into Landing several times with the fishing boat crews. It was glorious. I wanted to be a fishing captain. I had my father talked into buying a boat, putting it to work, and selling the surplus to the food plants. Hard work but honest." He frowned. "But things changed, and I had to join the Militia."

"Had to, sir?"

"Ground car accident. A buffalo on the road. No one to blame, just one of those things. My father and elder brother were killed. My brother was going to join the

Militia when he was of age. We've—my family, that is—we've had somebody in the Imperial forces since the founding. My mother has records going back over three hundred years. The pictures are up on the wall, starting with my great, great, great, great-grandmother. Since the abandonment, it's been the Militia, before that, usually the navy. So, mother just told me that I had to join the Militia. And here I am." The sails started to flap, and Roi turned the wheel to harden them. "Why did you join up, Sergeant?"

"Patriotism, sir."

"Sergeant Russell, I think you are a patriot, but I don't think that was your reason at eighteen years of age."

"Dental work," Sergeant Russell said. "We were poor. I had bad teeth. The Militia said they'd fix them up."

"Did they?"

Sergeant Russell gritted his teeth at the commander. "Did what they promised, sir."

"So, that's why you stayed?"

"They did what they promised, so I did what I promised. Seemed reasonable. Then, all of a sudden, I was in seven years, and it just seemed easier to sign another seven and then it was almost twenty, then it was just too easy, so here I am."

"Well, I'm glad you're here with us, Sergeant. You and your troops. There are challenging times ahead for all of us, and a few good men and women are what we need to right the wrongs of this corporation and return us to a proper Imperial government."

"The officers' council, sir?"

"Yes, once we have cleared out this nest of vipers that calls itself the Delta Council, we'll be able to fix things up and take our proper place."

"As you say, sir. What about the fires and the damage and suchlike?"

"I blame the corporations. Their greed and short sightedness has led us to this."

"Wasn't the corporations that blew up an orbital station, sir? Wasn't that Colonel Savard and his men?"

"Yes, the colonel did tend to get a little overenthusiastic from time to time. But his motives were pure, and who can fault him that?"

"All the people who were killed in the explosion," Sergeant Russell muttered.

"What's that, Sergeant?"

"All the people surely want more exposition, more explanations on what is to come next."

"Fear not, Sergeant! We will meet with our colleagues down south, collect our resources, and we will yet counter this cancer among us."

"Yes, sir."

"Cheer up, Sergeant! It is to glory, glory that we steer!"

The wind had whipped the waves up, and at the first of the commander's promise, steep waves crashed over the boat. Swirling white water washed down the deck. The seasick squad squawked from the far side of the boat as it soaked them, and Sergeant Russell caught a face full of water that knocked him down.

The motion increased considerably. Russell lurched to the side of the boat and barfed his entire day's breakfast out in a series of monumental heaves. The boat's motion changed, and he looked forward just in time to catch another wave slamming down the boat and into his face. It splashed water and vomit all over his uniform.

Sergeant Russell slumped on the side of the boat, staring at the colonel.

"Glory. As you say, sir, glory," he said before hanging over the side to vomit again.

CHAPTER 15

"Jake Stewart," Yvette said. "They are closing on us. Will we get away in time?" By common consent, Yvette had taken over as the primary pilot, with Odette as sensors and comm. The two were used to working together. Jake got the impression that they divided all their tasks into "thinking" and "doing" and that Yvette was the brains, and Odette was the brawn. Either way, Odette kept a wary eye on Jake and Major Shutt while Yvette was busy flying.

"I'm just checking something," Jake said, tapping through his board. "Give me a moment."

Yvette pushed the throttle for the main engines, but instead of it accelerating, a buzzer bonged and lights flashed.

"Insufficient fuel flow to complete command," Odette read off her screen. "Looks like you didn't configure these old Empire electronics properly, army girl."

Major Shutt was also looking at her screen. "Electronics are fine. It's this eighty- or hundred-year-old valve that's causing the problem. Where do we keep the wrenches?"

Yvette looked over her shoulder. Shutt was at one of the upper-level consoles next to Jake. "I know we talked about kneecapping each other, but why now? For Empire's sake. We're all busy, including you."

"For the valve, merchie, for the valve. I need to fix that."

"D'accord. Tool locker in engineering is unlocked," Yvette said.

Shutt turned and climbed down the ladder in the

central corridor. They still had enough acceleration that "down" was toward the rear of the ship.

"That's nice of you, trusting her enough to open up the engineering lockers," Jake said.

"Don't trust her at all. But there are no locks on the lockers, and I need more accel if that Militia ship is not to be catching us." Yvette's standard was fluent, but when she was stressed, she sometimes spoke oddly. "But she is being suspiciously helpful."

"Suspiciously?" Jake asked.

"And have you finished your checks?"

"No, they will take about another twenty minutes, I think," Jake said.

"Jake Stewart," Odette said, "run that command faster somehow. We need to find out if the Militia will catch us."

"Catch us?" Jake said.

"Get close enough to dock," Odette said.

"I don't need to wait for that to complete," Jake said. "They will definitely catch us, get close enough to be able to board or to dock if we were willing. I was checking something else."

Yvette and Odette exchanged glances. "Jake Stewart, did you not think that it was important to tell us that they would get into boarding range?"

"No. It's all part of my plan," Jake said.

Yvette shook her head. "I begin to see why all those other women want to shoot you or hit you."

"Really? You do?" Jake asked.

"Yes."

"Could you explain it?" Jake frowned. "Because, it's a bit of a puzzle to me. I set up these plans, and people always get so angry with me when I explain them, even when it's obvious that they will work."

Yvette turned and glared at him.

"Very angry," Jake said.

***

"Heads up, boss lady," Jammy said over the radio. The six of them were hanging in the air lock together. Perlins had put them all on a private channel before locking down the helmets. "I'm still hooked into the pilot's board. Storm warning. Radiation is rising."

Perlins looked down. The air lock was about two-thirds full of water. Cold water, if her suit was to be believed.

"Water's rising. We should be okay," she said. The other five figures in the air lock hung onto grab bars as the water swished. Sympathetic vibration shook the water's surface.

"We can always duck down under the water if you're worried," the medic said.

"What's your name?" Perlins asked.

"Merced."

"Merced, you know something about hard radiation?"

"Yes, we had to study it in school. But it was all academic—the only known cases in the last fifty years or so were miners whose ships malfunctioned and ended up on really strange orbits—orbits that took a year or something to come back down. They either died of burns or got strange cancers. Or starved to death."

"Good to know. But the water will protect us."

"According to the books, yes. But we have to be in the water, these waves lapping around aren't good."

"Jammy," Perlins said. "Give me that weather report again."

"Cold, cloudy, with rapidly increasing chances of death by solar flare. Got a bunch of new alarms over my channel while we're talking."

"Krikweigh," Perlins said. She looked over at the tug pilot, who was staring down at the water. No answer. "Krikweigh," she repeated. He didn't move, so she leaned over and tapped his shoulder. He looked up, and his lips moved. She tapped the radio on her neck, and he reached up and turned his on.

"Sorry, didn't want the radio to get wet."

"We're going to get totally wet. At least on the outside. Why do you care?"

"Water shorts out electronics. I don't want the radio destroyed," Krikweigh said.

"Water destroys electronics?" Jammy asked.

"Didn't you know that?" Krikweigh said.

"I've never even seen this much water before, never mind been in it. How does it work?"

"The water creates a temporary short circuit, and the electronics cut out. The power goes direct from the power source into the water."

"Hey, tug guy," Jammy said. "If the water makes the power go directly into the water, what about things in the water?"

"Electrical things? They stop working," Krikweigh said.

"And people in the water, do they stop working, too?" Jammy said.

Perlins frowned. "Medic-Merced right?"

"Yes, ma'am?"

"What happens to people who are in water with electricity."

"They get shocked."

"Is that bad?"

"Depends on the power sent into it. Could be nothing. Could be very bad."

"What's very bad?"

"Heart stops."

"How much power do we need for that?"

"Ship's main electric power can stop a heart if you're not in good shape."

Perlins looked around the air lock. "Any main electrics in here?"

Krikweigh pointed to the air vent on the dorsal surface of the ship, where the blower was. "Right up there. Main power to fans and the heater unit."

"You don't need main power to run a fan," Jammy said.

"No, you need main power to run all the command boards, the sensor processors, and the flight controls in the control room up ahead," Krikweigh said. "And since you're running a major power line to the front of the ship, just tap off a few lower voltage lines from a junction box. The fan power won't kill us. What it's plugged into will."

"How truly good," Perlins said. "So, we need to make sure that we don't fill this air lock up totally." The water was mostly pooling toward the air lock's rear, which, since it was "down" for everyone, was fine. The fan power unit combo was closer to the front of the ship, so the water wasn't regularly hitting the fan unit at that time. There had been a few splutters and sparks, but it was still running.

"Won't work. The splashes will hit that power line," Krikweigh said. "Short it out."

"So, we're conducting a field test on how much electricity we need to kill people?" Perlins asked.

"Always wanted to be a scientist," Daav said. "As a kid."

"Given your piloting skills, would have been a better option," Jammy said.

"Why don't they make those things water safe?" Daav asked.

"Most people don't fill their cutters with air locks full of water. Not a standard practice," Krikweigh said.

"Good point," Daav said. He fell over as a wave of water sloshed onto him. "Water is heavy. And why is it moving?"

"Vibration—makes standing waves in the water. And it's not attached to the ship, so it sloshes forward as the acceleration changes," Krikweigh said. "Have to watch that. Otherwise, it will destabilize the thrust, and we'll start yo-yoing."

"What's that mean?" Perlins said.

"These waves get high enough, and we'll end up being bounced around as it changes the center of gravity of the ship."

"How high?" Perlins asked.

The ship buckled left, and the water surged toward the right side, then down, then flipped back. The ship spun from side to side.

Perlins was caught as the water flipped back and forth and lost her footing, dropping below the water level. Her external suit lights shorted out, and red warnings appeared on her collar display.

"That high ought to do it," Krikweigh said. "Everybody, hang on."

The ship's yaw increased, left, right, left, right. Each time, the ship spun farther to one side, causing the correction to grow more violent as it spun back. It also pitched backward, causing the acceleration-based gravity to fluctuate from below, to one side, to another, then forward and backward. The different corrections became unsynchronized, and the crew grasped with their arms as their legs waved up and down and left and right as the gravity changed direction.

"Jammy, what's with the movement?" Perlins yelled.

"Center of gravity keeps changing, boss. Thrust pushes us off. I'm trying to compensate, but the automatic controls don't catch it fast enough."

"Cut the water, then."

"Can't, the radiation alarms are all redlining," Jammy said. "We need more water, not less."

A thrashing wave hit Perlins. She stuck against the port air lock as the ship pivoted three hundred sixty degrees when the yaw became unmanageable. "Do something with the water."

"Radiation," Jammy said.

"Captain," Merced said. "My colonel wants to talk to you. He wants to know what's going on."

"Tell him to bite my Imperial behind."

"He says he has casualties, and what are you playing at?"

"Cut him off, cut him off," Perlins said.

"I can't—"

Perlins peered through the splashes. Merced lolled and flailed in the water, banging against the bulkhead. Perlins held tight as a wave crashed into her. "It's the sloshing. Get more water in here. Now."

"How?" Jammy said.

"Increase the flow, break off the pipe, something," Perlins said.

"Unscrew the hose," Jammy said. "The hose is going to the pump to regulate the water. Let the whole tank vent into the air lock."

Krikweigh untangled one arm from the locker support he had been grasping, reached up and forward, and unscrewed the pipe fitting. Water under pressure spewed from the fitting, then the hose flapped completely off, and water flowed, unencumbered. The surface foamed.

"Daav, see to Merced," Perlins said. Daav leaned over from the hatch he was grasping and pulled Merced's flapping body toward him. "He's still breathing but lots of red indicators," Daav said.

As the compartment filled up with water, the waves dampened. The ship ceased, yawing, and the pitching leveled out.

"Just fill us up completely," Perlins said.

"Gonna happen whether you want to or not," Krikweigh said. "The valve is on that piece I unscrewed, and I don't see it. It's floating here somewhere."

"We'll be fine, then."

"Except for the power, the electricity," Krikweigh said.

"Imperial vagina, I forgot about that," Perlins said. "When does that happen?"

The lights died with a flash of sparks and smoke as the water lapped against the front of the compartment.

***

"But what are they doing, Jake Stewart?" Yvette asked. "I have never seen a course like that. They are spiraling out of control."

"No idea," Jake said. "I didn't expect that. But at least they're doing it fast."

"Why is that good?"

"Faster burns more fuel. This is a big ship, and we have big tanks. My plan was to have them chase me and burn a lot of fuel. At some point, they would have to give up the chase and turn back because, otherwise, they wouldn't have enough reserves to get back to Delta."

"When will that happen?" Yvette asked.

"Should have happened about ten minutes ago," Jake said. "Don't know why they haven't turned back already."

"Because they don't have anything to go back to," Shutt said. "They started a war, lost a war, tried to retreat; most of them got killed, and now, they're stuck out here. They'll end up freezing to death out here if they don't do something."

"But what are they trying to do?" Jake asked. "That course doesn't take them anywhere."

"Die with honor," Shutt said. "Attacking the last outpost of the false Empire they rose up to fight against."

"Who?" Jake said.

"Us, you idiot," Shutt said. "Us. We're the last outpost of their enemies. Why do you think I'm helping these stupid merchies rather than lounging in my bunk? Those Militia want to capture us or die gloriously in the attempt."

"Well, if they don't have better radiation shielding than most cutters, they're going to die gloriously all right, from radiation poisoning from those solar flares," Jake said.

"What about us? Does that affect us?" Yvette asked.

"No, we're designed to operate in interplanetary space. We've got heavier shielding, and we've got refuge spaces. We're okay now, but if the radiation gets any higher, we'll have to retreat to the computer room."

"I didn't mean the radiation; I mean the Empire-rising folks. Can they affect us."

"Well, if they catch us, but why would they do that?"

"To die gloriously, as army girl said."

"But they can do that without our help," Jake said. "They don't need to catch us. They're probably dead already."

"You're not getting it," Shutt said. "What if they decide that we need to die gloriously as well?"

Jake looked at his board again and tapped a key. "They have to get close enough to board to do that."

"Can they?"

Jake paged through to a screen and stared at it. "Ooops."

CHAPTER 16

"Daav, I'm tingling all over. Cut the power," Perlins said over the radio, floating in the air lock. The engines were still pushing them forward, so the rear hatch was down. Her feet banged the side walls as the ship slewed around. The compartment lights were out, and only the glow of suit lights and her helmet light showed the splashing water.

"Are you sure it's the power? Could be the swimming," Daav said. He was gripping Merced, floating next to him. Merced was still alive, but red lights showed on his suit status.

"Or maybe I'm just sexually stimulated by the water rushing between my legs. Kill the power, now."

"Okay, boss lady, but—"

"Urrrrup—that hurts," Corporal Dalon said. "I'm getting something in my neck. Uh." He had been at one side of the air lock, holding onto a locking wheel. "It feels strange." His body went rigid, and his suit status lights flashed red.

"KILL THE POWER," Perlins yelled.

Corporal Dalon's body unfolded, and he floated in the compartment. Perlins's tingling disappeared, but she found herself rising off the ground and rolling around.

"Power cut, boss lady. But we have another problem."

"Let me guess, the emergency power cut also turns the engines off."

"When all the control boards go dark, all the systems go into standby unless they are overridden by the board in engineering. Which we have locked."

"Turn the boards back on. Just kill the power to this air lock."

"Can't do that, boss lady."

"Right, the main power bars or whatever is here, and they're all linked. Isn't there a battery or some sort of standby on the main board?"

"Well, yeah, but I'm not sure if it works."

"Try it and see."

"About that, so when I cut off the power to this compartment—"

"I know. You cut off the power to the boards. You said that. Just restart one remotely on battery."

"It's kind of the remote thing that's the problem, boss lady."

Perlins stared at Daav across the compartment, also floating. The ship had started to tumble, so they sloshed around in the air lock with all the water. She turned to focus her helmet light on him. "Let me guess, your radio link is down, too."

"Got it in one, boss lady."

"Okay, but at least we're protected from the storm, right?"

"That's what that Merced guy said."

"How is he?" Perlins turned but didn't see him. "Where is he?" She looked up. Merced and Corporal Dalon had floated higher than her. Krikweigh was rolling them over and checking the status. "Krikweigh, how are they?"

"Knocked out. Unconscious. Suits say they're breathing but shallow breaths. We need to get them out of this water so I can look at them."

"We can't. We need to keep them shielded from the storm. Daav, how long 'til that storm passes, you think?"

"An hour or two should do it."

"That's not very exact."

"I'm a pilot, not a cosmic weatherman. Space weatherman. Whatever. I'm a pilot, not any of those."

"We'll wait two hours then drain the water then see where we're at. If we wait that long, we'll miss the worst of it, anyway. Correct?"

"Yes, boss lady."

The radio channel was silent. Daav, Jammy, Perlins, and Krikweigh floated, all with their helmet lights on. Krikweigh had engaged Merced and Corporal Dalon's magnetic grips and had them attached to the hull. They swayed in the water. The currents were much gentler than before.

"Read any good books lately?" Daav asked.

"Shut up, Daav," Perlins said.

"Boss lady?" Jammy asked.

"Not now, Jammy."

"I have a question, boss lady."

Perlins's sighed into the radio. "What is it, Jammy?"

"How much water is in here?"

"A lot. Shut up."

"But how many? Ten Tons? Twenty?"

"A lot. Water is one ton per cubic meter. We've got lots of cubic meters in here. Maybe twenty? Why do you care?"

"Well, the power's off now, right?"

"Are you basing that observation on the fact that we're not dying of electrocution or that all the lights are out?"

"Heaters run off main power, right?"

"Yes, Jammy, the heaters use electricity, so they run off main power."

"So, boss lady, with no heat, how long will it take for twenty tons of water to freeze solid?"

***

"But why were they moving like that?" Yvette asked. "They're making these constant S-turns, and there's no good reason for that. Now, they're just tumbling."

"Don't know," Jake said. "But the storm power is increasing. We should go to the Jump computer section.

It's better shielded down there."

Yvette tapped the intercom. "Army girl, Jake Stewart says we should go to the refuge."

"And yes, I did manage to successfully open that valve," Shutt said over the radio, "so you should have more power. You were calling to say thank you for me fixing that, weren't you?"

Yvette looked at her screen. "So, it is. But it is your job to fix these things. Why would I thank you?"

"Politeness? Professionalism? Or don't you do that in the Free Traders?"

"Thank you, Major Shutt," Jake said. "We will need the power later, but the storm is increasing now, and we should move to the better shielded parts of the ship."

"See? Even Jake can be polite."

"We need to go below," Jake said.

"Are you sure we have to?"

"Not really," Jake said. "I'm just going by what I've read. I think the control room might actually have enough shielding, but I'm not sure. I'll be able to tell after the field strength drops—compare the readings outside and inside and see how effective the shielding is. I know that the best shielding is protecting the Jump computer, so if we go in there, we'll be safe for sure."

"So, this is in the nature of an experiment, then," Shutt said over the radio.

"I'm just being cautious," Jake said.

"Are the Free Trader chickies going as well?"

"Chickies?" Odette said. "We're not chickies."

"I'm not army girl, either, but I answer to it."

Odette shook her head. "These Militia people." She shut her console down. "We will be there in five minutes, Major Shutt. Meet us there."

"Wilco," Major Shutt said over the radio.

Odette looked at Yvette, who shrugged. Odette turned to Jake. "What does this 'wilco' mean?"

***

The Jump module was different from anything Jake had seen on any ship before, which made sense. He'd never been on a Jump ship. Like most ship modules that people lived in, it was a cylinder. It had a standard coupling fore and aft where it would clip onto a ship's truss system, with a hatch between it, and the next module. Power and sensor couplings on both ends allowed it to plug in between the hab module and the first fuel tankage module. The standard merchant ships Jake had worked on in the past started at the bow with a control room, then a universal air lock, then a standard two-level hab module with living floors—the top one offering a lounge, fresher, and food preparation area, along with some acceleration couches. The next level had all acceleration couches, either in groups or in private rooms. The couches were pivoted so that, when sitting in them, the back of the couch could either face the stern to press passengers into them when the main engines were running or could be pointed outward. When the ship was spun for gravity, out was down, so the occupant would be pressed back into their seat.

Merchant ships followed the hab module with numerous container trusses. Six containers were arranged in a circle around a central truss system that they were chained to. The center held an access passageway that allowed access to the engineering module, where the main drives, fusion reactor, and fuel were located. Two sets of thruster trusses were inserted somewhere, an H-shaped truss that held thrusters on the outside, with fuel, power, and control lines attached. Most merchant ships had four or six container modules between the hab and the engineering module.

The Jump ship was different. Every cylinder was of a larger diameter than Jake was used to. At least twice as large, which cubed the space out substantially. The control cabin was bigger and had six consoles rather than the four he was used to. The hab module was more extensive as well. It had four levels—one level being a lounge, and the rest was all cabins, except for one group of eight accel couches on one side. The only single container truss held twelve containers rather than the usual six, and the engineering unit was larger and roomier than Jake was used to. The fusion plant and main drive matched the increase.

The biggest difference was the Jump module and the fuel tankage, drive, and weapons. There were two fuel tank modules the same size as the container module, but instead of twelve containers surrounding an access passage, there were just giant fuel tanks. The Jump module was as long as both fuel tanks combined. The outer rim of it was more fuel, either as an emergency reserve or as more shielding. The fuel surrounded rows and rows of computer modules. Toward the stern of the unit was an extra fusion reactor, then the Jump unit right in front of it. The fusion reactor was directly coupled to the Jump unit—all the power produced went directly to the Jump drive. In the middle of the Jump unit, the access way widened into a control station with four couches, each with its own console. This was the only place on the ship you could control the Jump drive, but you could access all the other systems from here.

The ship used standard trusses to carry sensors. They were almost identical to the thruster trusses—a box of girders with power and data couplings for sensors of different types. One of the trusses was labeled Weapon Hardpoints on Jake's screens. He hadn't had time to investigate that yet.

"I'm going to set up the jump while we're waiting," Jake said. "We're not close to the jump limit yet, but the calculations take a lot of time." He was seated at a control console in front of a large board.

"What do you need to do?" Yvette asked.

"Pick a destination, put us somewhere that we have a clear line to it, somewhere that doesn't take us through a star or a planet, or through their gravitational shadow."

"A gravitational shadow?" Yvette asked.

"It's based on mass. The bigger the object, the more it affects things."

"But I thought jump space was different."

"We create a bubble of exotic space with us inside it," Jake said. "The jump space. The drive uses an Alcubierre field to compress space in front of us. We move across that space propelled by the Jump drive. Since the space is compressed, the same speed in jump space moves us faster in regular space."

"Less distance, less time," Major Shutt said. "Like if we were moving at one thousand kilometers per hour, it would take us an hour to cross one thousand kilometers. But if it was only ten kilometers, we'd do it in one one-hundredth of the time."

"Right," Jake said. "We cross the shrunk space at sublight speed, so we don't break any laws of nature. But to an outside observer, we're traveling at supralight speed."

"How fast can we go?"

"Depends on the Jump drive. The more they compress space, the farther you go."

"You mean the faster," Odette said.

"No, our relative speed to us is the same. It's how much we compress—to use Major Shutt's example, our speed stays the same, but the distance we have to cross gets smaller and smaller. According to my reading, this is a moderate quality merchant grade Jump drive. It will take us about a week to move a few parsecs. The military ones could go much farther in the same amount of time."

"How long to get set up to jump?"

"Hours to do the calculations," Jake said. "I started them a while ago. ETA right now says almost an hour 'til completion."

"So, we should just watch some vids while you do this?" Major Shutt said.

"I can see all pilot and navigator functions here," Yvette said.

"Good for you, merchie," Shutt said. She paged through her screens. "Engineering is here as well, not every single control but most of them."

"I think the ship was designed so that this was the backup control room," Jake said. "It should have the same functions as the other consoles. There are a couple of things that can only be done from engineering, but we should be able to fly and maintain status."

"Do we have sensors?" Odette asked.

"Great sensors." Yvette said. "We have two telescopes, an infrared sensor. Three radars—short-range, long-range, and some sort of directed one. And lots and lots of general sensors. Cosmic ray detector. Gamma ray detector. A spectrometer. Something to collect dust for some reason."

"You can control them?" Odette asked.

"Standard controls," Jake said. "Same as on the cutters."

Odette paged through her screens. "Exactly the same. I've used these before."

"See," Jake said. "I can see that Militia cutter. And look at the resolution and the zoom. See the detail of the hull."

"I see some sort of cloud from their air lock," Yvette said. She tapped her screen. "Spectrometer says it's water. Wow, we have a spectrometer. Only seen that once before."

"I see people climbing out," Odette said. "And when I use this zoom feature, I see they've got guns. Shotguns." She zoomed in more. "Loaded shotguns, with solid slugs from the color."

"And using this directional radar, I see that the distance is way closer than you said it would be. While we've been talking, they've been speeding up, and it looks like they're going to catch us," Shutt said.

"Oh," Jake said. "But we'll be fine. They won't be able to shoot out an air lock. Not even with solid slugs."

Major Shutt tapped her screen. "No, but that ax the first person is carrying might help them open something."

The Jump Ship

CHAPTER 17

"I can't see anything," Krikweigh said over the radio, pausing at the outer air lock door. He had used the ax as a lever to force the door open and climbed onto the hull. "There's frozen water on my faceplate."

"What did you expect would happen when you vent a couple of tons of water at once?" Jammy asked. He climbed out behind Krikweigh.

"Wipe it off or something," Krikweigh said.

"The only thing I've got is this shotgun," Jammy said. "Not designed as an ice scraper."

"Krikweigh, get outside and point your faceplate at the primary. Get some solar radiation on it," Perlins said. "That will sublime it. Jammy, get out there and swap your shotgun with Krikweigh for that ax. We'll need the ax to clear things in here. Daav, what's your status?"

"I'm kind of stuck in this slush," Daav said. The water in the extended air lock had begun to freeze, and Perlins had ordered Krikweigh to vent the air lock to let them out, radiation or no radiation. They hadn't acted fast enough to avoid being stuck. "It's sticky, but I think I could pull myself out."

"Wait for Jammy," Perlins said. "If you damage your suit or your boots, we won't be able to get to you to fix them."

"Ice ax here, boss lady," Jammy said, coming back in. "Want somebody chopped?"

"Use the ax to clear the ice from us first," Perlins said. "Get us out of here."

"Can I hack Daav's legs off?" Jammy said.

"We need a spare pilot," Perlins said.

"He can fly with just his hands."

"Not only can I fly with just my hands," Daav said. "I can fly better than you with just my pinky finger."

Jammy hefted the ax. "Want me to test that theory?"

"Shut up, both of you," Perlins said. "Jammy, cut us loose."

Jammy banged the ax on the ice. He was able to beat a path around the slush of Daav's left leg. "Can you lift out now?"

Daav leaned against the bulkhead and pulled the leg up. He was able to lift it, but a large chunk of ice came with it. "As long as I bring my frozen friends, yeah."

"That's good enough," Perlins said. "Chip some off. Just enough to get him moving. Daav, get in the control room, get us some power back here, and get our course after that ship."

"Got it, boss lady, have to close the air lock, though."

"Krikweigh, what's going on out there?" Perlins asked. "Can you see?"

"Not yet. Some. I'm stuck on, and I have a tether on, so don't mind me."

"We need to close a hatch. Standby out there. Daav, control room. Jammy, close the lock."

Daav struggled with the forward hatch. Jammy went and closed the air lock, then had to go back and help Daav lever the control room hatch open. Atmosphere gushed in from the aired-up control room, and new steam rose as the water evaporated in the sudden heat. Daav clumped forward to the control boards and began the startup sequence.

"Emperor's balls," Perlins said, waving the steam away. "Now I can't see."

"Me, either," Jammy said. "Boss lady, should I still hack you out?" He came back to Perlins. "It's up to your knees. You're stuck hard. This will take a while."

"When did we start calling her boss lady?" Daav said.

"It's a natural progression since you started doing what I said, because I'm smarter than you," Perlins said.

Jammy swung the ax, and it hit the frozen slush around her knees, bounced, and struck her leg.

"Imperial vagina," she screamed. "You idiot. Are you trying to break my leg?"

"Sorry, sorry," Jammy said. "Just bounced off, is all."

A light in the air lock came back on. "Power," Daav said. "Got air blowing in, too."

Perlins waited. "And?"

"And?"

"Power is nice, but where's the heat?"

Daav cursed. "It's turned on, but I've got malfunctions showing."

"We shorted out everything except the air vents when we pushed all that water in," Perlins said. "I'll bet the air and heat is coming from the control room, and we're all bust back here."

"Got it in one, boss lady," Daav said.

Jammy held up the ax. "Should I—"

"No. Pump the air back. Things will warm up. I'll melt out." Perlins unclipped her helmet and flipped the visor up. She gasped. "Imperial testicles, that's cold." She coughed some more.

"Breathe through your nose," Jammy said. He had also opened his faceplate.

"Up your nose. What's that noise?"

"Coming from the aft hatch," Jammy said. "Somebody banging on the hatch with something metal."

"All the internal channels are lit up, boss lady," Daav said. "Lots of people want to talk to us on the radio. And the intercom."

"Ignore them. Where's that Jump ship?"

"Right ahead. Right dead ahead where I left them. We're on target for a flyby in about thirty minutes."

"How did you manage to account for their evading while we were watered up?"

"I didn't. They didn't evade."

"Everybody evades."

"They didn't. Straight push, accell unchanged since I checked before. One-G when we 'watered up' as you put it, and one-G when we came out. And they didn't evade 'cause our intercept course is exactly the same."

"Maybe the storm killed them?" Jammy said.

The rear hatch twisted a few inches with a screeching sound as the jamming bar was dragged across the lock.

"We can only hope," Perlins said.

***

"We must avoid them, Jake Stewart," Yvette said. "They are coming too close. They will be able to board."

"The Jump computer is running," Jake said.

"Good for the Jump computer," Yvette said. "But we cannot let them come closer."

Jake tapped buttons on his screen. "It's too dangerous to change course right now." He hit another. "We just need to hang on 'til we get higher. Once we're clear of the ecliptic, we'll have a clear view to that adjacent system we're aiming for, so we can do our jump. That has to be where that other Jump ship is going. Otherwise, its course doesn't make sense."

"You make no sense, Jake Stewart," Yvette said. She tapped her board, and a red light flashed. She tapped again, then flipped screens. Red lights flashed again. She turned to Odette and spoke rapidly in Francais. Odette nodded, reached down her boot, pulled out a small revolver, and pointed it at Jake.

"Unlock her board so she can make the course correction," Odette said.

"You had that in your boot the whole time?" Jake said.

"Fix the board, or I will shoot you."

"I should have known," Jake said. "Nadine always had a gun down there." He turned to Shutt, who was lounging in her chair with her hands behind her head. "Do you have a boot gun, too? Is this some sort of fashion accessory that all women carry?"

Odette cocked the gun with a click.

Jake turned back to her. "No."

"I will shoot."

"Get it over with," Jake said. He leaned back in his chair and closed his eyes.

Nothing happened.

He opened an eye. "Could you hurry along, please? I've got things to do."

Shutt raised her eyebrows and smiled. "You know, Stewart, for such a wimp, sometimes, you're pretty cool in the face of danger."

"I've been shot before," Jake said. "Bunch of times. It hurts a lot. But there doesn't seem to be any way to stop it. As soon as a woman gets the slightest bit attracted to me, she either shoots me or hits me or ties me up."

"I'm not attracted to you," Odette said. "I want to shoot you."

"Same thing," Jake said. "From my side anyway. 'Do what we say, Stewart, or we'll shoot you.' Next thing I know, I've got bandages on, and I'm getting a back massage."

"That's pretty weird courting behavior, Stewart," Shutt said. "You impress girls by letting them shoot you?"

"It's not that I want to. I don't really let them. They're going to do it whether I let them or not, but it does seem to impress them. It's like a necessary step. After they shoot me a time or two, we get along much better."

"Wouldn't it be easier to just take them to dinner or buy them a drink?"

"I tried that. The few times I've bought them drinks or dinner, I've ended up in jail or trapped on a pirate base or things like that."

"Pirate base?" Odette asked.

"It's a secret. We don't need to go into it now," Jake said.

Shutt turned to Odette. "You know you can't risk shooting him. He's the only one who can run the Jump drive."

Odette lowered her gun. "I know. Maybe I should shoot you."

"I'm the engineer," Shutt said. "You need me. And, unfortunately, we need pilots, so I can't shoot you." She eyed the two women. "Well, not both of you. One of you, sure."

Odette leaned down and holstered her gun. "But what would you shoot me with?" she asked.

Shutt unclasped her hands from behind her head, revealing a shiny revolver similar to Odette's clasped in her hand. "I've got options."

"Have you been hiding that the whole time?" Jake said.

Shutt spun the revolver around a finger. "Small enough to fit in the palm of my hand. Big enough to put a hole in you."

Jake leaned back for a better view. "That's a nice one. Bright. Shiny. Much nicer than Odette's."

"Now you are making fun of my weapon?" Odette asked.

"Can I see yours?" Jake asked Yvette.

"What?" Yvette said.

Jake looked her up and down. Her skin suit was quite trim, and she had a fancy neck scarf. "You dress kind of girly. I'll bet it's pink. A pink revolver."

Odette giggled. "She does have a pink revolver."

"It's not a pink revolver," Yvette said. "It has a pink grip. My mother gave it to me. It's old Empire."

"Your mother gave you a pre-abandonment revolver?" Shutt asked.

"Why not? Didn't your mother give you anything?" Yvette asked.

"My dad gave me his old boots. Or left them to me after he died," Jake said.

"You wear dead people's clothes?" Shutt asked.

"All the time," Jake said. "We're not like you spoiled Militia types, always getting new things."

"And here I was starting to like you," Shutt said.

"I am starting to like him," Yvette said. "You are braver than you look. And smarter than I gave you credit for. I think I understand. We can't change course because, if we do, you'll have to restart the Jump computer, correct?"

"Yes," Jake said. "We give it our current vector and destination, and it calculates when we can safely start the jump. If we change anything, it has to the start the calculation again. We just have to wait for it to finish, and we're out of here."

"And I will bet you picked the first jump that would get us away from here when you started that computer, didn't you?"

"It's easy here," Jake said. "There were only three possible systems in jump distance. One's blocked by the primary, one's on the other side of the ecliptic, but this one is just above us. We just need to get clear of the rings, and we've got a straight shot. And that other ship seems to be heading for it."

"How long until the jump?" Shutt asked.

"We've been talking a while. Let me see. ETA is twenty minutes. It will bong when it has a solution, and if we're happy, I put in a sequence, and we jump."

"So, we wait for a bong?" Shutt said.

The ship shuddered, the walls twanged, and the sensor boards lit up.

"What was that?" Shutt asked.

"Not a bong," Odette said.

***

"Did it hit?" Perlins asked. Krikweigh had fired his magnetic grapple at the pursued Jump ship.

"Yes, but that is the longest, thinnest line that we have, and it won't hold under any thrust," Krikweigh said.

"Daav?" Perlins asked.

"We're creeping up slowly. I'll need to do some sort of station keeping eventually," he said.

"You promised the single pivot would work," Jammy said. They had been set for a flyby but had pushed everybody back inside the air lock, spun, and used the main drive to bring them to rest relative to the Jump ship.

"It did, we're here," Daav said.

"I could have got us closer," Jammy said. "Should have let a real pilot do the job."

"Shut up, Jammy," Perlins said. "We don't have time." She looked behind her. The rear air lock's locking handle had spun another quarter turn. The metal strut blocking it had bent. "Our former friends have found a lever or something. That hatch is moving."

"What's going on?" Merced asked. He was awake but confused.

"We've got a line on that Jump ship," Perlins said. "We're going over there and taking it over."

"What happened with the storm?"

"It happened."

"How bad was it?"

Daav spoke from the cockpit where he was driving. "Really bad. Radiation levels were above survivable if you weren't shielded."

"What's going to happen to the rest back there?"

The rear hatch wheel clicked another inch. "Forget that," Perlins said. "Focus on what's going to happen to us if they get that hatch open. Everybody out and clip onto that line."

"Then what?"

"What?"

"We clip onto the line," Merced said. "And then what?"

"Board the other ship."

"They're just going to let us?"

"Yeah, they said they warmed the basic up and heated

some trays," Perlins said. "They're making a party of it. Get going."

"What about Dalon here?" Merced said.

"Hook him up to you."

"He'll be work."

"Don't care. He's with us now. And we won't be coming back. What does he need?"

"Some rest and oxygen. More oxygen will help. Not sure if that will be enough."

"You don't know that. You're not a doctor."

"I kind of am," Merced said. "Or as close as you have, and you're definitely not a doctor. Are you sure we should take him?"

"If we leave him here, once they get that door open, the rest will kill him."

"If the radiation was as bad as your minion says, then they won't be killing anybody even if they get the door open."

"Imperial anus," Perlins yelled. "Enough talking. Get moving. More talking doesn't help. We need to get out of here. I've had enough of you muttering whining types. I'm the leader here, and I say we go. This type of indecision is what got us in this mess in the first place."

"Boss lady," Jammy said.

"Shut up, Daav. Get moving."

"He's right, Perlins," Daav said from the control room. "Running blindly forward with no plan is what has got us in this mess."

"If we don't get out of here, we're going to die."

"What happens if we go over there?" Daav said. "Won't they fight us?"

"And we don't have any weapons, boss lady," Jammy said.

"Everybody, shut up," Perlins said. "There is no need for weapons. That ship hasn't changed course in an hour. Everybody must be dead or asleep or something. We get over there, pop the air lock, and we're free and clear. We get there, and we're fine. Otherwise, we starve here, freeze here, or get beaten to death by the crew behind us." Perlins took a deep breath. "Choose now."

***

"Jake Stewart, then this is a race," Yvette said. "We can't change course unless we want the Jump computer to restart."

"Right," Jake said.

"Why don't we avoid them now—make a course correction that will take us away from them and then restart the jump calculation," Shutt asked.

"Because we don't want them to crash into us," Jake said. "They're too close now. We could start up engines again, but they are close enough that they could catch us and damage something useful before we get far enough away."

"Shoot at them, then," Shutt said. "Didn't you say we have weapons?"

"Something called a positron beam. Don't know how that works. And they do have a laser."

"Do they?" Yvette asked.

"They're a cutter. They're supposed to have some sort of weapons," Shutt said. "And if they shoot, they could hit something important."

"Like what?" Yvette said.

Shutt pointed at Jake. "No idea. Ask our jump expert."

Jake shook his head. "I have no idea, either. Look, the ten-minute countdown is on. If we just keep quiet, we can jump in ten minutes."

"With them attached?" Shutt said.

"If they're within the jump field, they'll come with us. If not, we'll cut the line. I know that much from my reading."

"They are coming back onto the hull," Odette said. "I can see them clearly. These old Empire sensors are amazing. Four—no, five of them. Wait—six, they are carrying one. I see a shotgun, an ax, and a medical kit."

"You can see that they're carrying a medical kit?" Shutt asked.

"Yes. These scanning sensors show me size and dimensions, as well as a rough view of inside. It automatically cross-references that with a database of ship supplies."

"Wow. That's impressive," Shutt said.

"Also, it's a big box with a red cross on it. What else would it be?" Odette asked.

"Bite me, merchie," Shutt said. "Are they all going to cross that line?"

"They are clipping on," Odette said.

"What's the breaking strength of those lines?" Jakes asked. "Those messenger lines?"

"Five hundred kilos? Two hundred? No idea, and it doesn't matter," Shutt said. "We're not towing them, it's just being used to give them a bridge."

"We're not towing them yet," Jake said.

"You said we couldn't change course," Yvette said.

"We can't change course, but we can change aspect," Jake said.

***

"Everybody clipped on?" Perlins asked. Daav, Jammy, and Krikweigh answered in the affirmative.

"Almost," Merced said. "I'm just getting Dalon on, then I'll clip in front and tow him."

"Get ready to—whoa," Perlins said. The line tightened, and they were all lifted off the hull.

"They're maneuvering," Krikweigh said. They lifted slightly. "Should I hold on—"

"Let us float," Perlins said. "Somethings off."

The group of six slowly rose above the cutter.

"They're not maneuvering. They're rolling," Perlins said.

"That's it?"

"Never mind, everybody across," Perlins said.

"A little help here?" Merced asked. Dalon was clamped on the line, and Merced was grasping his belt harness. "I don't have any free hands here."

"If you weren't a medic," Jammy muttered.

"I'd already be dead," Merced said. "Still plenty of time for that for all of us."

***

"They're all on the line," Odette said, watching her screen. She had become the de facto sensor operator. "They've lifted off and are pulling across. At least the front ones are. There is some sort of jam at the back."

"Jake Stewart, how long 'til the jump?" Yvette said.

"Nearly ... seven minutes," Jake said.

"We need to fire the other thrusters."

"If we yaw or pitch, there will be a point where we change our vector slightly, change our forward momentum," Jake said.

"Changing our roll does that, too," Shutt said.

"Not our forward momentum, and that's the most important. Rolling makes the least impact on our course. The rolling thrusters are better balanced according to the flight computer," Jake said. "Plus, look at where they hit. If we roll, there isn't anything that line can damage."

"Aren't we kind of reeling them in?" Yvette said.

"Like a yo-yo," Jake agreed.

The women looked at him blankly. "An old Earth yo-yo?" Jake said.

They shook their heads.

"A ya-ya?" Yvette asked.

"Yo-yo. We're spinning them, but there is some friction on the line. We're not only pushing them around. We're kind of rolling them in."

"Only Jake Stewart could protect us from boarders by helping them get aboard more quickly." Yvette said.

"Status change," Odette said. "Pursing ship is leaking

vapor. Big leak. Changing their course."

Yvette, Odette, and Jake busied themselves, checking sensors, vectors, and screens.

"I can see a ventral air lock hatch open," Odette said. "A different one from before."

"That ship is coming closer," Yvette said. "Vapor loss pushed it toward us."

"Five minutes to jump at Mark. Mark." Jake said.

"More people coming out the ventral lock. At least two," Odette said.

"Are they firing a harpoon as well?" Yvette asked.

"No, they are walking along the surface. Looks like they are going to the bow. Wait—they're firing a shotgun," Odette said.

"They're firing a shotgun at us? At a ship? At this distance?" Shutt asked.

"No. Somewhere else."

"Hey, Free Trader chickie number two, that's you." Shutt pointed at Odette. "What's the status of the line crew?"

"Free Trader chickie?"

"Free Trader chickie number two." Shutt pointed at Yvette. "She's Free Trader chickie number one. You're Free Trader chickie number two."

"Why is she number one?"

"Cause she's smarter and better-looking."

Odette flicked her revolver into her hand. "I don't like you very much."

Shutt rolled her hand open, where she had been concealing her own revolver. "I thought I made it clear that I don't like you, either."

"Ladies," Jake said.

"Shut up, Jake Stewart," Yvette said. She had produced her own revolver. As described, it was pink. "We have a situation here. We are in some peril. Put your guns down and get back to work."

"That's very bright pink," Shutt said. "There's no way

you'd ever hide it. And it's so big. That won't fit under a dress. Of course, that assumes that you even own a dress."

"I have some very nice dresses, thank you mon ami," Yvette said. "And unlike you, I don't always wear coveralls."

"We're on a mission. We wear coveralls," Shutt said.

"She has no taste in clothes," Odette said. "She is always borrowing mine."

"Ladies—" Jake said.

"Shut up, Jake Stewart," Yvette said. She turned to Odette. "I am not always borrowing your dresses."

"And my makeup. Could you not at least buy some of your own lipstick?"

"I'm with her on that," Shutt said. "Lipstick is expensive."

"Girls—" Jake said.

"Shut up, Jake," all three women said.

"We are women, not girls," Yvette said.

"You should not call us that. Pig," Shutt said.

"Stupid man. Cochon," Odette said.

Jake pointed at the screens in front of him. The women paused, looked at each other, then looked down and typed.

"We continue to roll," Yvette said. "Thrusters neutral. I can correct."

"The two figures are still on the ventral side of the pursuing ship," Odette said. "One continues to fire a shotgun at the group trapped on the line. The other has proceeded to the bow and is working on a hatch there."

"Jake's clock shows two minutes to jump," Shutt said. "How is that line group doing?"

"They are more than three-quarters of the way here. Our rolling has reeled some of the line onto the ship, and they have also pulled along it. There is one group of four nearly onboard, and one group of two at the far end. The far group is moving very slowly. I think one is towing the other."

"Whatever weapons they have on the cutter, they have

to control them from the control room," Shutt said. "I don't know why the first group didn't shoot at us, but they could have. They obviously want to board."

"The second group doesn't look like it wants to board. It looks like it wants to shoot the first group. Or us."

"Or us," Shutt agreed. Her screen bonged. "For the love of the Emperor, there's another ship out there."

"Where?" Yvette asked.

"Right ahead of us. Running ballistic. Dark. Wow, these sensors are good. I'd never have seen that on a Militia cutter."

"What is it doing?" Yvette asked.

"Just drifting at speed."

"Is it on a collision course."

"No," Shutt said. "In fact, it's on the same course as us, just farther along."

"Farther along?"

"Yes. Same course. It must be going to the same place we are. It's like we're chasing it."

"What should we do?" Yvette asked. She and Odette looked at each other and shrugged. Shutt shook her head and typed some more numbers on her screen. She looked at the other women for a moment, then turned to Jake.

"Jake?"

"Shutting up," Jake said. He didn't look from his board.

"What's going on?" Shutt said.

"I'm being quiet so I don't get shot. Again. That's what."

"Jake, what are you doing?"

"Our mission."

"Our mission."

"Yes, as Dashi briefed me."

Shutt opened her hands. "And that was to ..."

"Investigate the other Jump ship."

"The other Jump ship?"

"The one you forgot about," Jake said.

Shutt snapped her fingers. "I did forget. There was another Jump ship."

"There it is," Jake said, pointing at the screen. "We're following it, like Dashi told me."

"What else did he tell you?" Shutt said.

"Test our jump capabilities. Don't let us get caught by any of the other factions. And if possible, flush out and neutralize any mutinous Militia assets in the far rings that might cause problems later."

"Well, we found some mutinous Militia assets, that's for sure," Shutt said. "And from the looks of how they're climbing on the outside of that ship, that storm did some sort of neutralizing."

The control board tinged.

"What's that?" Yvette said.

"That's our sensors confirming a course lock on the other Jump ship," Jake said.

A double bong rung from the control board.

"And that?" Odette said.

"That's the one-minute warning for jump. I've set the ship to auto jump as soon as it has a solution."

A loud thud followed, then three more.

"And that?" Shutt said.

Jake frowned. "Not exactly sure, but I think that's an armed boarding party clamping on to the ship, so they can force the air lock."

CHAPTER 18

"Has Admiral Edmunds provided an agenda for this meeting?" Dashi asked, levering himself out of the ground car.

"Not to me, sir," Jose said. "But I imagine we'll find out." They had driven to the ministry of agriculture building, where Edmunds had his headquarters, to discuss ongoing power and security issues. The door guards had shuffled them into a second-floor conference room and sat them down, but not before they had seen scores of Militia-uniformed troops loading equipment and supplies onto electric trucks and driving them away.

"Mr. Dashi. Jose," Admiral Edmunds said, arriving from an adjacent room.

"Admiral," Dashi said.

"Sir," Jose said.

Edmunds stared at them in silence. Finally, he said, "Thank you for coming here. I didn't think you would."

"Why ever not?" Dashi said.

"You're supposedly the Emperor presumptive. I would think that your dignity requires you to have others attend you, so to speak."

"My dignity, as you call it, is based on a disputed entry in a database, and your own personal willingness to be faithful to an Empire that hasn't been heard from in nearly a hundred years. Standing on said dignity strikes me as unreasonable and unrealistic. My power is purely theoretical."

"Theoretical?"

"You, Admiral, control the only effective military force

on the planetary surface right now. Your power is real."

Edmunds got up and walked to a window. Another truck loaded with boxes arrived. "The key there is effective. We control most of the city. The Galactic Growing mobs are defeated."

"Are they?" Dashi asked.

Edmunds turned to him. "Interesting question. They've stopped fighting us."

"Not the same thing," Jose said. "Maybe they just went home? Or ran out of ammunition."

Edmunds shook his head. "Why do I always feel like you two are way ahead of me any time I do anything?"

"You don't appear to lack self-confidence," Jose said. "More the other direction, in fact."

"It was excessive self-confidence on the part of Galactic Growers and certain members of the Militia that got us in this mess. They thought they understood how to run a revolution, how to run an economy, how to run a government. They didn't. I don't plan to make that mistake."

"Economies are complicated," Dashi said. "Governments are complicated. I can't speak of revolutions. I've never been in charge of one."

"And yet, Dashi, you seem to have come out on top of this one," Edmunds said.

"I have no idea what you mean. The current government of Delta is a council composed of TGI, the unaligned corporations, and the Free Traders. And the ... loyalist Militia. We share ministries almost equally."

"I can't kill you. I figured that out," Edmunds said. "Whether you're the real Emperor or not, enough people believe it that I can't do it. Or have it done, or have an accident. You're bulletproof. If I have you shot, half my officer Corp will shoot the other half and shoot me as well." Edmunds turned back to the window. "And I'm not sure that they would be wrong."

Dashi and Jose looked at each other.

"When will your control of the city be complete?" Jose asked. "The riots are disrupting repairs."

"Now, you, Jose, you I could kill. And that Jake Stewart fellow. I could kill him, too. I don't think anybody would say anything to me about that."

"Except your granddaughter," Dashi said. "She's not particularly well disposed to you under normal circumstances. Killing her current lover would dramatically alter that equation, for the worst, probably. And as far as Mr. Jose goes, he is my designated assistant. I would be upset. And I think you may find that he has developed resources of his own that he could deploy against you."

"Threatening you is hard work, Dashi," Edmunds said. "I always sound so coarse, and you're always so smooth. I get tired afterwards just trying to figure out what you said. You're under arrest."

"I don't threaten people," Dashi said. "I just point out alternatives."

"I'm taking you into custody. Protective custody."

"And if people don't understand which alternative is best, I do provide gentle guidance."

"You don't care that I'm arresting you, do you?"

"Something like this was bound to happen, one way or another," Dashi said. "But I'm curious what you think is going to happen. As you have so thoughtfully pointed out, we're bulletproof. Killing us would ensure your defeat and probable demise from this mortal coil."

"Emperor's balls, Dashi. 'Demise from this mortal coil.' Really? Do you have to talk that way?"

Dashi smiled. "Jose and I were talking about that earlier. It's a habit of mine. I find it hard to break."

"What's going to happen to me, to the Militia, to Delta?" Edmunds asked.

"That's an odd question coming from somebody who just arrested us," Jose said. "We should be asking you."

"Six months, a year ago, TGI, and its 'chairman presumptive,'" Edmunds said, "had two main enemies and a host of minor ones. Galactic Growers and the Empire-Rising Officers' council, plus a bunch of smaller corps and organizations. They were much more powerful and likely to prevail. Somehow, Galactic Growing got all the weapons and apparent support needed to start a civil war, started one, and were completely destroyed. Their senior people are all dead, their assets are either destroyed or have been handed over to their rivals. Again, including TGI."

"The Militia received a generous allotment," Dashi said.

"That's after the officers' council also started a civil war, within the Militia. We lost ships, resources, people. The items you gifted us didn't make up for our losses in the ... what did you call it in the last meeting, Jose?"

"The current unpleasantness."

Edmunds snapped his fingers. "That's it. Unpleasantness. So, after this unpleasantness, TGI reigns supreme. Most of its resources are in orbit, guarded by its allies, where I can't reach, and its chairman appears to be the Emperor of the known galaxy. The other corps are all too scared of what might happen to challenge you and have fallen in line. Oh, and you seem to have possession of the only Jump ship found in the last eighty years."

"The Jump ship was a fortuitous occurrence," Dashi said. "There was a low probability of it being found. Still, I felt it necessary to allocate some resources to the search."

"How long were you watching this Stewart fellow?"

"I knew his father long before Mr. Stewart was born," Dashi said. Jose looked at Dashi for a moment, creased his brow, then nodded.

"Meanwhile," Edmunds said. "I'm the hero of the revolution, saved the planet from the mutineers, and rallied the loyal Militia. As a reward, I have a burned city with no utilities to manage, gangs of armed toughs to fight without enough weapons or troops, and there are still groups of rogue officers who want to throw me out an air lock without a suit."

"The rogue Militia units are defeated," Dashi said. "You said so yourself."

"I lied. Not all of them. There's still lots of them running around."

"They hate us as well." Dashi went to look out the window. "I'm sure they would kill Mr. Jose and I without a thought. Presumably they have some sort of enemies list."

"It's a numbered list. My number is higher than yours. They'll come after me first."

"I assume you are taking precautions?"

"The officers' council are at the top of my list, that's for sure. I've got a plan to take care of them. Get them before they get me, as it were. But for it to work, you can't be here. You need to be somewhere else. So, I'm saying that the city has become too unsafe. As a precaution, your Imperial highness, I'm removing you and your assistant from the dangerous environment that is present in the city."

"If you're going to call Mr. Dashi his Imperial highness, then you should be referring to me as 'Tribune,' Admiral," Jose said.

"Tribune? What's a tribune?"

"In old Empire usage, a tribune is an officer appointed directly by the Emperor and reporting only to him. It comes from old Earth history."

"A tribune is a senior position, Jose. I would think you'd be more of a legate, wouldn't you?" Dashi said.

"You've empowered me to act independently in your absence, sir," Jose said. "In that respect, I felt I possess my own Imperium, thus not a mere legate."

"The addition of Imperium does make your position more like tribune, I agree," Dashi said. "You've been reading up, I see."

"So, you have Imperium, Jose?" Edmunds said. "Does that change the color of your skin suit or something?"

"It means, in the absence of the Emperor, I can rule by decree."

"You're a dictator now?"

"Dictator would be a different office, but I have many of the same powers. My person is sacred against violence. I can be preceded by an honor guard, and I can command legions."

"Legions? That's a military formation. Special infantry, correct?"

"Yes. Infantry raised by a tribune, a legate, or directly by the Emperor."

"Well, if I come across any legions, I'll send them to you for instructions right away," Edmunds said.

"Thank you, Admiral. That's very kind," Jose said.

Edmunds shook his head. "You two clearly don't understand irony when you hear it, do you?"

"I haven't heard any yet," Jose said.

"You haven't even asked why you're getting arrested," Edmunds said. Somebody shouted outside, and he walked to the window to look out.

"Galactic Growing is completely removed as a factor in the current conflict," Jose said. "Your troops concentrated on the household troops of GG during the current unpleasantness and eliminated most of them. GG has lost almost all of its weapons and armed security, and the rest have retreated to remote ranches and won't be causing any problems anymore. But in order to do that, you had to utilize substantial numbers of disloyal Militia troops. You have a core group of loyalists, but there are many other troops that you are not sure of. At least twenty percent, perhaps a quarter of the mutinous officers escaped and about a third of your current troops are suspect. There is a good chance that the remaining officers' council could reappear and challenge you for control."

"Go on," Edmunds said. A bell rang in the distance, and groups of armed men and women ran through the courtyard toward the entrance.

"The city is in worse shape than you thought. The lack of utilities is the main problem. You can't fix that, you lack the technical expertise. TGI has the technical expertise but insufficient security forces on planet to protect our work parties. If you stay and protect TGI staff while they fix things, TGI will get the credit for bringing the city back online, and there is an even chance that you will lose out to a counter-countercoup from the old Empire rising officers. The resultant fighting will destroy your loyal Militia cadre but leave us unaffected. When the dust settles, you might be dead, or, at best, in charge of a small local security force while TGI and their allies achieve hegemony over the entire system."

"Hegemony? Really?" Edmunds said. Somebody knocked at the door. Edmunds ignored it. "That's quite an assessment. So, what should I do?"

"What you are doing now?" Jose said. "Abandoning Landing. It will burn. Or freeze, I should say, for the next few weeks of winter. Concentrate on consolidating your power in the Militia by destroying your rivals. Once you have removed the remaining mutinous Militia forces, you will be free to reorganize and reenter Landing. After a period of anarchy, you'll be seen as the only valid leader of the planet, and TGI as purely a technical appendage."

Edmunds stared at them for a long time, then nodded. "You were right. You hadn't heard any irony there, had you?"

"Not as of yet, no," Jose said.

A larger group of men armed with shotguns sped by in the courtyard. The knocking at the door got louder, then ceased. "Well, I'm taking you out of the city. At least I'll be able to keep an eye on you. And once you're separate from your security troops, I'll bet you sing a different tune."

The door opened, and a Militia officer stepped in and saluted. "Apologies, admiral."

"When I said I didn't want to be interrupted for anything," Edmunds said, "I didn't think I needed to qualify what anything meant."

"Sir, a large group of armed troops have surrounded

the building, and their leader is demanding to see Mr. Jose here."

"Troops? Whose troops? You mean one of those mobs? Put a squad on them."

"Sir, a squad will not do. Several squads will not do. We're outnumbered, I believe."

"Outnumbered? All the mobs got together at once?"

"It's not a mob, sir. They're wearing uniforms, of a sort, and have weapons. Revolvers and shocksticks. Approximately one in ten is carrying boarding shotguns. They've deployed around the building in an organized fashion, and they are maintaining fire discipline. Their leader claims the title 'Legate,' and she says there will be fighting if they do not speak to Mr. Jose."

"Legate, huh?" Edmunds said. "Sure, send the legate in."

The Militia officer stepped out. Edmunds stared at Jose and Dashi in silence. Dashi reached into his coat. Edmunds dropped his hands to his holstered revolver, then removed it. "You don't have a gun with you."

Dashi produced a bottle of pills. "Of course not. I don't even own one." He shook a pill out and put it in his mouth.

"Breath mints?" Edmunds asked.

"Pain," Dashi said. "The physiotherapy helps, but my legs still hurt."

A knock sounded at the door, and Marianne stepped in. She was wearing a standard skin suit, but it was covered with a snazzy belted vest with loops for a holstered revolver and shock stick.

"Ms. Marianne," Edmunds said. "How truly good to see you."

"Marianne is my name, Admiral, but in this circumstance, I think Legate or Legate Marianne is more appropriate."

"We've all given ourselves fancy new titles, have we? Legate of what?"

"Of the Emperor's forces," Marianne said.

"As you say, Legate." Edmunds peered at the badge on her breast. "Is that Francais?"

"Yes. Liberte, Eqaulite, and Fraternite. They mean—"

"I know what they mean. I even know where they come from. Is that also Francais on your shoulder?"

"No, that is an old Earth language called Latin. It was used in the old Empire."

Edmunds read the shoulder tag. "Legio X, Sigma Draconis." He shook his head, then turned to Jose. "Tribune. Your resources are here."

CHAPTER 19

"You look like death, Sergeant," Commander Roi said.

"Feel like it, sir," Sergeant Russell said. He stared around him. The overnight storm had passed, and the waves had lessened, but he still had to hold on to a rail to stand upright.

He turned to a noise behind him. Nadine groped her way up to the cockpit from down below. Her hair was matted, full of vomit, and she was covered with a greasy green sludge down the front of her outfit. She crawled over to the side of the boat. A large bucket with a rope attached sat there. She dipped the bucket overboard and let it fill up. Then she pulled it back in and dumped the entire bucket over her head. She hissed as the cold water hit her.

She did this three more times before stopping.

"What was that green crud?" Sergeant Russell asked.

"Food trays. They got mixed into the water," she said.

"I don't think we have any green food trays," Sergeant Russell said.

"They're all green once you partially digest them." She rolled her hair into a ponytail and wrung it out. "I am never, ever, never, ever getting on a sailboat again."

"You get used to it," Commander Roi said.

"No, you do not," Nadine said. "When can I get off this boat?"

"Perhaps three, four hours," Commander Roi said. "We didn't get blown too far off course. We need only a short while to locate the base."

"Where's the brother's grim sailors?"

"They are sleeping," Commander Roi said. "They were up most of the night, steering and handling the storm. They are excellent sailors, I must say. Far better than me. One of them even went up the mast after the storm tangled the sails on the aerials. When the weather moderated, I could handle her for a while. They deserve their rest."

"Aerials?" Sergeant Russell asked.

"For the radio. Regular personal comms don't work out of sight of land. We have a special system on the boat, but the sails damaged the antennas, it is out. We cannot call anybody."

"That's unfortunate," Sergeant Russell said.

"Indeed. Especially since, on this base, they do not like unannounced visitors. I hope they don't react badly when we appear with no warning."

"What would constitute reacting badly?" Sergeant Russell said.

"Firing on the boat and sinking us," Commander Roi said.

***

"Red right returning." Balthazar pointed at a red stick poking out of the water. "When you are coming from the ocean, you keep the red markers to your right, and you won't run aground."

"That seems too simple," Sergeant Russell said. Melchior and Estephan were fussing with ropes on the front deck, and he was at the back with Balthazar watching the shoreline.

"Come all the way back from old Earth," Balthazar said. "Every sailor on Delta learns it. Every sailor in the Empire, as far as I know."

"Don't you have a plan, or a map, or something?" Nadine said. She was pale but moving. Most of the squad was asleep in the cabin.

"You look like the Empress's hairy anus," Russell said.

"I feel like it."

"Take a nap."

"Have you smelled what it's like down there? And by the way, I'm not cleaning it up. That was the Militia's finest there."

"Once they're awake, I'll have them clean it up," Sergeant Russell said. "But that's a good question—do we really need our glorious leader up there to drive us in? Isn't there a map of this area?"

"Not one hundred percent fond of the commander, are you Sergeant Russell?"

"He's the boss, but he's a bit of a twit. And he has a tendency to let his enthusiasms for what he thinks the Empire should be like to overcome the reality of what things are like right in front of him. Sometimes it's best if ... cooler heads prevail."

"Cooler heads like yourself?" Balthazar said.

"And your brothers. You're businesspeople, and I'm just a simple sergeant trying to keep his squad alive."

"And your commander is a bit of a—"

"Crazed lunatic fanatic mutineer," Nadine said. "I say the three of us take things over."

"First, there is no three of us," Sergeant Russell said. "You're a prisoner. Second, my squad, as sick as they are, have all the firepower. And third, Balt, can we find this base without the commander's help if we need to?"

"I don't know where we are," Balthazar said.

"I thought you sailing people just looked up at the stars, and they told you where you were and what time it was and what you should have for dinner?" Nadine said.

"That was on old Earth, where man had been charting the stars for thousands of years. Here, we're lucky if we can see the stars through the ring debris."

"We've got navigation satellites," Nadine said.

"There are only three working, and they're in very eccentric polar orbits, where all the settlements are. Even up there, we can't always cross-reference where you are.

Down here, we're lucky if we see one. And we can't figure out where we are with one. And even if we could, so what?"

"You don't want to know where you are?" Nadine asked.

"We need to know where to go, not where we are. We don't have maps. So, spin a globe and point to somewhere and say, 'We're here.' What happens next? Where is this base? And how do we get there?"

"You suck as a captain," Nadine said.

"Shut up, prisoner," Balthazar said.

"Bite me. This prisoner thing sucks, too," Nadine said.

"You can change that if you want," Sergeant Russell said. "You could swim to shore from here."

Nadine looked across the blue-green water. They were in a group of small sandy islands. None seemed more than ten feet tall, and all the beaches were covered with masses of green seaweed that floated in beds. Each bed was ten times longer and wider than the boat. In clear water, the boat ghosted along, up and down the swells, but as soon as it ran into a pile of seaweed, it slowed and trundled through. "I don't see any people or buildings here."

"Or trees," Sergeant Russell said.

"Or potable water," Balthazar said. "Hopefully, they have water and food at this base."

"I'll wait 'til we're closer and then I'll escape," Nadine said. "And you two are such Imperial turds I'm telling you in advance, and you won't do anything about it."

"Go with my blessing," Sergeant Russell said. "One less person to feed and water, and I am seriously wondering what's making that seaweed bob up and down like that." He pointed to a section of seaweed about twenty feet away.

"That's just the waves," Nadine said.

"Could be. Or could be a blond-girl-eating type of sea monster that's just watching the boat, trying to figure out if there is anything edible on it," Sergeant Russell said.

Nadine cursed some more. Another big red stick was up ahead. "So, we just watch Commander The-Empire-Will-Return up there follow red sticks?"

"That's the plan for now," Balthazar said.

"Everybody knows about this red stick thing, how to follow them?" Sergeant Russell asked.

"All sailors do, yes. It's a standard thing. Keep the red to your right." The boat approached the red stick in the middle of the channel. It was between two small islands, both of which were higher than the others so far, maybe twenty foot tall sand dunes covered with seaweed.

"If I was hiding a base, and I had a marked trail into it, I'd move one of those sticks, or put one in the wrong place. Somewhere that my trusted people would know so they would skip that one. Somewhere that would catch strangers, make them run aground or hit the rocks, get eaten by monsters or something, before they got too close."

"Why would you do that?" Nadine asked.

The boat approached the red stick. As they passed it, the keel ground on the bottom, and they all jerked forward as the boat slowed, then stuck. It hung there, five feet from the stick. Shouting burst from the right. The seaweed on the side of the sandbanks was fake. It had been woven into a net. The net had been pushed down, revealing a dugout. Three soldiers stood there. One had a shotgun across his chest. The other two pointed some sort of cannon on a tripod at the boat. They were yelling across the water.

"No reason," Sergeant Russell said. "Just something I'd do. I think they want us to put our hands up."

CHAPTER 20

"Daav, it's impossible for you to be hit by a shotgun. In space. Hundreds of meters away," Perlins said. She and the others were pulling down the harpoon line toward the Jump ship.

"Don't care. Hurts a lot," Daav said. A solid slug had hit him hard in his shoulder. His left arm dangled, and he was using his right to pull along the line in a series of jerks. Pull, release, reach forward, clamp, pull, release, etc. He huffed in pain every time he yanked.

"They're probably sick back there and never fired a shotgun. And you say they hit you?"

"That's why he's such a great guy to play poker with," Jammy said. "His continual bad luck."

"Shut up about luck," Perlins said. "Is he bleeding?"

"Doesn't look like it," Jammy said. "His arm is the only thing hit, but he's kind of slowing me down. Can I shoot him? Put him out of his misery?"

"Shut up. Krikweigh?"

"I'm fine. I'll be locked on momentarily."

"Merced?"

"I'm going as fast as I can. Couldn't you have got us closer?"

"Everybody's a critic," Jammy muttered. "But when I want help ..."

"Shut up, I said." Perlins said.

"You say that a lot," Jammy said. "If you're going to be senior officer, you need to find another catch phrase."

"Glad you agree I'm senior," Perlins said.

"That's not what I said."

"It kinda is," Krikweigh said. "Locking." He jumped the last few meters and impacted onto the hull. His magnetic boots held him. "Find an air lock, boss lady?"

"And get it open," Perlins agreed. "I'll help the desperate duo here. Jammy, help me get Daav locked on, then we'll help Krikweigh board."

"With what? Our hidden stash of ship-killing weapons that we keep in our boots?"

"That's the plan. I'm hopping," Perlins said. She leaped off the line and thunked into the Jump ship. She skidded for two inches, but then her magnetic boots gripped. "Now, just get him down and clamped."

"I don't need any help," Daav said. "I'm fine." He yanked himself forward and rushed at the ship. He didn't quite stop himself from thumping into the side headfirst. He groaned over the radio but managed to get a boot onto the ship, then lay there, panting.

"Face first with lots of screams," Jammy said. "A typical Daav Landing." He thumped next to him, clicked both his boots on, bent over, and grabbed Daav.

"Better than some, actually," Daav said. He yowled as Jammy levered him upright.

"You almost pulled off insouciant," Perlins said. "Until the scream."

"We could try again?" Jammy said. "I can just slam him to the deck, start it all over. Think you've got another scream in you, Daav?"

"To the Imperial hells with you," Daav said. "Just give me a moment."

"Krikweigh?"

"Air lock isn't locked. I think it's just stuck. There's a lever rod here, but I need more people."

"I'm coming. Jammy, leave Daav alone. Let him work things out. Help Krikweigh and me get that air lock open."

"We've only got the one shotgun, boss lady," Krikweigh said.

"Leave it out here," Perlins said. "We come in peace."

"Really?" Jammy said.

Light sparkled in the distance, and a bullet trail flashed in their field of vision.

"That's amazing shooting," Krikweigh said. "To hit us from that far."

"More reason to get inside, fast," Perlins said.

"Shotgun will help that," Daav said. "Getting inside, I mean. Protect us from whoever's inside right now. If we take it."

"Which do you prefer?" Perlins said. "That whoever is inside this beast is trying to repel boarders and not watching their sensors or that they are manning the control room and see that whoever over there is almost into our old control room?"

"Who cares about a control room?" Krikweigh asked.

"Anybody who wants to ram us or shoot us with that laser that we didn't try very hard to get working."

"We didn't try to get it working because we couldn't hit anything with it."

"We couldn't hit anything with it. We also had no hope of hitting a nearby ship with a shotgun, but whoever survived that storm has done it twice. I wonder if they are as good a shot with the laser as with their shotguns?"

"That's a point," Krikweigh said. "I need all the help I can get to get inside before anything happens." He pulled a long metal rod out of a hull locker and threaded it through the hatch's locking wheel. It stuck out several meters, close to the ship's hull. "Get over here and push."

Perlins and Jammy moved beside him. All three leaned down and grasped the bar. "On three, push. One, two ..."

"Wait," Jammy said. "Is it one, two, push on three, or is it one, two, three, push ...?"

"Shut up, Jammy," Perlins said. She crouched over, set her boots, and tried to push. Her boots lost lock, and she flipped up. "Too low." She rolled in space and brought her boots down. "I don't have the angle. Krikweigh, rack it up."

Krikweigh unthreaded the bar from the wheel and fitted it back in, going through only half of the wheel mechanism. Now the angle was much greater, but it stuck up higher. Krikweigh set himself in the middle where it was at his waist. Jammy stood next to him, pushing at shoulder-height. Perlins reached upward. "Merced?" she yelled over the radio.

"Just getting Dalon locked on," he said. "He really needs some fresh air. And a lot of it. I'm checking your friend, Daav, next.

"Leave Daav. Get over here and let me stand on your shoulders.

"What?" Merced said.

"I can't reach the bar. The guys need more help and leverage. I'm light enough. I can brace on you."

"I don't think—" Merced said. A bright flash of blue light ahead of them. "What was that?"

"That was the first recorded intersystem jump from Delta in maybe eighty years, that's what that was. Get over here and help."

"Are we going to jump?" Merced asked.

"Probably."

"What happens to us if we're on the hull when this ship jumps?"

"A, I don't know. B, I don't want to find out, and C, get over here and help."

Merced made sure that Dalon and Daav were locked on and skipped over. "What do I do?"

"Jammy, choke up," Perlins said. "Close to the start of this bar as you can." Jammy moved closer to the hatch, leaned down, and grasped the bar at knee-level to him. "Have you got leverage?" she asked.

Jammy set himself and pushed with his hands. "Yes. I'm set."

"Krikweigh, as you were. At waist-level." Krikweigh set his feet, then leaned into the bar. "Ready?"

"Merced, stand here and lean forward. Lock your

boots. I'm getting up on your shoulders and leaning into that bar. When I say push, you lean in and start walking if you can."

"Walking?"

"I'm going to be pushing, but I need you to propel me along."

"We won't have much force at this angle."

"That's how levers work, force times distance. We won't have much force, but we'll have lots of distance."

The ship vibrated.

"What's that?" Jammy asked.

"I think that's a Jump drive warming up. Everybody ready? Push," Perlins said.

***

"Jake Stewart, what is that vibration?" Yvette said.

"And the noise?" Odette said. "We're ... thrumming?"

Jake paged through his screens. "I don't know. But the Jump drive is running through its preliminary sequence."

"That other ship is gone," Odette said.

"In a flash of blue light," Shutt said. "Just like in the old vids. Must have jumped."

"Have you got their course?" Jake asked.

"Yes, Jake Stewart, and before you ask, it's the same as ours. We will follow them into jump."

"And will we follow them out of jump?" Shutt asked.

"Yes," Jake said. "Same course—we'll drop out of jump behind them."

"How do you know we'll be behind them?" Shutt asked. "If I understand this right, we go into jump space, we keep our velocity, but space itself is smaller, so we go farther in the same period of time."

"Right," Jake said.

"And when we get out of jump space, we drop back into normal space with our same velocity."

"Still right," Jake said.

"And all these super-duper calculations are to account

for the gravity of stars and planets along the way."

"I don't hear a question here," Jake said.

"Because their gravity still affects us, even in jump space. Just not for as long. And if we hit any of them directly, even in jump space, we're dead." The vibration increased and Shutt looked down at her screen. "Jump fusion reactor is spooling up. Some big capacitors charging up, too. So, your course is designed to avoid planets, stars, asteroids, dwarf planets, comets, all that stuff. Make sure all the different gravity is accounted for and that we don't hit anything before our exit point." Shutt looked at her screen again. "Where is our exit point, Jake?"

"It's at a place called the jump limit. As close to the planet Cygni-61 in the next system as I can get without the planet's gravity messing up the jump."

"And there is nothing between us and that jump limit exit point right now?"

"Nope."

"So, since we're on the exact same course as that ship in front of us, what's going to happen if they drop out of jump before we do, short of the jump point, and we overrun them in jump space?"

Jake's eyes widened, and he looked at his screen. "Emperor's balls."

***

"Push," Perlins said.

"That's what your mom said," Daav and Jammy chorused together over the radio.

"I hate pilots," Perlins said.

"You're a pilot," Krikweigh grunted. "Why did you become a pilot if you hated them?"

"It's just male pilots I hate. Stop everyone. Take a breath." Perlins gasped over the radio. "It almost moved. I felt it flex."

"Almost doesn't count," Krikweigh said.

"Two things. First, it's jammed. We need to crack it

loose, not push it loose." Perlins gasped for air over the channel again.

"And the second thing, boss lady?" Daav asked.

"Neither of you could handle my mom. She'd chew you up and spit you out. Then she'd polish your bones and use them for knitting needles."

"Pretty big words," Merced said.

"Very true," Jammy said. "I've met her mom. She's quite a handful. If you know what I mean."

"Handful of what?" Daav asked, his voice weak over the radio.

"Daav, you okay?" Perlins asked.

"Don't mind me, boss lady. Keep going."

Perlins looked back to where Daav stood, swaying next to an unconscious Dalon. A single red light blinked on his collar. Something had gone wrong.

"We need a better plan," Perlins said. "Jammy, Krikweigh, brace yourselves. Take up tension but don't give a hundred percent. Merced and I are backing up, and we're going to do a running dive and hit that pole as hard as we can. When you feel me hit it, hit hard yourself."

"I'm a medic," Merced said. "I'm not good at these outside maneuvers."

"Boss lady," Krikweigh said, pointing at the cutter. "They're maneuvering over there."

Everyone turned. The cutter was coming closer and spinning on its axis.

"They're clearing the laser," Perlins said. "Merced, just put a long tether on."

"Don't have one," Merced said. "I left it with the others."

"Then don't miss." Perlins turned, grabbed Merced by the arm, and propelled him back an easy ten meters. "We're going to do a running start and jump on three. Krikweigh and Jammy, brace when you hear us start and snap me a push when you feel us hit. Merced, just snap into the bar. Ready? Go."

***

"Thirty seconds," Jake said.

"Are we going to crash into that other ship or not?" Yvette asked.

"I don't know. There is a small random factor and a section in the manual on avoiding other ships in convoy," Jake said.

"And?"

"And I didn't read it. I didn't think we'd ever be in convoy. But the drives aren't aligned perfectly. We should randomly drift above or below our course, which means that, even if they stop short, we'll miss them."

"Or they might randomly drift into your course, if the two randoms cancel out," Shutt said.

"That other ship is maneuvering," Odette said. "They should have a laser or a mass driver or something. They are probably trying to get an angle."

"We've got all sorts of weapons here," Shutt said.

"So fire them," Yvette said.

"I don't know how. And I'm not going to figure it out in the next—how long, Jake?"

"Fifteen seconds," Jake said. He pressed a button. "We're committed now. Full auto once we're in the right spot."

***

Perlins flew through the air. Right away, she knew that they had botched it. Merced had been a step behind jumping off the ship, and she was too low. She hit the lever bar at full throttle, with her arms close to her chest. Her momentum made the bar bend, and she felt it bend farther as Krikweigh and Jammy pushed on it. It wasn't enough.

"Empress's vagina," she screamed. "Get ready—"

Merced hit the bar. Perlins felt a crack as something gave way, and the bar suddenly pivoted forward. She hung on tight as they rotated. Merced rolled up and over the bar, scrabbling with his hands. She wrapped one arm around the bar and the other around his legs. "I got you, I got you."

"Get down," Krikweigh said. "I'm opening."

"Jammy," Perlins said. "Get the others."

"I'm on it. Daav—"

"Coming," Daav said. He reached down and unsnapped Dalon's magnetic boots, then his own. Unlike Merced, he had no problem pushing off and heading directly for the air lock. "Emperor's balls, my arm hurts." He mouthed a series of curses as he flew toward the lock.

Krikweigh dragged the lever bar free from the locking wheel and spun the wheel to open the outer lock. A cursing Daav smacked into a cursing Jammy, and Jammy shoved first Daav, then Dalon, into the hatch and dove after them. Krikweigh hopped down next.

Perlins dragged a stumbling Merced over to the open hatch. She hesitated, since Krikweigh's head and shoulder blocked the entrance. The vibrations had increased so much one of her feet wouldn't stay locked on.

"Move," Perlins yelled. She spun Merced upside down and stuffed him in headfirst. Complaints, curses, and yells filled the radio channel. When she met resistance, she pushed harder until something gave way, and she felt him punch through. She jumped into the now clear hatch, but her feet struck something. Probably a shoulder or head. She struggled to pull the hatch closed behind her. "Move, move, move." She kicked, and more curses came over the channel. The ship vibrated enough that her vision was affected as she held onto the hatch wheel. She pushed harder, and something gave. She pushed herself feet-first through the hatch. The locking wheel came behind her, just as a bright blue light filled the air lock. It cut off as she slammed the hatch shut and spun the locking wheel.

CHAPTER 21

"Who are all these people?" Admiral Edmunds asked Sergeant Sumita. A line of soldiers stepped onto the train.

"I know some, sir," Sergeant Sumita said. "Some former Militia, but they're mostly Free Traders. They call themselves—"

"Legion X Sigma Draconis, yes I heard. What do you think of all this, Sergeant?"

"They're disciplined, for sure. Much better than those toughs roaming the streets."

"A gang of drunken tabbos stampeding the northern plains is more disciplined than those mobs."

"Well armed, too, sir. Everybody has a revolver. Half have shock sticks. And a boarding shotgun per squad." Sumita pointed at a stocky woman with a shotgun and a bandolier of ammunition across her chest. The colors of the rounds showed she had solid slugs and buckshot.

"Weapons do not make the man, Sergeant."

"They take good care of them, too, sir. Nice and shiny. Better than our conscripts."

"Conscripts are not renowned for their willingness to clean things."

"And their uniforms are pretty spiffy," Sumita said.

"Spiffy?" The admiral rounded on the sergeant. "You think the uniforms are spiffy? Are you interested in a transfer, then? Do you serve the Empire?"

"They are Imperial troops, sir."

"Raised by a corporate vice president and his henchman."

"Word is this Mr. Dashi is actually Emperor Dashi."

"You going to take his orders over mine, Sergeant?"

"Will I have to, sir?" Sumita shrugged. "I mean, I'm kind of over all this fighting, sir. I joined the Militia to get away from turnip-picking and delivery. Not shooting drunken kids in the streets."

"Are you telling me you actually fell off the turnip truck, Sergeant?"

"Dropped right off in front of Militia HQ almost twenty years ago. Signed up, haven't looked back. Haven't eaten any turnips since then, either. Can't even stand the smell."

Edmunds watched a group of Legionnaires secure heavy boxes onto a flatcar. "What's in the boxes?"

"No idea, sir. Provisions? They've said we don't need to feed them. They have their own rations and supplies."

"That's good news."

"And they've indicated where we'll be dropping them off, what size of units, and so on. And they've shown where we can put some of our troops as well. They say if we put our troops with theirs, we don't have to feed ours, either. They'll take care of it."

"We can feed our own troops. This planet is awash with food," the admiral said.

The sergeant didn't say anything.

"Isn't it?" the admiral asked.

"We're not in distress, Admiral, but we haven't had time to load enough supplies onto the trains. Wasn't enough space, anyway."

The admiral looked around. A group of Militia boarded the train. In contrast to the Legionnaires, their uniforms were torn and soot-stained, and their uniform accessories were a mix of different types, and not all had firearms.

"Trooper, come here," the admiral called.

A surprised trooper looked up, then jogged over and saluted. "Trooper Davis Monthan reporting, sir."

"What type of shock stick is that?" the admiral asked, pointing at her belt.

"Not a shock stick, sir. It's a stick stick."

"Stick stick? Are you stuttering, trooper?"

"No, sir. No shock component. It's just a metal stick."

"It's called a baton, sir," the sergeant said. "Trooper. Give it to me."

The trooper removed the stick from her belt and handed it over. It was, as described, simply a metal pipe with a handle attached.

"What happened to your issue weapon?" the admiral asked.

"This is my issue weapon, sir," the trooper said.

Edmunds looked at the sergeant. "We're using sticks now?"

"Had to give them something when we ran out of ammunition, sir," Sumita said.

The admiral swung it experimentally. "Good up close."

"We used them with the mobs, sir. Sergeant said he didn't trust us not to shoot people, but with the sticks, we could defend ourself."

"You were out fighting the mobs?"

"Didn't do much fighting, sir. Mostly, when we came on site, everybody ran off. Went home."

"They just went home?"

"Set some fires first, sir. Broke stuff. But yeah, I'd not want to get caught in an alley with those folks, but none would hang around when a squad showed up. They just ran away."

The admiral handed the stick back. "Carry on, Trooper." She saluted and ran to board the train.

The last of the Militia squads boarded. "How many more?"

"Fifty of our troops left in town. Next train is the last."

"How many of ours total are going west?"

"When the next train leaves—total, about two hundred."

"And the ... legion?"

"About the same. Hard to tell exactly."

A horn honked as the train left. "We don't split up our troops," Edmunds said. "All of them go to the end of the line, to that TGI base. What's it called?"

"Point 37."

"All of us there."

"Might not be enough food."

"Don't care. Everybody goes there. We sit with these legion people, and we stare at them. Then we wait for one of us to blink."

***

Dashi and Jose watched the countryside roll by. The monorail hung off the side of a cliff as it rolled past a headland. Dashi and Jose were sipping tea.

"How is this train even working?" Dashi said. "Given our problems with the fusion plant."

"We connected the hydro dam to this side, sir," Jose said. "And isolated the rest of the system from it. That gives us enough power to run the western legs of the monorails."

"And the eastern side?"

"Where Galactic Growing was strong, sir? Because of the security situation, we were unable to effect repairs, sir."

Dashi smiled. "Of course we haven't. How long before the remaining GG troops cave in and agree to our leadership, then?"

"Truthfully, sir, there really aren't any GG troops left. I was being truthful when I spoke to the admiral. They really have given up. Just some unorganized groups of locals defending scattered ranches."

"The admiral is not a man for half measures, that is for sure. Now that he's crushed GG, how long until he completely removes the remaining rebel officers?"

"He has to find them first, sir."

"Where are they?"

"Secret base on south continent. We have a man there."

"I assume the admiral does as well?"

"Woman, actually. Ms. Nadine is supposed to be there, along with that rogue squad. I haven't confirmed their arrival, but they were on their way. She hasn't been able to contact the admiral yet. Once she does, he'll have to do something."

"Ms. Nadine was supposed to be his agent on the Jump ship."

"That task has fallen to her backup, Major Clarisse Shutt. She's the admiral's woman on the spot, as it was," Jose said. "And of course, the Free Traders have their own crew there."

"And we have Mr. Stewart."

"Indeed, sir."

Dashi put his cup down. "Any news from Mr. Stewart?"

"They appear to have escaped the pursuing Militia cutter. Both they and the other Jump ship, which they were following, have left the system. We're assuming by a jump."

"Successful?"

"No way to tell. They could all be dead. I don't think it's likely, though."

"You trust the technology?"

"I trust Mr. Stewart, sir. Jump drives seem to be something he's competent in. I expect he wouldn't have engaged his if he hadn't had a high expectation of success."

"I expect that as well."

"The other Militia ship may be damaged, or the crew incapacitated. It's on a strange orbit, long duration orbit. Unless there is a lot more in the way of supplies there, all the remaining Militia officers on that ship are going to die."

"Removing them from the equation. Are we personally secure here?"

"There are enough Free Trader troops here—sorry,

Legionnaires—along with a small TGI security detachment, to make the admiral think very carefully before he does anything. Plus, of course, your personal notoriety is a shield."

"Notoriety? The notorious Mr. Dashi. I like that. Good morning, Ms. Marianne," Dashi said. Marianne had stepped into their compartment.

"Your Imperial Highness." She sat across from Dashi, next to Jose. Her thigh almost touched his.

"Just 'Dashi' will do. And since, according to Jose, you are now a legate, and he is a tribune, I suppose we should all be on a first name basis. May I call you Ms. Marianne?"

"Marianne is fine. And Mr. Jose?"

"Jose is fine, Marianne," Jose said. "And you, sir? Can we call you by your first name?"

"You always have been, Jose. It's Dashi."

"Just Dashi?"

"Indeed."

Dashi smiled at Marianne. "Would you like some tea?" He offered a cup. She nodded, and he poured her a generous mixture. "How goes your plotting to overthrow the admiral, Ms. Marianne?"

"Who says I am plotting?" Marianne asked.

"It's the appropriate thing to do in the moment. But perhaps not 'overthrow,' more like 'diminish.' You need him to run the Militia, you just need their strength reduced. Has he complained about you stealing his troops by recruiting some of them into your legions yet?"

"If we are recruiting Militia officers and troops with the promise of honorable service in a well-organized unit, why not? Especially in a unit recognized by the Empire?"

"As a point of interest," Dashi said. "Where did the idea for forming your own military unit come from? And where did you hear of legions?"

"That Shutt woman gave me the idea. Earlier, she had said that we were untrained, and she was right. We have weapons, and we have people, but we do not have experience." Marianne slurped the tea. "I just contacted current and former Militia members from Free Trader families who had training with the ground forces. They have become our—cadre, I think is the term?" Marianne looked at Jose, who nodded. "Our cadre. Then I contacted the leading Free Trader families and convinced them to provide manpower for training. Mostly youngsters who like a good fight."

"And the Legion part?"

"Mr. Stewart mentioned that in one of his ... discourses ... on Imperial history," Jose said. "I did a little research and mentioned the idea to Ms. Marianne. She took it further than I expected."

"Why would Free Traders swear personal loyalty to you?" Dashi asked. "They're not known for being interested in discipline."

Marianne shook her head. "They didn't swear loyalty to me. They swore loyalty to the Empire, to the Emperor. To you. We are all patriotic Imperial citizens, always have been. It's the Emperor's good laws that protect independent merchants from the—"

"You call yourself 'Legate,'" Dashi said. "I don't recall granting you that title."

"Mr. Jose granted it to me. I have a paper from him." Marianne reached inside her coveralls and produced a thick folded sheet, and extended it to Dashi.

Dashi didn't take it. He looked at Jose. "How is it you can grant her a title?"

"Sir, you made me tribune, under your authority. Planetary governor in effect. Governors can raise legions under legates. At least in the old Empire, and that is the lineage you claim to represent."

"I see," Dashi said.

"So, these troops were raised by Ms. Marianne under my direction, in your name," Jose said. "The Emperor's first legion."

"I command troops now," Dashi said. "Really?"

"Of course, sir. It would be unseemly for the Emperor, whoever he is," Jose said, "to deal directly with such mundane matters as military deployments. He makes his wishes known to his tribunes, and they pass them along to the troops."

"As filtered through their commander of course," Marianne said. "That would be me."

Dashi shook his head. "The student exceeds the master." He looked from face to face. "Or in this case, students, plural." He shrugged. "What if the admiral tries to shoot you?"

"He's welcome to try. Our new legion is mostly Free Traders. They are tired of having to put up with the Militia's posturing for the last few years. They feel that you will be a better leader than the old council."

"Oh, I shall be. But what if you, personally, don't believe? Where does that leave me?"

"I can't kill you. Too many people respect you as a symbol of the old Empire. You're bulletproof," Marianne said.

"You're the second person to say that," Dashi said. "Must be a trend of some sort. What about my assistants, Mr. Jose and Mr. Stewart?"

"Mr. Stewart is far away, and I have good friends keeping an eye on him. Whatever happens there, I will be represented. Mr. Jose is much more of a threat to me."

"Really?" Jose asked.

"Yes. Your defense of TGI Main is widely admired. You succeeded where others failed, and you used no violence. Your work in bringing the city back from the brink is acclaimed. Most of my troops see you as a hardworking technocrat who wants only what is best for everybody."

"Sounds dangerous to you." Mr. Dashi smiled. "Wouldn't take much for him to replace you in your troops' affections. When is the assassination scheduled?"

"I left my planning too late," Marianne said. "He is

already affectionate enough to them. Is that the right word? He is already untouchable. Besides, he is cute." She smiled at Jose.

Jose smiled back, then frowned. "You had planned to have me assassinated?"

"It wasn't so much a plan, more of an idea. In any event, don't worry. Not going to happen right now. Mr. Dashi, what are you going to do about Landing and the admiral?"

"Myself? Nothing. For security reasons, I'm relocating to Point-37. Which is also where our greatest corporate strength is, and our only functioning orbital lift. I will remain there until the security situation improves."

"When will that be?" Marianne asked.

"I suppose that depends on when the paid mobs that both you and Mr. Jose employ stop trying to destabilize the streets."

Marianne looked at Jose. "You know about that?"

"I do now," Jose said. He looked at Dashi. "It seems the master still has skills that we need to learn."

Dashi smiled and steepled his hands. "Thank you for your confidence, Jose."

"What are you going to do about the admiral and the Militia?" Marianne said. "How are you going to rein them in?"

"I'm going to seek advice from my main advisers. That would be you two. Jose, what should we do about the admiral?"

"The absence of the admiral's troops will lead to a brief period of anarchy, but the mass of people will not put up with it. There are enough free weapons floating around that some sort of popular group will eventually re-establish order. Probably a council of the more reliable citizens. I am in touch with a few. They will, in effect, rule the city. But they will lack the necessary technical and logistical depth to continue maintaining it. After asserting control, they will have to seek some arrangement with the other factions to survive. Most probably contact us and ask for our return."

"Interesting," Dashi said. He reached into his pocket and produced a pill bottle. He put one in his mouth and swallowed. "Ms. Marianne, what is your opinion of what the admiral is doing right now?"

"His retreat from the city is a masterstroke. If he had stayed, he would have ended up fighting the locals, which would have destroyed any legitimacy he gained. At least a third of his troops and the rebel Militia are undecided, ready to stick the knife in his back when given the chance."

"What should he do?"

"His idea for now is good. He is conserving his power, and as soon as he is sure he has located the rebel troops— and more importantly, their leaders—he will move to defeat them soundly. Without a sanctuary, they will surrender to his ways."

"What happens then?"

"We will be in a difficult situation, sir," Jose said. "There will be three main competing groups of power. The remaining Militia will be smaller but more supportive of the admiral. The Free Traders and their allies remain united. TGI and the allied corps continue in orbit. And I suppose whoever comes out on top in the city will be a fourth."

"And don't forget Mr. Stewart and whatever comes out of this Jump ship experiment. That will add another factor."

"So, we'll be left with multiple groups who don't trust each other, all with arms or resources that the others desire, who are forced to work together to survive."

"A very astute analysis, Marianne." Jose smiled at Marianne.

She smiled back. "As was yours, Jose."

"So, with all these different groups, Marianne," Jose said. "Who do you predict will seize control?

"A charismatic figure, Jose, one who can unite all the diverse factions but beholden to none." Marianne grasped Jose's hand for a moment, then smiled and looked at Dashi. Jose also turned to gaze at him.

Dashi smiled and steepled his hands. "Would you two like   more   tea?

CHAPTER 22

"Why did you throw your guns in the water, Sergeant?" Commander Roi said. He was staring at the bubbles formed when Sergeant Russell's entire squad had thrown all their weapons in the ocean.

Sergeant Russell pointed at the three men, pointing a cannon at them from across the water. "They said, 'Hands up' and 'throw down your guns.'"

"But did you have to throw them in the water?"

"They were pointing that big cannon thing at us, sir."

"Well, yes, I suppose so."

"And they did tell us to throw them down. The water is down, isn't it, sir."

"Well, yes."

"Quite a bit far down, too. And really, sir, it's all water here. I suppose we could have swum ashore to one of those sand bars and thrown them down there. Chaudhari?"

"Sergeant?"

"Swim ashore to that sandbar over there and throw down your weapons."

"Can't swim, Sergeant."

"Why not?"

"Not an in-demand skill on an orbital mining station, Sergeant."

"Huh. Anybody here swim?"

Nadine waved. "I do. Can I swim over there?"

"I think we've had enough of your swimming for one trip," Sergeant Russell said. He looked over. "Sorry, sir, throwing down in the water was all we could do. Why did you want me to throw those away, sir? I think we could have used them."

"That's what I was saying, Sergeant. We could have used them."

"If we could have used them, then why did you want them in the water?"

"I didn't. I mean, that's not what I wanted."

"As you say, sir. And you did mention earlier that I sometimes don't obey things with as much dispatching as is necessary."

"Dispatch, Sergeant."

"Dispatch? Of course, sir. Who?"

"What?"

"Who should I dispatch, sir?"

"I mean you should obey orders with more dispatch."

"More dispatch, no problem, sir. Kim and Kim, get up here. You're being dispatched."

The two troopers walked over to the sergeant. Their hands were up, and they had thrown their weapons in the water. "Yes, Sergeant. Where are we being dispatched to?"

"Let me ask." He turned to the three troops across the water.

"Hey, we dropped our weapons. Can we put our hands down now?"

The troops conferred, and one yelled back, "Yes. Why did you throw your guns in the water?"

"It was part of our dispatch procedure," Sergeant Russell yelled back.

"Your dispatch procedure?"

"Yes. I've been practicing my dispatching."

"Just get yourself over here, Imperial moron."

"Sure. How?"

"What?"

"We've run aground. We can't move."

"Use your boat."

"What boat?"

"Your tender."

"Who are you calling tender? I'm tough. Come over here. I'll show you tender." Sergeant Russell turned to Commander Roi. "Can you believe that, sir? Calling me tender."

"Tender is what a small boat that serves a larger boat is called," Roi said.

"A small boat is called a tender?"

"Yes."

"Why?"

"I don't know. It just is."

"Well, it should be called something else," Russell said. "A tough, or a spongy."

Balthazar, Melchior, and Estephan had been listening to the conversation.

"A spongy. That's a great name. We have a rigid hull inflatable spongy, Commander, if you want to use it," Balthazar said.

"I suppose we should go see them," Commander Roi said.

***

After fifteen minutes, the inflatable boat was only half inflated. They were using the hand pump found in the bottom. After twenty minutes, Roi got impatient and rowed over, even though the boat wasn't fully inflated.

The three brothers watched as Commander Roi tried to pull the rowboat across to the rebel Militia.

"You'd think there would be some sort of motor for that, to pump it up," Sergeant Russell said.

"Oh, there is," Estephan said. "It's down in the hold. Electric recharges by solar. Very quiet. Not fast but reliable."

Sergeant Russell watched the commander row across the water. "So, how badly screwed are we being hung up on this reef or whatever you call it?"

"Just have to wait," Estephan said. "We grounded on soft sand. Tides rising. Another ten minutes, and we'll be floating free."

"Really? Are the propellers damaged?"

"Nope. Sand, remember? We're fine. We ground deliberately all the time. We've got metal plates protecting the propellers, so we'll just move along.

"Didn't think about telling the commander this?"

"He never asked," Estephan said.

"He never does," Sergeant Russell agreed.

***

"I am Commander Roi, acting head of the officers' council," Commander Roi said, after having rowed over to the three Militia.

"Acting head? Who made you that?" The corporal said. His nametag said Conkal. The two others were labeled Abaco and Brunkee.

"Colonel Savard appointed me in his stead."

"The colonel? He was a great man," Corporal Conkal said. Abaco and Brunkee nodded.

"Yes, I was appointed in his stead."

"His stead? What's a stead? Is that like a room in a house?" Conkal asked.

"Isn't that a fancy name for a kind of bedroom, Corporal?" Abaco asked. "A steadroom? A steading."

"No, a steading is a ranch," Brunkee said.

"Right. So, you're the colonel's ranch hand?" Corporal Conkal said.

"Are you sure steading isn't a bed?" Abaco said.

"That's homesteading," Brunkee said.

"Got it," Corporal Conkal said. "Okay, so you were home on the ranch in bed with Colonel Savard, Commander. And he made you the head of the officers' council."

"I was not in his bed, it was in his stead—never mind, it was before he died."

"Colonel Savard died in bed? I didn't know that," Abaco said. "What a great way to go, though. I want to die in my bed."

"Me, too," Corporal Conkal said. "In my bed. With wine and a pretty girl. Say, Commander, did the colonel have a girl with him? In his stead?"

"A girl?" Commander Roi asked. "A girl in bed with him?"

"I knew it," Brunkee said. "Trust the colonel. He always had an eye for a pretty lady. What did she look like? Was she blond or brunette?"

"The colonel had neither a blond nor a brunette with him when he died," Commander Roi said.

"Redhead! I knew it. High five for the colonel," Brunkee said. The two troopers and the corporal exchanged hand slaps.

"He was my favorite officer," the corporal said. "Why, when he gave that speech about 'publishing the neverless desserts,' that was just outstanding."

"Publishing the desserts?" Commander Roi asked.

"The neverless desserts," Corporal Conkal said. "Great speech."

"Are you sure he said publishing?" Commander Roi said.

"Now that I think about it, maybe it was punishing."

"And I think that other word is wrong," Abaco said. "Wasn't it nefarious? Publishing the nefarious desserts?"

"No," Brunkee said. "I heard that speech. It was punishing the neverless."

"Punishing the nefarious desserts—that was it," Corporal Conkal said. "Say, Commander, what did the colonel have against desserts, anyway?"

"Yeah, I like a good apple pie when I can get it," Abaco said.

"So hard to get, though," Brunkee said. "Haven't seen a dessert in weeks."

"Did you bring any desserts, Commander?" Conkal asked.

"What?" Roi said.

"Food. Desserts. Apple pie. That pear thing they make."

"I like blueberry crumble," Abaco said.

"Nothing like that out here in the desert," Corporal Conkal said. The three Militia troopers looked at each other, and all three said at the same time, "Punishing the nefarious deserters!"

"That was the speech. I remember now," Corporal Conkal said.

Commander Roi expelled some air. "This is well and good, but I need you to take me to the base. Row me down there."

"Can't do it, Commander, sorry," Corporal Conkal said.

"Are you refusing an order, Corporal?" Commander Roi said.

"I'd never do that, sir. I'm loyal to the Empire."

"The Empire," all three troopers chorused.

"Then take me."

"Not possible."

"I order you to take me."

"Understand, sir, but I still won't do it."

"Why do you insist on disobeying me at this time, Corporal?"

"Not disobeying you, sir. I just can't."

"Why, in the name of the Imperial scrotum, not?"

"Your boat, sir." Corporal Conkal pointed. "It's filling up with water. You have a leak, and you'll start sinking any second now."

Commander Roi looked down just in time to see the deflated edge of his rowboat finally give up as the ocean water   rushed   in.

CHAPTER 23

"Did we jump?" Jammy asked. The six of them were jammed in the air lock, unlocking heads, arms, and legs from where they had been jammed when Perlins forced the hatch.

"You kicked my head," Krikweigh said to Perlins.

"Next time, get your fat head out of the way and clear the air lock," Perlins said. "And also, next time, you can be the one outside while we start to jump."

"Humming's stopped," Jammy said, "and there was that blue light. We must have jumped. Are we in jump space?"

"I don't feel different," Krikweigh said.

"I do," Daav said. "I feel sick. My arm hurts, and I'm upside down."

"There's no gravity in space, idiot," Perlins said.

"Upside down relative to you five," Daav said. "And my arm does hurt when I lean on it, so there is a down. We've got some sort of spin."

"Right, who's hurt?"

"As I said, boss lady—"

"Shup up. Merced. Check Dalon. Krikweigh? Jammy?"

"I'm fine, boss," Jammy said.

"Good as rain, boss lady," Krikweigh said.

"Never heard that phrase before," Perlins said. "Merced?"

"Dalon's really bad, ma'am," Merced said. "He needs more air. Something's wrong with his supply."

"It's ma'am now, is it?" Jammy asked. "Quite the little

suck-up you are."

"Everybody. Helmets off." Perlins popped hers and lifted it free. She sniffed the air. "Green lights. Smells good, too. Is that lemon?"

"Orange," Jammy said.

"Shouldn't we keep them on, as like, protection?" Daav asked.

"Are you wearing old Empire Imperial combat armor?" Jammy said, "because, if you're not, a shotgun slug will go right through your chest otherwise."

"I just don't want this beautiful face marred," Daav said.

"You don't sound good, Daav. There's a lot of red on that suit display," Perlins said.

"I can deal with it."

"How's your arm?"

"Fine, boss lady."

"Take your helmet off."

"Like I said, skipper, I'm worried about appearing in front of my fans with a bit of a mussed hair. Messes up my image."

"You can't lift your arm, can you?"

"Actually, no."

"Jammy, help him get his helmet off. No, take it off for him. He's hurt bad enough already. We want to be looking innocent when they open that inner hatch."

"We don't have the shotgun anymore," Jammy asked.

"It was left outside, as I requested. Finally, you people are taking orders," Perlins said.

"Meant to bring it with me but forgot about it during all the excitement," Krikweigh said. "Sorry about that." He had removed his helmet, sniffing the air. "This is the best-smelling ship I've been on in a long time. Maybe ever."

"Never mind your delicate nose. Can't you even just pretend to follow instructions for a while?" Perlins asked. She shook her hair loose and grasped her helmet in one hand. "Not even this once?"

"Sorry," Krikweigh said. "Next time, I'll lie." He sniffed again. "I think that's lemon."

"It's orange scent," Jammy said.

"What's an orange?" Krikweigh said.

"You've never had an orange?" Jammy asked.

"Is that one of those fruits? Too expensive for me."

Jammy had rotated Daav and sat him upright, relative to the others, and took both their helmets off. They both sniffed the air. "Not Jammy's stinking armpits for sure," Daav said. "He smells like the Emperor's anus most of the time."

"That would be you. And I'm sure now that you are on board that the place will start to stink up quick," Daav said.

"Ma'am, Dalon, he just stopped breathing," Merced said. "Just now."

"What do we do?"

Merced was doing something to Dalon's chest. "I need a defibrillator."

"I don't know what that is," Perlins said. "I'm a pilot, not a doctor."

"They'll have one on board near the med equipment. Get us inside, please."

"Saying please, too?" Jammy said. "Total suck-up."

"Shut up, Jammy," Merced said. They all laughed.

The inner lock swung open. A shotgun barrel poked through, and they all turned to it. A dark-haired woman stood behind the lock.

"Bonjour," she said.

"Uh, bonjour," Perlins said.

"Why are you all laughing?"

"Our friend is dying," Merced said. "We need a defibrillator."

"And that is funny?" the voice asked.

Perlins looked at her crew, jammed into the air lock, and shrugged. "Given the day we've had so far, kinda, yeah."

***

"We can't just shoot them all," Jake said.

"Of course we can," Yvette said. "They are Militia mutineers. They supported the coup, and they are trying to capture the ship.

"We don't know that," Jake said. His board bonged. "We got message traffic before we left. I sent Dashi a short update, and he responded. It might have an update." Jake perused his screen. "Strange-looking format, though."

"Now isn't really the time for discussing communication protocols," Shutt said over the intercom.

"Dashi wouldn't send me something unless it was important," Jake said. He tapped through his screens.

Yvette pushed the button on the intercom. "Do you see guns?"

Odette answered. "No shotguns. Perhaps a revolver hidden somewhere, but none visible."

"See?" Jake said. "We can lock them up."

"We can't lock them up. We have no locks," Yvette said. "There are no cells."

"No shooting," Shutt said over the intercom. "They are Militia troops."

"Rebel Militia troops," Yvette said.

"Mutinous Militia troops," Odette's voice said.

"If you start shooting them, I'll start shooting you," Shutt said.

"Here we go again," Jake said.

"You are not really in charge here, Mr. Jake. We are the ones with experience," Yvette said.

"Keep thinking that," Shutt said. "But try to shoot my colleagues, and we'll see who is really in charge."

"Everybody knows I'm in charge, right?" Jake said. "I was appointed and all that?"

"Be quiet, Jake Stewart. The adults are talking," Yvette said.

"We need a defibrillator," Odette's voice said.

"A what?" Yvette said.

"One of them is dead. It will bring him back to life."

"We can resurrect dead people?" Yvette asked.

"It's a heart thing," Jake said. "Major Shutt, there is a medical pod the next level up. You need to take the hurt man there. Let me give you directions." Jake told her where to go, and Shutt said she would take care of it before clicking off.

"This machine will bring the dead man back to life?" Yvette asked.

"No, it restarts his heart. Didn't you have one on your Trader ships?"

"Maybe. We had a basic pod. I don't remember having to start a heart, though. Us, mostly crush injuries. I had one myself."

"You were crushed?"

"I broke some ribs." Yvette looked at him. "I can take off my skin suit sometime if you want to see?"

"Uh, maybe later." Jake blushed.

Yvette laughed. "Well, then, Jake Stewart, we will fix this man up in the medic pod."

"Good," Jake said.

"Then we shoot him."

***

"We jump her on three," Perlins whispered, softly enough that the three others in the lock could hear her, but Odette, who was listening to the conversation on the intercom, could not.

"Is that one, two, three we go on three or one, two, three, then jump?" Jammy said.

"Shut up, Jammy," Perlins said. "Everybody ready?"

"Too tight, boss lady," Krikweigh said. "We'll just get in each other's way."

"I'm not good for much jumping," Daav said.

"Daav, stay back but be ready to do what you can. Spread out. Krikweigh, hit them from the left, Jammy, right." Perlins set her feet, flexed a bit, waited a beat, then yelled, "Now." She pushed off from the middle, Krikweigh from her left. The two of them flew through the low gravity. There was no sign of Jammy. Krikweigh bumped into her as they reached the one-person air lock, and she was pushed aside, hitting the door frame. She lost control and smacked off the door. She saw a flash and a puff of dust as a frangible slug hit metal.

Perlins rolled up and over after she bounced off the air lock frame and impacted the open air lock door. Krikweigh and Odette were locked together in front of her. Krikweigh had his arms around the shotgun and was forcing it up. Odette still had her hands on the trigger and had wrapped her legs around Krikweigh's waist, forcing them to tumble. The shotgun fired again into the air lock, and something punched Shutt's back hard. The momentum kept her rolling, and she smacked into the rolling pair in front of her.

The impact broke Odette's hold on the shotgun, and she flipped back. Krikweigh pulled up and out and claimed the shotgun. Odette rolled slightly as she went backward and caught herself on the far side of the corridor. Krikweigh leaned back and brought his legs underneath him and managed a controlled collision with the far bulkhead. He hit and bounced back, grunted, and slammed back-first to the deck.

He kept hold of the shotgun.

Odette paused, her eyes assessing the situation, then she pushed off the wall toward the central corridor, snagged a grab bar, and pivoted up toward the control room. She pushed the upper hatch down with a clang.

Perlins looked around. Krikweigh seemed stunned, lying on his back, but he had kept a firm grip on the shotgun with both hands. She sat beside him. Now that the adrenaline was wearing off, pain throbbed in her shoulder.

The air lock door had rebounded shut after she and

Krikweigh had banged through it. It swung open slowly, with a quiet squeal.

Jammy stuck his head around the side of the air lock. "Did   we   win?"

CHAPTER 24

"They jumped Odette," Shutt said over the radio. "While she was distracted looking after this guy here. Got her shotgun. But she says got a piece of one of them."

"What's happening now?" Yvette asked. She and Jake sat at the control stations in the Jump module. She glanced sideways at Jake, who was paging through various screens.

"Hatch is locked. Their guy is in the med pod. There's a lot of red lights. He looks bad."

"Can't they just open the hatch?" Yvette said.

"Nope. This fancy-dancy Imperial ship has locks. Not even computer-controlled locks, either—manual locks. I just slid this lever shut, and this door isn't going anywhere. They might be able to crack it enough to leak air, maybe, but no way can they open it."

"We are secure, then. Put Odette on." Odette and Yvette conversed for a perhaps twenty seconds in Francais. Jake didn't understand what they said, but Yvette glanced at him from time to time and frowned. After a long pause, she turned to Jake.

"Odette says they have two rounds left in the shotgun. If they know how to use it."

"They're Militia. Of course they know how to use a shotgun," Shutt said over the intercom.

"Perhaps. In any event, they are locked behind that hatch. Jake Stewart, can they do us any damage?"

"They can't move forward internally with that hatch locked," Jake said. "They could, in theory, go back to engineering and try to shut things down, but it's on a different system, and I've got that locked remotely. I suppose they could try to break in. There's a standard tool kit in the air lock and some fire suppression tools. They could try to use those. But we can see them."

"We can?" Shutt said.

"The cameras on this ship actually work," Jake said. "Unlike every Militia ship I've been on. And I can page through them. Look here." Jake paged through his screen.

Shutt and Odette were standing next to a hatch. Then various other locations, then a group of one woman and two men standing and gesturing at each other. The three of them wore tattered Militia skin suits. The largest man had the add-on plates for external work, but the other two wore the lightweight ones favored by pilots or others who never left atmosphere.

"Let's talk to them," Jake said.

"I don't think that's a good idea," Shutt said.

Jake ignored her. "Hello, mutinous Militia rebels."

All three of the Militia's heads swiveled toward the camera.

"We're not rebels. Or mutinous," the woman said.

"What are you, then?" Jake asked.

"I can't see you," the woman said.

Jake tapped some buttons. "Now you can. I'm Jake. I'm the captain. Who are you?"

"Really?" the woman said. "You don't look like any captain I've ever seen."

"It's a Jump ship," Jake said. "We do things differently here. Do you have a name?"

"Call me Perlins," she said. "Lieutenant Perlins."

"What about your friend in the med pod?"

"That's Corporal Dalon. How is he?"

"Pod's working on him. You attacked us."

"You pointed a shotgun at us."

"Boarding a ship was kind of unfriendly. As was shooting at us. And that ship you had, that was a Militia ship. That makes you mutineers. The admiral ordered all Militia ships to dock at a station and await orders."

"The admiral doesn't—" Jammy said.

Perlins put her hand over Jammy's mouth. "Shut up, Jammy. Yes, we heard the admiral's broadcast. We wanted to follow his orders, but we couldn't. There were too many of those Empire-rising people on the ship. They kept us out in the outer rings and told us to chase you. We were outnumbered and couldn't do anything."

"That's an interesting story. Does your friend disagree?"

Perlins took her hand off Jammy's mouth. "That's the way of it, right, Jammy?"

Jammy nodded. "We've been saying what we had to say to live. We thought things would be different here."

"But you boarded us, and your ship shot at us," Jake said.

"Our ship shot at you after we left, and we weren't boarding," Perlins said. "We were running away. We saw you and took the opportunity to get away from those losers. We want to rejoin the Militia."

"Couldn't you just have sent a message?" Jake asked.

"They would have heard us and gotten rid of us."

"Gotten rid of?"

"Shot us, or threw us out an air lo—" Perlins said.

Shutt said, "You say you're still in the Militia?"

Perlins looked at the camera. "Who are you?"

"Major Clarisse Shutt, Delta Militia, that's who," she said. "And if you want to rejoin, you have to follow orders. So, I'm ordering you to drop that shotgun by the air lock and retreat back down the hallway while we collect it."

Perlins looked at the camera again, then turned to her companions and raised an eyebrow. Jammy addressed the camera. "I'm Lieutenant Jammy. Our other pilot, Daav, is hurt. He's in the air lock."

"We can help him. We have another pod."

"We don't—" Jake said.

Yvette gripped his arm and shook her head off camera.

"We don't have a problem with that," Jake finished. "But your other friend isn't in very good shape."

"Is he going to make it? I'm Merced. I'm a medic," Merced said.

"Are you going to follow orders?" Shutt asked.

Perlins nodded. "We didn't know that this was a real Militia ship. We're ready to be with you. Krikweigh, give them the shotgun."

"Boss lady," Jammy said, "Are you sure that—"

"Yes. Shut up, Jammy," Perlins said. "Krikweigh, do it."

Krikweigh used his fingertips and toes to push himself down the corridor—their slow spin didn't impart much gravity—put the shotgun on the deck next to the air lock, then turned and slunk back to the group. Jake and Yvette watched the air lock door swing open on the camera, and Shutt stepped through. She picked up the shotgun and held it at across her chest. She didn't point it at the newcomers, but her posture wasn't welcoming.

Perlins started to give the crossed chest Empire-rising salute but caught herself and instead gave the Militia hand to hat. "Senior Lieutenants Perlins, Jammy, and Daav reporting for duty."

Perlins looked at Krikweigh. "You're Daav?"

"Daav's in the air lock," Perlins said. "This is ... Mr. Krikweigh. He was a tug pilot."

Shutt looked him over. "Not Militia?"

"Nope," Krikweigh said.

"He helped us escape them. He can be trusted," Perlins said.

"But can you be trusted?" Shutt said. She looked at Krikweigh. "What's your story?"

"I was collected up by the Empire-rising crowd. They made me fly tugs for them. I didn't want to."

"That's it? You didn't want to?" Shutt asked.

"They had guns, and there was a lot of them," Krikweigh said. "What would you have done?"

"Followed the admiral's orders, like I did," Shutt said. "Welcome aboard the Jump ship."

"The Jump ship? That's its name?" Perlins said.

"That's all we got for now," Shutt said.

"One other thing," Krikweigh said.

"What?" Shutt said. She didn't change her stance, but something seemed different in the way she grasped the shotgun.

Krikweigh leaned onto the wall and braced himself with his hand, then vomited onto the deck. "I don't feel very well at all."

***

There were two medical pods on the Jump ship. Dalon was occupying the first, so they put Krikweigh in the other. Perlins and Jammy carried Krikweigh with Merced fussing over him. Daav stumbled behind them, cursing as he banged his arm.

"Boss lady," Jammy said. "This isn't a good idea."

"Follow my lead. I'll get us through this."

"But these guys are our enemies. Once they figure out that we're rebel Militia, we're for the next air lock—"

"We're not rebels. Not anymore. We're escaped prisoners. The officers' council captured us and forced us to work for them, like they did Krikweigh here. Daav got injured while we were escaping."

"That's not going to fly. They'll know we were on the officers' council or at least in touch with it."

"We've just escaped one ship of incompetent maniacs. The losing maniacs. These are the winners. We need to join up."

"Is this the ethical thing to do?" Daav said from behind them. "I mean, we all thought the officers' council was right to—"

Perlins stopped and hissed at the two of them. "Shut up. Shut up, both of you. Ethics? You want to talk about ethics?" She dropped her side of Krikweigh, and Jammy staggered as the weight came on him. Perlins stepped back and smacked Jammy hard across the face.

"Hey, that's—"

"Exactly what you deserve. A low life like you. You're despicable." She pointed at Daav. "He's despicable. I'm despicable. We're all despicable. We helped start a war that we lost. All those people on GG Main and all those cutters would still be alive—and all those people in the city, if this war hadn't started. Remember, we did this not because we were great patriots—we're just stinking, weaselly low lifes who thought we could get more money or a better rank or more fame or whatever by joining the winning side. We guessed wrong, and now we're stuck with that guess. We left all those officer council types to die, die in a very gruesome manner. Slow death from radiation poisoning is not the way to go."

Perlins took a moment to take a breath, then grabbed her end of Krikweigh. "We never were rebels. Never ever. We were captured and did the best we could, and first chance we could we escaped to the forces of truth and glory—the regular Militia, the admiral, and this sanctimonious Major Shutt."

"You killed everyone on the cutter?" Merced whispered.

"What do you think all that raw radiation did to them?" Perlins asked. "Gave them a slight tan? They're baked through and through, and they'll be lucky to live that long. Actually, they'll be lucky to not live that long. Dying because your insides are boiled solid isn't a fun way to go."

"I didn't know they all died," Merced said.

"Doesn't matter whether you did or not," Perlins said. "You helped. You're alive, they're not. Or won't be. Our story is we escaped. We don't know anything about solar flares or dead troops. We're just escaped Militia people who are reentering the fold. We didn't know which side they were on, so that's why the shotgun. But now that we're here, up the Militia, up the admiral, up TGI, and thanks for giving us a ride away from those nasty Militia people. You three got it?" Perlins glared at them.

"Did you have to hit me, boss lady?" Jammy said.

Perlins hit him again. "Yes. You on board or not?"

Jammy rubbed his face and nodded.

Perlins rounded on Daav. "Well?"

"Don't hit me. I hurt a lot already," Daav said. "I'm with you."

"I'm not sure," Merced said. Perlins turned toward him. She slipped a hand into a pouch on her belt and pulled a small screwdriver out before pointing it at his face. "You're not sure of what? You can't go back now—those people back there are dead. You helped. Ratting us out won't help you but will hurt us. What's it going to be?"

Merced swallowed. His face was white. He nodded slowly. "I'll keep my mouth shut."

"What's the holdup back there?" Shutt's voice came from above through the hatch.

"Sorry, Major, we're having some problems carrying Krikweigh here. He's pretty heavy. And we don't want anyone else to get hurt." Perlins looked at the others with her. "We surely don't want anybody else to get hurt, do we?"

CHAPTER 25

The two groups met in the small lounge next to the medical area. Shutt kept the shotgun with her, and she had reloaded it. Yvette and Odette stood, facing Jammy and Perlins. Merced moved back and forth from one pod to the other, checking readouts and accepting suggestions from the medical pod software for treatment.

Shutt gestured her shotgun at Daav, slumped in a chair. "What's wrong with you?"

"Dislocated shoulder, I think," Daav said. "I got shot as we were escaping."

"Who shot you?"

"The last of the officers' council was on that ship," Daav said.

"At least the last of them that were orbital," Perlins said. "After that fiasco at GG Main, and after the admiral rallied the troops and called everybody back to their duties, they seized that last cutter and headed for the rings. They were still arguing which outer rim station to take over when you guys appeared."

"What were you three, wait, you six, doing on that cutter?"

"Can we give him something for his arm?" Perlins asked. "Some sort of shot to knock him out or something?"

"I don't need to be knocked out, skipper," Daav said. "I just want some pain meds."

"I think the pod can do that," Merced said. "Give me a minute."

Jake stepped through the hatch. "The pod can do it. Why do you need it? Who's hurt? What's going on?"

Merced pointed to the medical pod. "Dalon in the pod here is in rough shape. His air cut out back on our ship, and he passed out. He might be brain damaged. The med pod says there isn't much brain activity."

"What treatment is it recommending?" Jake asked.

"It isn't. It just says he's comatose and to transport to a hospital."

"I don't suppose you have a hospital tucked away here on this ship?" Perlins said.

"Nope. What about the others?" Jake said. "What about that guy in pod number two?"

"That's Krikweigh. He just puked and passed out a few minutes ago. Pod says increased heartbeat, low blood pressure, and high fever. The diagnosis is either stomach flu, food poisoning, or radiation exposure."

"How were you shielded when you got into high orbit?" Jake said. "There was a big increase in cosmic rays and a corona ejection."

"The computer called it a corona expulsion," Daav said, "And said we should hide inside Delta's magnetosphere or go to a shielded part of the ship."

"There's no special shielded parts of the ship on a cutter as small as yours," Jake said.

Daav sat on the deck. "No, there isn't. I don't feel so good."

"We put the ship on auto," Perlins said. "And we hid out in the air lock. We pumped some water in for better shielding."

Daav put his hands on his knees. He retched for a moment, then a stream of vomit blew out and impacted the deck. "Not enough shielding, obviously."

"Water? That was clever," Jake said. "What about the rest of the crew?"

"We didn't tell them," Jammy said. "There wasn't enough room for all of us in the air lock, so we just let them sleep."

"You left them there?" Shutt said.

"We couldn't hide the ship anywhere. We were too far out, nowhere to hide. And there wasn't enough room in the air lock."

"But just the five of you? How many in the crew?"

"Thirty-two, total," Jammy said.

"You Imperial vaginas," Shutt said. "The radiation exposure would be fatal."

"What could we have done?" Perlins said. "We couldn't save them all. And besides, these were the rebel Militia, the mutineers, as you call them. They'd been holding us on gunpoint. They killed all of Krikweigh's family. Ask him when he wakes up. There was just us. We did what we had to do."

"But kill them?" Perlins asked.

"You would have shot them all or blown the ship up if you could, Ms. I-never-left-the-Militia. We didn't have your options."

"Were all five of you in that air lock?" Jake asked.

"Yes."

"Two of you, of five, are down with what looks like hard radiation poisoning," Jake said. "How do you two feel?"

Jammy looked at Perlins, then Jake. "Not so good, actually. I've been nauseous for a while. I thought it was just the stress. I'm not used to fighting." Jammy smiled at the Francais girls. "More of a lover than a fighter, really. We haven't been introduced. I'm Jammy."

"More of a lover? That's what your mom said," Daav said from where he was lying on the floor. He retched again.

"Shut up, you two," Perlins said.

"Look, if you got hit by hard radiation, we need to give you some shots," Jake said. "Your white blood cells are getting murdered. We need to boost them up. Otherwise, you're going to die." Jake turned toward the pod and paged through the screens. "I think the medical pod can make up some doses."

"The medical pod can't make medicines," Yvette said. "At least the one on our trading ships couldn't."

"That was the basic model," Jake said. "This one is more advanced. At least according to the manual. I just need to find out how."

"You know," Daav said from the floor. "I'm withdrawing my objection. I'll take that anti-pain shot now. Or the knockout shot. Or both. This feeling isn't pleasant at all."

"I don't know how to do that. Give me a minute," Jake said. "I'll check on the med pod."

"I know how to do that," Merced said. "How to make the pain shot. I've worked with the med pods at the university. The Militia trained us there. One of the things was how to compound standard medicines."

"I'll take all the help I can get," Jake said. "Pain shot for your friend here, and anti-radiation for the rest of us."

"The rest of us?" Shutt said.

"Yes," Jake said. "An air lock and water should have stopped the radiation from affecting these five. If it didn't, it must have been stronger than we expected or recorded or something. In any event, it's just a white-cell booster. Just a precaution, we can all take it without any ill effects. Let me check something." Jake walked over to the other pod and tapped screens. Shutt, Yvette, and Odette huddled to discuss this.

Perlins pulled Merced close and spoke into his ear. "Swap the shots. Give them all the knockout shots. Can you do that?"

Merced looked at Jake, then back at Perlins. He shook his head. "Can't."

"Or won't. I've still got the screwdriver, and if the story comes out, you'll be in trouble."

Merced nodded.

"I can see how to mix up each dose," Jake said. "But not how to combine them."

"Let me," Merced said. He stepped over, leaned past

Jake, and tapped the screen. "It's just like the one I learned on. I'm going to give us a stronger dose of the anti-radiation than your crew. You all seem fine."

"For now," Jake said. "Who knows what will happen?"

"Are you sure this is a good idea? I don't think this is necessary." Shutt said.

"Stop your worrying. What's that?" Jake pointed at the screen.

"Anti-nausea for the four of us," Merced said. "It will keep us from puking more. I'm mixing it with the anti-radiation mix. And the other is pain meds for Daav. Make him sleepy."

"Good enough."

Merced tapped a few more screens, then tapped again. The screen bonged. "It says it needs a control code," Merced said.

"Sorry." Jake stepped to the other console. "I've encrypted everything, and turned on all the security protocols." He tapped the screen, acknowledging choices. "That's there. Now we need a delivery system." He opened a drawer under the medical pod and rummaged through it.

"Delivery system?" Perlins asked.

"A glass. It's a liquid," Merced said.

Jake stood, holding a box. "Got it. Package of twelve medical cups. And it's not glass. It's steel. Easier to sterilize."

He opened a windowed panel in the side and snapped the metal cup into a holder below twenty-four small spouts and one large one. He closed the door and tapped his screen. The machine whooshed, and the door snapped open. Jake pulled the cup out and sat it on a ledge next to the med pod. "Red for me and the jump space crew, and blue for our visitors. Daav gets a pleasing yellow." He cycled the other seven steel cups.

"Why the color change?" Shutt asked.

"Red is just a booster dose of anti-radiation meds. Blue

is a much stronger dose, and the anti-nausea drug Merced put in." Jake handed out the cups.

"No time like the present," Merced kneeled and helped Daav tilt his cup up and drink it. Daav slurped it down. Merced stood and turned so only Perlins could see his face. He winked at her and drank.

"Bottoms up," Perlins toasted and drank. Jammy followed suit.

"Free Trades," Jake said, then tossed his own down.

"I still don't think this is necessary," Shutt said.

"Why?" Jake said. "You want radiation sickness or not?"

She drank. Yvette and Odette followed.

Jake collected the cups. "Just have to sterilize these beauties. Great thing about metal, you can expose it to vacuum with no ill effects, but it kills any microbes or bacteria, and all of the liquid will boil off."

"You just carry them out?" Perlins asked.

"No," Jake said. "There's a medical locker in one of the air locks. It takes trays of stuff, we just pop it in there, and then pull the locker outside. Between the vacuum, the radiation, and the cold, it kills everything."

"Naughty," Yvette said.

"What?" Odette said.

"I mean, nighty. No, nifty."

"Nifty? Sacre bleu," Odette said. "I feel funny. I need to sit down." She leaned against the wall and slid down.

"So do I," Yvette said.

"Emperor's testicles," Shutt said. She leaned against a wall. "You drugged us."

"Sorry," Merced said. "I gave you a sedative instead of the anti-radiation drug. I'll boost you up when I have a moment."

"We don't mean anything bad by it," Perlins said. "We just don't entirely trust you not to kill us, that's all."

"Militia mutineers," Shutt said. "Should have spaced you from the start." She slid to the ground.

"That's what we were afraid of," Perlins said. She looked at Jake. "Time to go sleepy time."

Jake sat and lolled but didn't pass out. "What are you going to do with us?"

"Should space you, like your friend suggested," Perlins said. "Jammy, help me with girl number one here." She slid over and grabbed Yvette's shoulder. "Gravity is low, but she's still got mass. I need help moving her." She maneuvered Yvette down the corridor.

"Boss lady, I don't think," Jammy said. "I mean, they really didn't do anything to us, and we did kind of come into their ship."

"What do you mean?"

"We can't, I mean, we shouldn't. They're not the officers' council. We don't need to do this."

"We need to do this. Get them out of the way."

Jammy took a deep breath. "Boss lady. I won't. I won't help. We shouldn't do this. I won't do it. We're not going to kill them. There's been too much killing, anyway." He straightened his shoulders. "I'm not going to help you throw them out the air lock."

"Throw them out the air lock?" Perlins grinned. "So, now you're getting noble on me? You won't help me space them?"

"I won't. It's not right, boss. I won't do it. You've been good at getting us out of this mess up to now, but enough is enough."

"You weren't so squeamish before. With the storm."

"The storm wasn't my fault. And I didn't understand. I'm not going to do anything. Merced, help me out here." Jammy turned to Merced.

"I won't help you kill them," Merced said. "They don't deserve it. I could have killed them with the drugs, but I won't."

"You two must think I'm a pretty cold-hearted Imperial bitch, don't you?" Perlins said.

"I don't want to cross you," Jammy said. "But I won't

help you do this."

"You're sure you won't help me to throw them out the air lock."

"No. No more killing. We have to figure something out."

"Merced, how long will they be out?"

"Long time," Merced said. "Two shifts at least, probably three."

"Good. So, we have plenty of time to think of another solution. By the way, Jammy, which way is the air lock?"

Jammy turned and pointed the other way down the corridor. "It's that way."

"Not this way?" Perlins pointed to the direction she was dragging Yvette.

"No, it's the other direction." Jammy looked down the corridor. "You weren't going to space them."

"Nope. Just drag them to their quarters and let them sleep it off. Great speech, though."

CHAPTER 26

It took all of twenty minutes to maneuver the three women back to a stateroom and strap them in.

"Do they need to be strapped in? Do we bounce in jump space?" Jammy asked.

"No idea," Perlins said, stepping out of Yvette's room. "But better safe than sorry. They have been decent to us. They could have spaced us from the start."

"You could have stopped my speech back there," Jammy said as they slid down the ladder to the lower decks. He was going feet-first, and Perlins was headfirst, so they were facing each other.

"Naw, you were so serious while you were doing it. It was kind of cute. Besides, I had to know we were on the same page."

"No more killing?"

"Didn't want any from the start but kind of got overtaken by circumstances. Look, this is a new place. They don't know our history. We'll just figure out where this ship is going, and see what happens when we get there. We can go ashore. We can put these four ashore if it's safe for them to stay there. There are all sorts of options. I just want it to be our decision, is all." She reached the med pod deck, swung around, and pushed off toward them. The spin gravity was so low she was able to grab the med pod and examine the readouts before she drifted down.

"Drugging them helped?"

"Those Francais girls were Free Traders. They're not fond of Militia, mutinous or otherwise. And that Major Shutt isn't fond of us. This takes them out of the loop.

Merced, what do these red lights mean?"

Merced spun through the hatch opening down the hall. He pushed over and grabbed the med pod next to Perlins. "No change, Lieutenant. Krikweigh has had his anti-radiation meds, and he's still out. Dalon is, well, he's still nearly dead."

"Will he get better?"

"Have to ask a real doctor, in a real hospital," Merced said. "All I do in these cases is stabilize and transport."

"Maybe there's a hospital where we're going," Perlins said.

"This may not be a hospital, but there's drugs here. This arm hurts, and I'm still awake."

Perlins looked at Merced, who nodded and stepped to the medical console.

Perlins floated over to Daav. "Stand by, Daav. What about his arm?" She called back to Merced.

Merced pulled a steel cup out of the panel and slid back. "Drink this." He stooped by Daav. "It will deaden the pain. I can fix your shoulder, but I'll need somewhere to wrench it back into place."

"So, if I drink this, I won't feel it when you pull it back?" Daav said.

"Sure, yeah, that's it. Won't feel it," Merced said. He looked at Perlins, caught her eye, and shook his head.

Perlins grimaced. "Jammy, you and Merced take Daav up to a stateroom, and you help fix his shoulder when you get up there."

"Skipper, this Jake guy's still awake, I think. He's making noises." Perlins looked at Merced, who shrugged. "Different responses to the drug. I'll give him another dose when we get Daav dealt with.

"I'll take care of it. You two go." Perlins helped them maneuver a now relaxed Daav up the ladder toward the crew deck, then returned to contemplate the muttering Jake.

"I think you're fooling," Perlins said.

Jake opened his eyes. "A little."

She put her hands on her hips. "Are you really drugged?"

"A little," Jake said.

Perlins yawned. "Did you see Daav swap the drugs?"

"I kind of figure he'd do that, so I made sure that my dose was different from everybody else's."

A scream and a string of curses rang out from the hatchway.

"Good. They fixed his arm," Jake said.

"I thought he wouldn't feel any pain with the drugs?" Perlins asked.

"Dislocated shoulders hurt when they go back in," Jake said. "But it's done now. Just have to wait for the drugs to take effect. Why'd you do it?"

"I had to drug them all. I couldn't trust them not to do something."

"All of them?"

Perlins yawned again, harder. "They're pretty dangerous to us. An angry Militia officer and some bitter Free Traders. And whatever you are. But I don't have any bad feelings about you. Get us where you're going. If it's safe, one group will leave the ship, and the other will stay."

"Do I get to choose?" Jake asked.

"Maybe. Will you behave?"

"Absolutely. Will you?"

"Can you stop me if I don't want to?" She yawned again. Then again. "I feel sleepy. Why do I feel sleepy? Imperial anus. You drugged us."

"Technically, you drugged yourself," Jake said. "I figured that your guy, Merced, would doctor everybody's dose, so I just made sure you got a slower-acting sedative. And everybody really did need to get the anti-radiation shot, so I wanted to make sure everybody would drink."

"You're going to kill me, aren't you?"

"No, you're just going to sleep this off while I sort things out. And your folks as well. But they're already in a stateroom, so they should just nap there."

"I was worried about the wrong people. The quiet ones are way more dangerous."

"With me, that's often the case," Jake said. He pushed himself up and caught Perlins as she slumped down. "Sleep tight, mutinous Militia rebel."

***

Perlins had no idea where she was when she woke up. She established that it was a stateroom, that everything except her clothes were missing, and that, according to the clock on the comm in her room, she'd slept for three shifts. The door to her stateroom wasn't locked, and after using the fresher, she walked around the ship. Jammy was asleep in the next stateroom over, and she found Merced, Daav, and Krikweigh sitting at a table in the lounge.

"Enjoy your nap, skipper?" Daav asked.

"Didn't you have a dislocated shoulder?" Perlins asked.

Daav rotated his shoulder up in a circle. He gasped a little as he did, and sweat broke out on his brow, but he seemed to have full range of motion.

"Good as new, skipper," Daav said.

"If new is him nearly screaming every time he moves," Merced said. "If he doesn't take his pain meds, he'll never be able to do the physio he needs to do."

"You don't want any pain meds?" Perlins asked.

"Didn't work out so well last time," Daav said. "Think I'll just tough it out."

"Toughing it out is the same as saying that he wants a permanent reduction in range of motion," Merced said.

"I can handle it."

"Aren't you a pilot? Don't you need to move your arms to pilot a ship?"

"Take the pain meds," Perlins said.

"Skipper, I—"

"Shut up, Daav. Krikweigh, you don't look so good."

He didn't. He was pale and wan.

"I'm not. That radiation has knocked me out. I feel really sick, and I'm very weak. Our medic, here"—he pointed at Merced—"he says I'll get over it. Eventually."

Perlins faced Merced. "Eventually. How long is that?"

"Eventually is as long as it takes," Merced said.

Perlins saw something in his eyes, so she didn't press it further. "Where's Jammy?" she asked.

"Jammy is asleep in the stateroom next to mine," Merced said.

"Always said he was a lazy Imperial turd," Daav said. "But you wouldn't believe me, skipper."

"I'll kick him up, then, put him to work," Perlins said. Daav laughed. "What is it, Daav?"

"Jammy and I used to argue about who should be in charge, who had seniority, who had more command presence. We never thought about you. Now you tell us to come, and we come. You tell us to go, and we go. Somehow, you're in charge."

"It's the excellent training I had at command college."

"You went to command college?"

"Of course not," Perlins said. "Only those Empire-rising dorks did. I wasn't ... mutinous enough for them. Are those Francais women going to shoot us for drugging them?"

"Funny thing," Daav said. "They don't know it was us."

"That's not possible. I don't like them that much, but they're not stupid. They'll figure it out."

"That Jake Stewart guy told them he did it. He said he knocked everybody out to 'stabilize the situation.' They believe him."

"What? Why would he say that?"

"Don't know, but those other three women are all armed now. We're not. That Jake guy searched us while we were sleeping and took all our stuff. Comms, hidden weapons, course chips, everything. He gave them back their stuff. They've all got guns. At least one in a holster that we can see. Probably others."

Perlins clapped her hand on her thigh. "My knife is missing. The holster, too."

"Which means he had your pants off," Daav said. "The little pervert."

"Can't blame him for searching us, I guess," Perlins said. "But why is he lying about it?"

"He didn't say, but he wants to talk to you when you're up. He's down in the Jump module. Said to go down and see him after you're up and eaten."

"Where are we now?"

"He says jump space, says we'll be here for three to four more days, then onto another system. He also says he'll make you an offer you can't refuse if you go see him."

"Then, I guess I'll go see him and not refuse it," Perlins said. The microwave bonged. "But I'll take a tray first."

***

"Lieutenant Perlins," Jake said as Perlins climbed into the Jump computer room. "Welcome to my kingdom. The first Jump ship in either of these systems in eighty years."

"I thought you were chasing another Jump ship out here?"

"Okay, the second Jump ship in eighty years. I'm going back to engineering to check some of the monitors on the drive. Come with me." Jake slid over to the stern hatch and swung it open.

Clarisse followed him over. "What's wrong with having our talk here?"

"I can echo most things on my screens out here, but there are some actions I need to be on the engineering console for." Jake pulled himself over the hatch rim and pulled himself down the center corridor.

"I've never seen a Jump drive before," Perlins said.

"Me neither 'til I got on board. But truthfully, it's the Jump computer that's way more impressive. The computing power needed to calculate an obstacle free course between systems is pretty awesome—all those forces to keep track of, planets, suns, systems, all their gravity, and the changes it makes on our course as we travel between systems."

"I thought there was no gravity in jump space."

"Plenty of gravity, but we're just moving so fast relative to regular space it has different effects."

"How so?"

"It's kind of like. Well"—Jake stopped and held onto a ladder rung, then turned to face Perlins—"gravity is like this big pool of water that we live in. When we travel through it at regular, sublight speeds, it holds us back—pushes or pulls at us. But when we go supralight, not only does it hold us back, but we have to push it out of the way to get by it. So, it affects us differently. It's hard to explain, but the software on the computer accounts for it. It's an amazing system."

Perlins gripped her own rung. "You didn't kill us while we slept."

"Could have. Didn't."

"And your other crew believe that it was you who drugged them."

"I told them that, yes."

"Nobody is that stupid."

"They're not stupid. They're all very smart. Argumentative perhaps, but smart. And they believe me. Or they pretend to." Jake spun forward and continued pulling himself along the ladder.

"You're good in low gravity," Perlins said. "Better than me, even, and I was a pilot for years."

"Grew up on a rim station," Jake said. "Zero-G drills every month, playing netball in the inner rings in zero-G, and worked outside after school until I left."

"You went to the university?"

"No. Merchant's academy."

"What was your specialization? Engineering? Deck?"

"Accounting. I'm an auditor," Jake said. He pulled up

at a hatch blocking the corridor and typed in a code.

"Accountants don't run ships," Perlins said.

"This one does. It's my ship. I own it. I'm leasing it to my boss, Mr. Dashi. Or I should say Emperor Dashi."

"He's no Emperor."

"Planetary computer confirmed it. DNA sample and everything. He's seventeenth in line or something, but he's the Emperor we have right now. He's putting Delta back together."

"Before we left, we heard there was some crisis on the surface."

Jake was having problems with his code. He started over. "The GG-Militia battles damaged a lot of infrastructure. The monorail is mostly down, and more importantly, the mass driver won't lift food to orbit. We can't provide electric power for it until we get some parts."

"Sounds bad. I'm glad I wasn't there."

Jake finally got the code to work, and the door swung open. "This is the air lock in front of engineering. Come on in." He swung over the threshold and went to the far door, waiting 'til Perlins swung the other door shut before punching in a new code.

"You going to share those codes with us?" Perlins asked.

"Nope. I'll give you some later, so you can use them to work the ship when we hit normal space."

"What makes you think we'll help you?"

Jake swung the engineering door open. "I read your message chips. The encrypted ones, too. I have code-breaking software. And the transcripts of some channels you were talking on. You're not refugees who were forced into helping the rebels. You're all criminals who supported them out of self-interest. Oh, I don't think you were big supporters of the Empire-rising thing, and you certainly didn't start the war, but when it came, you followed along, and when you lost, you escaped with the others."

Perlins stared at Jake. "I see. But that still doesn't make

me want to help you."

"You're rebels, but you're not murderers. You did leave those others to die, but frankly, they were dead as soon as that orbit crested the magnetosphere. You just acted to save yourselves. And your little speech with Jammy on not killing people was very effective. I think your killing days are over, if they ever even started." Jake stepped into engineering and went over to a console. He typed another code in and looked at the screens.

"You seem pretty cold about this." Jake didn't respond. "What's in it for us?" she asked. She stepped into the room. "I've never seen a setup like this before."

"Nobody in this system has. Here's your situation. Major Shutt and the regular Militia will hang you if they find out you were rebels, particularly since you were officers. They're systematically hunting down all the rebel officers who were on that officers' council. Sooner or later, your real story will come out, and they'll get you. If the Free Traders don't get you first. They suffered at the hands of the Militia quite a bit before and during the coup. They're all related, so every one of them has a cousin or an uncle who was killed in the fighting, and they want revenge. Even if those two groups don't get you, there still might be some hidden rebel groups left, and they'll want to get you for frying your old crewmates with cosmic radiation."

Perlins grimaced. "That wasn't our plan. We were told to chase you."

"You can try to convince them of that if you want, or ..."

"Or what?"

"Here's my offer. No more funny business for the rest of the trip. Stand watches. Help with the ship. Help dock and land if necessary. I have some items I have to acquire. To help with the problems on Landing and bring them back. When I take this ship back to Delta, I'll keep things quiet. I won't tell anybody who you were. You'll just be

Militia troops we rescued from the Empire-rising rebels." A screen bonged, and Jake paged through. "I thought so. Energy fields are a bit unbalanced. We'll be a tad out of position when we arrive."

"Is that bad?"

"Good, actually. We'll miss the ship that went in ahead of us. Our position will be farther out from the planet I'm targeting, but we'll be fine."

Perlins bit her lip. "The only thing that bothers me is that I can't figure out what's in it for you."

"The rest of the crew believes that I drugged them, not you."

"Yeah, I don't get that."

"They believe it because I'm known for overly complex plans that seem very confusing at first go, but ultimately give me what I need."

"Is that what's happening here?"

"I'm also known for not explaining things in advance," Jake said. "They just end up working out for me and for the people involved."

"We work for you?"

"You treat me like the captain. In fact, you all call me Captain Jake."

Perlins thought about it. "It's a good offer. We go with you to this system, come back, act as your crew, keep our mouths shut?"

"That's it. And one more thing."

"Yes?"

"You need to support me against any other threats to my authority."

"Who's after your job? The Francais girls or the Militia?"

"Any threats. At all. You in, or do I turn you over to Shutt?"

Perlins looked at Jake's control board. The cooling fan hummed for ten seconds, then stopped. Finally, she nodded. "I'm onboard. And the others will follow my lead."

"I thought so."

Perlins saluted. She remembered to do the hand-to-head old style Militia salute. "Your orders, Captain?"

"Square up the others, then go see Major Shutt in the control room. She has a watch schedule."

"Understood, Captain." She turned and went into the air lock but hesitated at the edge. "One question, Captain?"

"Yes?" Jake said, looking up from the console.

"Did you enjoy taking my pants off?"

CHAPTER 27

"Really like these motor things," Sergeant Russell said. "Much easier than rowing." He sat at the back of the inflatable boat next to Balthazar. Balthazar and his brothers had produced a rechargeable electric motor from the hold of their sailboat and clamped it to the back of the tender. They sped up the channel, away from their grounded boat. Sand islands with lush vegetation ringed the channel.

"It's pre-abandonment, not many of them on this moon," Balthazar said. "So, we treat it carefully. It runs the compressor as well, so it's easy to pump up the boat."

"Great idea, don't you think, sir?" Sergeant Russell asked Commander Roi. "These electric things."

Commander Roi scowled but didn't say anything. Sergeant Russell and Balthazar sat at the back next to the motor. Commander Roi sat across from a smiling trooper from the outpost. The name tag on his breast said Luzja. Chaudhari and Nadine lounged at the front.

"This is fun," Nadine said. She'd stripped down to her skin suit and sat on the dinghy's bow, letting the wind stream through her hair. "Being out on the water like this is way better than being on that stupid boat in a storm."

"The boat is more fun than you think," Balthazar said. "The storms don't come often, and besides, that's real sailing in those storms. Not just gliding along."

"It's so warm." Nadine stretched in the sun. "Not like up north at all."

"Small moon, but big climate difference," Chaudhari said. "South continent is equatorial, and with our axial tilt, it gets a lot more sun this time of the year. At least during this part of the Dragon's cycle.

"Turn here,"Lujza said, pointing to a channel marker coming up. "The channel splits here. This one goes to the base."

"Will your brothers be able to bring the ship up here?" Sergeant Russell asked Balthazar.

"No problem at all. Estephan is watching us through binoculars right now, and he's charting our course."

"Will you great navigators run us aground again?" Nadine asked.

"We're used to this," Balthazar said. "We've had lots of experience with, uh, non-standard deliveries. We usually have to run up some difficult estuaries to do our deliveries or pickups."

"What's an estuary?" Sergeant Russell asked.

"That's where a river widens as it meets the ocean," Nadine said. "It's a river, but it's still subject to tidal effects from the world ocean. Tidal bores and large depth changes."

All the men on the boat looked at her.

"What? I can't know about rivers?" Nadine asked.

"It's out of character for an orbital pilot, that's for sure," Balthazar said.

"I'm just naturally curious about all things ocean," Nadine said.

Sergeant Russell and Balthazar looked at each other, shook their heads, then turned back to Nadine. "Nah," Sergeant Russell said. "Doesn't track."

Nadine shrugged. "Fine. My friend, Jake Stewart, told me all about this. He knows all sorts of obscure facts."

"Your friend, the guy with the Jump ship?" Sergeant Russell asked.

"That's Jakey. Jump ship man."

"Friend or boyfriend?" Balthazar asked.

Nadine looked him up and down. "Could be a friend. Why are you asking?"

"I thought he was 'boyfriend,'" Sergeant Russell said.

"Friend," Nadine said. "But you never answered my question about running us aground. You going to do that again?"

"We rely on the information provided to us," Balthazar said. He looked at Commander Roi. "If that information isn't very reliable, problems occur."

Commander Roi scowled. "Colonel Savard had provided me with what I needed to do my job, and I provided it to you."

"Kind of odd that the colonel didn't mention that turn to you," Balthazar said. "Kind of like he didn't expect you to make it here."

"What are you insinuating?" Commander Roi asked.

"Just that maybe you're not supposed to be here," Balthazar said.

"Commander Roi is the new head of the officers' council," Sergeant Russell said. "So, here is where he should be. And I'm sure Colonel Savard had his own reasons for adding this extra wrinkle into things. The colonel was a very smart man, don't you agree, commander?"

"The smartest," Commander Roi said.

"So, there must have been a reason," Sergeant Russell said.

"Indeed."

"Would be nice to ask him a few questions, though," Balthazar said. "Firm up a few things."

"Well, Colonel Savard is dead, so depending on your religion, there might be a way to start a conversation," Sergeant Russell said. "You believe in life after death, Balthazar?"

Balthazar grimaced. "Don't want to find out."

"Well, if you ever change your mind about that," Sergeant Russell said, "And you want to get some answers from Colonel Savard, me, and the squad, we have no problem arranging a meeting."

Balthazar grimaced again.

"Here we go," the smiling Lujza said. "Around this corner, at the head of the bay." The boat swung past another low island, and a large bay opened up ahead of them. The island ahead was much larger and had trees on it that came down to the water's edge. "There," he pointed, "ground on the beach there."

Balthazar pointed the boat's nose at the shore, and a few quick instructions had everyone splashing out into the warm water as it ran into the shallows. He pulled a lever, and the motor on the back swiveled up and clear of the sand. The six of them had no problem pulling the now empty boat onto the shore.

"Up into the trees,"Lujza said. "The satellites only cover here once a day, but we don't want any chance of them noticing something unusual." They all complied.

"Won't they see the drag marks?" Balthazar asked.

"Tide erases them,"Lujza said.

"Well, Commander," Sergeant Russell turned and saluted the silent Commander Roi. "Mission accomplished. As ordered by Colonel Savard, I've delivered you here. The new head of the officers' council."

Commander Roi frowned. "There doesn't seem to be anything here."

"More than you think,"Lujza said. "But I'll let the bigwigs set you up." He pointed to a group of men and women coming toward them in tattered Militia uniforms. "I'll go and report in. Will you accompany me, sir?" He walked over with Commander Roi. Sergeant Russell stayed behind.

"Not going along with your friends, Sergeant?" Nadine asked once the group was out of earshot.

"Call me Scott," Sergeant Russell said. "I've done my job, got him here."

"And Scott's probably worried that whoever is in charge here right now might not be so happy to see the commander," Balthazar said. "And might, perhaps, stab him in the eye and anyone with him."

Commander Roi had reached the group of officers, and a loud discussion had commenced. Lujza stepped to one side and spoke to a non-uniformed man, who strolled toward them.

"No drawn weapons," Chaudhari said, "but some of them have revolvers in holsters. Is Roi armed?"

"Nope," Sergeant Russell said. "He lost his revolver when he was arrested, and we didn't have a spare for him."

"How convenient for you," Nadine said. "Let him push himself forward. If he takes over, well and good. If not, there's a fait-accompli, and he's not your problem anymore."

"I serve the Empire," Sergeant Russell said.

Nadine giggled. "And yourself."

Sergeant Russell shrugged. "Are you going to try to escape again?"

"Not right away. Why?" Nadine looked at Russell. "You have a job for me?"

"Maybe," Russell said. "You interested?"

"Always. What's it pay?"

"I thought you worked for this admiral guy?"

"He's not here right now." Nadine looked at the non-uniformed man approaching them. "Well, that's a surprise."

"Hello, Nadine," Vince Pletcher said. "Have you come for the dinner you promised me?"

***

They all sat at dinner.

"More wine?" Vince asked. He had led them to a table on the sand under a group of palm trees.

"Yes, please," Nadine said. "This is different from the last one."

"This one's white," Vince said. "And from Delta. The old one was red from the Empire."

"Pre-abandonment?" Sergeant Russell said. "Need a pile of cash for that."

"Nothing but the finest for a pretty girl like Ms. Nadine," Vince said.

"Good job, Vinny," Nadine said. "That's the spirit. Buy me wine and tell me I'm pretty. That'll get you somewhere."

"This one's pretty good, though," Sergeant Russell said. "You agree, Balthazar?"

"I do, I do. You sure your troops don't want some?" He gestured at the half squad, who was relaxing under another group of trees.

"They're still too sick. Right now, they're just happy to be on land and not puking all the time. I told them to sleep for a couple of hours, and once they've had some down time and a solid meal in them, we'll give 'em some booze. Then we'll assign them duties."

"How long will that take 'til they're ready for duty?" Vince asked. "I have some things need to be unloaded."

"Funny question from a ship salesman," Sergeant Russell said. "And I've got a few questions of my own, for that matter."

"Vinny isn't just a ship salesman. He also sells other things," Nadine said.

"Like what?"

"What do you need?" Vince asked.

"Enough weapons to start a revolution," Sergeant Russell asked.

"I think somebody tried that already," Vince said. "It didn't work out so well for them. I made decent money, though."

"So, who are you working for, Mr. Pletcher?" Sergeant Russell asked.

"I could ask the same of you, Sergeant Russell," Vince said. "My information was that you were initially part of the mutiny, then against it. But my information must be wrong because, now, you're for it again."

"And my information was that you sold weapons to the Growers to fight the Militia, and yet now you're here with the Militia," Sergeant Russell said. "I guess my information was wrong, too."

"Sounds like you both had bad information," Balthazar said.

"And what's your story, then?" Chaudhari said. "You boat people? You and your brothers."

"We're neutral in this," Balthazar said. "Just transport. We're a supplier to the Militia. And Mr. Pletcher. We supplied him, or them, with some items, and they've taken delivery."

"So, you're going to sail away and leave us here?" Chaudhari said.

"Maybe," Balthazar said.

"No, because you're my prisoner," Sergeant Russell said. "Try to sail away, and my squad will fill you and your electric motors full of holes."

"How can we be your prisoner if we work for Mr. Pletcher? He's obviously a distinguished guest. Of your officers' council. For which you work?" Balthazar said. "Besides, my brothers are bringing the ship and the rest of your squad into here. They'll be here in about an hour."

"I think I can vouch for them, Sergeant Russell," Vince said.

"Yeah, but who's vouching for you?"

"Your commander, Roi, if he ends up being the new Imperial leader," Vince said.

"What are they doing over there?" Chaudhari asked.

"Discussing the rules of succession for the leader of Delta," Vince said.

"Do they understand that they don't actually lead Delta?" Chaudhari asked. "That they're just a bunch of people on a beach with a few sailboats, and a wrecked suborbital boat?" He pointed at an airplane-like vehicle behind them. The front of it had impacted a tree. "What happened there, anyway?"

"Pilots didn't have much experience," Vince said. "They're the officers' council to free Delta. Whoever wins,

I'm their main supplier for food and munitions, as long as the money lasts. Balthazar and company are my delivery service. You're loyal to Colonel Savard's designated successor, right?"

"That's the plan," Sergeant Russell said.

"And if that designated successor isn't your boy, Roi?" Vince asked.

"Whoever the officers' council appoints, we'll follow their lead," Sergeant Russell said.

"What about your squad there?" Vince asked.

"We all owe Sergeant Russell," Chaudhari said. "He just seems like a loitering screw up. He saved all of us from getting killed in several stupid, useless, suicidal battles or going to jail afterword. We'll just follow him along. Thank you very much."

"I guess we're all friends here, then," Sergeant Russell said. They all ate in silence for a moment, then all turned to the end of the table.

Nadine looked up at them. "What?" She gulped wine. "I really like this wine. I'm not going anywhere." She took another glug. "At least as long as the wine holds out."

CHAPTER 28

Jake sat on the bed in his quarters. The Jump ship was bigger and in better shape than any other he'd been in. The quarters didn't differ much from a single cube in an older station. All it contained was an acceleration couch pivoted so that it could adapt to either spin or propulsion gravity and a few lockers that he could stash clothes in. The Jump engines were running, so the back of the ship and associated decks were currently down. He had just finished the mandated daily workout of pull-ups and resistance training and was sitting sweating on the bed. On small ships, you would only shower on alternate days. That day was his off-water day, so didn't rate a shower. To cover the stink, he used ship perfume—a generic anti-odor spray. He preferred to wait 'til the sweat dried before smearing himself.

Jake lay back on his pillow and stared at the ceiling, then took out his comm. He opened a file, and pictures of Nadine appeared. Nadine smiling next to the shuttle. Nadine holding a handful of silver bars. His favorite was Nadine in her shiniest skin suit, hips cocked, with a leather holster slung low, as she blows smoke from revolver barrel. Jake smiled as he remembered that night.

He also remembered that revolver. She'd shot him with it. Twice.

His door slipped open.

"Jake"—Major Shutt stepped inside—"we need to talk." She was carrying a bottle.

"Can't you knock? And it's Captain Jake to you."

"You're as much a captain as I'm a carnivorous sea hippo," Shutt said. She sat on the bed next to Jake.

"What's a sea hippo?" Jake asked.

"Those big sea animals on Delta that eat people."

"I don't think those exist. It's just a rumor."

"I've seen pictures."

"So have I," Jake said. "And those pictures were of buffalo swimming in rivers. Again, why didn't you knock?"

Shutt took a swig from her bottle and raised it in salute. "Wives and sweethearts," she said.

"What's that?"

"Traditional Militia toast," Shutt said. "You're supposed to say 'May they never meet.'"

"That's your favorite toast?"

"Nope. My favorite is 'A bloody war and or a sickly season.'"

"That's gruesome."

"It's how you get promoted," Shutt said. "People above you die. Of course, that's in other organizations. In the Delta Militia, you only get promoted if you're from a corporate family, and they buy your spot. Competence doesn't matter." Shutt took another swig, then passed the bottle to Jake.

Jake took a drink. It was sweet and sickly but not harsh. He handed it back. "How long have you been in the Militia?"

"Fifteen years. Fifteen glorious years," Shutt said. "I need to talk to you about those new Militia people."

"What about them?"

"You know that they're rebels?"

"We have no proof of that. They could just be regular Militia people caught up in the rebellion. That's what they say."

"I think they're rebels."

"That's for a court to decide, and besides, right now, they are very helpful in operating this Jump ship."

"I will agree they know their jobs. They know their jobs so well, in fact," Shutt said. "Well, enough that we could fix another problem."

"What other problem?" Jake said.

"Those Francais girls. We can't trust them. They should be locked up."

"They're part of the crew," Jake said. "They were appointed here."

"They're as bad as the rebels, even worse."

"You've hated them since you met them. What have you got against Free Traders? They're hard working, smart. On the station I grew up on, they were the only ones who ever visited. We were too small for the corporate ship."

"Which is why they were there. Wasn't enough for the corporations to steal, but they took the rest."

"They didn't steal anything," Jake said. "They sold us things."

"Happy with the prices they charged, were you?"

Jake frowned. When he'd gotten to the merchant's academy and studied cargo rates, he was amazed at how profitable the smaller stations actually were for the Free Traders.

Shutt saw his look. "Thought so. You know that you can't just become a Free Trader, right? You have to be born into it. And they limit the number of ships. So, even if you're in a Free Trader family, if you're not the shipmaster, you're stuck with being crew for your whole life, doing the same boring job forever, while lazier, dumber people are promoted ahead of you because of who they know or how much money they have." She swigged from the bottle. "Just like the Militia."

"Why'd you join the Militia?" Jake asked.

"It was my best option." Shutt said.

"So, it worked out for you?"

"I said it was my best option, not that it was a good option. I hear you worked your way into the core on a tramp ship, and Dashi has been sending you all across the rim."

"I'm fortunate to be working for him," Jake said.

"Really?" Shutt said. She took another swig from her

bottle, then put it on the floor.

"The Free Traders. I think they're going to try to seize control of the ship."

"What evidence do you have for this?" Jake asked.

"No real evidence, just a feeling," Shutt said.

"Well, we'll talk more about it when you have evidence. In the meantime, the subject is closed. Maybe go outside and knock next time."

Shutt looked at him, then beamed a smile at him. "Fine, that subject is closed. Let's talk about something else I've been meaning to bring up." She smiled and leaned forward. Her sweat-slicked arms gleamed in the light as she leaned on her bare legs. "I just finished my workout." She leaned farther forward and stretched her shoulders. It tightened over her breasts, outlining her figure. She wanted Jake to notice, and he did.

"I, uh, just finished my workout as well," Jake said. Shutt smiled at him. "I sweat."

I sweat? Jake thought. Why are you such an idiot when there's a pretty woman around?

Shutt put an arm on his shoulder, leaned in, and sniffed. "I like guys who exercise. Their sweat smells very ... masculine." She toyed with his shoulder.

Jake swallowed. "Why are you here, Clarisse? This isn't like you."

"Oh, you do know my name," Shutt said.

"It's in the records," Jake said.

"So, you looked me up. Any questions about my past you want to know?"

"Um, no, it seemed pretty complete," Jake said.

"I'm single, if that isn't in there," Shutt said. "No boyfriend."

"That's hard to believe," Jake said. "An attractive girl like you, without a boyfriend."

"I had one," Shutt said. She slumped a little. "Before the fighting. He was killed when they stormed GG Main. Those Emperor-rising people did him in."

"Oh," Jake said. "Oh. Sorry."

Shutt nodded.

"Oh," Jake said again.

"You say that a lot," Shutt said.

"You're not the first one to notice that," Jake said. "My girlfriend, Nadine, says that."

"Nadine? The admiral's bimbo?"

"His granddaughter."

"Just cause she's related to somebody important doesn't mean she isn't a bimbo."

"She's not like that," Jake said.

"Really? I've watched her interact with the admiral and his officers and some Militia guys and pilots and guys she met in bars and guys she met in corridors—"

"She's just friendly," Jake said.

"What's that phrase? When you sleep with a lot of guys just for fun? Isn't it sport f—"

"Maybe she is like that, a bit," Jake said. "But we're dating now."

"Exclusively dating?"

"Uh, yes?"

"Does she know that?" Shutt asked.

Jake started to speak, then stopped. He wondered about that himself sometimes. Nadine wasn't malicious, but he could see her getting caught up in the moment.

"Of course she does," he said.

"That pause was way too long," Shutt said. "You're wondering what she's doing right now."

"She was supposed to be here, but apparently, she disappeared with a Militia squad."

"A squad with a handsome, aggressive, take-charge Militia guy in it?"

"Um ..."

"We talked about your ums," Shutt said. She caressed his hair. "You must have been working hard, even your head is sweaty." She reached out and rubbed his biceps. "Feels strong."

"I have a girlfriend," Jake said.

"She's not here right now," Shutt said. "I am. Your girlfriend has disappeared with a bunch of handsome Militia troopers. Handsome rebel Militia troopers. I wonder what she's doing? Doesn't she have a reputation for being a mercenary?"

"Her parents are dead. She's had to look out for herself," Jake said.

"And is she looking out for you when she's with you?" Shutt said.

Jake had wondered that himself.

"Jake, how did you get appointed to captain? Dashi's not a guy that I'd like to cross. He's always smiling, but I think he could probably slice me into small pieces without getting any blood on his skin suit, then sell the pieces to a tabbo food-processing plant."

"Probably," Jake said. "And get a good price, too."

"And the admiral respects you. He doesn't like you, but he wasn't upset that you were recommended. He wasn't willing to cross Dashi on that."

"There's more to me than meets the eye, I guess," Jake said.

"And those Free Trader girls, they listen to you. They know ten times as much about ships and trading and things than it seems you do, but they pay attention when you talk."

"Maybe it's my sterling intellect," Jake said.

"It's not your looks. Oh, you're attractive in a sweaty-male sort of way, but you're not Mr. Right."

"I'm not? That's kind of offensive," Jake said.

"You're not Mr. Right, but you'll do fine as Mr. Right Now," Shutt said. "And it's a long trip."

"I have a girlfriend."

"Wonder what she's doing right now? And who's she doing it with?"

Jake pictured Nadine. Nadine smiling. Nadine kissing him. Nadine seeing him with Shutt. Nadine breaking his arm off and beating him to death with the stump. He shivered and slid into the corner of his bed.

"Why are you here, Clarisse?"

Clarisse smiled at him, hiding in the corner. "Came on too strong, did I? Well, don't worry, Jake. It's a long trip. We can talk more about this later." She smiled. "Just remember, I'm here."

"What do you want? Truthfully?"

Clarisse looked at him. "Truth? Okay. Those Militia people? They're going out an air lock or in front of a firing squad first chance I get. My boyfriend is dead, along with lots of others, because of the likes of them. So, first chance, they're going to be gone. But you know, I'm willing to get some work out of them. They can be helpful getting to this other system and getting back to Delta. Once they're there, the admiral can take care of them."

"They're very helpful with taking care of the ship. And they claim they escaped from the Empire-rising people."

"They can claim what they want. But I can wait. The admiral will deal with them when we're back.

"Good," Jake said.

"And those Free Trader girls," Shutt said. "Same deal. They're useful for now, but we—you and me—we don't really need them."

"We need them to get to 61 Cygni," Jake said.

"And back. But after the jump," Shutt smiled. "Don't worry, Jake, I'm on your side. But remember this, if it's just you and me when we get back to Delta, I doubt there will be very many questions. I've worked very hard to get where I'm at. So have you. This might be a chance. It might be our chance. Remember that."

"I'll keep that in mind," Jake said. "But for now, can you not kill, space, hang or shoot anybody until we get those reactor parts? That's more important."

"Oh, I agree with that," Shutt said. "No hanging or shooting 'til we're back to Delta."

"Thank you."

Shutt saluted him.

"This isn't like you, Clarisse," Jake said. "This seduction thing. Why now?"

"I thought you were a total dweeb. But you handled that jump and those Militia people. And you were very cool when that other Militia ship was chasing us, and when they boarded us. That sedative was genius. How did you think of that?"

"I'm pretty creative," Jake said.

Shutt looked at him. "There's not much in your history in the records. In fact, all it says is, 'Employed by TGI as a special auditor, accounting division.' That's it. What have you actually done?"

"Well," Jake said. "I've stolen several ships, been shot at least four times, committed multiple insurance frauds, taken over a pirate base, stolen a shuttle, released dozens of indentured slaves, falsified computer records, shot my Militia commander, caused several GG ships to explode, recovered a Jump ship from the rings, evaded multiple Militia cutters, sold weapons, bought weapons, evaded trading restrictions, falsified accounting and banking documents, and managed to acquire a small fortune in ships, precious metals, and goods."

Shutt stared at him, then laughed. "Good story. I should have known you'd never tell me the truth."

Jake shrugged. "Well, you know." It was all true.

Shutt got up. "Remember, we can continue this ... conversation whenever you want. In the meantime, I'm watching those others. As soon as you want to really take control of this mission, I'm there for you."

"Thanks," Jake said.

***

Jake sat and reflected for a while after Shutt had left. He was playing a dangerous game. Dashi's last message had stressed the need for the replacement parts was critical and had alluded to the tensions between the different factions of the Delta government. He needed to complete his mission without upsetting either the Militia or the Free Traders.

A knock rapped his door.

"Come in, Clarisse," Jake said. "But I'm not ready to continue our discussion yet."

Yvette walked in and shut the door. "You are expecting Ms. Army? Is that so. Am I a surprise?"

"Um, Um ..."

"You say that a lot," Yvette said.

"I have to fix that habit," Jake said. "I stutter a bit when I'm surprised."

"You are surprised to see me?" Yvette said. She frowned. "But not surprised to continue a conversation with Ms. Army girl. Was she here earlier?"

"Yes," Jake said. He shook his head. "Emperor's testicles. Why did I tell you that? Why can't I lie to women?"

"It's one of your more endearing qualities," Yvette said. "You always tell the truth."

"It always gets me in trouble, especially with women," Jake said. "I need to learn how to lie better."

"Well, let's begin your lesson," Yvette said. "You're only wearing workout clothes, so ..." She unzipped her coveralls and stepped out of them, revealing a bra and panties. "Now we match. Would you like to make love to me?"

Jake looked her up and down. "No?"

Yvette patted his cheek. "See? Your first lie. That wasn't so difficult."

"I don't—I don't want ... this is complicated."

"Not for us. I think it would be more fun than complicated."

"I'm sure it would be fun, but I don't want to upset you or upset Nadine."

"I would very much like to upset that one," Yvette said. "I don't like or trust her. But right now, let's talk about you. Don't you find me attractive?"

"Yes. No. Yes. Very much. Why are you here?"

"Perhaps you like Odette better? I can send her?"

"What is this? Some sort of Free Trader love pact?"

"Exactly," Yvette said. "We both decided we liked you, so we cut cards. I won, so I get to try first."

"That's kind of weird, cutting cards over who gets to sleep with me."

"Not cutting cards over who gets to sleep with you. It's who gets to sleep with you first. After I'm done, Odette will be along as well."

"Uh, uh ..."

"You really do say that a lot."

"Will everybody please stop telling me that? Why are you here?"

"I thought I told you? To sleep with you. That means that we—"

"I know what that means. But why me? Am I some bastion of masculine attractiveness?"

"Truthfully no. You are a bit scrawny for my taste."

"Thanks."

"And not very tall. I like tall men."

"Thanks again."

"You are not pretty. I do like a pretty man. You are at best average, but—"

"If I'm a short, scrawny, average guy, why are you half dressed in my bedroom?" Jake said.

"You have the most attractive of attributes. Power. You are captain. Dashi has taken control of this system, and he trusts you. The admiral has the power of the Militia behind him, but he fears you. Jose watches you carefully. You are his rival. Your friend, Nadine, she can beat you, chase you—"

"Shoot me."

"Shoot you, steal from you. She is a formidable opponent. A worthy opponent but not a match for Odette and I. Yet, she does not challenge you. She believes you are a match for her. She has gone head-to-head with you, in many matters, and by her own judgment, she has lost. You win. How do you win? I do not know. But you always do. So, I would like to learn this."

"By sleeping with me?" Jake asked.

"You will support your lovers. You support that Nadine girl, and she is an uncouth, violent, unthinking, irresponsible idiot."

Jake worked through the adjectives. "She's not uncouth."

"That's the best you have? "Not uncouth?"

"What do you want?"

"Those other Militia dead," Yvette said. "I agree with that Shutt person on this. Once a rebel, always a rebel, and ..."

"Yes?"

"That army girl, Shutt,"

"She's Militia," Jake said.

"Army. Militia. Same thing. They are not our friends."

"They're friendly enough to me," Jake said.

"They are not my and Odette's friends."

"You're not in charge here."

"We could be, together with you. With our support, you could remove all of them. That Shutt. And those rebels."

"I'm already in charge. And you can't know they are rebels," Jake said.

"Do you really believe that?"

Jake was silent.

"Things could go well for you, Jake Stewart. Work with us, with the Free Traders. We have some friends who would like very much to inspect this ship. Return to the Delta system, finish your mission. But before that, just take it to see them."

"Dashi needs those supplies," Jake said. "Those parts."

"That is fine. We will release those supplies, but you must allow us to have use of the ship. You will remain the owner, but we have some activities we want to perform."

"What you mean is, don't let the Militia take control of the ship."

"D'accord. Everyone says you are smart."

Jake sighed. "I'll think about this. But I must get Dashi his parts."

"Of course you will," Yvette said. "Everyone also says you manage to make everyone happy." She giggled. "Of course, in this case, I am promising to make you happy."

Jake stared at the wall. Nadine was far away. Why is it so hard to do the right thing for the right reason?

The door swung open. "Oh," Odette said, "I thought you two would be finished by now."

"We haven't started yet, chéri," Yvette said.

Odette looked at them. "Can I help?"

"I've got to go," Jake said. "Work to do." He ran out of his cube.

CHAPTER 29

The improvised shuttle didn't look like it was going to lift off. Water fountained behind it as it raced down the river's estuary, but it was smacking the wave tops, not rising over them.

"Not enough speed, and it's going the wrong way, upstream," Marianne said.

"Patience. It's supposed to go into the current," Jose said. "That's the plan." The two of them were standing on the dock by the water. A fishing boat had towed the shuttle out to the center of the estuary.

"It's going to just skip along until it hits that beach," Marianne said.

"Just watch."

A rocket blasted and flashed behind the shuttle. The shuttle lifted about a meter off the water on tiny fins. It came up out of the water, stabilized, and accelerated.

"What are those fins?" Marianne asked.

"Hydrofoil cradle. The regular shuttles use a cradle propelled by electromagnets from the mass driver. We use hydrogen rockets for the initial push."

The shuttle and cradle lifted higher, then a series of clamps snapped open, and the shuttle—actually a repurposed lifting body—climbed under its own power. The cradle flared along for about another two seconds, then the rockets shut off. As the cradle slowed, it dipped back into the water and drifted to a halt.

Marianne shaded her eyes against the suns. "It's climbing. But not fast enough. It will hit those hills."

"It will just skim past them," Jose said.

The shuttle climbed slowly. It skimmed over the hills

that walled the valley and the river and continued off into the distance.

"Are you sure it will make orbit?"

"We'll know if it doesn't. If it doesn't have enough velocity, it will impact that mountain over there." Jose pointed to the horizon.

"That fin thing. Was that your idea?"

"Jake Stewart's. He read about it in some old book."

"Why not launch in the other direction? Away from ship-crushing mountains?"

"Has to do with the getting out of the water. These fins—they're called hydrofoils, need a certain velocity of water over them to lift up. Once it's lifted, it speeds up quickly, but getting up and on them is the hard part. That's why it always runs into the current."

"Clever."

"Jake is clever," Jose said.

"What's the latest on him?"

"Nothing new. His ship jumped. Or appeared to. He acknowledged Dashi's last message to him just before he did with his personal code, so we know he was alive and kicking before they jumped. But it's days to the nearest system. He'll need some time there, and several days to come back. Maybe a month round trip? Maybe less. Nobody's used a Jump ship here since the abandonment."

Marianne looked at the workers unloading fish from the ship at the docks and carting it up the hill to the processing plant.

"Will we survive here?"

"Plenty to eat here," Jose said.

"I mean civilization, on Delta. Or is this the beginning of the end?"

"An excellent question," Dashi said from behind.

Turning, Jose and Marianne saw him limping onto the dock.

"Sir, how is your leg?" Jose asked.

"Getting better. Slowly." He leaned heavily on his cane

and took a deep breath. "Very slowly. The shuttle launched appropriately?"

"No problem, sir."

"Good. And the cargo? Sufficient quantities?"

"No, sir," Jose said. "Not nearly enough."

"I see," Dashi said. "Ms. Marianne, I heard your last question. The answer is yes. We will survive. We might get cold. But we will survive. At least here at Land's End."

"Land's End?" Jose asked.

"We needed a name rather than point 37. I wonder if those fisherman will take me out." Dashi walked to the end of the dock.

"He doesn't look good," Marianne said.

"Doesn't look well," Jose said.

"Same thing," Marianne said.

"Not really, it's not proper grammar—never mind. Where did you learn your standard?"

"Where did you learn yours?"

Jose laughed. "I was too young to remember. Parents? Friends?"

"I did, also. All the Free Traders learn Francais and standard as children."

Jose watched Dashi speak to the fishermen. "Why are you helping us? With the legion and the political support?"

"We're helping us, not you. Dashi is our best bet for survival. We know how serious things are. Dashi is not our friend, but he is not our enemy. And we have many enemies. Other corps. The Militia. GG hated the Free Traders."

"And look where that got them," Jose said.

Dashi limped back. "They'll take me out now. I just have to go back to my room and change. They say the weather will freshen once we're clear of the headland and in the world ocean. I'll need to dress warmly. I'll see you after I get back, Jose."

A horn blasted from the river. A fishing boat had come too close to the boat assigned as tender to the hydrofoil cradle. Yells echoed from the valley walls.

"Noisy bunch," Jose said.

"It does seem that they can't catch fish without a lot of yelling and cursing," Dashi said.

"Yes, sir," Jose said. "I'll need your decision on that other matter as quickly as possible, if we're to take my second option."

"I'll let you know upon my return, Jose. I just need some time to relax and think things through. In fact, I'm calling a council meeting for when I'm back. I will inform everyone then."

Dashi limped back toward their quarters in the containerized housing.

"If he's going to be the Emperor," Marianne said, "and there are decisions to be made, I don't think this is the right time for him to be going on a fishing trip."

"I think the decision has already been made, and he's just coming to terms with it."

"What decision is that?"

"Who starves first."

***

"Jake Stewart contacted us just before the jump. They were chasing him, and he ... dealt with them," Dashi said. The Militia was meeting in the conference room at Land's End. They had a beautiful view of the headland. The tide was running out, so the cliffs were exposed, and spray shrouded the large waterfall upstream. They weren't quite high enough or far enough past the sheltering mountains to feel the wind, but the large swells impacting the cliffs gave notice of the offshore wind's strength.

"Dealt with them? What does that mean?" Admiral Edmunds asked. He was looking at the shore's side windows, toward the monorail station, the container houses, and the small food factories on the riverside.

"Mr. Stewart didn't give details, but he said everybody on the other ship was dead and that the ship itself was intact and could be retrieved when it came back on its orbit. That will be some time. Jose?"

"Years, sir. It's a very, very high orbit."

"Well, make a note."

"How did that little punk kill thirty plus Militia troops without harming the ship they were in?" Admiral Edmunds said.

"Mr. Stewart is very resourceful," Dashi said. "But he didn't give details. You'll have to ask him."

The admiral frowned. "I don't know what my granddaughter sees in him. I thought he was a little ... soft."

"You call killing thirty people soft?" Marianne asked.

"We're not sure they're dead," Admiral Edmunds said. "We only have his word."

"If Jake says they're dead, they're dead," Jose said. "He's precise about those types of things."

"Any updates on arrivals of spare parts?" Edmunds asked.

"We are scheduling the refurb and testing of the repairs to the switching station in a few days," Jose said.

"Too bad you couldn't have done it sooner," Edmunds said.

"You could also say too bad we had to retreat out here because the security situation in the city was too difficult," Marianne said. "Doesn't make the Militia look very good that they had to run away, does it?"

"Funny how, since we've left, things have quieted down," Edmunds said. "Makes you wonder who was behind those riots."

"Regardless of who was behind them, you were responsible for maintaining order," Dashi said.

"Did you start any riots, Dashi?" Edmunds asked.

"I did not. How could I? I was removed from Landing, under guard, by Militia troops. Surely, I could not be responsible for anything while almost under house arrest."

"Didn't think that through before you did it, did you,

Admiral?" Marianne grinned at him.

Edmunds returned to gazing out the window.

"I have authorized some adjustments in Jose's shipping schedule," Dashi said. "Affecting where the food will be delivered orbitally. I present them to you as information only."

"Some council," Edmunds said without turning. "You do what you like."

"In consultation with my advisers, yes," Dashi agreed. "That is the purpose of an advisory council. I believe that you supported my appointment as head last time. Have you changed your mind?"

"I think you're enjoying this," Edmunds said. "This crisis."

"Well, you know what they say," Jose said. "Never let a good crisis go to waste."

CHAPTER 30

"We should be coming out of jump in a few minutes," Jake said over the ship wide intercom. "I'm putting a timer up on your screens." The crew had mixed the jobs and shift coverage up between them, since each group didn't trust the other, even with Jake saying that everything was fine.

Jake had announced that the Militia troops would be augmenting the crew for now. Shutt had protested, and the Free Traders had complained. But the group of four healthy Militia tacitly siding with Jake had muted their proposals. Perlins had publicly announced she and her crew was going to take orders from Captain Jake, which made the others pause.

Jake hadn't given the Militia their guns back, though.

Daav was seated at the pilot's console in the control room. He had taken over as primary pilot on first shift. Even Major Shutt agreed he was the best pilot on the ship, and it was obvious to everybody that, rebellion or not, he just wanted to fly ships. Odette was sitting next to him. After Jake, she was the best navigator, and she and Daav worked well together. Plus, she and Daav were about the same size, and Yvette and Odette figured she could probably take him in a fight.

Jammy and Odette were seated behind them, monitoring the other systems. Both had lots of ship time and were versatile enough to back up the others if necessary. And they could keep an eye on each other. They handled the second shift, and the two groups worked shift-on, shift-off to keep an eye on the systems.

Jake had appointed Merced to be in charge of all things

medical and the galley. Since the galley was made of trays, anybody could reheat, and the only drink was basic. That part of his job was just recordkeeping and some minor cleaning. Corporal Dalon was still in a medical pod, his prognosis grim. Merced couldn't do anything for him except look at the colored lights.

Krikweigh was still too sick to work. Merced was trying to convince him to go back into the medical pod. He was losing weight because he wasn't eating but said he had no intention of going back under the pod's care. When Merced asked why, he had a one-word answer. "Nightmares."

Major Shutt and Lieutenant Perlins shared the Jump control room with Jake. Their jobs seemed to consist solely of watching each other suspiciously, trying to get Jake to show them how to use the Jump drive. Jake refused to answer any questions except innocuous ones and didn't attempt to make them do anything at all, with the exception of making them promise not to shoot each other.

"Three, two, one. Back in normal space," Jake said. "Anybody with a sensor board of any sort, check things and sing out."

In the control room, Jammy checked his board. "Planet dead ahead. This kid can navigate, I'll give him that."

"Can he navigate better than you?" Yvette asked.

"Nobody can navigate better than me," Jammy said.

"Didn't you ram an ore barge once on a run to a smelter?" Daav asked.

"I gently tapped one in passing a long time ago," Jammy said.

"Crunched the entire port truss, as I recall. Knocked all the sensors off, and crushed the thrusters," Daav said.

"Getting a course to the planet," Jammy said.

"Mr. Navigator there navigated us right into a line of about twenty barges on a continuous cycle between a mine and a smelter." Daav used his hands to illustrate. "Big line of them. Could have gone over, could have gone under, but no, we had to hit them right broadside," Daav said.

"You want me to dislocate your arm again?" Jammy said. "Here's a course. Steer it."

Daav punched the intercom. "Maneuvering. Stay strapped in 'til we're on one-G acceleration." He consulted his board, tapped the thrusters, then fired the mains. The ship accelerated smoothly.

Jake's voice came over the intercom. "Welcome to 61 Cygni and the local K-type dwarf stars A and B. Our destination is 61 Cygni-B-III, third planet of the second star. Stellar mass—"

"We got it. Thank you," Daav said. "It's on our screens." Jake shut up.

"Very relaxing startup," Odette said. "Very smooth."

"I think it's more the ship than the pilot," Jammy muttered. "I've got an orbital beacon. A station. Small one."

"You can tell it's small this far out?" Daav asked.

"I can't. Computer can. It has a database of Imperial stations, apparently. Even puts a map up on the screen. Three rings. Three small rings—one for shuttles, one for interstellar ships, and a habitation one in the middle."

"Three rings isn't bad."

"Only six docking ports. Two for shuttles, four for ships. Something at two of the shuttle ports. Nothing else."

"That's small. Any traffic control?" Daav asked.

"Contacting them now. We won't be there for two days, with turnaround, so plenty of time for them to reply."

Odette was tapping through her board. "I see a beacon for this station."

"I just said that," Jammy said. "Weren't you listening?"

"You don't say much that I need to pay attention to," Odette said. "But in this case, yes. I did hear you. What I mean is, we see a beacon for this station. We all see this beacon, mais oui?"

"Unless we're having some sort of jump-induced psychosis, then, yes, we all see it," Jammy said.

"But why didn't we see a beacon when we were leaving Delta? Don't the Delta stations have beacons?"

"Since we're in another system, we should now probably start saying 'in the Sigma Draconis system,' instead of Delta. Delta is just the name of the fourth moon of Sigma Draconis IV."

"Fourth of the fourth star, and there's four of us. Kind of poetic, isn't it?" Daav said.

"Shut up, Mr. Daav. What I mean is, why didn't we see a beacon like this when we left Delta? That was an Imperial outpost as well, wasn't it?"

"Was. Is. Maybe it's turned off."

"Or maybe there is something different about this planet here, and this outpost is different. Different enough to get a special listing in Imperial databases," Odette said. "Something dangerous."

***

Jake was paging through his screens, appearing absorbed in a graph labeled "Variable flow reactor temperature changes by minute." Major Shutt and Lieutenant Perlins watched as Jammy's displays echoed on their own screens, working on their own systems.

"These sensors are great," Perlins said. "I've got the telescope focused on that planet already."

"Is that how you report a sensor reading to your superior?" Shutt asked. "How long were you in the Militia?"

"Too long," Perlins said. "I've forgotten how to deal with Imperial anus officers like you."

"I'll remind you that I'm your superior," Shutt said.

"We're not in the Militia anymore."

"Oh, yes, you are. Either you're back in the Militia and subject to Militia discipline, or you're still a rebel. And we shoot rebels."

"No shooting," Jake said. "And no Militia discipline, either."

"I'm the highest-ranking Militia officer on this ship. I'm in charge."

"You're not in charge, I am," Jake said. "And what makes you think that you're the highest-ranking Militia officer on the ship?"

"I'm a major," Major Shutt said.

"The question stands, but we'll deal with it later," Jake said. "For now, let's put that planet on the screens and let everybody look at it."

Perlins tapped her screen, and a picture appeared. The day-night terminator was present about one-third of the way across.

"Small but dense," Shutt said. "And cold, if the infrared is to be believed.

"No clusters of artificial lights on the night side, no cities," Perlins said. "Are there any people?"

"There's some people," Jake said. "Not many. Should be a few hundred or thousand, according to records."

"Not much water, either," Shutt said. "Looks like deserts."

"High plains," Jake said. "Grasslands with rolling hills, punctuated by deep-cut ravines. There's water in the bottom of the ravines."

Perlins raised an eyebrow. "You know a lot about this place. Have you visited or something?"

"Not me," Jake said. "But I've talked to somebody who has."

"And who would that be?"

Jake shrugged.

Shutt looked at Perlins, then at Jake. "Jake, who were you talking to? What are you not telling us?"

Jake ignored the question again.

Shutt opened her mouth. "Shouldn't—"

The intercom crackled. "Heads up," Jammy said. "We

found that other Jump ship, and it's on a collision course to that orbital station."

***

Jammy was typing. The others in the control room were watching him or looking at their own screens.

Perlins's voice came over the intercom. "How'd you find that ship?"

"I'm the greatest sensor tech ever," Jammy said.

Daav laughed and tapped his intercom key. "There's a beacon, just like for the station. It popped up on our display automatically."

"Stop stealing my glory," Jammy said. "Confirmed. It's going to hit that station. Should we shoot it down?"

"Stand by," Perlins said.

"How come the first thing you Militia people want to do is shoot something down? Did you think of trying to talk to them first?" Yvette asked.

Jammy and Daav looked at each other. "Actually, no, we didn't think of that," Jammy said. "We don't normally make those kinds of decisions."

"Try to talk to them," Yvette said. She tapped her screen to send a message. "Let's see if they answer."

Daav waited for a return message. "They don't seem to be friendly."

"You only waited ten seconds," Yvette said. "Be patient. Let's try the station as well."

"We already called traffic control," Jammy said.

"Try them again."

"You're not my boss," Jammy said.

Yvette shook her head. "Boss or not, it's a good idea. Hail that ship, hail that station. Is there anything on the planet?"

"I see satellites," Odette said. "Half dozen. Maybe more hidden behind the planet. This fancy database says, 'Standard Imperial colony satellite constellation number 47.' It does weather forecasting, communication, imagery, and looks like ground navigation as well."

"Then, try to contact anything you can find. See if we can bounce a signal off a satellite or onto a satellite or through them. Hit the station, hit that ship. Do a broad beam to the planet."

"On what frequency?" Jammy asked.

"You're the greatest sensor tech ever. You figure it out," Yvette said.

***

"Right, time to shoot it down," Major Shutt said. They had waited an hour and there had been no response from anywhere.

"We're not shooting anything down," Jake said. "It looks like a docking maneuver."

"That other Jump ship is on profile to impact that station. It's been almost constantly accelerating since we've seen it. It's going to impact like a comet."

"The profile could still be a rendezvous or a flyby. It doesn't have to be a collision."

"Who heads into a station at five-G and climbing?" Major Shutt said.

"Somebody who is in a hurry and doesn't care about fuel," Jake said.

"That would be a pretty rough ride for the crew," Major Shutt said. "You ever been at five-G?"

"Not for very long," Jake said. "I didn't like it." He paged through his screens. "These indexes are difficult. I can't find what I'm looking for."

"Why were you at five-G?" Perlins asked.

"A bunch of station security on a tug had boarded us and were trying to force their way in. We spun as much as we could to fling them off." He typed again. "I think I'm in the wrong database. I'll try a global search."

"Why were they boarding you?"

"They thought we were harboring a fugitive and had stolen the ship."

"Had you?" Perlins asked.

"What?" Jake looked up. "Yes, of course. And I guess, technically, I had stolen it, and Nadine was the fugitive, but they didn't seem to make a distinction."

"We should shoot it down," Major Shutt said. "Before it destroys that station."

"You harbored a fugitive and stole a ship?" Perlins asked.

"For a short period," Jake said. "We won't shoot anybody until we communicate with them."

"What if we the don't answer our communications?" Perlins asked.

"I'll decide then," Jake said.

"We need to be prudent. We should shoot now," Shutt said.

"That's not your decision to make," Jake said.

"I'm the senior Militia officer on board."

"Yes, but I'm the captain," Jake said.

"This is a combat situation and a Militia asset. I'm taking control."

"A Militia asset? It's my personal asset. The Militia doesn't own it."

"This is a combat situation. As the senior Militia officer on board, I'm declaring force majeure and taking over."

"Force majeure? What does that mean?" Perlins asked.

"It's a military term. It means I can take control of private assets in a public emergency," Shutt said.

"Actually, it's an insurance term," Jake said. "It means overwhelming force and says that an insurance claim will not be paid."

"That's what it means? Are you sure?" Shutt asked.

"Positive. I'm an auditor, remember?" Jake said.

"Didn't pay close attention at command college, did you, Major?" Perlins asked.

"Shut up," Shutt said.

"I think what you meant," Jake said, "was eminent domain, the right of a government to take control of private property, but that doesn't apply because you're military, not civil."

"That sounds interesting," Perlins said. "Bet you wish you'd paid more attention in school now, huh?"

"Shut up, Jake, and you shut up, too, Perlins. We're going to destroy that ship."

Jake looked at Shutt. "Are you going to shoot me?"

"What?"

"It's just that, it seems anytime two pretty girls are arguing near me, I end up getting shot."

"You think I'm pretty?" Perlins asked. "Thanks. That and a glass of wine might get you somewhere."

Shutt scowled at Perlins. "I wasn't planning on shooting you, but I'll think about it if you don't bring up the weapons."

"Okay," Jake said. He typed for a moment. "On your screen. There you go. Fire away." He swapped screens and typed again.

Shutt looked down at her screen, up at Jake, then down again. Her hands didn't move.

"You don't know how to fire the weapons, do you?" Perlins asked.

"Never was a weapons officer," Shutt admitted. "And these screens look different than Militia ones."

"Can any of your folks fire them?" Perlins asked.

Shutt's silence was the answer.

Perlins gave a big grin. "I was a weapons officer. Bet I could figure them out."

"Do it, then," Shutt said.

"Well, Major," Perlins said. "I really think I should let the captain make that decision. Captain Jake, what should I do?"

"Stand by," Jake said. "I'm looking through the document indexes now."

Jammy's voice came over the intercom. "Status change. That Jump ship just flipped, and now it's decelerating relative to the station. Decelerating at six-Gs, no less. Hate to be not in an accel couch there right now."

"What sort of ship puts that much strain on the crew?" Shutt asked.

"Gotcha," Jake said and slapped his screen. He peered at the results. "One without a crew. Finally figured out how to send a coded Imperial request for identification. That's an Imperial courier ship. Automated." He tapped another screen. "And that station was an Imperial station. There's a research laboratory here and an experimental farm on the surface as well."

"An experimental farm? What for?" Perlins asked.

"Buffalo, moose, elk, and cows, apparently. Some sort of animal breeding program here."

"And the station? Are there people there?"

"Not right now," Jake said. "There were. But there aren't any there now, according to the log."

"Does the log say where they went?" Shutt asked.

"It does," Jake said. "Sort of." He tapped his screen again. "If I'm reading this right, it says they're all dead."

CHAPTER 31

Commander Roi called all the troops to give a speech under the palm trees. The original group of mutinous Militia officers and their few followers stood to his left. Sergeant Russel, Nadine, Vince, and the squad stood to his right. "Fellow liberators of Delta!" Commander Roi said. "I salute you on your glorious crusade. It has been a long, hard struggle, with reverses, but we will prevail."

"Three weeks is long?" Chaudhari asked Sergeant Russell.

"For officers, it is," Russell said.

Roi waved his hands. "Friends. Soldiers. Fellow patriots. Things have not been easy for us. We have been scattered, we have starved, and we have seen many good men and women killed by the perfidiousness of our enemies."

"What's a perfidiousness?" Kim One asked.

"It's a sea monster, I think," Chaudhari said. "A baby perfidiousaurus. They're called perfidiousnesses."

"We have sea monsters? On Delta?" Kim One asked.

"Everybody has sea monsters," Chaudhari said.

"Perfidiousness is not a sea monster," Commander Roi said.

"Sorry, sir," Chaudhari said. "You are correct. It's not a monster. It's just a naturally occurring part of the Delta ecosystem. Fills a niche. Nature at work, and all that."

"Ecosystem or not," Balthazar said. "I've been sailing all my life, and I've never seen one."

"Absence of proof is not proof of absence," Vince said.

"Huh," Nadine said. She looked at Vince. "That's

actually pretty smart. Did you go to the university?"

"Nope, just my natural talent and intelligence shining through," Vince said.

Nadine gave him a once-over. "What else do you know?"

"Come over for dinner, and I'll regale you with my wisdom."

Nadine furrowed her brow and mouthed "regale."

Kim One was still confused. "I don't understand, sir. Why would the Empire bring sea monsters to a new planet?"

"The Empire did not bring sea monsters to Delta," Commander Roi yelled.

"You mean they're native here? An alien sea monster race?" Kim One said. "Right here on Delta."

"An alien race here? How come I didn't hear about this?" Chaudhari said.

"You didn't go to the university, like Vinny here," Nadine said. "He majored in regaling."

"Is that what they call it now?" Sergeant Russell said. "We used different words when I was in school. I've done some regaling myself, in my time. Why, I remember this one girl, worked for the water department—"

"Sergeant, you are not going to talk about this," Commander Roi said. "If there is any regaling to be done here, I will be doing it."

The troopers looked at each other, then back to Commander Roi.

"You're going to be doing the regaling, sir?" Sergeant Russell asked. "Right here, with everybody watching?"

"Listening. They will be listening to me regale. Listen to my regaling."

"If you say so, sir," Sergeant Russell said. "But that's, well, that's just kind of weird, sir. The listening and all. Do people really get into that sort of thing?"

"It takes all kinds," Chaudhari said.

"What about these alien space monsters?" Nadine

asked.

"Yeah, are you going to regale us about those, Commander?" Vince asked.

"Gross," Nadine said. "You want to hear that? Him regaling those aliens."

"That's not for tender eyes. Or ears," Sergeant Russell said. "Chaudhari. Kim Two. Plug your ears, you don't need to hear this regaling. You're too young."

"I'm twenty-seven," Chaudhari said. "What can't I hear?"

"Well, Kim Two. You're the youngest, aren't you?"

"I'm thirty-four next birthday, Sergeant."

"Thirty-four?" Nadine leaned over and looked at her. "Really? But you look so young. Ten years younger."

"Thanks," Kim Two said.

"Your skin is amazing. What's your secret?" Nadine asked.

"Rather than eating it, I use the seaweed from the red-green-blue trays as a facial mask and scrub."

"The seaweed? It does that? Opens up your pores?"

Kim ran her hand over her face. "Smooth as a tabbo's butt."

"Wow," Nadine said. "I've got to try that. I'm so dry since we've been down south. You'd think that it would be humid here, with all this sea water. Hey, Vinny," She turned to Vince. "You got any red-green-blue trays?"

Vince sidled up to her and stroked her hair. "For somebody as pretty as you , whatever you need, Ms. Nadine, Vincent Pletcher and Owl ship sales can acquire it for you. There is the small question about repayment ..."

Nadine smiled, leaned toward Vince, and patted him on the cheek. "I can make it worth your while, Vinny." She dropped her hand to his arm and yanked him toward her. She stepped inside the pull, twisted his arm up and back, 'til his arm was pushed up high between his shoulder blades, and he was standing on his toes. "For example, get me a tray, and I won't break your arm for touching my hair this time."

Sergeant Russell and the others giggled, then laughed. They chortled, they snickered, they gave a big belly laugh. Nadine didn't release Vince. Vince twisted a bit, but couldn't break the hold.

"Is that a yes, Vinny?" Nadine asked.

Vince was having some trouble talking but managed to shake a yes out. Nadine let him go, and he dropped down. An ominous silence lingered, then everybody looked left. Commander Roi was regarding them with a frown, as were the other officers to their left. The officers looked angry. The troops looked curious.

"Sorry, Commander," Sergeant Russell said. "Just some residual stress from the storm yesterday. Troops need a little relaxing. You were saying, you were going to have us listen to you regale the alien sea monsters? We'll keep quiet so we can hear better. Kim Two, take notes."

"Take notes, Sergeant?"

"Yes, on, um, new regaling techniques."

"To be used if I ever find myself attracted to alien sea monsters?"

"I'm not judging, Kim Two. Live your life the way you want."

One of the random officers in front of Roi spoke up. "Sergeant, this is the worst example of undisciplined troops I have ever seen. Have you not instructed them in the proper procedures for troops standing in formation?"

"Nobody to blame but myself, sir," Sergeant Russell said. "Why, with my squad spending their time storming the Grower positions at the monorail station, fighting in orbit, capturing the TGI station with Commander Roi here, I just plain forget to instill a sense of discipline in the troops here." Sergeant Russell regarded the officer. "You are correct, sir. I should have taken the time to do it when we were breaking Commander Roi out of his prison back at Landing. Or before it. Of course, we couldn't let Commander Roi know what we were doing, so it would have looked a little odd, trying to do formation when we were supposed to be rescuing the true head of the Delta Militia from the rebel factions." Sergeant Russell turned to Commander Roi. "No excuse, sir. We'll submit ourselves to the orders of these officers over here. They've been here long enough to have set up some sort of training program, I'm sure. How long have you been here, sir?" Sergeant Russell said, turning to the red-faced officer. "A week? Two?"

"The major has been here for three weeks, Sergeant."

"Just after we left the fighting in the city to go to orbit," Sergeant Russell said. "Very good, sir. I'm sure the ... Garrison troops here, have had ample time to practice their formations."

"Garrison troops," the major said. "I'll have you know—"

"That you are under my command now," Commander Roi said. "And that I am ... comfortable ... with Sergeant Russell's methods, unusual that they be. They are fighting troops and must be given some leeway. Now, let me talk about how we will secure our moon's patrimony ..."

The commander droned on. Chaudhari slid next to Sergeant Russell. "Look at you, Sergeant, fighting troops. I actually am kind of starting to like this guy. It feels weird."

"Maybe it's just indigestion?" Sergeant Russell wondered.

Chaudhari burped out a long blast of gas. "You're right, that was most of it. But still ..."

***

The commander had finished his harangue and called on all the troops to follow him. They turned and walked into the trees. Up until that point, they'd been in tents, a short walk from the sandy bay where the Gaspar, Balthazar's boat, under the palm trees was. The group walked along a path that paralleled the water. The bay narrowed, and a strip of salt water separated the island they were on from another, perhaps ten meters away. Palm trees from the other island overhung the channel.

They edged out of the clearing to another beach. This fronted a large round bay, but unlike the other bay, where the sand slowly dipped into the water, this beach had a steep slope. The sand ran down from the trees into the water within two meters, and the bay looked deep.

"More boats," Chaudhari said to Sergeant Russell. There were two new boats in the bay, grounded on the beaches. They were square-sided barges, with low sides and blocky lines, contrasting Gaspar's sleek lines.

"Hidden as well," Sergeant Russell said. "Under those trees. Won't see them from a satellite."

"Infrared would see them," Chaudhari said. "If they have a heat signature."

"If anybody's watching. Think anybody is reviewing the imagery from down here?"

"Computer can do it automatically."

"Maybe. Nobody on board, though. With the trees above, and with those solar panels, are they actually generating any heat?"

"What's that over there?" Chaudhari pointed to the four odd-looking holes that were spread evenly around the bay's edge. Piles of sand and trees covered them on the top and the sides, but the front was open.

"You call 'em bunkers," Vince said. "And those are docks in front of them."

"There's no docks here on south continent," Sergeant Russell said. "There's no houses or facilities on south. Everybody knows that."

They watched as Balthazar edged his boat up to the sand and realized it wasn't sand. It was a casket of trees built into a square, filled with sand. So, from above or the side, it looked like a pile of dirt with some fallen trees but was actually a loading dock with a pier that stuck out into deep water. The land side of the pier faced one of the empty black doors.

"You sure about that?" Vince asked. "I've been delivering stuff here for years. We sail down, tie up at one of those piers, unload some crates into those storage bunkers, and sail out. If we time it right, there's no chance of us getting caught, satellite or otherwise."

"Better hope Roi doesn't figure that out. He'll be upset with you running him aground," Sergeant Russell said.

"I didn't run him aground. You did," Vince said.

"Your boy, Balthazar, better get tied up quick," Sergeant Russell said. "And get his unloading done."

Vince pursed his lips. "We don't have any unloading to do. Everything that these guys asked for has already been delivered. Nothing on B's boat that we wanted. Just you folks and Roi. We were waiting for you."

"You were waiting for Roi?" Sergeant Russell said. "What for? How did you know he was coming?"

"I don't think they did. Or I don't think they thought it was him. But they were talking about needing something that only that colonel guy had. Apparently, he gave it to somebody."

"He didn't give Roi anything," Sergeant Russell said. "I know because I had him searched, and those aren't his original clothes or comm unit or even his belt. Everything is new. Anything that he was supposed to have is gone."

"And yet," Vince said, "these guys have been sitting down here for weeks, waiting for something, getting sunburned and angry and then your guy Roi arrives, and suddenly, he's in charge."

"It is odd," Chaudhari agreed. "But hardly relevant."

They all arrived under the trees next to B's boat, and Roi began another speech. A squad of the original southern troopers ran into a bunker and came out carrying a variety of metal boxes. They placed them on the ground and flipped the covers open and pulled out components. First, they put three large metal plates down on the ground, then attached legs, leveling jacks, and metal supports. They also put a small radar antenna on a side plate.

"What's that? Directional radar?" Chaudhari wondered.

"How's that work?" Vince asked. "What do you need directional radar for?"

"To get range and bearing to something," Sergeant Russell said.

"What's the use of that?"

"No idea," Chaudhari said. Another crew brought a large tube out and attached it to the contraption. "Is that a gun?"

"Nowhere to put rounds in, no ammunition. Can't be a gun." The squad attached a rounded nose cone to the front of the cylinder and attached fins and a smaller cylinder on the back.

"Missile," Chaudhari and Sergeant Russell said.

"What?"

"Surface-to-air missile," Sergeant Russell said. "Old Empire model. Used to shoot down aircraft."

"Or landing shuttles," Chaudhari said.

"I didn't know the Militia had missiles," Vince said.

"Neither did we," Sergeant Russell said. He looked at Chaudhari, who shook his head.

"How come they didn't use it during that war you guys fought, then?" Vince asked.

One of the squad members pulled out an L-shaped piece of metal, slid it in a crack on the side of the missile, and twisted. A panel popped open, and a keypad with a series of red lights was visible. Sergeant Russell let out a breath with a whoosh.

"Didn't use it because they probably couldn't arm it. They all had unique arming codes, as I recall from my reading."

"You've never used one before?" Vince asked.

"Never touched one, never even seen one. It was just referenced in some manual I read once—that's a surface-to-air missile, model 137. Good to several thousand meters, seeking, that type of thing. But all the sensor software and tracking software is encrypted. If you don't have the password, you can't even reverse engineer what the sensors are doing. It's all gibberish. That way, if it was captured, it couldn't be used against Imperial forces."

"Or against Imperial shuttles. Or Delta shuttles," Chaudhari said.

"Those red lights mean that it's still encrypted," Sergeant Russell said. "Which is good. Means they can't shoot anything down."

"You're a Militia guy," Vince said. "Empire-rising and all that. I would have thought you'd want the Militia to be able to shoot down shuttles."

"We've already blown up enough important infrastructure," Sergeant Russell said. "Shuttles bring food to orbit, and they bring materials dirtside. Like spare parts for food plants that make the food that I eat. I like to eat."

"Me, too," Chaudhari said. "I want to be on the winning side, but I don't want to win and then starve to death a week later."

"We're fine. If these clowns had the codes, they would have used this already," Sergeant Russell said.

Vince reacted to the clown comment for a second, then shrugged. "So, we're safe, then?"

"Safe unless somebody gives them the codes. No problems otherwise," Sergeant Russell said.

The squad assembling the missile system stepped back, and Commander Roi stepped forward. He leaned over the keypad on the missile and typed in a long numeric code. A very long numeric code. It didn't work the first time. Nor the second time.

"He's just guessing," Sergeant Russell said. "He can't possibly know it."

"Pretty long guess to keep trying," Chaudhari said. "If he's just guessing a sixty-four-character code, it wouldn't even be worth trying again."

"Third try will lock it if it's wrong."

"Still no problems, then?" Vince asked.

"No problems," Sergeant Russell agreed. Commander Roi typed on the keypad again, pressing each key once, hard.

"Sixty-two," Chaudhari said, counting presses. "Sixty-three. Sixty-four." Commander Roi stopped and stared at the panel. The lights remained stubbornly red. Chaudhari and Sergeant Russell let out big breaths.

After three seconds, the panel bonged, and the lights turned green. The other troops all cheered. "The Emperor's hairy anus," Sergeant Russell said.

Vince turned to him. "Do we have a problem now?"

Sergeant Russell nodded. "We have a very, very big problem right now. One I don't know how to fix."

CHAPTER 32

"We'll close with the station and dock," Jake said. "There should be a shuttle there, and we can take it down to the surface." Jake had come up to the lounge to speak to the crew.

Shutt got up from her chair. "I'm sure your excellent crew of Free Traders can take care of that. I'll leave you in their capable hands." She walked out of the room.

"Must be hard for her," Perlins said.

"Really?" Jake said. "You're the one defending her?"

"I'm with her about working for idiots. Her and I, we just worked for different groups of idiots. Mine got lots of people killed for no reason. Almost got me and the guys as well. I sympathize with her not wanting to be run by amateurs."

"Amateur?" Jake asked.

"Like you. And these Trader chicks," Perlins said. "We in the Militia are the professionals."

"Jake Stewart is not an amateur," Yvette said. "He is unconventional, but he has many admirers in the Free Traders, and the Militia as well. He gets things done. He works for Dashi. Dashi has been a friend to the Free Traders. And unlike many others, Jake Stewart rarely gets anyone killed. And whenever there is danger, he is there."

"Thanks," Jake said.

"He is there, reading some sort of manual or talking about historical trivia," Yvette said.

"Not so much. Thanks," Jake said.

"But it seems to work." She turned to Perlins. "He has seen to your crew, has he not? And given you a second chance."

"What do you mean?" Perlins asked. "What second chance?"

"We don't believe the 'escaped' tale you told us. You were true mutineers. You lost, so you ran away, and now you want forgiveness and forgetness."

"You don't know that," Perlins said. "We were kept hostage—"

"No, you weren't." Yvette said. "Nobody believes that. Jake doesn't believe it, but he accepts your story for his own reasons. We support him, so we accept your story. For now."

"Thanks," Perlins said.

"Remember this," Yvette said. "With your situation, you may need some more help in the future. So might we. We could help each other."

"How so?" Perlins asked.

"We don't have time right now. Later." She turned to Jake. "What do we do now?"

"When we dock with that station," Jake said, "we have to get down to the surface. If my information is correct, there are some small shuttles. Space for some passengers, a little cargo. We need to land, pick up some boxes, come back up, and jump back to Delta."

"What crew do you need?"

"I need a great pilot, a good sensor ops, somebody who is good with a gun, and myself. The others have to be the best at what they do."

"Take Daav," Jammy said. "He's the best pilot."

"You just said that?" Daav said. "Admitted it? In public?"

"Best pilot for this. You learned groundside. I learned orbital. You're just the touch bit faster than me in atmosphere. Something instinctive. And take one of the Free Trader women as sensor operators. They're better than any of us Militia people. Working with those crap systems has made them better. I'm not as intuitive."

Yvette pointed at Odette. "She's better. I'm a better

engineer, but she's had more experience on sensors."

"Who's the gun hand, then?" Jake asked.

All five looked at each other.

"Perlins," Jammy said. "Take her."

"Why?" Jake asked.

"She's the most ruthless of all of us. She won't hesitate to shoot somebody. She'll shoot first and shoot straight. The rest of us are too timid. She's a killer."

Jake looked at Perlins. "You're a killer?"

"Wasn't before. I am now," Perlins said.

Jake looked around. "We have our shuttle crew. We dock in about three shifts. Everybody get a lot of rest. We need to be in tip-top shape when we get there. We're going to get those boxes, examine that other Jump ship, then head back to Delta posthaste."

"Whatever that means," Yvette said.

Jake ignored her. "Just make sure you're ready." Merced came running into the room. "What is it?"

"Dalon just died. And Krikweigh doesn't look too good, either."

***

"On the subject of dead people," Daav said, manipulating the controls. "I don't like having a dead guy on board."

They were coasting to the 61 Cygni station—or "Siggys," as Jammy had dubbed it. It was shift handover, and he, Daav, Yvette, and Odette were in the control room. "Makes me think about life and time and death." He burped. "And gives me gas."

"Be respectful," Jammy said. "No corpse belching. And he's not actually dead yet. Merced says he's just flatlined for brain function, and the med pod is keeping him alive."

"As good as dead, then."

"What did you want us to do? Dump him out an air lock?"

"That is what we normally do," Yvette said. "We have

a ceremony of life, then we have a solemn launch, sending him on an orbit that will impact the Dragon."

Everyone contemplated this in silence. "What type of rocket do you use to launch them out?" Daav asked. "Seems like the waste of a good rocket."

"We don't use a rocket."

"No?"

"We do not need one. We just throw them."

"You just heave the corpse out? Like broken furniture?"

"Perhaps toss is a better word. We find it's best to get the body above the orbital plane, give them a bit of a rising inclination."

"That's horrifying," Daav said. "You just toss them out the lock?"

"Out and up, as I said. Why is it horrifying? If we didn't get a bit of up-orbit, they'd just bounce around the rings, probably end up orbiting one of the bigger asteroids or the bigger stations. This way they loop down toward the Dragon 'til they burn up."

"You just leave them out there, orbiting, as frozen corpses? What if somebody runs into them?"

"Running into a frozen corpse, now that's horrifying," Odette said. "Really impacts your day."

"Scares you, does it?" Daav asked.

"What? Scared? No. They're frozen, just big blocks of ice, so when you hit them, they break up into pieces. The collision heats them up a bit, and they smush all over the hull, then freeze there. You spend the entire next cleaning period scraping frozen body parts off the hull. Messes up your maintenance schedule."

"You Free Traders sure think differently than the norm," Daav said.

"From our point of view, you think differently from the norm. Anything to report, other than you have stomach gas?"

"On target for docking with the station in four hours,"

Daav said.

"Should be interesting," Jammy said. "I wonder if it will be difficult."

***

It wasn't. "And, locked," Jammy said. "Hard seal."

"Any issues?" Jake asked over the intercom.

"Totally Delta standard docking bay. Or I guess, I should say, totally standard Imperial docking bay, since we're rejoining the Empire now."

"We are rejoining the Empire, aren't we?" Daav said.

"Not if we can help it," Yvette said. "The Empire has not exactly been good to us."

"Rather starve and freeze back in Delta orbit, then?" Jammy asked. "Some problems back there, so we're told."

"We wouldn't have these problems if you two and your like hadn't started them."

Jammy shrugged. "Good point."

Jake's voice came over the intercom. "Could everybody meet in the lounge?"

The control room crew swarmed down the central corridor, meeting Jake, Perlins, and Merced there. Shutt arrived back within a moment.

"Major, thanks for joining us," Jake said.

"I want to give you the benefit of my professional opinion."

"Or you were bored," Daav said.

"Shut up," Shutt said.

"She's taking a leaf out of your officer's manner book, boss lady," Daav said to Perlins.

"Shut up, Daav." Perlins turned to Jake. "What's the plan, Jake?"

"That's Captain Jake to you, army girl," Yvette said.

Shutt glared at Yvette. Yvette glared back. "Captain," Shutt said.

"I'm sure you've all been studying the sensors on our way in," Jake said. "But I'll let the specialists give their report. Yvette?"

"The station is powered down," Yvette said. "The fusion reactor is lit, but the heating system is set on standby. It's warm enough to keep water from freezing, but that's it."

"And no comm answers from anybody on the station?" Jake asked.

"Nobody. I don't think anybody is here. It's too cold to live. There is plenty of power. They could turn up the heat if they want to. Same with the settlement on the surface. There's a single location with a working fusion reactor. There's what looks like a small mass driver next to it, but the mass driver isn't powered. There are what could be houses nearby. A small town. Maybe a village."

"What's the temperature down there?

"Reasonable. The planet's surface is cool and dry, and there are some lakes, mostly in deep valleys. There are big winds blowing on the plains and big fires. They whip up dust storms. The settlement is near a lake, in the biggest valley. It's almost warm there."

"Is it summer down there?" Perlins.

"No seasons," Yvette said. "No orbital tilt. But those winds almost create their own weather patterns. But once you get into the valleys, out of the wind, things warm up a lot."

"So, just a single abandoned village, and lots of empty space."

"With some strange local wildlife," Odette said. "We see heat sources, huge herds of them out on the plains. Big ones, but I don't know what they are. We can't get good resolution yet. The atmosphere's pretty dusty."

"Cattle," Jake said. "Lots and lots of cattle."

"Like buffalo? Like you see back on Delta?"

"Close, I think," Jake said. "What about population?"

"Well, no industry, but there could be people. People give off heat, but so do cattle. Hard to separate people from cattle at a distance. And if the people stuck to using wood fires, we'd never notice different energy sources. There's enough natural fires on the plains." She tapped to the next screen. "No strange chemicals or radio waves or magnetic indications."

"This is great and all, Mr. Captain," Perlins said. "But why are we here and what are we doing? Some of us weren't part of your original mission briefing, remember?"

"I haven't forgotten," Jake said. "We—and by we, I mean Major Shutt and Yvette and Odette—had been given instructions by the council. First, test this ship by making a jump to a safe adjacent system. This was one of two that was suggested. Second, track the other Jump ship to see where it was going and what it was doing and when. It jumped here, so I followed it."

"And third, intercept the biggest group of remaining mutinous Militia, and kill them all?" Perlins asked.

"That wasn't in our orders, no," Jake said.

"Bet you're glad it happened, though," Perlins said.

"It does make things ... simpler," Yvette said.

"Glad we made it easy for you," Perlins said.

"Would have been easiest if you all died," Shutt said. "I suppose you could still do that for us."

Perlins looked at Daav, Jammy, and Merced. "We're sorry to disappoint."

"Could you try harder next time?" Shutt said. "If it's not too much trouble."

Perlins turned back to Jake. "Okay, so your orders said to jump here, follow that other ship, then report back. Why are we going down to the surface, then?"

"Because Mr. Dashi. Emperor Dashi. My boss. Because my boss gave me additional orders. To come here, to this system, dock at this station, take a shuttle to the surface. He told me there would be that reactor down there, and he told me to go down and collect some parts. Reactor parts."

"When did you get this order?" Major Shutt asked. "That wasn't part of our briefing."

"I had some verbal indications before we lifted, but he

sent me an encrypted message just before we jumped," Jake said. "With more details. Everything about this system checked out with what he said. The station. The shuttles. The fusion plant on the surface—it's a standard Imperial colony package incidentally—the smallest set of Imperial infrastructure built on any planet that was to have permanent population. There were a lot of interesting notes in the files. Documentation on the building and the procurement methods. And even a history of the standardized design methods that—"

Shutt had crossed her arms. Jammy and Daav raised their eyebrows. Yvette and Odette rolled their eyes at each other.

"Sorry," Jake said. "That sort of stuff interests me. Bottom line, Dashi described everything, including the cattle, and he told me where to get a bunch of reactor parts. He even told me why. The situation on Delta is critical. The power distribution system was heavily damaged in the fighting, worse than they thought. There's a strong possibility that it can't be put back online without replacement components. If it doesn't come back online, everybody in orbit will starve, and the surface will go into serious decline with the loss of orbital metals and other industrial items. The whole civilization will collapse."

"And bringing back a few boxes of spare parts will fix this?" Shutt asked.

"Dashi's in charge," Jake said.

"He's not here right now, Jake Stewart," Yvette said. She looked at Perlins, then Shutt, then back to Jake. "You could make your own decisions right now,"

Something passed between everyone in the room, and they all sat up straight. Hands moved and hovered near pockets, holsters, or drawers. No weapons were actually produced, but they felt their presence.

"You could disobey Dashi's orders," Shutt said.

"We got in this mess by people thinking they knew better than the people in charge," Jake said. "It didn't work and has nearly destroyed us. Dashi's in charge, everybody agrees on that. If he's in charge on Delta, then I'm in charge here."

Jake looked at Perlins.

She nodded once. "Captain's in charge."

Shutt frowned. Yvette looked at Odette and shrugged. "Later." She turned to Jake. "So, what do we do now?"

"Daav, Odette, Perlins, and I are going to the surface. Yvette, take Jammy with you and check out the other ship docks on this level. Get into that other Jump ship if you can. Then walk the hab section.

"Got it, skipper," Jammy said.

"Merced, how's Krikweigh?

"He's in his cabin. He sleeps all the time. The radiation really messed him up. I think he's dying slowly. And before you ask, I can't do anything for him. I looked it up. Nothing cures too much radiation exposure. He's got good pain meds, and he can still move. I think I should stay here." Merced shrugged. "I'm not good on stations or ships. I'd just get in the way."

"What about me?" Shutt asked.

"Guard the ship," Jake said.

"Against what?"

"Ghosts," Jake said. "Or maybe zombies."

CHAPTER 33

The monorail train glided to a halt about five kilometers outside of Landing. The Dragon lit up the night sky with reflected light, but the primary was obscured. Delta's orbit about Sigma Draconis IV had begun its every eighty-seven-day transit of the planet's penumbra. It wasn't facing a full solar eclipse for almost ten days, but the cold season had begun. This wasn't a true winter, since the moon had almost no axial tilt, but as it spent more and more of its rotation in shadow, the solar radiation would decrease. Snow would fall and accumulate in the dark until rising daylight temperatures melted it.

The cold season only lasted three weeks, but snow could fall in that time, and people outside could freeze to death in a single night if they weren't prepared.

Thirty Legionnaires and an equal number of Militia had begun their trudge along the rail line. Lights in the distance were only a fraction of what would have been a few months prior.

"Trust this to happen during winter," Dunlop said.

"It doesn't matter when it happened," Jose said. "One time is as bad as another."

"You sure we have to wait for those folks to get there?"

"We're only five km away—maybe two hours' walk. Our reports indicate that the city is quiet. Everybody is huddling inside, mostly. But there are still gangs and a lot of weapons around. We don't want them damaging the train. The troops will just secure the station."

"Seems strange, soldiers in the streets," Dunlop said. "People won't react well. But at least we're bringing them food."

"They don't need food, not really. Plenty in the town. And the warehouses will last for years."

"Never did figure out why we have so many food production facilities."

"We were an intersystem fuel station," Jose said. "We're on the crossroads of two different jump trading routes. They funneled down near here, and longer-range merchant ships could take a shortcut through Delta. Before the abandonment, they'd all stop here and pick up consumables. Hydrogen and oxygen from the rings. Food grown from the surface. And since we had the infrastructure, repair companies set up shop. Then mining companies to make parts for the repair companies. We're designed to feed and fuel starships, not a planet."

"Explains the weather," Dunlop said. "No sane person would live here."

"No sane person did. At the time of the abandonment, it was mostly transients, station staff on short-term contracts, merchants traveling through. Refugees from fighting elsewhere in the Empire. Just people passing by."

"And we could feed 'em," Dunlop said.

Jose nodded. "That's why we don't have any real industry. We didn't make things. Nothing too technological. We imported all that from the bigger systems, farther away. We can do some repairs of intersystem ships, but anything big, like fusion plants or Jump drives, and we're out of luck."

"The Imperial engineers built well, to have things running so long without parts and maintenance."

"Well, we're counting on you to follow the Imperial tradition and fix this mess."

"I'm not an engineer," Dunlop said. "I'm a fireman who learned electrical maintenance."

"You're what we've got."

"I'm not enough."

"You'll have to be."

***

Nothing happened when the troops arrived at the station, and the train rolled in unopposed three hours later.

"It's too cold," the Sergeant leading the Militia said. "Nobody cares. They're all huddling inside around whatever battery- or solar-powered heaters they have."

"One problem solved, then. Less and less sun, next few weeks," Jose said. "That will keep the mobs out of our hair."

"We have another problem," Dunlop said

"Of course we do. What now?"

"Train can't go far enough into the station. Tracks aren't electrified all the way in. We're running on the west grid, the one run by that hydro plant. Central and East grids are down— they're the ones that switch from the fusion plant. West grid tracks stop about twenty meters too soon."

Jose looked at the back of the train. A large flat car carried heavy copper beams in cradles. Those were the new power switching bars that had been machined in orbit and brought down on the lifting-body shuttle. Directly behind it was a train-mounted crane. The crane's arm was long enough to reach the flat car and lift the cradles up and out. The plan had been to swing the beams onto an electric ground truck that had been charged at the fusion plant.

"Let me guess, the road where the truck can get to is too far for the crane."

"Right in one," Dunlop agreed.

"And the truck is too far from the tracks and can't cross close enough?"

A city street paralleled the tracks near the station. The flatbed truck was parked there. If the train could have moved forward a few dozen meters, they could have loaded the power switching bars directly onto the truck. But the tracks hadn't curved in yet.

"Why can't the truck drive up next to the train? It's self-propelled."

"It's also heavy, and that's dirt with melted snow on top of it. Also called mud. We can load it, but getting it to move after that might be a problem."

"How will you move it off the truck on the far end?"

"There's a work crane on rails there, used for lifting containers and shuttles and stuff. But it's fixed. Can't get it here."

"So, we carry them."

"Some of them. But the biggest two weigh about two thousand kilos each, give or take."

Jose shook his head and stomped off to stand by himself for a moment. Being in charge is hard. He looked around. There were no other cranes in Landing that he knew of. Delta didn't do any new construction. Everything in the city had been built pre-abandonment. Landing didn't have suburbs, and the town ended right at the monorail station. Fields and farms stretched all the way up to the foothills, a few kilometers away. The foothills had orchards. He walked back to Dunlop and pointed. "What do they grow over there?"

Dunlop looked up at the hills. "Apples."

Jose nodded. "Send your crews into town and get as many chainsaws as you can find."

***

The crews worked three shifts. Not everyone could work because Jose kept a guard detachment on standby. It was long, tiring work, but at least they got a warm place to rest inside the train. It stayed where it was and had power from the west grid.

The second day, they shifted perhaps two dozen smaller copper pieces, secondary switching bars, and switching bars to the fusion plant. They were small enough to be carried out to the road and loaded onto the trucks. When they got to the switching station, Dunlop's crew

289

installed them. The two heaviest pieces stayed on the train.

Jose sent crews into the woods outside town with detailed instructions. It was three days before they returned.

The crews dragged a set of two-meter logs into place. "I have never, ever heard of this before," Dunlop said.

"This is how the Egyptians built the pyramids," Jose said.

"I don't know what a pyramid is. Or who Egyptians are, for that matter. And I don't care. Will those logs take the weight?"

The crews had cut down a dozen apple trees, at great expense in compensation to the owners, trimmed the branches and the bark, and cut the trunks into two-meter lengths. They were arranged in a group right below where the train crane could reach. The crane operator lowered the first switching bar and its cradle onto the rounded logs. The logs creaked and cracked but held. Once the cradle settled, ground crews unhooked the chain from the crane, walked it over to the power switching bar, and attached it to the front. The foreman yelled, and the group strained. The cradle rolled forward. The logs underneath rolled as the copper switching bars rolled over them. Teams of four men picked the last log up and ran it to the front of the line of logs, extending the support. They repeated the process, pulling from behind and putting in front as it rolled. The walking crew pulled the switching bars slowly, stopping occasionally when they ran out of logs in front. The crews struggled to keep up.

"Yes," Jose said. "On old Earth, they moved ten-ton stones with this method."

"What about the mud?"

"The weight is distributed between twenty wide logs, not four skinny tires. Surface pressure is so much lower they won't sink."

The pulling group stopped just short of the truck. A long ramp had been constructed up to the truck bed.

Pulleys had been rigged so that the switching bars could be winched up onto the truck.

"That worked lickety-split," Dunlop said. "Get that to the switching plant, and we'll have it installed in a couple of shifts."

"That long?" Jose asked.

"Alignment is a problem—and grounding. Don't want a hundred thousand volts going through until we're ready."

***

Two days later, Jose watched a worker on top of the switching bar turning the final nut with a wrench as long as her arm. Past fires had blackened the structure, and it had taken an extra three shifts to cut the remains of the previous switching bar off. Some of it had been hammered free, some cut with a torch. Dunlop's people had done nothing for an entire shift while three stuck parts were heated to expand enough that they could be pried off.

Dunlop walked up to Jose. "Once the boys and girls get that one bolted on tight, we attach the sub-bars back on and then we try the switches."

"Is your other man going to be okay?"

"It's just frostbite. He'll live, but he won't be using those fingers for a while."

"I would have thought he'd know not to touch bare metal like that."

"He does orbital work. Vacuum they understand, but he thought in an atmosphere nothing could be that cold."

Jose looked around. Snow covered the ground, and more fell. "Everybody's staying inside. I thought they'd be out to watch."

"As soon as we get power to the city, they'll know, so why watch out in the cold?"

"True," Jose said.

The worker finished tightening the giant bolt with the giant wrench and gave the thumbs-up to her colleagues. A half dozen other workers in teams of two bolted smaller bars on ninety-degree angles. One end of each bar was bolted onto the switching bar, the other end onto a switching mechanism. The switches were all conspicuously open and tagged with green covers to indicate they were safe to work on.

"Speaking of, let's go inside to the fusion control room and wait there. It's warm, and all the monitors are there." He led the way through the switching station, past the burned-out switching bar remains, and under a bunch of heavy electrical wires. They climbed up a set of metal stairs and went through a metal door. Down a hall, the room opened up.

"How long will this take?" Jose asked, rubbing his hands.

"Minutes," Dunlop said. "The feeder bars aren't that heavy. We'll have them on in a jiffy."

"Tell me again how this works," Jose said.

"When the main switching bar is back on, we switch fusion number one output onto the main power bar. And since, this time, we have the transformers attached forward, not backward, the correct voltage will hit the switching bars. That's our heaviest power circuit. Big thing we're looking for there is that circuit to reach fusion number two. Then we use the electricity to restart it. That works. We've got two running reactors and one can restart the other from now on."

"Then we can launch a shuttle?"

"Nope. Then we turn on the primary circuits, which power a bunch of things in the plant here. Then we can switch the secondary switching bars on with those big mechanical solenoids. That activates a whole bunch of feeder circuits. Most of the city. The university. The monorail. We'll have planet-side power back on. Mostly."

"So, nobody freezes."

"Right."

"Then we launch the shuttle."

"Nope. Then we bring on the tertiary switches. They

power the mass driver, and we can launch containers and shuttles."

"Good. What do you anticipate happening?"

Dunlop didn't say anything. "Yes?" Jose said.

"We've inspected the main and secondary switches and switching bars. They're mostly mechanical, just big hunks of metal. Those I'm pretty confident will work. We just needed big hunks of copper to take the current. But we got a big surge when that stupid truck hit. We might have damaged some of the secondary switches. Maybe. But the big problem is the tertiary switches."

"You talked about those before, said you needed spares. What about them?"

"They control flow to the mass drivers. They're not switches really, they're computers. The magnets have to be magnetized in exactly the right sequence for the right amount of time. Otherwise, the mass driver ... just kind of flails around."

"What does flail around mean?"

"It will blow up or shred any shuttle we put into it. But we'll know before that starts. Did you get any spares?"

"I don't have any right now. Dashi has been working on something."

"Your boss has a secret stash of pre-abandonment equipment?"

"He has lots of things. Let's get this test over with."

A number of technicians came up to confer with Dunlop. They spoke technician speak for a while, then the group and Dunlop went to one side of the room, where a large board with a circuit diagram and lights was. From left to right, it was labeled Fusion One, Fusion Two, Main Dist, Second Dist, Mass Drv. Fusion One's lights were green. The rest were all red.

"Everybody got the checklist?" Dunlop asked. There were yells of assent. He turned to a man at the center control station. "Evay, ready on number seventeen."

Jose walked over to Dunlop. "You start at seventeen?

What's wrong with one?"

"First sixteen were field tests. Seventeen is the first powered item. Evay, go."

Evay tapped his screen. The lights under Fusion Two went orange. Everybody cheered.

"Orange is good? I thought green was good?"

"Green means it's running, orange means it's functional but not on. As they start the second reactor, orange will be green."

Dunlop walked over to confer with another technician at a side station. As they talked, the orange lights changed to green, except for two at the end, which didn't seem to bother anybody.

Dunlop came back to Jose. "Right, Fusion Two is good. Evan, steps forty-six."

"What happened to the other steps?" Jose asked.

"You want a copy of the runbook? We can give you a job. Somebody needs to be out in the cold, manually closing some switches. We're short there."

"Sorry I asked," Jose said.

The lights on Main Dist changed from orange to red, except one, labeled Secondary Pumps. Dunlop, again, cornered another tech, and they talked. Evay yelled out numbers every few seconds, and the orange lights switched to green over the next few minutes, except for the errant pump. "Try it again," Dunlop said from his station. "Once more." Evay tapped his screen. The pump light turned green.

More cheers erupted.

"Carry on. Item ninety-six," Dunlop said. Evay, again, tapped his screen, and all the Second Dist lights went orange and then to green in a few seconds. The room clapped and cheered.

"About time we had a break," Dunlop said. "And now the finish." He nodded at Evay, who reached down and tapped his screen. The red lights under Mass Drv flashed red.

"Is that normal?" Jose asked.

"Shss," Dunlop said before his lips moved again. Jose realized he was counting. He reached eight, and the flashing red changed to flashing orange. The entire room counted again as the lights flashed orange.

"Six, seven, eight ..." The lights stopped flashing any color and went out. The control room held their collective breath.

All the lights under Mass Drv were back to red.

"The Emperor's hairy testicles," Dunlop said. "That's bad."

CHAPTER 34

"We have to stop them getting those missiles back to the mainland," Nadine said.

"We're on the mainland," Vince said. "This is the biggest continent on Delta."

"This is south continent. Not the mainland. The mainland is north."

"Kind of northern-hemisphere centric, aren't you?" Vince asked. "They're both continents. This could be the mainland."

"The northern continent has the shuttle launch facility, the mass driver, the only big fusion plant on this moon, the monorail, and all of the population. What's here?"

"Neat beaches and lots of cool palm trees."

"That's all you got? Palm trees?"

"South continent is bigger," Vince insisted.

Nadine rolled her eyes. "All your money is on north continent."

"Well ..." Vince bit his lip.

"And your wine," Nadine said. "That's all up north."

"Okay, that's the mainland," Vince agreed. "But why do we have to stop Roi getting that up north? To the mainland, I mean."

"Aren't you a loyal Delta citizen?" Nadine asked.

"Now you're sounding like our glorious leader over there."

"He does have a distinct speaking style," Nadine said. "But are you loyal?"

"Loyal to who?" Vince pointed at Roi. "Crazed Militia leader president-for-life number four over there? The corporate fat cats who split this system up between them, kept the small guys from earning an honest living."

"You sell stolen food to rebels," Sergeant Russell said. "And weapons to anybody. That's hardly an honest living."

"I'll have you know I paid for all that food. And they weren't rebels when they started buying, just some Militia guys who paid their bills on time."

"Is that all you're interested in, money?" Sergeant Russell asked.

"Feel free to donate your salary to charity, Sergeant, and work for the joy of serving the Empire. I'd be curious to see how long you last without any cash coming in. And why are you supporting the Militia at all? Didn't you used to be a Master Sergeant?"

"That was a misunderstanding," Sergeant Russell said.

"Speaking of salary," Chaudhari said. "Are we getting paid? Are we in the Militia? Or are we rebels now? And if we're rebels, how do we eat?"

"Mr. Vince here will deliver you all the food you need, for a price," Nadine said.

"If I don't pay the people who sell me the food, they can't pay the people who bring it to them, and if they don't pay the people who make it, no food gets made. So, yes, if the price is right, I'll get you food," Vince said.

"Doesn't it bother you only doing this for money? And trying to make the most money possible?" Nadine asked.

"Funny hearing that from you," Russell said.

"It's what I do," Vince said. "And why shouldn't I be good at it? I work hard at getting better at what I do." He pointed at Sergeant Russell and Chaudhari and the rest of the Militia. "You guys shoot people. And practice shooting people so that you can get better at it. Are you ashamed of that?"

"It's not the same thing," Chaudhari said.

"And you, the lovely Miss Nadine. What do you do? Just twist people's arms and steal things from them. Like ships, revolvers, and metal? That's what I heard."

"Those things shouldn't have belonged to them in the first place," Nadine said.

"You get to decide who gets what?" Sergeant Russell asked. "Who elected you?"

"I ..." Nadine frowned. "I work for the admiral. For the Militia, I suppose. For the Delta council."

"Which one?" Chaudhari asked. "The current council, the one they fought off, or the Militia appointed council over there? Some other one?"

"Sergeant Rusell is a patriot," Vince said. "He works for whichever Militia council he thinks is going to win. And Ms. Nadine works for whichever one pays her."

"Bite me," Nadine said.

"I agree. Bite her," Chaudhari said.

Sergeant Russell cleared his throat. "Fine. We've got the femme fatale female mercenary agent—"

Nadine raised her hand. "That's me! Femme fatale. I like that. Right here, baby!"

Sergeant Russell shook his head. "Then the uncaring, greedy businessman—"

"Present," Vince said. "After our discussion here, I'm going to go back to the tent and roll around in a bed full of money."

Sergeant Russell tapped his chest. "The hardworking, level-headed Militia sergeant—"

"Level-headed? I once saw you shoot a man for knocking over your beer," Chaudhari said.

"Who is just trying to make his way in a cruel world," Sergeant Russell finished.

"What am I, then?" Chaudhari asked.

"The dedicated sidekick," Sergeant Russell said.

"I don't want to be a sidekick. I want the story to be about me," Chaudhari said.

"Nobody cares what you think," Sergeant Russell said. "That's why you're a sidekick."

"Sounds like the plot for a cheap vid," Vince said. "Maybe even a series."

"It'll never work. Nobody would ever believe it," Nadine said.

"And even if they did, it wouldn't last beyond the first book. Not enough depth," Chaudhari said.

Metal clanked on metal in the distance. They turned. The crew was disassembling the missiles and putting them in travel boxes.

"Why are we even having this conversation?" Nadine asked.

"Because we're the only non-crazy people here," Vince said. "We're all working people, just trying to make our way through life. We work hard, try to get things done. We appreciate the possible. Different jobs. We sell things that need to be sold, steal things that need to be stolen, and sometimes, kill people who need killing. We're pragmatists. We work things out." Vince pointed at the group. "Those folks are lunatics. They think they're idealists when, in fact, they're just idiots with a poor grasp on reality. They've already gotten a bunch of people killed, and our only city mostly destroyed. We'll be lucky if the remaining half of the population doesn't freeze or starve to death in the next month. Or both at the same time. Anybody, anybody else—the old Militia council, the corps, even the Free Traders council is better than them. Missiles or no, they have no chance of winning. But they can cause a lot of damage with their glorious revolution. Not only to themselves but to us. We need to stop them."

Nadine, Sergeant Russell, and Chaudhari clapped. "A very enlightened high-sounding call to look out for our own self-interest in this case," Chaudhari said. "Well done."

"He's right," Sergeant Russell said. "Regardless of what's going on, we need to stop them from continuing this fight."

"You're the one who brought the glorious leader down here," Nadine said.

"I know. That was a bad idea."

"And you're the one who kidnapped me," Nadine said.

"Another bad idea," Sergeant Russell agreed.

Vince smiled at Nadine. "I don't think so. I kinda like having her around."

"You're sweet, Vinny," Nadine said. "Have any of that wine left?"

"But how do we stop them?" Chaudhari asked.

"I'll stab them all," Nadine said.

"What do you want for lunch?" Sergeant Russell asked.

"Lunch?"

"It takes a minute or more to stab a man with a knife. Longer if you want to make sure he's dead. There's about fifty, sixty over there. It will take you two hours to kill them all. It will be lunchtime by then."

"I'll use two knives," Nadine said. "Stab 'em twice as fast."

"Put your knives away. I've got a plan."

***

"I always knew I could count on you, Sergeant," Commander Roi said to Sergeant Russell. They, along with Nadine, Vince, Balthazar, and Chaudhari, were standing near the Gaspar's helm, watching the activity on the bow. A technician was welding a mounting bracket just behind the windlass, and teams of troops were carrying boxes of food and supplies to an aft hatch.

"I serve the Empire, sir," Sergeant Russell said.

"The Empire," the troops in earshot said. They gave the crossed chest salute. Sergeant Russell rolled his eyes at Chaudhari but mirrored the motion.

"It only makes sense, sir, the Gaspar is the fastest, most seaworthy ship down here, and Balthazar is the most experienced captain—"

"I'm not—" Balthazar said.

"Used to being praised in public, I know," Sergeant Russell said. "But we needed the weapons onboard our best managed boat, and you were our best manager."

"I'm a captain, not a manager," Balthazar said.

"And our best one, too!" Sergeant Russell said. "Soon as that mounting setting is set, we'll test our new weapon. Death to the traitors."

"Death to traitors," the crew members chorused. They knew a leading line when they heard it.

"Death," Vince said, executing a badly mangled salute. Roi nodded approvingly, then frowned at the silent Nadine. She caught the look, beamed a smile, then gave a cross-breast salute. "Yay. Death. Yay."

Roi frowned. "Could you excuse us for a moment, Ms.?"

"Excuse you? For kidnapping me? Not really," Nadine said. "But I do need a drink. I'm going over there." She sauntered down the gangplank. A group of soldiers were issuing food and drinks from a portable kitchen set up in the trees.

Roi waited 'til she was out of earshot, then turned to Sergeant Russell. "Are you sure that we can trust Ms. Nadine over there? She was one of the admiral's lovers."

"His granddaughter," Chaudhari said.

"She was one of his granddaughter's lovers as well?" Roi's frown deepened. "Is there no end to his perfidy? These are the types of creatures he employs. Why, never minding the ... unnaturalness of the relationship with the granddaughter. You would think if she was his lover, his paid lover, at least she would remain faithful to her duties with that mutinous dog of a so-called admiral."

Chaudhari, Vince, and Sergeant Russell exchanged glances. "Commander," Vince said. "Just so I understand, you believe she was a prostitute hired for sexual services by the admiral?"

"Everybody knows this. I myself saw them cavorting together in restaurants in Landing," Roi said.

"Cavorting? Is that like regaling?" Chaudhari asked.

"Not at all the same thing," Vince said. "I regale, but you won't see me cavorting. At least, not at the same time.

But Commander, you're upset because the Adm—I mean that, even though Mr. Edmunds hired her for sexual services, you think she was two-timing him with Mr. Edmunds's granddaughter?"

"If somebody pays you to perform a task, you should perform it as specified, to the extent of your abilities. It's a matter of honor."

"There's an honorable way to sleep with your granddaughter?" Chaudhari asked.

"His granddaughter? She's his granddaughter?" Roi asked.

"That's what she said," Sergeant Russell said. Vince raised an eyebrow. "No, I mean that literally," Russell said. "I was told that's what she said in the council meeting. She said she was his granddaughter."

"Beastly," Commander Roi said. "There is no end to the man's perversions. Cavorting with his own granddaughter. Beastly."

"I don't think we have exactly the same definition of cavorting," Sergeant Russell said. "But yes, they were definitely cavorting in public."

"Disgusting." Roi frowned again. "But I do find it somewhat strange, that, well." He looked at Sergeant Russell. "Why did he pay her? I mean, distasteful a relationship as it was, why would he pay his own granddaughter? I would think that, if it was some sort of family thing, it wouldn't be so, well, so commercial?" He shook his head again. "And the age difference? What does she see in him?"

The three other men looked at each other again. "Well, Commander," Vince said, "it's just another example of the venality of Mr. Edmunds and his staff, isn't it?"

"And their perfidy," Sergeant Russell said.

"And all that cavorting," Chaudhari said. Roi looked at Chaudhari for a moment, then shook his head.

"Sir," Russell said. "Are we clear on our plan? Stow the missiles here, with the launcher?"

"Yes, Sergeant, I'm going ashore to see that all is well in hand. I'll be back."

They watched him leave. "Chaudhari, if you don't know what a word means, keep your mouth shut."

"You didn't know what it means, either. You used it."

"I'm in charge. Hello, Ms. Nadine."

Nadine had returned from picking up her food. "Hello, boys. Try some of this." She extended a plate of steaming food.

"Looks like tabbo turds," Chaudhari said.

"Tastes like it, too," Nadine said. "How's the plan going?"

"Smooth as a tabbo's butt," Vince said. "Roi thinks you're a prostitute, who is also the admiral's granddaughter, and that you're sleeping with him for money."

"That's nothing new. Everybody already believes that. Wasn't that the point?"

"He thinks it's disgusting."

"Everybody thinks that."

"Oddly enough, he seems to think that, because you're his granddaughter, you should be doing him for free. At least that's what I think he means. That bothers him more than anything, the charging."

"He's upset about the age difference, too," Chaudhari said. "Thinks that the admiral's too old for you."

"If I wasn't his granddaughter," Nadine said. "Never mind the age difference. I'd absolutely sleep with him. I wouldn't charge him, either."

"Really?" Vince asked. "He's forty years older than you."

"But he's so masculine. So virile. He just exudes virility."

"Virility? Really." Vince thought about it for a moment. "Do you think I'm virile?"

"If you have to ask ..." Nadine laughed. "Can we focus on the plan? What's the latest?"

"Well," Sergeant Russell said. "The commander agreed to put the mounting here on this boat. Which means that the missiles will be here as well, in the hold. We'll just mount them on that turret thing, and during the night, we'll arrange for a big wave to hit us and wash them over or the salt water to damage them."

"How do you arrange a wave?"

"Bal says he can do it," Sergeant Russell said.

"Yes, the weather report is for rough seas. If I change the angle of the boat," Bal said, "I can make the same waves appear to hit harder, so it will be believable if the missile gets washed over."

"And without the missile, these posers won't last a minute against Edmunds's regular troops," Russell said. "He cleaned out Landing in a few days, and he took casualties. His boys and girls are rested now, and not well disposed to rebels. They'll cut these chowderheads down in a second."

"Is Roi really stupid enough to believe you when you tell him his best weapon was washed overboard?"

"Stupid and crazy. Shh. Here he comes." Sergeant Russell pointed to the shore. Roi was heading back to the ship. "You decide after we've heard what he has to say how crazy he really is."

Roi advanced up the gangplank. "Sergeant, are you ready to depart?"

Sergeant Russell looked at Balthazar, who shrugged.

"I'll have to talk to my brothers," Balthazar said. "Why so soon?"

"The weather is not looking advantageous," Roi said. "Not dangerous, just rough for novice sailors. Mr. Balthazar, you need to send your brothers to the other boats. We're short on real sailors here, so they'll be the captains of the other two. I've already sent them the rendezvous point off the northern coast. We'll all meet there. I want you and I together. We're the best sailors, and this ship has the most valuable cargo. Together, we'll make sure it's safe. Sergeant Russell?"

"Sir?" Sergeant Russell saluted.

"Split your squad in half and send half to each of the other ships. Send your man, Chaudhari, with the least reliable group." Roi leaned over and lowered his voice. "I hesitate to say this, but some of the other officers are not as ... secure in my leadership as they should be. Even after I pointed out that the great Colonel Savard appointed me. I fear the results if they are left by themselves. I know your troops to be loyal, efficient, and deadly. I can trust them to deal decisively with any attempt to misdirect the other ships from the specified rendezvous."

Sergeant Russell swallowed. "Shouldn't we keep them here to guard the ... valuable cargo, sir? Otherwise it's just me, and what use will I be by myself?"

Roi laughed. "What use will you be by yourself? That's a humorous statement, Sergeant. You are by far the most competent and deadly of the bunch. I've watched you control events around you for months now. Why, you were even able to manipulate me, and the fake officers' council members. What use will you be? Hah. I'd leave you here by yourself if it wasn't for the need of two sets of eyes to watch the potentially disruptive elements." Roi looked at Nadine. "We need to keep a close watch on some people, have them under our eyes. No, Sergeant, you yourself are enough. Balthazar's brothers will sail the other ships. Your troops will secure them and make sure any waverers arrive on time for our glorious battle. You and I will guard our most precious of assets, and we will stride forward to victory." He raised his hands. "The Empire will return! Victory!"

Everybody in earshot raised their hands. "Victory."

"What about me?" Vince asked. "I'm not really a combat type of guy."

"You don't want to be a part of our glorious revolutionary rebirth?" Roi asked.

"I tend to avoid birthings," Vince said. "Pretty messy

events. Lots of shouting. I should stay back here. Deal with supplies. Sort out communications." He turned so that Roi couldn't see him and winked at Russell and Nadine. "Communications are important."

Russell and Nadine nodded.

"Well, it is to be expected," Roi said. "You are only a merchant, after all."

"They also serve who stand and wait," Vince said.

"What?" Roi said.

"He'll be standing by, awaiting our glorious return, sir," Russell said. He and Nadine shook Vince's hand as he departed.

Roi slapped Sergeant Russell on the back. "I'm so glad you're with me on this trip, Sergeant. Knowing that someone as loyal and competent as you is along warms my heart." He smiled. "Captain Balthazar, make preparations to leave at once."

Roi climbed down below. Everybody stared after him, then looked at Sergeant Russell.

"Crazy," Sergeant Russell said.

"Crazy like a fox," Nadine said. "How long has Vince been working for you?"

"I thought he was working for you?" Russell said. "The Militia. The admiral."

"I thought he was working for you, personally, that you had some sort of deal to get him down here."

"I wonder who he's going to communicate with," Russell said.

"Probably whoever has the best wine," Nadine said.

CHAPTER 35

"Standard Imperial shuttle," Daav said. He was looking out the viewport next to the air lock. "I've seen this type before."

"During training?" Jake asked.

"In a museum," Daav said. The group of four had left their Jump ship, taken the nearest stairs to the core, floated down to the shuttle ring, and taken the stairs down. This shuttle was docked at the next spinward lock. A second one was docked right after it, but they hadn't bothered to investigate it yet.

"You can fly it?" Jake asked.

"I can fly anything. I'm the best pilot in the universe," Daav said. "Why, I'll bet you twenty credits that I can go in there, sit down, and I'll have all those controls figured out in ten minutes and be ready to fly us down, no problem."

"Really? I'm impressed," Jake said.

"I'm not," Perlins said. She had a holstered revolver on her belt and carried a loaded boarding shotgun over one shoulder. "It's the same controls as the ones on Delta, isn't it, hotshot?"

"Well, yeah. But I'd have to adjust the screens to my style. That takes time."

Perlins looked at Jake. "All the Imperial shuttles had the same type of controls. Made it easier for training. Once you learned to fly one, you could fly twenty different types. All set up the same. The Imperials were big on standardization."

"Which is why we're here," Jake said. "Standard reactor parts as well."

Daav swung the air lock door open. "There's only room for one in the air lock." He latched on his helmet and put on his gloves. "I'll go on board and make sure all the systems are good. I'll check atmo, then you three can come in."

"Can you turn on the heating?" Odette said, shivering.

"Will do," Daav latched his helmet down, then stepped into the air lock.

Jake's comm bonged. "Jammy, Yvette, did you find that other Jump ship?"

"We did. It's small. The hab module is only three couches. No lounge. There is a small control room, but it only has one station. And that one is locked."

"Can you login to it?" Jake asked.

"If you give me a code, El Supremo."

"It should be captain—never mind. How did you get onboard?"

"Through the air lock. Nothing was locked. We just pulled 'em open."

"Is it attached to the station properly?"

"It's here. It's docked. Magnets engaged. Station power and comm are attached. No fuel lines. Lights and environmental are on. It's much warmer than the station. Nice in here."

"Anything else?"

"It smells of lemon, like our ship."

"So, it smells nice. Anything else important?"

"Well. Sort of. Yvette?"

Yvette's voice came on the board. "A lot of this station has never been used. It's brand new."

"You mean not used recently?" Jake asked.

"No, never used. The other docks, they looked brand new. Shiny. No dents. No scratches. Even on the cargo doors. Nothing. The chains weren't even scratched. Who loads cargo without at least dropping a chain or two?"

Perlins, Odette, and Jake looked. They hadn't paid attention before, but the shuttle dock looked brand new.

Perlins looked up. "All the lights are working. No circuits out."

Odette scuffed her feet on the floor. "No marks or scratches. It does look brand new."

"In fact," Perlins said. "It looks new and clean. Like the people who left were going to come back." She turned to Jake. "I thought you said everybody died."

"That's what I thought," Jake said. "But maybe the log meant they just left."

"So, the station and the Jump ship look like they have been sitting here since they were abandoned during the, er, abandonment," Perlins said.

"Looks that way," Jake said. He keyed his comm. "Jammy, any chance of figuring out why that Jump ship shuttled back here from Delta, or what it was doing in Delta?"

"Have you got a code for me?"

"No."

"Then I don't have any chance, no. We're going to walk the hab module now."

"Fine, we're heading off to the surface soon." The air lock door swung open. "Right now, in fact. Talk later."

"All set," Daav said. "Systems are hot. Reactor is in fine shape. Those Imperials knew how to build 'em."

"Too bad we don't," Jake said.

"Is the heat on?" Odette said.

"Running right now. Should we wait?"

"No," Jake said. "I don't know what's going on back at Delta, but I'm sure it's not good. We don't need to be reckless, but we need to move briskly."

"Good enough," Daav said. "Other pilots would say they need a full orbit to assess the landing, but I can take us straight down."

"I'm sticking with my don't be reckless," Jake said. "We'll make two orbits to assess."

"Two orbits?"

"Measure twice. Land once," Jake said.

***

Two orbits took eighty-seven minutes each. Odette checked the landing area with the sensors, and all she could add to her previous discussion was that there was definitely a village there. It looked abandoned. There were more trees on the hills than expected, possibly pines. Daav said they were spruce. They argued until Perlins pointed out that, since both lived and worked in space, they didn't know anything about trees. She also smacked Daav's head.

Smoke from wildfires obscured most of the view elsewhere on the planet, but there was a truly awesome number of the cows or buffalo or whatever they were.

"Could be millions on the planet," she said.

"How did they get so many?" Perlins asked.

"They let loose some breeding pairs a hundred years ago and haven't controlled them since the abandonment," Jake said. "They reproduce, and here you go."

"Coming up on our landing," Daav said. "According to the computer, but all I see is grass and those cow things. Odette?"

"Look for a river," Odette said. "It should show up straight ahead of you, then you'll see it drop down into a valley. The lake is at the bottom there."

"Got it," Daav said. He flew them between two low hills. The river below widened.

"Those are impressive waterfalls," Perlins said. The water cascaded down the hill side.

"And those are houses," Jake pointed. What looked like buildings appeared occasionally on the hillsides, surrounded by trees. "There, in the trees."

Odette manipulated her board. "Don't show up on the scans. Not enough metal. Are they plastic?"

"Those are wood," Jake said. "Wooden houses. No wonder the scans didn't pick them up. They look like part of the forest."

"Why would they hide them like that?" Perlins said.

"They didn't," Jake said. "We're just not used to this much wood or houses made of wood. We didn't look for them."

"They're not giving off any heat," Odette said.

"Lake coming up. Landing in one minute," Daav said. "Make sure you're belted in."

Jake had a thought. "How—how do we handle the lake? Won't we sink? How do we get to shore? How do we take off again?"

Daav grinned and turned back to Perlins, who winked back. "Didn't think of that, did you, Mr. El Supremo. Should have given it some thought."

"The Emperor's hairy testicles," Jake said. "We're going to be trapped here."

"Take it easy, Mr. El Supremo," she said. "Daav and I have you covered. We talked about it earlier."

"This model shuttle has a planning body and vectored thrusters," Daav said. "When we land, as long as we keep moving, we won't sink. The thrusters can be manipulated to steer us. And we looked at the imagery of the fusion plant. There's a cradle there on rails. We steer for that and hit it right, we'll roll right up onto land. We can turn there and come back when we're ready to launch. Standard Imperial launch-recovery facility."

"Gravity's on the edge for launching, but mass driver should help us out."

"Oh. Thanks," Jake said. He thought for a moment. "Have you ever landed like this before?"

"Sure. In simulations," Daav said. The lake loomed in front of them. "Brace, brace, brace."

They hit the water fast. Everybody was flung forward against their restraints. Steam exploded around them as the heated shuttle skin boiled the water away.

"Whoops. Can't see the cradle," Daav said.

"You marked the direction before you landed, didn't you?" Jake said.

"Of course he did," Perlins said. She turned to Odette

and shook her head.

Daav throttled the engines down, and the apparent motion slowed, but the steam remained. He kept glancing at the monitor, but nothing showed for the next few seconds. Then the steam cleared, and the fusion installation loomed ahead of them. The cradle with the rails was clearly visible. Far, far to their right. In front of them was a rocky beach that would strand them, if not tear out the bottom of the shuttle.

Daav firewalled the left engine, and the shuttle swung hard to the right with the unbalanced thrust. Everyone snapped back into their seats. Then, as they crossed the rail lines, he dampened the left engine, and firewalled the right to correct. They rocked in their seats. The shuttle corrected its path and slammed into the cradle, then skidded onto the beach. Daav cut both engines. Their momentum rode them up onto the cradle. The cradle roared down the rails, up the shingle beach, along a paved forecourt, and through the open doors into a large hangar. The hangar's wall loomed in front. They were slowing down but not fast enough. The hangar filled the entire viewport when they hit the spring at the end. Everybody snapped forward against their restraints, and the shuttle rocked forward for a moment before sliding back and stopping.

"Welcome to 61-Cygni-B-III," Daav said. "Another great landing!"

CHAPTER 36

"Does this look like a cafeteria to you?" Jammy asked.

Yvette looked at all the metal tables surrounding them. "No, it looks like that place you keep the dead bodies. What's that called?"

"A morgue."

"Why have a morgue on a station?"

"To keep the zombies fed?"

"Phfffft," Yvette said. "If this is a morgue, the people who lived here were much taller than us." The room they were in resembled a cafeteria, with a half dozen tables, and some sort of counter at one end. The tables were too long for people and too wide. "And heavier. That looks like a small cargo crane." She pointed up. There was a winch fixed to a rail. "Looks like that winch can lift things off these tables. And those rails run out into the corridor. Probably all the way to the cargo lock. If you have something heavy, you can drag it along those rails, all the way in here, and drop it on these tables."

"A morgue for aliens. Too high to sit at," Jammy said, standing next to one of the tables. "But the right height to work on. If you were cutting brains out."

"Why would you cut brains out?"

"Zombies eat brains," Jammy said. "Everybody knows that."

"You watch too many vids," Yvette said. "But it is strange here. What's that behind the counter?"

"They look like freezers. That's where they keep the fresh corpses," Jammy said.

"Funny," Yvette said.

"You'll see," Jammy said.

"They're too big for corpses. They look more like industrial freezers." She walked to the freezer. "There's a mechanical combination lock. Need a code."

"So, we can't get in. Too bad. Let's look at the rest of the station," Jammy said.

"Not yet. We need to open one of these and see what's in it."

"We don't. We really don't," Jammy said. "This place gives me the creeps. Just let it alone."

"I'm going to see what's in here. Let me try some codes," Yvette said. She fiddled with the lock.

"We have no right doing this. Breaking into people's freezers, that's not civilized. There's no good reason to open that," Jammy said. "Let's just leave. Now."

Yvette looked at him. "We just jumped in here from another star system, flew for days, docked with an apparently abandoned station over a planet that we haven't heard from in eighty years, send an expedition dirtside, and you don't want to open a drawer. After we've come all this way and done all these things?"

Jammy looked around. "Well, if you put it that way."

"I do. One-two-three didn't work. Maybe all ones ..."

"We weren't told explicitly to open fridges."

"Why are you so scared?"

"I just—I don't. I don't know. Something about here gives me the creeps. Why aren't there people? And if they're dead, why aren't there corpses?"

"I don't know."

"What if something ate them?"

Yvette clicked the lock again. "You think space zombies came on board and ate all the people? Where did they go, then?"

"Maybe they weren't space zombies, maybe they were space cannibals, and they are hiding, waiting for us to drop our guard, and they'll catch us and eat us."

"Emperor's testicles. Nobody is eating anybody." She clicked the lock. "Three, three, three. Come over here and see what's in this freezer."

Jammy slid over and looked at her. "I—"

"Don't be scared." She put her hand on the drawer handle. "Ready?"

Jammy nodded.

Yvette pulled the drawer open. Vapor boiled out. "See, it's nothing but—yeeeeeeaaaaah!"

The freezer was full of frozen body parts.

***

"I still say it was a great landing," Daav said. The four of them had climbed out of the shuttle and wandered through the fusion plant. It was much smaller than the plant on Delta. It had only one reactor, and the switching station was tiny. Only a single power cable ran to the houses in the distance. The mass driver wouldn't have lifted a standard size container. It was just big enough for their mini shuttle. It ran straight into the distance for perhaps a kilometer. Rather than curving up into a series of circular tunnels like the Delta one, it was simply attached to the valley wall.

"Lots of smoke." Perlins coughed. "And dust or ash or something in the air. And on everything else." A layer of gray dust covered everything in view.

"It's those fires," Odette coughed as well. "Every one of those high plains burns every few years. The fires are big, and the smoke circles the whole planet. Cools it."

"Do we need filter masks?" Perlins asked.

"Yes," Jake said. "If we had them."

"Where are the people?" Perlins said. "If a shuttle landed on my doorstep, I'd certainly try to find out what was happening."

"We didn't see any," Odette said. "Maybe the fires killed them all."

"Let's move along, then." Perlins found the door to the control room, and they all went in. The control room was a small room with only four control consoles. "And Daav, if, by great landing, you mean we didn't die, then sure, it was a great landing," she said. She hopped on her feet and sprung up. "Gravity is much lower than I expected."

Odette also hopped up and floated back down. "I didn't look it up. This planet was bigger than Delta. I thought the gravity would be higher."

Jake was checking his comm. "Delta is very dense for its size. This planet is ... what's the opposite of dense? Undense? Lighter rock in the core, so its gravity is lower."

"We can have fun then," Daav said. "Whoop!" He jumped, crashed into the ceiling, then fell back down. "The Emperor's hairy anus, that hurt."

Everyone was laughing. "Our great pilot," Perlins said. "Can't figure out how to walk."

"I wasn't walking. I was jumping," Daav said.

"Just as bad," Odette said. "Probably worse."

Jake opened a door on the far side. "Jackpot. Here's the storage room. Wow. Check this out." They all crowded through behind him.

"This is a giant warehouse," Perlins said. "Must be hundreds of boxes here."

"Thousands," Jake said. "It's a standard Imperial colony supply depot. Enough supplies for a colony to replace parts for a fusion reactor for twenty years after it's founded." He coughed again. The air was clearer inside but still smoky enough to affect breathing.

"How come we don't have one of these on Delta?" Perlins asked.

"We did," Jake said. "But the parts were all used up, and the remaining ones were scattered between different corps over the years. The old Imperial warehouse is an apple storage facility now in Landing."

"And how do we know what your man, Dashi, needs?" Perlins said.

"I've got a list. Let me send it to your comms. There are a couple hundred part numbers. I'll give each of us about fifty."

"How do we find them in this pile?"

"Standard locater map, I've included that." He pointed to his comm. "Plus, see that console there?" A console hung on the wall. Jake walked over and typed in a part number. The screen lit up with a row and column indicator, plus a shelf number.

"Shouldn't we explore a bit more? See if we can find any people." Perlins said.

"Nobody on the station," Odette said. "Nobody answering comm calls. No houses with power. No visible settlements."

"This is a settlement," Perlins said.

"An ash-covered settlement with no people. You said yourself they should have come out to see us when we landed like that." She coughed again. "Isn't there a filter system in this plant?"

"I'll check," Jake said. "But given the air and the lack of people and the problems back on Delta, maybe we should get these parts as quick as we can and get out of here."

They piled the parts by the door. The labeling and storage system was so well organized that, in less than two hours, they had the bulk of the boxes piled by the door. Jake kept track on his comm.

"It looks like we'll have about eight cubic meters total," Jake said.

"How much mass?"

"Not even a thousand kilograms for everything, if these specs are to be believed."

"Then we'll cube out before we mass out," Daav said. "We can lift another ton, no problem, but we don't have eight cubic meters of space on that little shuttle."

"How much space do we have?"

"Maybe three? Could be a bit more."

"So, at least two, probably three lifts, then," Jake said. "Can we get one going right now? Everybody, help load up the shuttle, then Daav can lift up to the station. They can cross load to the Jump ship."

"We need a better name than that," Yvette said. "Ships should have names."

"Militia ships didn't," Perlins said. "Just numbers."

"Exactly," Yvette said. "Exactly." She picked up an armful of boxes and pushed through the door.

"I think I've been insulted," Perlins said. "But I'm not sure how." She piled her arms with boxes and followed Yvette out the door.

"Take as many as you can first lift," Jake said. "How long will it take for turnaround?"

"Couple hours," Daav said, loading his arms up. "Now that I don't have to do your double orbits, I can come straight down. It's an easy drop. That station up there is set up to make it easy to hit the surface. I should be back here three hours after takeoff. We have to fuel first. If you can find the beacons and turn them on, that would speed things up even more."

"I'll do that," Jake said. He collected his own pile of boxes and followed Daav out the door. As they crossed the control room, Jake saw the outer door was wide open.

"We need to shut that." Jake coughed. "It's letting that smoke in, and the filter system doesn't seem to be working."

He and Daav nosed through the open outer door. Yvette and Perlins had stopped a few meters past the door. Jake came up behind them. "Listen, we need to keep that door closed, the smoke—"

"We have a problem, El Supremo," Perlins said.

"The smoke—" Jake said.

"Not the smoke, over there." Perlins dropped her boxes, pulled out her revolver, and pointed it into the dust. Her shotgun was leaning against the wall in the warehouse.

Jake blinked. He could see something in the smoke. He blinked again, and it resolved. Five human figures were looming in the smoke, dressed in gray, covered in gray dust. Their faces were blank, like nothing was there. They didn't speak, just stared at the crew.

"I think—" Jake said. Then his comm bonged an emergency signal.

"Zombies!" Jammy's voice screamed.

CHAPTER 37

"I've decided I hate the world ocean," Nadine said, leaning over the rail to puke again.

"Took you long enough," Sergeant Russell said. He was also leaning on the rail, but he'd emptied his stomach over the side hours before. "Didn't you say you'd never get on a boat again?"

"And I hate Roi, the smug Imperial anus," Nadine said. "Look at him over there."

Roi was at the helm, conning the sailboat up over the waves. He was smiling as he gently slid the wheel side to side, bringing it up and over the different waves. He saw the two looking at him. His smile got wider, and he waved.

"That Imperial anus," Nadine said, smiling and waving back. "When do we get to shoot him?"

"We don't have to kill him," Sergeant Russell said. "We just need to wait until it gets dark and then get on deck and dump those rockets overboard."

Another large wave hit them, and the boat shook. "How are we going to get them out of the hold?"

"Just open it, right?" Sergeant Russell said.

"So, shoot him first, then dump the rockets overboard. Or dump the rockets and shoot him. Or shoot him, dump the rockets, and shoot him again," Nadine said. "Lots of choices."

Balthazar came out on deck. He was dressed as they'd never seen him before, in a heavy rain jacket and pants. He had some sort of contraption buckled on over his jacket. "The barometer is dropping like a rock."

"Good for the barometer," Nadine said. "We're discussing whether we're going to shoot Roi just once or twice tonight. Me, think I can get it in one."

"That's not a good idea," Balthazar said.

Nadine nodded. "You're right. Better be safe. Twice it is."

"What's a barometer, and why did you bring it up?" Sergeant Russell asked.

"And that's an interesting fashion accessory you have on there," Nadine said. "What's it for?"

"This is a harness. I can attach a chain here, on this clip."

"Didn't know you went that way, but your sexual proclivities aren't really our problem."

"Proclivities?" Sergeant Russell said.

"Damn you, Jake Stewart," Nadine said. "I'm talking like you now. I don't care what you do for fun, Bal. Good for you and your bondage harness."

"It's a sailing harness, and it's not for fun. It's to keep me from getting washed overboard in the middle of a storm. And a falling barometer means a storm is coming."

"How big a storm? And for how long?" Sergeant Russell asked.

"Depends on the barometer. How big a storm depends on how far down it drops. How long depends on when it stops."

"How far down has it dropped?"

"A lot."

"Has it stopped?"

Balthazar looked up at the flag at the boat's stern, flapping in the wind. "Not yet."

***

Four hours later, the boat was streaming up and down over ten-meter waves. Not only was it bobbing, it was rolling from side to side, causing a rollicking stomach destroying motion. Everybody except Roi and Balthazar had been sick for hours, until finally they had nothing left in their stomachs to retch up. Nadine and Sergeant Russell had wedged themselves into a settee behind a table. Even so, they had to grip the table with both hands to keep from being thrown violently across the cabin.

Balthazar and Roi had spent two hours wrestling with the sails and setting the boat up for heavy weather. The engine was on, but Balthazar and Roi kept the sails up because they stabilized the boat. Neither Nadine nor Sergeant Russell had been able to help. They had problems just keeping on their feet on the heaving boat, never mind trying to perform complex commands on one of the dozens of inexplicable ropes running on the boat. In the dark.

Balthazar had gone below for a nap, and was just returning to the main cabin.

"How can you sleep in this?" Nadine asked.

"Practice," Balthazar said. "I'm going to go up and take over from Roi. He needs a break."

"Can't we slow down or turn around or something?" Nadine asked.

"In this type of weather, it's safest to ride it out by heading into the storm. If we try to turn around, the waves could roll us over or hit us from behind and knock us sideways. Heading into the waves on a manageable course is the safest."

"If you think this is manageable, you're an Imperial anus," Nadine said. "I'm hating this. When do we shoot Roi?"

"You can't," Balthazar said. "Not in this weather."

"I can. I just need to get close," Nadine said. "I'll hold the pistol to his shoulder if I need to."

"It's too dangerous," Balthazar said.

"He'll be fine. Shoulder wounds are debilitating but rarely fatal."

"How do you know that?" Sergeant Russell asked.

"I've shot a shoulder or two in my time," Nadine said. "I'm a pretty versatile girl."

"It's not about versatility or his safety, it's about ours,"

Balthazar said. "This storm is dangerous. If we get pooped, we're in trouble, and Roi and I are the only two sailors on board. I can't control the boat by myself, not for twenty-four hours straight. I need him alive and healthy, helping drive this boat."

Nadine frowned but nodded. "Fine, but as soon as the weather moderates, I'm shooting him."

"Wonder if he will have something to say about that?" Russell asked.

"Say about what?" The cabin door opened, and a drenched Commander Roi appeared. "It's dirty weather out there. What were you talking about?"

"We wondered if you had anything to say about this storm, sir," Sergeant Russell said.

"I've been in worse," Roi said. "But you'll have to clip in when you go up top, Mr. Balthazar. Please go up soon. We can't leave the autopilot on long in this weather." Roi extended a line with a carbineer on the end. "I'm going down for some sleep. Wake me when my watch starts in four hours. Goodnight." Roi went below. He had to hold onto furniture and railings to make any headway.

"I'm going up to drive," Balthazar said. He clipped the carbineer to the metal ring on his harness. "Give him about an hour, then come up and do your thing. It will be dark by then."

"Free Trades Captain," Nadine said. She gave him a mock salute.

"On a sailboat, the correct phrase is 'fair winds and following seas' if you want to wish somebody well," Balthazar said.

"That, too," Nadine said.

Balthazar made sure his clip was in, then opened the hatch and climbed out. Salty water showered in until he closed it.

Nadine pulled her ponytail in front and squeezed the water out of it. "What's a following sea?" she asked.

Sergeant Russell wiped his face. "Dunno. What does

pooped mean?"

***

An hour later, Nadine opened the hatch and tried to climb out. The boat's motion had eased somewhat, but the water still crashed in.

"The Empress's hairy vagina," she said.

"Get out there, and let's get this done," Sergeant Russell said. "Before he notices us."

"Nobody will be able to see or hear anything in this weather." She was right. The wind howled through the rigging, the sails smacked as they flapped, and the water slapped the hull. She crawled out into the boat's rear cockpit.

Balthazar was sitting at the elevated helm station, watching the instruments and maneuvering the boat up and down the waves. He leaned down and handed her the end of a rope, then stuck his mouth next to her ear. "Tie this around your waist. You'll need it if you slip."

"I won't slip." She had to yell over the noise.

"Tie it anyway," Balthazar yelled. Nadine cursed at him quietly and tied the rope in a loose knot. Sergeant Russell followed, tying his own knot on a second rope Balthazar gave him.

The two of them stepped to the edge of the enclosed cockpit and climbed up on the exposed right side, the side the sailors called the starboard side.

Nadine was rocked back on her heels. The wind was a physical force, and the strength of it pushed her back. The boat was not moving as much as before, but its bobbing motion required her to use both hands on the railing. A sudden jag sideways tripped her to her knees, and she cursed as both kneecaps exploded with pain when she slammed into the deck. She yelled but held on, then flopped down onto her belly and crawled forward on the deck. The missiles were in the front hold, only four meters away, but opening the hatch was going to be a problem.

324

Sergeant Russell watched her crawl forward, then leaned to shout into Balthazar's ear. "How dangerous is this?"

Balthazar yelled back. "Don't get washed overboard. I'll never find you in this."

Sergeant Russell looked at Nadine, who was sprawled on the deck ahead of him. "That girl has an amazing ass."

"The next wave might flip this boat over, and you're looking at her ass? Not the time."

"Always time for a great ass," Sergeant Russell said. He followed Nadine's example and got down on his belly and low crawled behind her. Nadine managed to get level with the hatch, but it was in the center of the heaving deck, and she was hanging on to the side.

Sergeant Russell pulled up beside her. "Well?"

Nadine pointed at the hatch cover in the middle of the boat. "How do we get there?"

"Slide," Russell said. He waited 'til just after a roll and slid downhill across the deck. He spun like a drunken man on a frozen pond, but managed to snag the hatch cover handle as he went by. He held there, grasping the cover with both hands.

Nadine watched him swing, held only by his hands, his feet loose behind him. He was having some difficulty with the hatch. She waited 'til the boat surged in an approximately correct direction, then launched herself forward. But instead of sliding toward the hatch, she found herself spinning in place as the boat rotated under her, then sliding feet-first across the deck. She tried to rotate backward, and got her head up just in time to see her feet smack into Sergeant Russell's face. His mouth opened, but she didn't hear him yell. The waves were too loud. She continued to slide by him, but he grabbed her as she went by.

"Grab the edge here," he said.

Nadine grasped the raised edge of the hatch cover.

"What now?" Nadine asked.

"Slide around to the opposite side. I'm going to grab that handle on this side, turn it, and when I do that, you lever that hatch up and open on the other side."

"Not with your rope across it you won't," Nadine said. She pointed. Sergeant Russell's rope was stretched taut over the hatch, which held it down.

"The Emperor's hairy anus," he said. "I'll have to untie it." He reached down and pulled the knot loose. "Once it's loose, we can pull the hatch open." The rope came free, and he thrust it aside. "Ready?"

Nadine nodded, and Sergeant Russell climbed up on the far side of the hatch. She braced one hand on the edge of the hatch cover and put the other under it. Sergeant Russell slid forward, reached up with his hand, and pulled on the handle. He wasn't making any headway, so he reached over and used both to twist the handle. It spun grudgingly, and as soon as she felt a bit of give, she strained with one hand to push the hatch up. It was heavy and only lifted three inches.

"More, higher," Sergeant Rusell yelled.

Nadine rolled on her side, let go of the hatch coaming, rolled on her back, and used both hands to push the hatch up. Her arms strained, and she got it about a foot off the deck when the wind caught it, and the hatch snapped open, up, and over to slam open. Sergeant Russell was caught by surprise and propelled backward, slamming into the railing, just missing getting squashed by the hatch.

"Are you okay?" Nadine yelled. He looked at her, then above her, and his eyes widened. He pointed over her shoulder and then turned away and grasped the rail with both hands.

Nadine turned. The biggest wave she had ever seen was about to bear down on their tiny boat.

CHAPTER 38

"Stay back," Perlins yelled. She waved her revolver at the zombies advancing through the smoke toward them. "I'll shoot, I'll shoot." She backed away.

"Jammy, what do you mean, zombies?" Jake said over the comm.

"The freezers up here are full of frozen body parts," Jammy said. "It's got to be zombies."

"Zombies? Space zombies," Jake said. "Frozen body parts? That makes no sense."

"Stay away. What do you want?" Perlins waved her revolver at the figures in the dust. "Stay back."

"What are these?" Odette said. She dropped her boxes. "Where did they come from? Why didn't we see them? They didn't show up on sensors."

"Undead don't show up on sensors," Daav said. "They must be real, live zombies."

"Isn't that a contradiction in terms?" Jake said. "Live zombies. Aren't they supposed to be dead?"

"Undead. Real undead. Don't you watch the vids?"

"Not the same one you do, apparently," Jake said.

The crowd of zombies walked toward them. "Wooo RRRReuuu." The lead figure said. "Wooo RRReeuee."

"Shoot them Perlins, shoot them," Daav said.

"Don't shoot anybody," Jake said. "We don't know what's going on."

"They're zombies, shoot them."

"I thought zombies can't be hurt."

Jake's comm crackled. "Are the zombies there? Are you okay?" Jammy said.

"Cut off their heads. Keep them back," Daav shouted.

"Shoot, Perlins. Shoot. Shoot."

"Veeevo, veeevo," the lead zombie said. It stepped forward. They didn't have a nose or mouth, but their eyes glowed red in the dim light. "Wooo RRReuuu."

Perlins stopped retreating, pointed the revolver at the nearest zombie's feet, and fired. BANG. The shot kicked up a cloud of dust. The zombies checked, stared down, then turned as one and ran away. "Whahaaa." They all screamed as they dove behind the shuttle.

The zombies disappeared into the dust. Perlins looked at Jake. Jake shrugged. "That was easy," Perlins said.

"You saved us, Boss lady," Daav said.

"Saved us from what? Why did they all run away?" Odette asked.

The dust swirled for a moment and then cleared a little. A head poked up from behind the shuttle. "In the Emperor's name, what is wrong with you people? Why are you shooting at us?" a voice said.

The four crew members looked at each other. "I beg your pardon?" Jake yelled.

"Why are you shooting at us?"

"We're, uh, we didn't know who you are. Who are you?" Jake asked.

"We live here."

"You live here."

"Yes. On the ranches. Here."

"You're ... Cygnians?"

"We prefer Cygnites but sure. Who are you? Are you from the Empire?"

"Kind of," Jake said. "You live here? Why didn't you answer your comms?"

"There haven't been any ships here for fifty years. Not since the last one of ours left. Why bother to keep a radio watch?"

"There's nobody on the orbital station?"

"Of course not. Why live up there? No food. All the cattle are down here. And the last shuttle crew left with the last Jump ship, anyway."

"Your ship? You have a Jump ship."

"Had. But you didn't say who you are. Can we come out now? Are you going to shoot again?"

Perlins holstered her revolver. "Sorry," she said. "About the shooting. Sorry. We were confused."

A bald-headed, brown-skinned man came out from behind the shuttle. He was carrying a helmet partially wrapped in a cloth. "You sure you're not going to shoot me?"

"No, no. Sorry."

"So, you're from the Empire? Why did you abandon us?"

"We didn't. I mean, we aren't," Jake said. "Wait. Okay. We're from Sigma Draconis, the neighboring star system. We were abandoned as well." Jake explained about the abandonment, the lack of ships, finding the Jump ship, and the loss of industry. While he was talking, the group of Cygnites crowded around him. When they took off their helmets, Jake could see all their faces clearly. They had dark complexions, and several of the men were bald. Everyone was much shorter than Jake. Some stood slightly crooked. Everyone listened attentively.

"That's kind of a weird story," the man said. "I'm Derbi, by the way."

"I'm Jake." He introduced the rest.

"So, you're here to pick up parts for your reactor?" Derbi said. "How did you know the parts you needed would be here?"

"My boss knew you had a warehouse here, and he had an inventory list."

"How did he get that? From another system?"

"I don't know. He just sent me coordinates, a list, and instructions on what to do."

"Interesting. Well, regardless of what your boss says, this is stealing. These parts belong to us. To this planet anyway."

"Yes. We didn't know anybody was here. We didn't mean to steal them. We're sorry about that. We'll buy them."

"Buy them with what?"

"I have some banking drafts ..." Jake said.

"For another system, that we can't get to. Not much use here."

"Maybe trade," Jake said.

"Trade? What would you trade?" Derbi asked.

"I don't know," Jake said. "Food?"

Derbi shook his head. "We got plenty of food. In case you haven't noticed, there are millions of cattle here. That's why we took so long to get back here. We were moving a herd to a different pasture. One with less smoke cover. The smoke makes it harder for the cattle to find the grass they like. What else you got?"

"Surely, you don't just eat cattle. You must have other foods, vegetables or suchlike."

"The grass on the grassland is totally edible. Makes a great salad. It's a kind of wheat. We can grind it up and make bread if we want. It grows wild, so we don't even need to farm it. The tree leaves are edible. The berries are edible. There are bushes we can pick. Most of the trees are edible as well."

"Really?" Jake said. "Is everything that grows here edible?"

"Pretty much," Derbi said. "This planet was an Imperial agricultural research center. Developing different types of food crops. Staff at the research center made all these tasty types of grasses and bushes and the trees. We even made these really nutritious types of potatoes. Almost a meal in themselves."

"Superpotatoes?" Jake asked.

"That's what they're called, yeah," Derbi said. "They grow wild here. How have you heard of them?"

"We grow 'em on Delta," Jake said.

"And why were you shooting at us? You didn't say?"

"Well, the people up on the station—oh," Jake said. "Sorry, I cut them off. Gotta turn my comm back on." He fiddled with it.

Shutt must have been waiting for him to come back online because she called him right away, using the ship override code. "Jake? Are you okay?"

"We're fine. Are Jammy and Yvette there?"

"They came back with some crazy story about zombies."

"Yes. We met the zombies. Very friendly people," Jake said.

"Friendly zombies? Wait one.'" Shutt cut the connection for a moment, then came back. "I can't believe I'm saying this, but they are asking if there are cannibals there."

"Zombies? Cannibals? You think we're zombie cannibals?" Derbi said.

"Our other crew found something on the station. They said they found freezers full of frozen body parts."

"Sure they did," Derbi said.

"I didn't think it was true," Jake said.

"Oh, it's true," Derbi said. He smiled. "There are freezes and freezers full of body parts."

Jake looked sideways at Derbi, then pressed his comm. "Major Shutt, did they find freezers full of body parts?"

"Yes, they did. They're pretty freaked out about it."

Derbi laughed. "You thought we were cannibal zombies?"

"Well, we heard about the body parts, and we saw those blank-faced red eyes—" Jake said.

The crowd laughed harder. One of them flipped something down over her face. Jake realized it was a mask of some sort. She fiddled with it—it was a modified skin suit helmet, pitted gray with dust. She turned a knob, and the face turned opaque.

"Those are air filters," Derbi said.

"We saw red eyes," Daav said.

The women tilted her head sideways so that it caught the light of the suns. The reflected light created two pinpoints, like glowing red eyes. "We see em all the time," Derbi said. "We're used to them."

"Okay, you're clearly not zombies," Jake said. "But what about the freezers of body parts?"

"That's us. We did that back when we had a crew on the station, before they left. We packed those freezers full. Did any of your crew try them out?"

"Try them out?" Major Shutt said over the comm.

Jake realized he had left the channel open. "What do you mean?"

"You know, fry them up," Derbi said. "I like fresh meat myself, but the frozen stuff's good enough if that's all you can get. Cut up some ribs, or something like that. They're not half bad."

Major Shutt's voice choked with emotion. "You are sick. Sick and twisted. You should all be killed."

Derbi furrowed his brow. "Sick? Killed? Are you one of those vegetarian types?"

"Vegetarian?" Jake asked.

"Or those vegans?"

"What does being from Vega have to do with eating?" Jake asked.

"I get it, you have an opinion," Derbi said. "But I mean, we're a ranching planet. We've got millions of cows. I understand some people don't eat meat. But we're overrun with cows here. Eating them is our thing."

"You eat cows?" Jake said. "Wait, what's in the freezers again?"

"Beefsteaks," Derbi said. "Why? What did you think it was?"

CHAPTER 39

"I can't believe you thought we were zombies," Derbi said. "And cannibals. We're just ranchers." The two groups had retreated back into the fusion plant and closed the doors.

"The dust, the masks, the whole thing," Jake said.

"Even so. You Deltoids are weird." Derbi gave him a big grin. It reminded Jake of somebody.

"Deltoids?"

"You call your planet Delta, don't you?"

"Moon but yes."

"So, Deltoids."

"We prefer ... I don't know what we prefer," Jake said. "The topic has never come up. Can you get the air filters to work in here?"

"Nope. They broke long ago."

"How do you breathe in this dust?"

"First, we have personal filters. Second, we're not stupid enough to stay in the dust. The dust comes with the wind. We just stay out of the wind. And avoid the places where it's strongest. This is the bad fire season here, but it'll end soon."

"None of you have ever been off planet," Jake said.

"We've been off planet," Derbi said. "Some of us. We try to send a crew up to the station every year or so. I don't know who does it anymore. Since old man Murphy died a few years back, his family was supposed to take care of it. He was the last real shuttle pilot. He taught his kids a bit."

"Wow. And how many of you are there? On the planet, I mean?"

"Couple thousand," Derbi said. "Spread across the whole continent. There's plenty of ranches, but we're pretty far apart. We move a lot."

"You just ranch? Don't you want to go to space?"

"There's no reason to go. After the Empire left, only a couple hundred people stayed here. Our grandparents and great grandparents mostly. They were all scientists, at the Imperial research station. My grandparents were biologists. Everybody just decamped to the surface and continued their experiments."

"It must have been very traumatic," Jake said.

"Not according to them. They got to keep doing their experiments. We had plenty of food—they were all wildlife people and plant people, so they knew how to grow food. Everybody loved camping out and building houses out of wood. After ten years, they figured that something bad had happened to the Empire, and they weren't coming back. They didn't really care. Do you know what happened to the Empire?"

"No idea," Jake said. "Ships stopped coming about eighty years ago. We still don't know why. The ship we were on now came about fifty years ago, but it hid. We only discovered it a few months back."

"We had three ships left after the Empire was gone. One waited a year and left, with everybody who wanted to leave. Never heard from again. And after that, everybody who was here, wanted to be here. Well, almost. After a few dozen years, one group who wanted to see what happened to the Empire loaded up with a couple of families, their kids, and left. That was about fifty years ago. They didn't come back."

"Then, the only thing that was left was the courier ship?" Jake asked.

"What's a courier ship?" Derbi asked.

"Small ship. Room for like three people?"

"You mean the message probe? The automated message ship. It's back?" Derbi turned to his group. They nodded and talked among themselves. "Guess the automatic beacon didn't trigger down here."

"Message probe," Jake said. "One of those ships that just took messages and jumped back and forth."

"That's the one. It went away years ago with the second group. It was supposed to come back with messages about the state of the Empire. It never did."

"So, you've been isolated for fifty years?" Jake asked. "No contact with the Empire?"

"Nothing 'til you came. Why did you come here?"

"We followed the probe. It was hiding in the rings around Delta, powered down. It had been there for years."

"I wonder why it came now?"

Jake nodded slowly. "It was me. I did it."

"You started the probe up?"

"No. I ... discovered another Jump ship in Delta and boarded it. I was first on board, and I was playing with the systems. One of them I remember was called 'Message Handshake.' I remember looking at it and turning it on. The Jump ship must have handshaked with your probe ship, send it some sort of updates or something. The probe program probably decided since it had new messages and set a course to jump here and broadcast the new messages."

"That's neat. So, you sent it."

"I guess so," Jake said. "Have you ever seen the probe ship?"

"I've never even been to the station."

"How old are you?"

"Sixty-seven."

"You don't look it."

"You mean I look a lot older?"

Jake looked him over. "Well, kind of."

"Honest outdoor living. Lots of exercise. Working the plains. It can be hard sometimes. Maybe it ages us differently, compared to you space people."

"You're all kind of short," Jake said. "Is that a genetic

thing?"

"Genetics. The kids are tall, but we shrink quite a bit as we age. We have bone issues as we get older."

Jake contemplated that. "Don't you miss the Empire and, well, technology?"

"Never knew the Empire. And we have enough technology. We have personal comms and databases and stuff. The kids all take the same schooling my grandparents have. You can go all the way up to being a professor. The lectures are in the computer and the tests. Really, to live here all you need is an ax and a saw to build a house. You can eat the grass. You don't even need to hunt the cattle. Enough of them die by falling down into ravines. You get all the fresh meat you can eat. There's more trees than we'll ever use."

"Sounds like paradise," Jake said. "I'd love to see it."

"Come out to the ranch with us." He gestured to the group. "Too much smoke in the valley here, anyway. Can you ride a horse?"

"What's a horse?" Jake asked.

"That's a no, I guess." Derbi grinned again, still reminding Jake of somebody.

"I grew up on a space station," Jake said. "I don't think I ever saw a horse."

"You'd know if you'd seen one," Derbi said. "They're pretty distinctive." He surveyed the pile of boxes that Jake and his group had collected. "Busy little thieves, weren't you?"

"We didn't know you were here."

"Could have asked."

"We did. Sent messages on all the comm bands, repeatedly. Checked out the orbital station pretty thoroughly before we came down. Scanned for you. The scanner couldn't tell the difference between people and cattle."

"Not very good sensors if you can't tell people from cattle. You can't just take this stuff."

"We need it badly. There are thousands of people depending on us getting it back."

"Thousands of your people. Not of ours."

Jake stood and faced him. "You're not using it."

"We might in the future. Either way, it belongs to us."

"Are you trying to stop us?" Perlins asked. She had retrieved her shotgun and cradled it.

"Going to shoot us if we don't give it to you?" Derbi asked.

"Don't want to," Perlins said. "Could, though."

A Cygnian coughed in the background. "Derbi, can we have this discussion somewhere where there is less smoke? It's killing my throat."

"Here," Daav said. He extended a canteen he wore on his belt. "Have some of this."

The woman nodded her thanks and took a drink.

"Put your shotgun away, Perlins," Jake said. "We're not stealing anything. We'll trade. There must be something you need. Technology? Solar panels? Tools?"

"We have a warehouse full of stuff here." Derbi said. "In case you haven't noticed. Oh, wait, you were robbing it, so you had noticed."

"As I said before," Jake said. "We thought it was abandoned—"

"Derbi," the drinking woman said. "Taste this."

"Hey," Daav said. "That's not for everybody." The woman ignored him and handed it to Derbi. He sniffed the canteen, then took a quick swig. He smacked his lips and took a longer drink.

"You're welcome," Daav said. He extended his hand. "Could have asked."

"This is space drink," Derbi said. "Sugar. Citrus. Are there vitamins in it?"

"Vitamins and minerals," Jake said. "Everything a person needs for a healthy life. Daily amounts of everything. We call it basic."

"Iron?"

"Lots of iron," Jake said. He looked at the crowd. "Calcium, too. Lots of calcium. Calcium is good for bones."

"Where did you get it?" Derbi asked.

"We make it on Delta. There's a factory, makes it from plants, some salts. Minerals. Some of it is mined, like copper and iron. That's just micro amounts. And they evaporate saltwater to get potassium and some other salts. I don't remember which ones, but it's a complete package."

"Make it as a drink?"

"No, it comes as a powder. You just mix it in with water, and you're ready to go."

"How much do you have with you?" Derbi asked.

Jake looked at the pile of boxes, all the spare parts he needed. "How much do you need?" Jake asked.

***

The deal was easy to conclude after that. Derbi and his people had been dealing with ongoing vitamin and mineral deficiencies for years. Their scientist parents knew what minerals they were short of and had formulated diets to deal with that, but they had ongoing seasonal shortages of trace elements. Jake showed them the ingredients of basic and offered to trade all he was carrying, except for a small amount for the return trip, for all the parts they needed as a onetime deal.

"It's more in the way of a swap," Derbi said. "Not a trade. It's a lot easier for you to make basic than it is for us to get reactor parts, but we're interested in generating some goodwill to start with."

"Aren't you worried we'll come back and attack and take over or something?" Jake asked.

"With what? What does your ship hold? Maybe thirty people at a time? We've got thousands here. And now that we know you exist, we'll put somebody back on the orbital station and do a sensor watch. They're still manuals available, and some of the old folks know how to do it. And why would you do that? Come back and steal some cattle? There's millions here. Next time, come back and trade for them. We'll fill your ship up with cattle parts. Then you'll be the zombies." Derbi laughed.

Jake smiled at that. "Our pilots watched too many old vids."

"I have to go look those up," Derbi said. "The school comms have old vids. I can go watch some of them."

"Do you want to come back with us?" Jake asked.

"Nope. Somebody might eventually, but fifty years ago, there was a big discussion, and all the families that wanted to leave left, and the rest stayed. Maybe it's genetic or something, but most of us here are pretty happy. Would you leave your station and live here?"

Jake didn't have to think about that. "Nope. I like being on stations. In space. Planets are nice to visit, but they get tiresome after a while."

"What do you get tired of?" Derbi asked.

Jake thought for a moment. "The smells. There are so many, and so different. I'm always confused by how things smell."

"I never would have thought that," Derbi said.

"Me neither," Jake said. "Not 'til you asked me."

"You should be able to start your lifts soon. You sure you don't want to stay and see some horses?"

"Next time," Jake said. "It's important that we get these supplies back."

"Well, your people can come visit. We're all in the same Empire, now that you're back here."

"We're still isolated in Delta," Jake said.

"Seems like you're back to exploring," Derbi said. "So, you'll figure out what happened to the Empire before we do."

"True," Jake said. "My boss is pretty interested in reconnecting to the rest of the Empire."

"Your boss, what was his name again?" Derbi asked.

"Dashi," Jake said. "I call him Mr. Dashi, but he's really Emperor Dashi III."

"Is Dashi a common name where you come from?" Derbi asked.

"Nope."

"Any chance he's named after his father?"

"I never asked," Jake said. "Why?"

"Wondering. What did his dad do?"

"Don't know," Jake said. "He did say something about his dad had a ranch or grew up on a ranch or something." Jake looked closely at Derbi. Brown-skinned, bald head. Big smile.

"Well, tell him I said hello."

"You know Dashi? You've met him before?" Jake said.

"Course not. Nobody has left this system for like fifty years. I'm just being friendly."

"Right. True," Jake said. "Thanks."

"And," Derbi said. "I think he might be my cousin."

***

Jake had to sit at that point. Derbi presented him with a convoluted family tree, dating back a hundred years, dealing with the families that had stayed behind, their relationships to each other, and their relationships with each other.

"So, he's really the Emperor?" Jake asked.

"I don't know about that," Derbi said. "But his grandfather was an Imperial Duke, patron of the research station here. Before I was born, of course. Word was he wasn't the standard Imperial aristocrat. A bit shy, quiet, liked plants. They sent him and his family out here to keep him safe, so he didn't get mixed up with politics. When the abandonment happened, he was trapped here with his family. He was a botanist, so he was happy staying and breeding grasses. A lot of his family and friends came out. That's part of the reason why nobody really wanted to leave. They were all sick of the politics, but after thirty years, some of the family wanted to see what happened."

"Wow, that's quite a story."

"Yeah, I figure they didn't mind being 'trapped' here, away from whatever was the drama."

"But if he's the Emperor," Jake said. "Then, aren't you a duke or something?"

"I'm his third cousin twice removed," Derbi said. "He has other relatives here, but not close ones. Immediate family went with his grandad when they left. I'm not really anybody."

"But you're sure he's the Emperor?" Jake asked.

"If the dozen or so people ahead of him died during whatever happened to cause the abandonment, then congratulations." Derbi slapped Jake's shoulder. "You're the personal assistant to the legitimate Emperor of the known galaxy!"

CHAPTER 40

"How many are going to starve?" Admiral Edmunds asked the meeting. Dashi, Jose, Mariane and two of her Legionnaires, the admiral and his aides, and the two non-aligned members were having a board meeting of the Delta Corporation. Or perhaps an Imperial Council meeting, since Dashi, aka Emperor Dashi III, was present. They weren't quite sure.

"That is a complicated question," Jose said. He had returned with the monorail to Launch West as the small launch site was being called. "There is no immediate danger of starving or freezing, not dirtside. Orbit is another story."

"Can we bring everybody down?"

"Our shuttle, lifting bodies, can take a couple dozen at a time, and we can only do one lift a day, at best."

"We should be able to do more than one lift a day," Edmunds said. "The other shuttles could handle several."

"The other shuttles are giant mass lifting bodies. This one isn't. And fuel is the biggest problem," Jose said. He shot his cuffs. He had taken to wearing elaborate dress shirts over his skin suit. "We have a cracker here, but it's limited in how much it can make. It takes about thirty hours to do a full tank for launch."

"There's storage tanks of fuel at Landing," Admiral Edmunds said. "Big storage tanks. Full storage tanks."

"Yes, at Landing. Not here. How do we get it here? The monorail is for passenger, containers, and anything we can put on a flatcar. Other than ships and shuttles, everything we have is electric. I'm not sure there is a single hydrogen-powered vehicle on this moon, so we have no storage or transfer infrastructure."

"Can we move the shuttle to Landing?"

"That won't help. We can land it there, perhaps. Once. It won't fit on the mass driver, even if it was operating, and we'll have problems launching it on the river there. This bay is unique."

"So, you're letting them starve?" Admiral Edmunds said.

"I'm doing no such thing, Admiral," Jose said. "We're filling the shuttle with as much food as we can cram in, given weight and volume restrictions. And we're looking at taking non-essential personnel dirtside."

"How many?"

Jose hesitated. "Right now, we only dock at TGI Main, so we've been quietly taking families with young children down. But we'll run out soon enough. There are children everywhere in the rings. If we start asking them to meet us at the shuttle dock, there will be questions. And possibly riots. Probably riots."

"Who else knows how bad the situation is?" one of the unaligned reps asked.

"It's very closely held," Jose said. "Just this group here, and some key staff on TGI Main. And whoever you have told."

"Nobody," Marianne said. "But we will have to make a general announcement soon."

"Does it have to be general?" Admiral Edmunds asked. "Can't we keep it to a select few? Higher ranks."

"We're Free Traders," Marianne said. "We don't have ranks."

"Emperor's testicles," Admiral Edmunds said. "How do you get anything done on those ships?"

"People will figure it out," one of the Admiral's aides said.

"Eventually," Jose said. "But we got the lights back on in Landing like we said we would. We've gained a bit of a respite with that. Dunlop has said publicly he needs time to recondition the mass driver power system before it starts up. He's doing that now."

"Will it help?" Marianne asked.

"Absolutely not. It's just make work 'til we can find spare parts."

"What's the update on that?" Admiral Edmunds asked.

Jose turned to Dashi. "Sir?"

Dashi steepled his hands. "This delay is unfortunate but not critical. Before he jumped, I gave Mr. Stewart a preliminary list of spare parts that might be needed for the repairs here. The parts we need were on that list. He should have arrived at the ... facility that contains those parts by now. Once he loads up and comes back, we will have what we need."

"How long?"

"Even at best speed, he won't be back for at least ten more days. And he will need some time to load up and maneuver his ship at the far end. My estimate is that he will return in seventeen days."

"We have only twenty-one days of food up there, if I understand this youngster here correctly," the admiral said. "Did you people plan nothing?"

"I'm one of the planetary executives, Admiral," Jose said. "I deserve my titles. Tribune, or at very least, Mr."

"Well, excuse me, youngster, but I don't think arguing about titles is a good use of our time right now with people starving."

"But you do think criticizing the people who are trying to fix things is a good use of our time?"

"If I was in charge, this never would have happened."

"You were in charge during the revolt. And this is exactly what happened. I remind you that the Militia armed the gangs that destroyed the power system to start with."

"And all your orbital people are eating TGI food," the unaligned member muttered.

The admiral raised a finger and pointed it at Jose. Then dropped it. "Emperor's testicles. Never mind. What do we do?"

"Keep our mouths shut," Jose said.

"Yes, best if we keep our own counsel," Dashi said. "Mr. Stewart will be back with the replacement items we need. He has been reliable in the past. I see no reason he will not be in the current crisis."

"I have to tell the Free Traders," Marianne said. "They deserve to know. To make plans."

"What plans will they make?" Jose asked. "We're already distributing all the food we have up there, and whatever we can launch over the next few weeks won't make that much of a difference. All they can do is steal food from somebody else. If there's fighting ..."

"We know how much food is contained in the orbital stores," Dashi said. "It will feed everyone for perhaps three weeks, and people will start starving after that if we can't get bulk food deliveries restarted. We've already cut rations back by two-thirds, and we have problems as it is."

Dashi spun his chair to look at the picture of Landing on the well. "If we show any lack of confidence in our plans, there will be panic. If there is panic, people will die. Many people. Stations will be wrecked. More stations will be wrecked, I should say. This will occur even if Mr. Stewart arrives with our replacement components, and we restart food deliveries."

He swung back to face the group. "If Mr. Stewart does not arrive in time, or we have other problems restarting deliveries, then it will not matter what we have said up to that point. So, from a purely theoretical perspective, our least cost option is to insist that we will have food deliveries restarted in seventeen days from now, when Mr. Stewart arrives with components. If he does not, he does not."

"What is this place that he is getting the parts from?" Admiral Edmunds asked. "How did you know about it?"

"What if the parts aren't there?" Marianne said.

"What if something delays his return?" the unaligned

rep asked.

Dashi stood. "You might as well ask what if a herd of feral buffalos races into town and crushes us all under hoof. We can influence that as much as we can deal with those other questions. The die is cast. The plans are made. We feed all our people until we cannot. We have plans to fix our infrastructure if we receive what we need. If we do not receive, we cannot fix. This meeting is concluded. In the meantime, we must remain calm and perform the most difficult task that a leader must perform."

"What's that, sir?" Jose said.

"We must not lose our nerve," Dashi said.

CHAPTER 41

The wave rushing down on them blanketed the storm. The wind roar dropped five-fold, and the sails flapped. The wave was higher than the deck, higher than the cabin, and looked to be higher than the mast.

That's not possible, Nadine thought. The mast is twenty meters high.

Possible or not, the boat kept rising.

"Hang on," Balthazar yelled in the quiet. "I'm going to try to take her on the bows." The boat spun right, and the bows dug into the wave as it rose.

The boat lifted as the water surged underneath. This wave was a different color—green, not the gray-blue of the others. The wind roared as they rushed up. The sails snapped full as the mast rose above the crest, pushing the boat over on its side. The lean increased as the sails took the wind's force. The engine revved as Balthazar struggled to keep the boat pointed directly into the wave. Then they lifted higher, and the wind roared and pulsated.

The wave drove the boat to the left, presenting the broadside to the wave. Nadine didn't know much about boats, but she knew that was a bad sign. They were nearly at the crest when the top of the wave foamed over the bow. The boat tilted, and her grip slackened. Then the wave roiled over her and ripped her hands free from the hatch. She flailed down the deck, rolling over and over in the water. The water rushed past her and smashed Sergeant Russell free. It pushed them across the deck and into the metal lifelines on the lee side. Nadine continued rolling. Sergeant Russell smacked into the lifelines and held for an instant. Nadine looked up as she slid across the deck and saw the tail of the wave hit Balthazar in the face. He fell back with his arms flailing.

The wind increased as the boat topped out, and the extra strain of the lean caused the lifeline to snap.

Sergeant Russell fell feet-first into the water, and Nadine slid right after him. She felt herself drop on top of him, headfirst. Her body kept diving, but suddenly, she was jerked to a stop as her lifeline tautened. Sergeant Russell had been tangled with her, and he reached and grasped the loop around her waist with both hands and held on.

Nadine surfed under the water, then popped up and took a big breath of air. The boat was rolling heavily, and the sails were flapping. The motor still raced, but the boat didn't appear under control. She was dragging alongside, flapping in the waves.

"Hang on," Sergeant Russell screamed.

"Thanks for the great advice, professor boat," Nadine yelled back. A figure appeared above.

"Roi," Nadine yelled. "Get us out of here." A wave hit her in the face, and she spat salt.

Roi grasped the rail and peered down at them. He looked forward, then up, then away, then disappeared from view.

"You coward," Nadine yelled. "Help us out." But he was gone.

"Try to climb up," Sergeant Russell said. "Use both hands and pull us forward."

Nadine pulled on the taut lifeline. She strained as much as she could, but the pressure of the boat's speed kept her from moving at all.

"Nothing. I need your hands."

"My hands are all that's keeping me from being pulled back."

"You need to pull forward."

"I can't swim. I don't dare move them."

"I'm not strong enough to pull both of us."

"I'll let go."

"Don't. Not yet. We just need to get closer to the boat."

The boat did something, and the sail at the foresail snapped taut. The pressure change caused the sailboat to turn right, back into the wind, and Nadine and Russell slid sideways in the water, banging into the hull. Russell cursed as his shoulder hit.

"Get us up on deck," he yelled.

Nadine reached up, but the boat wasn't leaning toward them, more away. It seemed higher, too. She reached up as high as she could.

"Too high," she yelled. Sergeant Russell reached down and grabbed her butt.

"The Empress's vagina. Now is not the time, you pervert."

Sergeant Russell gripped her. He set his other hand on the rope, and she felt herself propelled up. "Get the rail. Try again." She managed to get one hand, then two, over the rail with his hand holding hers.

"Now roll on deck and pull us out," he yelled.

Nadine kicked and pulled herself up. She managed to get to shoulder-height when the foresail suddenly flapped, and the boat rolled. She held on as the boat swung to the left, then the foresail filled and cracked again, and the boat swung harder left, throwing her back into the water.

"That Imperial anus, Roi," Nadine said. "Shooting's too good for him. I'll cut him into pieces with my knives."

The boat swung even farther to the left, and they drifted away.

"I'll hold him for you," Sergeant Russell said.

"You're still grabbing my butt," Nadine said.

"I've always wanted to die holding a nice piece of ass," Sergeant Russell said.

"Worse ways to die," Nadine said.

***

Sergeant Russell was trying to decide if he should still hang on or just give up, when the boat tipped, and the boom that held the mainsail swung out over them, the sail rippling. The boat swung to the right again, but the motion had changed. The foresail was full of wind, driving the boat, but the mainsail just flapped. The roar of the engine faded. The boat's motion dropped completely. They floated next to a stationary boat. The wind roar had dropped as well.

Roi reappeared at the rail. He threw a long line at them. It slapped the water in front of Nadine and floated down. Two lifejackets kept it on the water's surface. "There's a loop in it. Put that around you, and I'll pull you in," he yelled.

"That wuss can't pull us in," Sergeant Russell said.

"Put the loop over your head. You can pull yourself in," Nadine said.

Sergeant Russell put the loop over his head and flailed toward the boat. The line tightened, towing Russell toward the side of the boat, much more rapidly than he could have pulled himself, never mind swim.

Roi appeared at the side and thrust a portable ladder over the edge. It attached to the side with hooks and two ropes. Roi leaned down and lashed the ladder to the boat. He waited 'til Sergeant Russell grabbed the ladder, then disappeared. The line slackened, then pulled taut as it pulled Russell in slowly. The line tightened 'til it was painful across his shoulders, but he was dragged into and up the side of the boat. When he got a foot on the ladder, he scrambled up and rolled onto the deck.

He rolled over onto his back. Roi was visible at the stern, working on something. That's a winch, Sergeant Russell thought. It pulls the sails up and down. Roi had disconnected the sail from the winch and replaced it with the lifeline rope. He had been using the mechanical advantage to drag Russell into the boat.

Roi stopped the winch. "Get that line off you. We need

to get it to Ms. Nadine," he said.

Sergeant Russell saw that Balthazar was sprawled on the deck in the cockpit, behind the wheel. "What happened to him."

"Did we take a rogue wave?"

"What?"

"A big wave. Did a big wave rush over the boat?"

"Yes. A big wave. What's wrong with Bal?"

"Knocked out. A wave must have knocked him off the helm. He was dragging along in the water at the end of his harness when I came up. I had to get him first. You two were conscious. You could keep your heads up."

"Is he okay?"

"He has a pulse and is breathing. More than that, I don't know. Get this line to Ms. Nadine. I need to adjust the sails so we don't crash gybe."

Sergeant Russell didn't know what a crash gybe was, but it sounded bad. He collected the looped rope in his hands and flung it out to Nadine. He tangled the life jackets with the rail, and it went only part way. He tried again, and this time got the whole line in the water but behind Nadine. She yelled something uncomplimentary at him.

Roi stepped up next to him. "Like this," he said. He picked up the rope and coiled it in his left hand. Then he grabbed the end with the life jacket in his right hand, made a few exploratory swings, then tossed it forward. The life jacket smacked beyond Nadine, and the rope draped directly over her head. Roi pulled the rope in until Nadine had it over her head. He then slid back to the winch and ratcheted her in.

Sergeant Russell waited 'til she slid into the boat and reached down to pull her in. She came up to the deck but got stuck getting over the rail. Sergeant Russell gave her a heave, making sure to grab her butt as she went by.

Nadine rolled onto the deck and pulled the rope over her head. She stepped over to Sergeant Russell and slapped him.

"I just hauled you in," he said.

"That's for grabbing my butt there."

"I needed to. I had to get you on board."

"Not the second time." She stepped forward, threw her arms around him, and gave him a big sloppy kiss on the mouth.

"What's that for?"

"That's for grabbing my butt the first time. You almost saved me."

"So, can I grab it or not?"

"Keep guessing," Nadine said. She looked over at Roi and Balthazar. "What's up with Bally?"

"Got knocked out. Let me get a medical kit." He dove below.

***

An hour later, Nadine and Sergeant Russell were back in the cabin. They tied Balthazar to his bunk and drank hot tea. They had barfed it and copious quantities of salt water up the first two times, but Roi insisted they keep drinking the hot, sweet liquid until they weren't so pale. Roi was up, fussing with the sails again.

"Is he going to be okay?" Nadine asked.

"He's not dead," Russell said. "I can't do anything else without a hospital, a diagnostic machine, and an awake patient."

"Some doctor you are," Nadine said.

"His ankle is swelling, so that's hurt. Other than that, I got nothing." Russell wrapped him tighter in blankets to keep him warm. "Let's go up to the cabin."

They went back to the ladder. "Why is there a hatch here? Aren't we under water?" Nadine pointed at a hatch protected by a metal locking bar on the hull. "That's a stupid place."

"Ask Roi," Russell said, climbing the ladder.

"And get another hour-long lecture on sailing terms?

No thanks," Nadine said. "No thanks."

They returned to the saloon and sat on the settee. "I have never been this tired, ever," Sergeant Russell said. "I'm cold, wet, and I'm bruised all over. I don't think I can move."

"Did you enjoy grabbing my butt?" Nadine asked.

"Very much so," Sergeant Russell agreed.

"You didn't ask permission," Nadine said.

"Didn't seem appropriate at the time."

"Next time, ask permission."

"Will there be a next time?"

Nadine smiled. "Won't know until you ask, will you?"

Roi opened the hatch and came in, accompanied by the expected saltwater shower. He was carrying a coil of knotted rope, possibly the one that he had used to rescue them. He dropped the coil on the salon table and sat.

"The wind is dropping but not very fast. The swell remains. The barometer is rising again, so the storm is passing. It will be some hours before we can continue on our journey."

"As you say, sir," Sergeant Russell said.

"Sergeant, I must thank you for your bravery. And your dedication to the cause. You are a true servant of the Empire."

"I am, sir? I mean, yes, I am, sir," Sergeant Russell said. He darted a glance at Nadine. She shrugged.

Sergeant Russell faced Roi. "How, uh, how did we serve the Empire this time, sir?"

Roi opened his jacket and produced a clasp knife. Sergeant Russell sat up straighter. He'd never seen Roi with a knife. Roi snapped one side open and extended a blunt spike. The spike was at least six inches long and came to a rounded point. It was mostly smooth but sharp enough to wound deeply if plunged into a person.

"The missiles," Roi said.

"Of course, the missiles," Sergeant Russell said.

"Yes, that's why you were out on deck, the two of

you."

Nadine pulled her ponytail forward and slowly squeezed the water out of it. "Two of us what?"

"Both of you. On the foredeck, I saw you there, after the wave hit, with the hatch open."

Nadine shook her hair out and turned sideways to squeeze it some more. Sergeant Russell saw her use the motion to cover dropping her left hand to her thigh, where she kept her knives.

"You did, sir?" Sergeant Russell said.

"Yes. What did you think you were going to accomplish there?" Roi asked. He reached down onto the deck.

"Well, we, I can explain, sir," Sergeant Russell said.

Commander Roi brandished the spike at Sergeant Russell. "No you can't. You can't explain. You should be ashamed of yourself."

Nadine twitched, and her left hand came up under the table. Roi saw the twitch and turned to her, brandishing the knife again. "And you. You should be ashamed as well. What were the two of you thinking?"

Sergeant Russell was trapped behind the table, so he dropped his hands and did what he normally did when he wanted to start a bar fight, which was flipping the table onto his assailant.

Except he wasn't in a bar—he was on a boat, and the table was welded to the floor.

"We did what we had to do," Nadine said. Her hand was under the table, but her eyes darted to Sergeant Russell. They were at a severe disadvantage, pinned behind the table, tired and freezing from their time in the water. Roi was free to move and had one weapon visible, with access to more.

"You didn't have to. You had a choice," Roi said. "You could have chosen not to."

Sergeant Russell saw Nadine stretch backward. He'd bet she could throw those knives, but she needed to get her hand behind her shoulder to get any distance.

"I don't think we had a choice," Nadine said.

"And yet, there you were, Ms. Nadine. You don't even believe in our cause. You think the Empire is not coming back.

"I did what I had to do," Nadine said.

"Me, too, sir," Sergeant Russell said. "I didn't think I had a choice, either."

Roi shook his head, pulled his spike back, and rubbed something off the end. "I will say it was very brave. Brave for both of you. In those seas, as inexperienced sailors, you had no idea what you were getting into when you went on the foredeck."

"I'd have done it even if I knew how risky it was," Sergeant Russell said.

"Me, too," Nadine said.

"Brave and foolhardy," Roi said. He rolled the spike in his hands. "Both of you. Why didn't you ask for my help?"

Sergeant Russell was nonplussed. "Your help, sir? With the missiles?"

"Yes. With the missiles. I would have helped. In fact, I would have done a better job than you would have."

Sergeant Russell looked at Nadine. She shrugged. "Sir, you think you would have done a better job than us."

"Of course. I know how to fix a hatch."

"Fix a hatch?" Sergeant Russell asked.

"Of course. When I heard that wave hit, I knew exactly what had happened."

Sergeant Russell pursed his lips. "You knew what had happened, sir? From below? Really."

"Of course I did. I'm an experienced seaman. I understand these things."

Nadine spoke. "What did you think or hear, happened?"

"Why, I heard the waves break the hatch open. Nothing against Balthazar and his preparations, it happens to the best of us in heavy weather. The storm blew the

Andrew Moriarty

hatch open, and the salt water was getting into the hold. It was brave of you to go on the deck, to try to secure the hatch. But you shouldn't have done so. You lack the experience."

"The hatch, sir? Experience."

"Oh, I don't blame you. You were brave, but as soon as I heard the noises, I knew that the hatch was open and water was getting in. I could feel the change in the motion of the boat. That's why I raced up top, to help secure things. I didn't expect to see you both there on the deck ahead of me." Roi pulled the coil of rope toward him and stabbed the spike into it. Nadine and Sergeant Russell jumped at the sudden motion. Sergeant Russell pushed on the table again, forgetting it was attached.

Roi continued. "Oh, I should have secured the hatch first, but when I saw that you two brave souls had already tried, and been washed overboard, I just had to save you. I knew it was wrong. I should have saved the weapons first, but I couldn't do it. You were so brave. So gallant." Tears welled in Roi's eyes. "With dedicated troops like you, we cannot but triumph. I am so proud to be serving with the likes of you, Sergeant Russell. Why, I would give you a medal if I could. And your friend, too." He pulled the spike free, pointed it at Nadine, then stabbed the rope coil again. Nadine didn't flinch this time, but Sergeant Russell winced.

"No need for a medal, sir. Just doing my duty."

"Nevertheless, Sergeant, if I can, I will see that you get your just reward."

"Justice can wait, sir."

"Indeed, but again, I am proud to be serving with the likes of you." Roi cocked his head. "I think the wind is moderating. I will go on deck and check. I need to see if the missiles were damaged." He stood, closed his knife, and pocketed it.

"That's quite a knife there," Sergeant Russell said.

"A knife? Oh, it's not a knife." Roi clicked it open

356

again. "It's called a marlin spike. It's used to loosen knots in ropes so they can be removed." He stabbed down and rocked the knife. Sergeant Russell saw that the blunt point was pushed into a knot. Roi worked his hand, and the knot loosened up.

"It's for working on ropes?" Nadine asked. She shifted a bit, and Sergeant Russell figured she had holstered her throwing knife.

"Yes. All sailors have one. Why?" Roi looked at Nadine. "What did you think it was for?"

CHAPTER 42

"Why are we carrying boxes around the station again?" Daav asked as he walked up the stairs from the shuttle ring to the core.

"Because our brilliant leaders couldn't get the cranes working properly," Jammy said.

"Or the self-described world's greatest pilot couldn't figure out how to dock a shuttle at a ship docking bay," Yvette said.

"They're totally different sizes," Daav protested. "Different shapes, different magnets. Besides, the pilot isn't responsible for docking maneuvers."

"Free Traders could have done it. Or we would have had things set up differently up here."

The original plan had been to dock the shuttle next to the Jump ship. But the shuttle was so small and the Jump ships so big they couldn't use the same docking mechanism. Next plan had been to collect the boxes on a pallet and use the cranes to swing the pallet around the ring to the stairs, load it on an elevator to the core through a cargo access tunnel, then back down another elevator.

Jake had traded almost all the basic on the ship for the three shuttle loads of parts. The remaining station crew had managed to get half of the promised bags of basic to the shuttle dock and unload the parts. Daav had brought up one of the Cygnites who thought she could get the cranes started because "her mother used to talk about it years ago." Her optimism proved false, and they were left carting bags and boxes in both directions on long, circuitous routes across the station. The Cygnite had returned to the surface to consult further with an elderly uncle.

They had taken a break to conduct a ceremony of life for Corporal Dalon. It was short, since nobody really knew him. Shutt read the Militia spaceborne burial service, and his companions had heaved him out an air lock door. Yvette told them what direction to throw him, and their tracking indicated he'd deorbit and burn up in 61 Cygni's atmo within a month.

Bringing the boxes through the shuttle ring and up through the core was easy. The gravity started out heavy and got lighter as they climbed into the transfer tubes. Coming back downstairs to the Jump ship was harder. The increasing weight caught everyone by surprise at least once. After Jammy dropped a box of indicator lights onto Odette's head, they waited their turn on the stairs.

Jake had appointed Perlins in charge of inventory. She stayed on the ship and checked the boxes in and the basic out.

Jake was puffing when he arrived at the lock. He proffered the box at Perlins. "Electronic Solenoids."

"Type 4645, it says here." Perlins read from her comm and entered them in the inventory. "Are we done?"

"We might need a final lift," Jake said. "There are two boxes down there we couldn't fit in. But they might be duplicates. Did you already get two boxes of 9973-4451? They're big but don't mass much. I'm sure that I saw something like them come onboard before."

Perlins looked at her comm and examined her screen. "I didn't check them in."

"Need to go down again, then," Jake said. "We need to move smartly. My calculations for making orbit said we've only got a few windows. With all these extra suns and moons, the calculations are complicated. If we don't get off at the next launch window, we'll have to wait five shifts."

"Well, move along, then. I found two extra bags of basic here," Perlins said. "Small ones. It's more than we promised, but as a gesture of good will, I think we could send them down with this trip."

"Good idea," Jake said. "I'll take 'em back." He frowned as Krikweigh came out of the ship carrying one of the bags. He nodded at Jake as he swept by with a bag.

"What's he doing out here?" Jake said. "He looks terrible. He must have lost sixty pounds."

"More than sixty. He wanted to help."

"How can he even stand?"

"Stimulants."

"He should be in bed."

"He doesn't want to die in bed. And he's going to die. Merced gave him super strong drugs. He's feeling no pain. And he doesn't puke anymore."

"His stomach is getting better?" Jake asked.

"Nope. He hasn't eaten anything in days. Here's your bag," Perlins said.

"Thanks," Jake said. "Another one to carry over."

"Soon as you and Krikweigh get that basic loaded, Daav can drop. I'll tell him to hustle."

Jake turned and trudged back to the stairs. He passed Jammy, Daav, and Yvette coming the other way.

Yvette checked her box in, turned, and trudged back toward the stairs. Jammy and Daav dropped their boxes. Perlins held her comm but watched Odette.

"Wait," she whispered. Jammy and Daav stood, panting. She gestured to them to come closer and stood quietly 'til Odette disappeared.

"Where are those two boxes I told you to hide?" she asked.

"The two big ones? Next bay over," Daav said.

"Get 'em and bring 'em. Now. Fast."

"What's going—" Jammy said.

"Shut up. Get them now."

"Yes, boss lady," Jammy said.

Perlins made a show of closely inspecting the two boxes in front of her before checking them in. She picked one up and walked into the Jump ship, carried it to the main lounge area, and dropped it off. Jake had asked her to put all the boxes in the main area so that they could triple-check before storing them in a container for dropping.

Shutt climbed up from below. "More?"

"More," Perlins agreed. "Still some coming."

Shutt scanned the boxes with her own scanner, checked her list, and carried them down the central corridor. She'd been loading them in their transit container as they arrived.

Perlins stepped over to the lounge and pulled a sip of basic. She waited 'til Shutt disappeared down the ladder, drained the basic, then raced to her cabin. She picked up two large bags labeled basic-50kg, threw both over her shoulder, and ran back to the air lock.

Jammy and Daav were each pushing a large box back to the ship. "Here they are. Big but not heavy," Jammy said.

Perlins dumped the two bags of basic in front of them. "Take these."

"More basic?" Daav asked.

"Extra clothes, your tool belts, any personal stuff I found in your rooms. Some food. Comms and entertainment cubes."

"What do we need this for?"

"Jake, Yvette and Odette are going back there to pick up the last of the boxes. Carry these over like they go on the shuttle. Once they're out of sight, you two and Krikweigh drop that shuttle with the three of you and the rest of the basic. I've undercounted the basic, so this won't show up. Get down to the surface. Tell 'em you're staying. Offer the extra basic for them to help you out."

"You want us to desert?" Daav asked.

"We're mutinous rebels. What's a little deserting going to do for us?"

"We've got a good gig here, sort of."

"Think, Daav. That Shutt lady is polishing her knives.

She's regular Militia, and she wants us out an air lock without a suit. Right now, she listens to him, but that ends when we get back to Delta. What do you think her admiral will say about us being rebel officers? The only question will be can we all be spaced in one go, or does she have to use two different locks."

Jammy looked around. "I don't want to be a farmer."

"Rancher," Perlins said. "They have cows."

"Same thing. I don't want to be on some undeveloped planet forever."

"You'd rather be a frozen corpse that gets smushed by passing Free Trader ships? Cause that's what you'll be if you stay. Besides, these Cygnites won't care about our problems. And now that there will be trade with Delta, they'll need you. They can't get even cranes or elevators working, and by the four-and twenty testicles of the Emperor's advisory council, they surely don't know how to pilot a shuttle."

"I thought the Imperial Council was mixed gender," Daav said. "That would mean that the number of testicles—"

"Shut up, Daav. Jammy, you and he are trained pilots, up on all the navigation systems here and also talented engineers."

"Actually, we're lousy engineers," Daav said. "But—"

"Shut up, Daav. Lie."

"What about Krikweigh?" Jammy said.

"He said he didn't want to die on a ship. He started dirtside. He's dying, and he just wants a planet under him for a day. And don't worry about Merced. He's not in trouble. He was actually kidnapped, and he'll get off free. These days, even the admiral won't mess with a trained medic."

"What about you?" Jammy asked. "You coming along?"

"Yes," Perlins said. "But not right away. I'll cover for you 'til you launch, then I'll run over and take the other shuttle. I'll be there in a few hours."

Jammy gave her a hard look. "Really?"

Perlins's eyes flickered to Daav for a moment, then back to Jammy. She put her hand on his shoulder. "Shut up, Jammy."

Jammy stared in her eyes and stepped back. He braced and saluted. "As you say, boss lady."

"I don't think—" Daav began.

Jammy grabbed Daav and dragged him away. "Shut up, Daav. Thinking only ever got you in trouble."

***

Unlike most of her plans that past year, everything went as it should for Perlins. She stayed in the control room to monitor the shuttle launch. Daav called her over the comm and said he was ready to drop and pick up the last two boxes and deliver the bags of basic dirtside.

"You have all your cargo? Everything?"

"All my assigned cargo," Daav agreed.

"Drop when ready," Perlins said. She waited to confirm he was dropping from the onboard sensors, then went back to the lounge.

Jake, Yvette, Odette, and Shutt were there, eating trays. "Shuttles on the way down," Perlins said. She looked at the food. "None of you tried to fry up a frozen beefsteak?"

"Seemed a little ... something," Jake said.

"Creepy," Yvette said. "I know that they're not zombies, but it is kind of odd. I don't entirely trust them."

"And we also don't know how to cook," Odette said.

"We're on a bit of a schedule," Jake said. "When will Daav be able to lift with the last two boxes?"

Shutt looked up. "What last two boxes? We've got everything on your list."

"I thought we were waiting for two large boxes," Jake said. "According to Perlins." Shutt shook her head, then checked her comm to double-check her inventory. Jake checked his inventory list, a duplicate of Perlins.

"I show everything here now," Jake said.

"Me, too," Shutt said. She looked at Jake. "So, why did Daav drop, then, if we have everything?"

"Give them a couple extra boxes of basic we found," Perlins said.

"Where's Jammy? And Krikweigh."

"Krikweigh shouldn't be out there," Yvette said. "He is not looking well."

Perlins shrugged. "His choice. He wanted off the ship." The silence stretched for a moment.

Shutt stood and drew her holstered revolver. She pointed it at Perlins. "They're all on the shuttle, aren't they?"

Perlins nodded. "Jammy and Daav are staying. So is Krikweigh, but in his case, it's definitely permanent."

"Give me your revolver, grip-first."

Perlins didn't try to fight it. She picked the revolver up from her holster with two fingers, twirled it, and handed it butt-first to Shutt. Shutt kept the revolver pointed at her. "What did you steal? What parts are we missing?"

"Nothing, and nothing. They took their clothes and comms. That's it. And we loaded everything on El Supremo Jake's list. If it's not on this ship, it's his fault."

"Hands up," Shutt said.

"Why bother? I'm not going to do anything."

"I should shoot you right now," Shutt said.

Jake used his spoon to scrape some super potatoes out of his tray. "Did Merced know?"

"I didn't tell him," Perlins said, "and neither did the guys, but he probably figured it out."

"He didn't say anything about it," Jake said. "He's in his cabin right now, I think."

"You never asked. And if it's just a suspicion, why should he bring it up?"

"How were you going to get away?" Jake asked.

"I told them I was going to take the other shuttle,"

Perlins said.

"You're good enough to land an unfamiliar shuttle?" Jake asked.

"No."

"Is it even serviceable?"

"Don't know. No fuel in it, so I couldn't test it."

"Thought so," Jake said. "You had no intention of going down, did you?"

"The boys got away. They've got basic, and skills, and they've got a whole planet to hide on now."

"We need to go after them," Shutt said. "I can take the other shuttle down and go after them."

"No time," Jake said. "We've got a launch window in a few hours. Next one is several days. We can't afford the delay now that we have what Dashi needs. What Delta needs."

"We can't just let them escape without any consequences," Shutt said.

Jake licked his spoon and pointed it at Perlins. "They'll want to trade with Delta, the Cygnians, now that we have a way, and we know each other exists," Jake said. "What if the admiral says delivering them is a requirement of starting trade?"

"He won't," Perlins said, "Or you and your Dashi won't let him. They're not worth bothering with. They're too far away, and they won't be coming back."

"True. I'll say I exiled them. That will make it official."

"Exile? Can you do that?" Perlins asked.

"I'm the captain," Jake said. "We make it an exile, saying we needed their skills to lift the goods and that they refused to help unless we left them behind. Make it official, then there's no blowback." He looked at Shutt. "And certain majors won't be censured for letting people escape. Because there was no escape."

Perlins looked at him. "You knew, didn't you?"

"Will they answer a comm call from you?"

"Yes. If it's me."

"Tell them that the rest of their skin suits, gear, and the stuff I confiscated is in the shuttle's locker. I swapped some stuff out earlier."

"Thanks."

"I kept all weapons, and their armored inserts. The ones Krikweigh had. They're left with just simple skin suits."

"I don't think they'll mind or care."

"Me neither," Jake said. He got up. "Yvette, can you and Odette drop us, please? There's a course set in the boards. Let me know when we're running to the jump limit. I've got a jump to plan." He looked at Shutt. "You might as well put that pistol away and go watch the boards in engineering."

"What happens to me?" Perlins asked.

"Consider yourself under arrest for disobeying a direct order, stealing basic, and… spitting on the deck," Jake said.

"Anything else?"

"Go lock yourself in your cabin, I guess," Jake said. He looked around. "But first, do you mind cleaning up the lounge? Everybody else is going to be busy for a while."

CHAPTER 43

Yvette and Odette waited 'til Shutt was busy checking the fusion plant before capturing the ship. Yvette went down to the engineering spaces and slid in behind Shutt. She drew her revolver and banged the barrel against the bulkhead to attract attention.

"Hands up," Yvette said, when Shutt turned.

"I don't think so," Shutt said. She reached for her own revolver. Yvette didn't let her finish. She aimed at Shutt's arm. Shutt folded onto the floor as the frangible hit her shoulder.

"Imperial anus, that hurts," she said. She tried to reach her revolver with her off hand, but Yvette reached out and collected it, then stepped back and held up a set of cuffs.

"Back to your stateroom," Yvette said. "It will hurt less if you can use at least one hand. I'll leave you uncuffed if you agree no funny business."

Shutt glared at her, then nodded. Yvette tapped a button on her comm. "Allez."

***

Odette pushed the button to open Jake's cube and stepped in, brandishing a pistol. Jake turned from his screen, swallowed, lifted his chest, and closed his eyes.

"What are you doing?" Odette said after a moment.

Jake opened one eye. "Aren't you going to shoot me?"

"Do I need to?"

"No, but every time I meet a pretty girl, she ends up shooting me."

"You should have taken my other offer. That would have been more fun than shooting."

"Where were you when I was single?"

"Shooting my cheating boyfriends."

Jake nodded. "That actually makes sense. Is this the long-delayed hijacking?"

"Long-delayed?"

"I expected it earlier. Before we got to the planet."

"Sorry we didn't work to your schedule."

"That's okay. I can compensate," Jake said. "I built some flexibility into my planning." He turned back to his screen and kept typing.

Odette watched him for a moment. "Aren't you going to complain or threaten, or something?"

"You've both got guns, and you have the drop on me. What should I do?"

"Aren't you going to threaten us with army girl?"

"She's Militia," Jake said. "Besides, you would have captured her first. You would have thought her the more dangerous."

"Thought her the more dangerous? She is more dangerous."

Jake shrugged. "If you're not going to shoot me, can you just lock the door on the way out? I've got work to do."

He didn't look up as his door hissed shut.

***

Perlins was on watch at the front console. She turned to see what the commotion was. Yvette and Odette had arrived, bringing Shutt. Shutt's wrists were cuffed in front of her, and she had a black eye.

"I thought you weren't going to cuff her if she cooperated," Odette said.

"I didn't. Then she didn't. So, I shot her again and cuffed her."

"And beat her up?"

"She tripped over a door jamb, and with both arms stunned, couldn't break her fall."

"You broke both my arms," Shutt said.

"No, she didn't," Yvette said. "But it's going to hurt a lot." Yvette looked at Perlins. "Air lock, or work with us?"

"Work," Perlins said. "I can stand a watch, and I'm a fair pilot, as you know."

"Any issues, and we'll space you," Yvette said.

"Got it," Perlins said. She tapped her intercom. "Merced?"

"Yes?" Merced's voice said.

"There is some fallout from the boys staying behind. Fallout with guns. I think you should stay in your cabin for a while."

"How long is a while?"

"Till we're back on Delta."

"Good. Enjoy cleaning the galley, I hated that. If you need a medic, you know where to find me. Call me when this is sorted out." The intercom clicked off.

"Coward,' Shutt said.

"You wanted to space me, too," Perlins said. "They're at least giving me the choice."

"And what do you think is going to happen when we get back to Delta?" Shutt asked.

"I'm going to disappear into the Free Trader work force on one of their ships. And you're going to be let free."

"They're going to space me," Shutt said.

Perlins turned to Yvette. "Are you?"

"She would do the same to us," Yvette said.

"That's going to make the admiral angry," Perlins said. "He won't let it go."

"We don't care about the admiral."

"It's going to make El Supremo captain Stewart there upset, too."

"We can handle Jake Stewart."

"And he's going to talk to his boss, the Mr. Dashi. The one who has come out on top of this rebellion. You think you can handle him, too?"

Odette looked at Yvette, and they rattled away in Francais.

"Which air lock?" Shutt said. "I can walk."

"Your cube," Odette said. "Try not to fall again."

***

"It's not a hijacking, exactly," Jake said. He and Major Shutt were locked in their cubes, but they could still use the intercom, and Jake had shown her how to use the internal cameras. Yvette and Odette had left them there while they were aft working on the engineering settings.

"Looks like it to me," Major Shutt said.

"All they did was search us and our quarters for weapons and confiscate them."

"That's not a hijacking?"

"No, in a hijacking, they storm the bridge. There are shots fired, you're tied up, then locked up. They turn the power off to your room, chain you to a bed, electronically lock your door. Or weld it shut. Or just put you in a part of the ship without an air lock and clamp the hatch down or jam the air lock and the hatch mechanically, or—"

"That's a lot of details relating to taking over a ship," Shutt said.

"I've lots of experience in being put in jail. People point guns at me and threaten me a lot. Usually, it's Nadine, though."

"Ms. Bimbo has locked you up?"

"Locked me up. Tied me up. Shot me. More than once."

"She shot you?" Major Shutt asked. "I thought she was your girlfriend."

"She was angry because I'd stolen a lot of money from her. But it's okay," Jake said. "After she shot me, I shot her back. Then locked her up in a jail cell for a few weeks in a pirate base. But that was before she stole my ship, though."

"You shot each other, lock each other in jail cells, and

steal ships from each other. This is your relationship?" Shutt asked.

"We're still in the honeymoon phase," Jake said. "We still do nice things for each other." Jake sniffed. "What is that smell? The Free Traders must have turned it on. The whole ship smells of it. It's invigorating."

"She's a very attractive girl," Major Shutt said. "Very active. Assertive." Jake heard her sniff. "Citrus?"

"Assertive is putting it mildly," Jake said. "Is that what an orange smells like? I've never had one."

"Could be an orange," Shutt agreed. "Never had one, either. Ms. Bimbo is very assertive. But, you're—"

"Thorough? Methodical? Responsible?" Jake said.

"Shy. Diffident. A wimp."

Jake grimaced. "I'm not a wimp."

"The way you talk, the way you act. Your lack of aggression."

"That's not what you were saying in my cabin a while back."

"As you suspected, that was somewhat of a ploy. I don't think you're really boyfriend material. Or captain material."

"And yet," Jake said. "Here I stand, captain of the first Jump ship in this system in eighty years. A Jump ship that I found, boarded, restarted, and brought into dock. Appointed by the planetary executive, who may be the Emperor waiting, approved by the head of the Militia, and even our Free Trader thugs here are letting me do my thing. Perhaps your characterization is incorrect."

"My characterization is incorrect? Who talks like that?"

"Sorry, I was rereading some messages from Dashi. Whenever I do that, I lapse into Dashi speak."

"Well, your characterizations aren't helping with these thugs."

"We're not thugs," Yvette said over the intercom. "More like concerned citizens. And we can hear you."

"So concerned they have guns," Shutt said. "Which

matches the thug category, doesn't it?"

"You know, Jake Stewart makes sense. If we are to have a real hijacking, we should be locking you up. We can handcuff you to your bed if you want, soldier girl."

"Militia."

"Soldier."

"Not the same."

"Is that a yes to handcuffing you, then?"

"Never mind," Shutt said. "Say, why haven't the two of you handcuffed Jake as well? He's not on your side."

"Jake Stewart is on his side," Yvette said. "We've had experience with him before. He's never violent, but somehow, he always manipulates us into doing what he wants."

"I don't believe that," Major Shutt said.

"Whether you do what he asks or not, somehow, you always end up giving him the thing he needs. He always wins. Best to just follow his lead."

"Are you saying that you hijacking this ship is all part of Jake's plan, not yours?"

"Yes. He will have some sort of contingency that involves the hijacking. We will do all the work hijacking and manipulating things, and probably fighting people and get shot, then Jake will come back and fix things."

"You can't believe that?" Major Shutt said.

"Let's find out," Yvette said. "Jake, what happens now?"

"After this burn, we have to cycle for a half orbit, then fire again. That will take an entire shift. We're moving up to higher orbits in stages. "

"What will you do next?"

"After the burn?" Jake thought for a moment. "I think I'll take a nap."

"What if we have a problem with the Jump drive?" Yvette said.

"Sorry." Jake said. "Prisoners and captives of hijackings don't take watches or fix problems. We're only doing things under duress. In fact, just call me if there is a problem with the burn. I'm going to lay down now. Don't forget to lock me into my room."

***

Jake slept only a half shift. He spent the rest of the time reading more system manuals. There were a number of systems he was still confused about, and he wanted to make sure he understood everything.

Odette's voice came over the intercom. "Jake Stewart, come up here."

"I can't," Jake said.

"Why not? You too busy to help us working people?"

"Isn't this supposed to be a hijacking?"

"Come up here, or it will go poorly for you."

"You locked me in, remember?" Jake said.

Odette cursed, and two minutes later, his door slid open. "D'accord. No more locking. Come to the Jump control room."

Jake pulled himself up to the Jump control room, using grab bars. They weren't under thrust, just coasting along their orbit. When he arrived, the Free Trader women were occupying two consoles. Perlins was nowhere in evidence.

"Where's Perlins?" Jake asked. "You didn't space her, did you?"

"Sleeping. She watches a board for a shift to spell us."

"What do you want?"

"We can't get the Jump computer to work," Yvette said.

"Not surprising," Jake said. "Took me a long time to figure it out."

"Show us."

"Give me your guns. Let Perlins out."

"No."

"Okay," Jake said. "I'm going back to bed, then."

"All those people on Delta will die, and it will be your fault."

"No, I'm the one bringing the parts back. You're the one stopping me. It will be your fault."

"Your friends will die."

"And yours. Your families. Still your fault."

Yvette and Odette fumed and glared at Jake. He shrugged, then tried it again in a different way. "I need to learn that Francais shrug. It's harder than it looks." He tried to shrug again but couldn't do it. "You thought you could just reverse my course, like with a regular nav computer, didn't you?" Jake said.

Yvette nodded. "It's much more complicated than we imagined."

"I'm good with complicated things." Jake waited. "Anything else?"

"Shutt stays locked up."

"No," Jake said. "We need her."

"Need me for what?" Shutt appeared behind them.

"How did you get out?" Yvette asked.

"My door was open."

Yvette turned to Jake. "Same controls for all of them," Jake said. "Opening mine opened hers. Yvette and Odette can't make the Jump computer work."

"So, we're stuck here?"

"No, I can get us back."

Everyone waited. Finally, Yvette reached under her shirt and produced a revolver. Odette did the same.

Jake took them both and put them on the console in front of him. "And?"

Yvette scowled but pulled a smaller pink revolver out of her boot. Jake took that as well. He collected the three revolvers and handed them to Shutt.

Yvette and Odette sucked their breath in. Shutt smiled and gingerly slid them into her belt, then pointed the largest one at the Free Traders.

"How's your arms?" Jake asked.

"Good enough to hold a revolver and shoot them," Shutt said.

"Just keep an eye on them while I program the Jump in," Jake said. "It will take a couple of hours. No shooting them before we jump."

"Okay."

"This will take a few items to work out. I have one more course burn to do, then we coast 'til we're at the Jump limit."

"Got it," Shutt said.

"Jake Stewart," Yvette said. "This one will shoot us both."

"Didn't you talk about spacing her?" Jake asked.

"They did," Shutt said. "But I promise I won't space them."

"Good," Jake said. "I'm going to the Jump station to work this out." He reached up and pulled himself along the grab bars.

Shutt glared at the women in silence, the revolver not wavering.

"You can't point that at us forever, you know," Yvette said. "And you promised Jake you wouldn't shoot us."

"I promised to not shoot you until we jump," Shutt said. "I can wait that long."

CHAPTER 44

"We can't just shoot him in cold blood," Nadine said. She and Sergeant Russell were sitting at the helm. The winds and swell had dropped. Roi had given them rudimentary instructions on what to do in an emergency if a big wave swept in. He told them they would feel better if they had something to do on deck and if they could see the horizon.

"I thought shooting people was your favorite thing in the world," Sergeant Russell said. "Right after stabbing them with your knives."

"I like hitting people, too," Nadine said. "It's exciting. But as far as shooting goes, I'm more of a 'shooting in hot blood' type."

"Does shooting people make you hot?" Sergeant Russell asked.

"Bite me."

"Talking about shooting them? Does that make you hot?"

"In your pathetic dreams. What are we going to do about Roi?"

They looked to the foredeck. Roi had finished fixing the hatch. It was closed, locked, and welded. He had said that was the only way to guarantee it wouldn't come open again. He saw them looking at him, smiled, and gave them a thumbs-up. Nadine gave him a thumbs-up.

"I could throw him overboard, I suppose," Sergeant Russell said.

"Could you really? After he saved your life?" Nadine said.

Sergeant Russell frowned. "That wouldn't feel right."

"He's pretty good with that torch welder thing. He knows how to fix things."

"That's not good for us. No way I'll get that hatch open now without a sledgehammer."

"I think if he hadn't been good at fixing things and tying things down, we'd have sunk in that storm."

"I hate dying in storms. It ruins your entire day," Sergeant Russell said.

"Well, Scotty, got any other ideas?"

"Scotty?"

"It's your name."

"Scott. Always Scott. Never Scotty."

The sails flapped. Nadine looked down and eased the wheel slightly to the left as she had been taught. "Got it, Scotty." The flapping stopped. Roi smiled back at Nadine and nodded, then went back to welding.

"Well, missy, any ideas on what to do next?"

"Don't call me missy," Nadine said.

"Make me stop," Sergeant Russell said.

Nadine gave him a glare, then looked at Roi, replacing his tools. "He looks happy."

"He's enjoying the weather. This trip is great fun for him."

"He knows sailing. And weather. And fixing a boat. Frankly, I feel more confident with him in charge than with Bal. Bal was experienced but lazy."

"Roi was the world's worse Militia officer," Sergeant Russell said. "Pompous. Arrogant. Belittling. He treated the troops like dirt."

"He's not a Militia officer anymore. He's a sea captain."

Roi returned to the cockpit. "Feeling better, both of you?" He asked. Both nodded. "It's often like that. The sooner you get to work in a storm, the sooner the seasickness passes. Well, that hatch won't open again. No matter what."

"We'll need a sledgehammer to get it open later," Sergeant Russell said.

"You are correct, Sergeant. Isn't it a glorious day? The wind, the sea, we're running before it, and making good time. You balanced the sails well, Ms. Nadine."

"Thanks, it's a lot like piloting a shuttle, in a way."

"I wouldn't know. I failed my pilot training class."

"You took a pilot's class, sir?" Russell asked.

"And an engineer's, and a navigator's, and the university entrance exam. Failed them all. My family was appalled."

"You don't seem," Nadine said, "well, you don't seem—"

"So incompetent?" Roi asked. "I assure you that I was the most incompetent officer in the Militia. Ask any of my superiors who wrote my fitness reports. Or those who read them."

"You're not incompetent," Nadine said. "You saved our life. You saved this ship and everybody on board in the storm."

Roi looked down at the helm controls, then up at the sails. He put a line on a winch and cranked it tighter. "It's kind of you to say so. But I only did what any good sailor would do in a storm."

"You did save our lives, sir," Sergeant Russell said. "Have to be competent to do that. Besides, you're a commander. They don't make anybody a commander."

Roi watched the sails as he turned the crank. "They do if you mutiny. I was a lieutenant, and a bad one, at that. If it wasn't for my sergeants, I never would have gotten anything done. Oh, don't look so surprised, Sergeant. I knew you were covering for me. I couldn't figure out how to make things happen. You fixed for me."

"I didn't think you noticed, sir." Sergeant Russell said.

"I noticed. I didn't know what to do about things. I commanded the troops, but I didn't know what orders to give. I was a pompous, arrogant ass—no, don't try to deny it."

Sergeant Russell had opened his mouth, then closed it.

"I was unfit to command. Oh, I wasn't a thief, like some others. I didn't steal Militia funds or sell parts off ships or use Militia resources to go mining, like some officers did. I just plodded along, doing my duty, poorly."

"Why didn't you quit?" Nadine asked. "Quit the Militia?"

"Members of my family had served the Empire for hundreds of years," Roi said. "Possibly farther back, if some of the old records are right. If I'd told my family that I was considering quitting, it would have been like me saying I was going to have sexual congress with a buffalo at noon in the town square. On camera. They wouldn't have understood what I was talking about. I wouldn't have understood what I was talking about. The Militia was my life, even if I was bad at it. Do you know why I joined this mutiny?"

"You mean the Empire Rising, sir?" Sergeant Russell asked. "That's not a mutiny, it's an attempt to bring back the true Empire—"

"Spare me the rhetoric, Sergeant. If it must be said, I'm better at it then you. No, I joined because Colonel Savard convinced me it was my duty. Serve the Empire. Exercise the disease."

"Excise the disease, sir," Sergeant Russell said. "Excise means to cut. Exercise is working out at a gym."

"I've been saying it wrong this whole time? Really?"

"I'm afraid so, sir."

"Another one of my failures, then." Roi unhooked the line he had been winching and reached for another. He let that one loosen about a foot, then tied it off again.

Nadine looked at her instruments. "We're going faster."

"Yes, we should get another knot or two as we go along."

"I don't know what a knot is, but the gauge says we've sped up. What did you do?"

"The sails were out of balance. I just rebalanced

everything."

"How did you know what to do?" Nadine asked.

Roi shrugged. "I just know. I can tell by the way the boat feels. This is something I'm good at. Unlike all Militia things. Oh, and poetry. I write poetry." Roi saw Nadine and Sergeant Russell exchange glances. "It's good. Even I can tell. I publish it anonymously in the university journals. It's very well received. In a perfect world I would sail a sailboat around the world ocean and write poetry at night."

Sergeant Russell smiled. "You never did say why you joined the rebellion, sir."

"Like you, I followed orders. You superiors told you what to do, and you did it. And did it well. Colonel Savard was lucky to have you, as was I. For me, it was duty. I convinced myself it was for duty. But it wasn't. It was just hubris and ambition and laziness."

Roi coiled up the loose end of a line. Silence descended.

"What happens now, sir?" Sergeant Russell asked.

"We sail north and west. Before we departed, I received information the Militia has decamped from the city to a western base. They receive supplies there. Some by a shuttle. These missiles will allow me to shoot down their shuttle, and without supplies, we may yet regain our strength and 'excise' the cancer. Did I say it right, Sergeant?"

"You did, sir."

"Outstanding."

The sails flapped, and Nadine turned the boat again. Roi nodded his approval. She checked her course on the helm and spoke to Roi. "Do you really believe that shooting down a single shuttle will save your rebellion?"

"Absolutely not," Roi said. "A one percent chance at best. But I have to do it."

"Why?"

"It's my duty."

"Your duty will get you killed."

"Duty often does. You may call me an incompetent idiot. You may say I can't pronounce the word 'excise.' You may say that I've led us to ruin. All that is true. But you'll never say I shirked my duty, even at the risk of my own life. I'm going below. I need sleep, and you two have turned into competent sailors I trust at the helm." He clapped them both on the shoulder, then went below.

Neither Sergeant Russell nor Nadine spoke for a moment.

"What do we do now?" Nadine asked.

"Our duty," Sergeant Russell said.

CHAPTER 45

Shutt sat in the Jump control room, pointing her revolver in the general direction of Yvette and Odette. The revolver was heavy. Her hand wavered.

"How long do you think you can keep that up?" Yvette asked.

"Long enough. If I get tired, I'll shoot you."

"You promised Jake you wouldn't shoot us," Yvette said.

"Nobody really believed that, did they?" Shutt asked. "After all the mayhem and revolts and mutinies, I'm just waiting 'til I make sure that Jake can get us out of here, then I'll do my proper duty, shoot you both, capture Jake, and bring the ship back to the Militia where it belongs."

"What will Jake do if we tell him that?" Odette asked.

"He won't believe you."

"He might."

"I can shoot him, too."

"You're a pirate," Yvette said.

"I'm a Militia officer. I follow orders from my proper superiors."

The boards in the control room bonged. Everybody looked down.

"My board is locked out," Odette said.

"Mine, too," Yvette said.

Jake's voice came back over the intercom. "I've shut things down for a moment. We're running ballistic to the jump limit, and we have plenty of time to discuss some matters. Perlins, please come back to the Jump station. I'll meet everyone there."

***

Perlins arrived in the Jump station where a bemused Yvette and Odette were listening to Major Shutt hold forth to Jake. "-Including Militia discipline. I've about had it with your lackadaisical command style, Mr. So-Called Captain. This is a Militia ship now."

Jake ignored the tirade and typed.

"Furthermore, as the senior Militia officer on board, I hereby requisition—"

"I thought we said that was the wrong term?" Perlins asked.

"That was force majeure," Yvette said. "And that other word—what was it?"

"Eminent domain," Shutt said. "But I looked it up. The military term is requisition, so I'm requisitioning—"

"Perlins, is this your comm code?" Jake pointed at his screen. "The one you're using on the ship. Perlins leaned over and nodded.

"As I said, as the senior Militia officer—" Shutt said.

"You keep saying that," Jake said.

"Because I am."

"I just sent everybody a comm," Jake said. "It's an encrypted message, encrypted with the Militia codes. I'm just forwarding it. I didn't create it. You should all be able to decrypt it with the Militia public keys."

"What does that have to do with anything?" Shutt asked.

Perlins was already sitting at her screen. She typed in a code and read.

"To all present. Greetings. I, Emperor Dashi the third—"

"There's three of him?" Yvette asked.

"Was in the past," Jake said. "Keep reading,"

"Emperor of all humanity, duke of the core systems," Perlins said.

"Just a bunch of titles," Shutt said.

"Lots of titles, though," Perlins said. "Tsar of all the Russians? Kaiser of the Germans?"

"Big historical Empires on old Earth," Jake said. "It's traditional that the Emperor is considered the heir of all royal titles on old Earth. It was part of the political maneuvering that created the early Empire. All of the historical Empires and kingdoms supported it out of a feeling that a royalist government system was the only proper one."

"King of the four-quarters?" Perlins said.

"Assyria," Jake said.

"Duke of Guernsey?"

"An island."

"Prince of Wales?"

"Another island."

"Shah of Zanzibar?"

"Island."

"Master of Sedge and Bee?"

"Egyptian Pharaoh."

"What's that?"

"It's like a king. King of England, Pharaoh of Egypt. They happened at the same time." Jake tilted his head. "I think they did."

"King of Australia?"

"Bigger island," Jake said.

"This is all very nice," Yvette said. "But I don't see how it applies. We're Free Traders, and we follow a different tradition. The Emperor was legitimate, and all ..."

"Your stuff is on page seventeen," Jake said. "I looked it up."

Everyone paged through the document.

"Bishop of Andorra," Yvette said. "What's an Andorra?"

"Farther down," Jake said. "You'll recognize it when you see it."

"I don't think so. Oh." Yvette looked up. "The Duke of Anjou?" She looked farther. "And ... the count of

Paris." The Free Trader girls exchanged glances.

"Who cares about the count of parties?" Shutt asked. "What do these ancient titles have to do with anything?"

"The titles authenticate Dashi's authority," Jake said. "Give him the Imperium to make decrees."

"And who is he decrying to?" Shutt asked. "And why should we care?"

"Master of Militia, Sigma Draconis," Perlins read. "Page eighteen. That's the official head of the Militia on Delta, right?"

"The commanding admiral acts in the name of the master of Militia, in their absence," Shutt said. "As appointed by the Delta Corporation during the current emergency."

"Well, Emperor Dashi, third of his name seems to be usurping that authority. Check the end, this is good," Perlins.

"What?" Shutt asked.

Perlins sat up and read out the end of the communication. "... reposing special trust and confidence in the patriotism, valor, fidelity, and abilities of Jake Stewart, I have nominated, and by and with the advice and consent of the Senate, do appoint him ..." She looked at Shutt. "What do you think?"

"Oh, no," Shutt said

"Admiral of the Delta Militia, as of this day. Done in the system of Sigma Draconis, Signed by my hand, on the first day of my reign."

Perlins laughed, stood, and snapped off a parade ground salute. "Your orders, Admiral."

CHAPTER 46

"We have received some good news," Dashi announced. "Jake Stewart is back in the system with the Jump ship. He has retrieved all the components I specified in quantities sufficient to repair the mass driver." He was addressing the group that had become known as "The Council." Leaving out whether it was the council for Delta or an as-yet-uncreated Empire. "Preliminary repairs are completed. As soon as we receive the components we need, the mass driver will be online in hours."

"Outstanding," Admiral Edmunds said. "What else?"

Jose jumped in. "We've got the remaining three shuttles loaded with food trays, and we have an entire train load of containers prepped for launch. They're all full of food. As soon as we get the mass driver loading, we'll start delivering tons of food right away. The crews at the shuttle launch facility are constantly updating launch windows and courses. We'll be able to launch a week's worth of food every two days."

"To where?" Edmunds asked.

"Everywhere." Jose brought up a display. "All the major stations will be getting containers, the shuttles will be docking at the transfer ports where the bulk of the independent ships are located. We'll even be sending a few containers into higher orbits to catch some of the rim stations."

"How do we get the parts from here to the mass driver?" an unaligned member asked.

"We're pulling the monorail train out here from Landing," Jose said. "It will be standing by here to receive the packages as we land them. As soon as it is loaded, it will head directly to Landing. We have plenty of workers standing by—Dunlop has multiple work-crews standing by, and they'll work straight shifts 'til it's done."

"How long to fix it? How long to get them to the train? With the lifting-body shuttle? Will they fit?"

"Everything is under control," Jose said. "We'll have the lifting-body shuttle in orbit waiting for the Jump ship to rendezvous. The volume of items is quite small. Eight or ten cubic meters. If they cross link air locks, even a small crew can carry them across and secure them in a quarter shift. None of the parts are heavy. They're mostly electronics."

"Outstanding," Edmunds said. "I'm hearing that, within hours of the Jump ship hitting orbit, we'll have the mass driver up and delivering food. That's all good news." He grimaced. "What's the catch?"

Marianne tapped the table. "Tribune Jose hasn't told us when that orbit rendezvous will take place."

Every head swiveled to Jose. He looked along the table, then back at Dashi. Dashi nodded. "Five days," Jose said. "They came out farther from the primary than expected."

Everybody reached for their comms and to run calculations. Except for Marianne. "Some of the outer stations will run out of food the day after tomorrow," she said.

"Some are nearly out of food already," one of her Legionnaires said.

"Yes," Jose said.

"The main stations have four days left," Marianne said.

"Yes," Jose said.

"That's it? Yes?"

"They'll be without food for a day," Jose said.

"We've already had incidents, a lot of incidents," Marianne said. "We've hushed them up as much as possible. But everybody expected the shuttles to start flying today. If we delay, they'll be riots."

"You mean that there'll be more riots," Edmunds said.

"Ones that we can't hide."

"We just have to tell everyone they have to wait a few more days," Jose said.

"That won't fly."

"Tell them we're delayed a day," Jose said. "Don't tell the truth."

"We need to tell the truth."

"In this case, the truth will get everyone killed," Jose said. "Just announce for general consumption that the food shipments are delayed a day. People can wait a day. Then another day. If we say five days, people will think a week. Nobody thinks they will starve in a day. Everybody thinks they'll starve in a week."

"So, we just keep saying a day then another day then another day," Marianne said.

"Yes, we can." Jose said.

"My people will not believe me after the second postponement," Marianne said. "I have to tell them the truth. If I don't, they will start the riots themselves. We'll end up with them breaking into the existing food stores."

"How?" Jose asked. "If we tell everyone the truth, they won't wait the five days. Everyone will know right away."

"I can trust my people to be quiet."

"But how can you trust your comm system?" the admiral asked. "Everybody and their pet tabbo has a Free Trader decryption key. There's no way to keep those secret."

Marianne started to say something, then frowned. She and her aides leaned together and spoke in low voices.

Dashi cleared his throat. "We will publicly announce a delay of two days for the shuttle launch. That will give everyone the ability to adjust. Then we will announce another delay. By then, the arrival of the Jump ship will be visible to everyone, and we will regain our credibility. But we do need a way to spread the message to ... supervisory elements, from all the parties represented here, the truth, so they do not lose faith. How can we do that?"

The admiral spoke. "We can send out messages with Militia codes. If we're careful about who I send them to, they can hand-deliver messages to your people all over the system. That way, only the people we want to know will know."

"You're sure your codes are secure?" Jose asked.

Admiral Edmunds shrugged. "Of course. Who has Militia codes?"

CHAPTER 47

"You can decrypt Militia codes?" Nadine asked Roi.

"Yes, Colonel Savard gave me the decryption keys during our abortive, um ..."

"During the failed rebellion," Sergeant Russell said.

"Yes," Roi agreed. "Hand me that hammer and chisel, please."

The three of them were sitting on the fore deck. A somewhat woozy Balthazar was manning the helm. Everybody agreed it was better he be doing something rather than sitting, holding his head on his bunk. Roi had finished chiseling the forward hatch open and was peering at the missiles in the hold. "That's how I knew that the perfidious remnants of the old Militia had retreated to that western base. As soon as I can contact them, we will join with our colleagues on the other boats to defeat them."

"Well, sir, not to put too fine a point on it," Sergeant Russell said, "but you did say you haven't been able to communicate with the other ships? Nothing since the storm."

"And shouldn't they be called ships?" Nadine asked. "Not boats?"

"Sailing vessels are always boats, it's a historic definition," Roi said. "From old Earth. And they could have suffered radio damage in the storm," Roi said.

"Or sunk and been eaten by carnivorous aquatic buffalo," Nadine said.

"Buffalo do not like to swim," Roi said.

"How do you know that?" Nadine asked.

"There was an embarrassing incident in my youth," Roi said.

"You tried to get a buffalo to swim?" Nadine asked.

"I tried to ride one into the water," Roi said. "I still have a scar. I will not discuss it further. Please help me lift this up." He jumped down into the hold and pushed the box with the missiles onto the fore deck. They attached to the mounting brackets. "We are lucky those did not bend in the storm," he said.

"Sir, you think the other ships sunk in the storm, didn't they?" Sergeant Russell said. "That's why you haven't heard anything from them since the storm happened?"

"They were well-found ships, with good crews," Roi said. "They will have managed."

"No, sir, they weren't," Sergeant Russell said. "You're lying."

"Sergeant, even with all we have been through, telling your commanding officer that he's a liar is beyond the pale."

"Who's pale?" Nadine asked. "I think I've got a very nice tan." She rolled the arms up on her shirt to show her sun-browned arms.

"Very nice, Ms. Nadine," Sergeant Russell said. "What about your legs? Can we see those?"

Nadine stuck her tongue out.

Russell looked at Roi. "Sir, I didn't understand before the storm, but now I do. Our boat was the smallest, and it looked the most dangerous, but it wasn't, was it? You picked this boat for the missiles because it was the most seaworthy and because you could sail it alone or with a small crew. You knew that Bal was the best sailor, after you."

"I claim no great skill, Sergeant."

"But we're alive. And they're not, are they? Those lectures you gave us about balance and freeboard and reserve buoyancy, and—and—"

"Righting moment," Nadine said. "That one was neat. It actually made sense, the part about this boat being hard to roll over because of the lead thingy on the bottom."

"The keel," Roi said. He stripped the cover off of the missiles. Each was a meter long, and perhaps five inches in diameter, clipped together in a two-by-two grid. A small control unit sat on the top. Roi flipped a panel up on the top of the unit, uncovering a number pad.

Nadine snapped her fingers. "Yes, the keel. But Scotty's right, we survived the storm because of you and Bal and because this was a better boat than the others."

"Scott," Sergeant Russell said.

"Scotty," Nadine said. "We're the last, aren't we? Did they all drown?"

"While you were ... indisposed ... at the beginning of this trip, as the storm was starting, Melchior called his brother and said they were going to run before the wind—" Roi held up his hand. "I know you don't know what that means. They turned back and sailed to south continent. With the wind where it was, it was a safer course for them. They may have survived." Roi keyed a code into the keypad.

"Even with the storm," Nadine said.

"If they got back before the full force of the storm hit them, yes. If not, no." Roi frowned. "Then we are alone here. Just us."

"What are you going to do?" Nadine asked.

"My duty," Roi said. He finished typing his code in. Four lights lit up next to the panel. Two red, two green. "Two have been damaged in the storm," Roi said. "The rest will have to do. From what I understand, this shuttle is special."

"What's so special about this ship again? Nadine asked.

"The message says 'Jump ship arriving with necessary reactor parts. Transfer to lifting-body shuttle on—' Let me check the date," Roi said. He pulled his comm out of his pocket.

"How long have we been on this stinking scow?" Nadine said. "I lost track."

"This stinking scow has saved your life, Ms. Nadine,"

Roi said. He patted the deck. "There, there, she didn't mean it."

"Are you talking to us, sir?" Sergeant Russell asked.

"The Gaspar, Sergeant. I'm talking to the boat."

"Do you do that a lot, sir?" Sergeant Russell asked. "Talk to inanimate objects?"

Roi ignored him. "I did lose track of the day-to-day date during the storms, but my comm has corrected me. This special shuttle will be arriving today with needed parts for the current usurping Militia government. Good. I plan to shoot it down with our missiles."

"Sir, that's a great idea," Sergeant Russell said. "But these missiles are pretty short-ranged. They can't hit an orbital shuttle.

"The shuttle will not be orbital. It will be landing," Roi said. "And I have been able to reconnect to one of the navigation satellites. I now know where we are. Exactly." He looked up at the sun. "Not far from the estuary where that shuttle will land." Roi pointed over the bow. "If you look over there, you will see land soon. At our current speed, in less than an hour, we will be in a perfect position to destroy that shuttle as it lands."

***

"So, we take him now?" Nadine asked. She and Sergeant Russell were conferring in the salon, under the cover of preparing a meal.

"I want to see land first," Sergeant Russell said. "Those missiles are no threat if we're not close to the landing point. But we can still drown or starve or what have you if we don't get this scow to a dock somewhere. I want to know what direction to go before we take him out of the picture."

"Just get up there, and we hit him," Nadine said. "Knock him out."

"You don't want to shoot him?"

"I told you he saved our lives. That would be ...

ungrateful," Nadine said.

Sergeant Russell laughed, then Nadine joined in.

Roi's head stuck down the hatch. "What's so funny?"

"Just—just been a long trip, sir."

"Too long for Bal, I think. He's fallen asleep. He's either tired or the concussion. If I lower him down, can you put him to bed? I have the helm."

"Of course, sir," Sergeant Russell said. He and Nadine grabbed Bal's legs as he was lowered into the salon, then maneuvered him down to his bunk. After he was settled, they returned to the cabin. Nadine made sure her knives were in place in their sheathes, and Sergeant Russell pulled out a big thermos and filled it with water. Its weight and heft would make a decent bludgeon.

"Right," Sergeant Russell said. "Let's do this thing." He and Nadine went to climb out of the cabin. He stopped.

"Move it," Nadine said. "No time like the present."

"It's locked," Sergeant Russell said. "The hatch is locked." He pointed. The flimsy plastic battens that had been in place during the storm had been replaced by metal ones. And they were bolted and locked in place.

"Maybe, just maybe, he's not as stupid as we thought," Nadine said.

***

Communication with Roi was short and to the point. "This operation is too important, Sergeant. I can't brook any interference. We're almost where we need to be. I can see the landing spot. A few minutes more sailing and then we can float and wait for that shuttle to land. It should appear any time."

"Let us out, please, sir. We can help."

"The thing is, Sergeant. There is no way to escape this. I believe that I can shoot down the shuttle, yes. But there are fishing boats nearby. I can see one in the distance. They have radios and better engines. We won't get away after this. They'll hunt us down and kill us."

"We can help, sir."

"Did you read the messages I showed you? If I understand correctly, if these parts don't get in, if the mass driver doesn't get repaired, thousands will starve. If I can stop that, then the rebellion has a chance. But I won't have a personal chance. I'll be the man who killed thousands. I plan to do my duty, then surrender. I assume I'll be executed after."

"Maybe, sir," Sergeant Russell said. "Maybe you've done enough. The rebellion or the mutiny or whatever you want to call it, is finished. You've lost."

"I know that, Sergeant. But I must do what I must do. I promised to oppose these people, and oppose them I will."

"Sir, thousands of innocent people will die."

"I know. That's why I locked you down there. Whatever happens, you cannot be held responsible, held below deck."

"The Emperor's hairy anus, sir. Don't do this."

"I'll let you up when I'm finished, Sergeant. Stand by."

Nadine came back up from below. "Tool locker is closed. Chained and padlocked. We'll need to batter it open."

"Batter it open with a heavy thermos?"

"Use a light thermos if you want," Nadine said. "It will be just as effective. What have we got for weapons?"

"My revolver," Sergeant Russell said. "Your knives. One of those marlin spike things."

"Glad to know, in the current emergency, we'll be able to get knots out of ropes. Shoot the locks off."

"Think again," Sergeant Russell said. He held up his revolver to flash its colors.

"Frangibles," Nadine said. "You're loaded with frangibles?"

"I wasn't originally. Roi must have swapped them. I would have noticed if he'd unloaded the gun, but with the weight the same, I didn't check."

"So, swap the reloads."

"The spares were in that cabinet over there." Sergeant Russell indicated an open locker. "Not there now."

"Give me that gun," Nadine said. "I'll try it on the chain on the tool locker. You take that spike and try to rip the hatch open."

"It's a revolver, not a gun. Revolvers are for shooting—"

"Shut up with your stupid marine stuff. Get prying." Nadine snatched the revolver out of his hand and went below to the arms locker.

Sergeant Russell tried pounding the marlin spike into the hatch. The hatch was metal and barely dented. He tried pushing it between the gaps on the sides, but it didn't fit. He cursed and banged it on the locking plate. Nadine's revolver cracked below. After five shots, she reappeared, covered with dust.

"No luck?"

"I've ruined a perfectly good hairband. I kept one shot for Roi. What about you?"

"This hatch is solid. We're not getting out this way."

"Ok." Nadine looked around. "Can we sail the boat away?"

"Controls are up there," Sergeant Russell said. "So, no."

"But the engine is down here," Nadine said. She pulled panels off the wall and floor. One uncovered the compartment with the engine.

"Stop it somehow?" Russell said.

"We're already in position, according to him. So, we need to get out of position." Nadine removed the last panel and examined the engine. "It's electric. If the repeating controls are up top, there must be controls on the engine." She crawled forward.

Russell pointed. "Next to your head, that bunch of wires are labeled 'helm.'"

Nadine squeezed a plug and pulled the wires off the

engine block.

"This must be the speed control here," Nadine said. She turned the knob counterclockwise, and the engine's noises faded.

"Never guess right first time," she said. She spun the knob fully in the other direction. The engine snapped to life, and she barely held on as the boat flew forward.

**

"Everything looking good?" Jake asked. He, Shutt, Yvette, and Odette occupied the four spots in the shuttle's control room. Perlins lurked in the back. Merced stayed in his cabin. Shutt had insisted that she pilot the shuttle down after they had transferred all the boxes from the Jump ship.

Yvette and Odette had agreed. "Atmosphere messes us up," Yvette said. "We're used to vacuum. She's a dirtsider. Let her do it."

"Piloting messes you up," Shutt said. "You Free Traders are lousy pilots. Take too long."

"We have to pay for things we break," Yvette said. "Unlike spendthrift Militia."

"Spendthrift?" Odette said. "You've been listening to Jake too much."

"It does stick on you," Perlins said from the passenger compartment. "His way of talking."

"Shut up back there," Shutt said. "You're lucky you're not chained up."

"Didn't want to chain me when I helped cross load or lash down the cargo," Perlins said. "Funny that."

"If it was up to me, you'd be locked up," Shutt said.

"If it was up to us, you'd be out an air lock," Yvette said.

"Good thing for me, it's up to Captain Jake there," Perlins said. "Say, El Supremo Captain Jake?"

"Yes, Ms. Perlins?"

"Since you're an admiral, you should get in the habit of

using ranks, so I'd be Lieutenant Perlins. But how do you do it? When I met you, it seemed like you were this wimpy techno geek, and now you're in charge of a Jump ship and keeping three different groups of people from shooting each other."

"Would you believe my natural animal magnetism?" Jake asked.

All four women laughed. "No, seriously, how do you do it?" Perlins asked.

"It could be my natural animal magnetism," Jake said. "It's possible."

"No, it's not," Shutt said.

"You hit on me."

"It was because you were the only one who would keep me from getting killed. It was more, calculation."

"Exploitation," Yvette said.

"Manipulation," Odette said.

"Desperation," Perlins said.

"Should I run an ad?" Jake said. "Are you a calculating, single woman good at exploiting and manipulating men? Are you desperate? Here's the guy for you. Think that's how I should advertise myself?"

The women were quiet. Shutt touched some controls, and the lifting body rolled slightly, then rolled back. "Well, you have to admit, it would save everybody some time," she said.

Jake shook his head. "Are we on course for the landing?"

"Yep. Just overfly those fishing boats there," Shutt said, pointing to a display screen, "and land in that estuary, and you can see two boats set up as tenders to tow us in."

A bad memory stirred in Jake's mind. "Is the tide going to be a problem?"

"No, it's slack water, but why are you asking about tides?"

"No reason," Jake said. He'd been in a shuttle that an incoming tidal bore had flipped.

They flew sedately forward. Their course was level, and they were slowing as they approached the touchdown point.

"What's that?" Jake pointed at a screen. One of the fishing boats had suddenly accelerated. It was kicking up a stream of water from the stern, spinning in a tight circle.

"That's weird," Shutt said. "Are they out of control or something?"

"Why would they do that?" Yvette said. "That's a very odd maneuver."

Smoke rose up from the sailboat, then exhaust gases flashed, and a bright point of light climbed into the air.

"Missile, missile, missile," Shutt said. She pulled on the controls. "Hang on."

CHAPTER 48

Nadine and Scott grabbed whatever they could as the boat rocketed in a tight turn. Roi was yelling something.

"Didn't expect this," Nadine said. "This spin." A boom shook the boat. "Sonic boom. That's a shuttle inbound."

Sergeant Russell managed to drag himself upright enough to look out a small window. "Well, we're definitely spinning. And not far from the shore. I think we threw him off."

A flash brightened the windows, and one of the missiles on the foredeck roared out and up.

"He fired," Nadine said.

"Thanks for the update," Sergeant Russell said. "Wouldn't have figured that out myself."

A boom shook the boat. "Did he hit it?" Nadine asked.

Sergeant Russell held on to the bulkhead and stared out the window. "I can't see. Wait. There it is. Parts of the missile, falling. No, it self-destructed or something. Hit the water."

"Good. Our maneuvering threw him off," Nadine said.

The boat swayed for a moment, then settled. The speed continued, but it executed a gentle turn. "He's fixed the helm or turned us. We've straightened up."

"He can get a better aim," Nadine said.

"And he's going to run us onto shore," Sergeant Russell said. "I see land ahead. We're going to ram the rocks."

"Before or after he fires that missile?"

"After," Sergeant Russell said. "We need to stop him."

"As you said, thanks for the update. I wouldn't have figured this out myself."

"So, what's your plan?"

"You're the military guy. You should have a plan."

"Give me artillery, some air cover, and two squads, and I'll give you a plan. A sailing ship on the ocean, not really my thing. What about you?"

"I'm a spy. I steal stuff."

"Can we steal this boat?"

"I think he stole it from us."

"How do we get it back?"

"Can't figure out how to stop him. Not before he fires or we hit the shore."

Nadine peered out the small window. "Stop him, or just stop?"

"What?"

"Follow me." She dashed below.

***

"Overfly it," Yvette yelled at Shutt. "Go up."

"We won't clear those mountains ahead if we go up," Shutt said. "We need to go down,"

"Maneuver around it," Odette said.

"I'm trying. Shut up."

The missile had been fired and was climbing toward them. But something had messed with its guidance. It was turning in tighter and tighter circles. Shutt threw the descending shuttle in a short sideways hop, and the missile tried to correct, then popped up vertically and exploded. The flash blanked their cameras for a moment, then they came back on.

"Good work," Jake said.

"Wasn't me. The guidance was corrupt or something."

"Get us back on course," Yvette said. "We don't have much room."

Shutt tapped the controls delicately until they were again online for the landing. "Relax. We're on course for landing. Straight ahead, and we'll be in the bay."

"Right over that boat that shot at us. We'll overfly it at

ten meters," Yvette said.

***

"That's a missile," Jose said. The council and followers was crowded on the dock to greet the returning lifting body. The vapor trail rose from the sailboat out in the estuary.

"Glad you're along, youngster," the admiral said. "Wouldn't have been able to figure that out myself."

"Where did it come from?" Marianne asked.

"Militia stores," Edmunds said. "There was a limited number of pre-abandonment items stored at Militia HQ.

"The Militia has a secret stock of missiles?" Jose said.

"Not really," Edmunds said. "Just some old boxes. They'd been there for years. Wasn't sure they worked."

"You didn't think this was important enough to tell us?"

"Lots of people knew about it." Edmunds shrugged. "It wasn't a secret."

The rising missile turned and headed for a collision with the descending lifting body.

"And you needed special codes to arm it." The missile corkscrewed, then veered upward, blowing up before the shuttle came close. "Which apparently somebody found."

"They'll shoot down the shuttle," Jose said.

"They could. Didn't expect that."

"Didn't expect them to shoot it down, or didn't expect them to be there?"

"Thought they were sunk," Edmunds said. "Just before that big storm, the last of the rebel fighting force on south continent headed north to attack us here. Two of the ships were damaged, and they lost most of their equipment and about half of their personnel."

"How do you know this?" Dashi asked.

"The remainder of their strength limped back there a few days ago, and I got some updates from my agent."

"I thought your agent was on the other boat?" Jose

said.

"She was. I thought she was sunk. Apparently not."

"How did they know that you would be here, so they could attack us?" Dashi asked.

"Oh, I told them," Edmunds said. "Not directly, of course, but I made sure that they knew we would be here. Once they knew we were here, within striking distance of their remaining troops, they were bound to try something. And screw it up."

"You expected them to try and fail?" Dashi said.

"I thought they had failed," Edmunds said. "Drowned."

"They didn't," Jose said. "They're right there."

"They are," Edmunds said. "And they might have three more of those missiles with them."

"You've killed us all," Jose said. "All these people are going to starve."

"Look." Marianne pointed. The sailboat that had launched the missile had sped up and was spinning in a tight circle, clearly out of control.

"We're not done yet," Edmunds said. "I still have some players on the board."

***

Nadine hammered at the pin on the side of the bar. She was strong, but she couldn't get a grip. "Use the marlin spike thing. Get it open."

"This is not a good idea," Sergeant Russell said.

"It's the only idea. Lever it open."

Sergeant Russell spun the lock on one side, then the other. A crossbar that had protected the hatch dropped off.

"You sure about this?"

"Yes," Nadine said. She grasped the locking handle on one side of the hatch and pulled.

Sergeant Russell had a moment to read the letters on the metal plate as she pulled. Rollover escape hatch. For use in knockdown emergency only. Danger of sinking. Do not open underway.

It is a rare event, but sailboats can flip upside down. Once the masts are completely underwater, the pressure of the masts and sails can hold the boat completely inverted. There is sufficient buoyancy in materials and sealed compartments to keep the boat afloat forever, upside down, but anybody below in the cabins are trapped. Many boats have an emergency hatch on the bottom of the hull. The idea is, if the boat flips over, the hatch will be out of the water, and the trapped crew could crawl up to the hatch, pop it open, and climb on the upturned hull. Of course, the hatch should be high and dry at that point.

Opening it while the boat was right side up meant it was under water. Deep underwater. And the hatch had to be big enough for people to escape through it, so it was a very hefty opening. By popping the hatch, Nadine had essentially blown a huge hole in the bottom of the boat.

The hatch snapped back, and water fountained in. The pressure of the water forced Nadine back. The sudden gush of the ocean and the extra weight had also changed the boat's course. The open hatch acted like a brake on the speed of the boat and slammed the bow to a stop. The stern wanted to keep going, so the net result was the boat stood on its bow and pushed the open hatch even deeper. The boat pivoted stern up, bow-down, and stayed that way as tons of water flooded in.

"Get Bal," Nadine yelled, as the two of them floundered away from the water jet. Bal had been banged out of his bunk, and Nadine and Russell grabbed him and hustled him into the main cabin. They clung to tables, chairs, wall fittings, anything to keep moving as the boat tipped up. The engine noise stopped. Something had jerked the throttle off.

They rocked back to a more even keel, but floated bow-down in the water, steadily sinking deeper as the water rushed in. Nadine could see the forward cabins were full of rising water. From the angle of the hull, she judged the bow was awash and dropping, but the missile launcher was still high enough to fire.

Roi's voice came from above. "A gallant effort, but I can still fire that missile before we sink."

"There's no time," Nadine said. "The water's rising in here. Unlock the hatch and let us out, or we'll drown."

"I have my duty," Roi said.

"To the Emperor's hairy nostrils with your duty," Nadine yelled. "Get us out."

The lights in the cabin shorted out as water reached the power distribution board. Sparks flew, then disappeared into the dark. Only a dim light from a window remained. Nadine and Sergeant Rusell clutched a bemused Bal, keeping his head above the water. The ocean gurgled into the cabin steadily, and Nadine had to kick her feet to keep her head above the water.

The light dimmed even farther as the water covered the final window. They were both swimming now in a green-tinged dark.

Nadine heard clanking. Was that the missile being tracked for a final shot?

Then light flooded in, and Roi's face appeared in the open hatch. "Give me your hand."

***

The shuttle floated behind the tender. The tender was a repurposed fishing boat, but the crew were old hands on retrieving this particular lifting-body shuttle. They'd gotten magnetic grapples and float bags on and under it within seconds after the shuttle came to a halt. They'd tied it up and towed it toward the dock professionally, even taking time to collect the four figures on the bow of a sinking sailboat as they drove by.

Minutes later, the shuttle was dragged up a cradle and onto shore, and the tender cast off to dock nearby. A crew swarmed onto the shuttle and raced the boxes out of the hold and onto the waiting monorail train. Jake realized he was superfluous and climbed out and walked to the steps leading to the settlement. A blond figure on the dock ran toward him.

"Jake," Nadine said. She gave him a big hug. "You're alive."

"So are you. What happened?"

"Kidnapped, went to a secret Militia base, almost died in a storm, sunk a boat. We'll talk later. I need to talk to the admiral. Did your jump work?"

"Perfectly. We went to the adjacent system, found a brand new station, saw herds of buffalo, and had dinner with some zombies. We got what Dashi wanted. I have to talk to him."

"Sounds like you did your normal, outstanding job."

"I did. I had a lot of help, though, a great crew."

The four women from Jake's crew had wandered along behind him. Major Shutt saw Nadine, and her eyes narrowed. Nadine glared right back. "You had a great crew, did you?" Nadine said.

"Yes. They were super," Jake said. "I couldn't have done it without them. They were the best."

Merced stepped out of the shuttle carrying a medical kit, and disappeared up the steps. Major Shutt gathered the three other women together, and they had a whispered conference. Then she turned and walked them toward Jake and Nadine.

"Nadine, you know Major Shutt," Jake said.

"I do," Nadine said.

"Thank you so much, Captain Jake," Shutt said. "Or should I say admiral."

"Admiral?" Nadine said.

"That's what we girls call him." Shutt leaned in and kissed Jake. "A great voyage. I learned so much."

"Um, thanks. Thank you," Jake said.

"I'm sorry we never finished that matter in your cabin," Shutt said.

"Your cabin?" Nadine said. "What was she doing in your cabin, Jakey?"

"She wasn't. I wasn't. I mean, I left." Jake said. He backed away from Nadine.

Yvette and Odette came over. Each stepped to one side of Jake and hugged him, then kissed his cheeks. "You were wonderful, Mr. Jake. We're so lucky to have worked with you," Odette said. She turned to Nadine. "He taught us so many things." She stepped back, smiled at Jake, and made the universal call me sign with her hands.

Nadine glared and crossed her arms across her chest. "What's going on here, Stewart?"

"Nothing, nothing," Jake said.

Perlins was next. She gave Jake a bear hug and kissed him on the lips, then stepped back. "Thank you so much, Captain. I'll never forget you."

Sergeant Russell arrived at that moment. Medics had collected Bal, and other troops had taken Roi in tow.

"You must be that Jake I've heard about," Sergeant Russell said.

"Um, yes."

"Nadine tells me a lot about you."

"She does. She's quite a girl, Nadine," Jake said. He was worried, recognizing Nadine's look.

"Yep, you're lucky to be with her."

"Yes," Nadine said. "He is, isn't he?"

"Nadine," Jake said. "It's not what you think."

"What do I think, Jakey?" Nadine asked. "Sergeant Russell, may I borrow your revolver?"

Sergeant Russell looked surprised. "Sure." He handed it to her.

"Now, Nadine, don't do anything hasty."

"Hasty?" She spun the revolvers. "Frangibles? Well, they'll have to do." She glared at Jake. "I leave you alone for a few weeks, and I see four women all over you."

"Nadine, I can explain," Jake said.

"Go ahead."

"They're just crew."

"Just crew? Wrong explanation," Nadine said.

"Don't do this again, Nadine?"

"Again? What's she going to do?" Russell asked.

Nadine raised her revolver. Jake closed his eyes. "Every time. Every single time."

Nadine shot him.

CHAPTER 49

"Stand for the council, Commander Roi," the bailiff said. The courtroom was packed. And since the courtroom had previously been an empty food pallet storage room, packed meant hundreds.

Roi stood from where he was sitting with his lawyer. The man's name was Strewth or Starth or something with an H at the end. Roi hadn't bothered to remember it. It wasn't relevant. Dashi, the admiral, Marianne, and two other judges walked in and sat at the table.

"Commander?" Roi said to the bailiff. "Why bother with my rank?"

"You're still a commander. For now," the bailiff said. "Until the court says otherwise."

"This isn't a court," Roi said. "It's a public lynching." But he stood.

"Commander Roi," Admiral Edmunds said, "we are gathered here today—"

"Guilty." Roi said.

"You need to wait 'til I read the charges."

"No, I don't. I'm guilty. Whatever they are. I stole Militia property. I fired on Militia troops. I rebelled. I attacked a space station. I misfiled fuel storage reports. I mixed colored and white laundry. I got a lot of people killed. Guilty."

"Well, this saves us some time," Edmunds said. "What does the council say?"

"Admiral," Strada said, rising.

"Shut up, Stwarth," Roi said. "I know what I'm doing."

"It's Strada, Commander," Strada said. "I don't think—"

"Sit down and shut up," Roi said. "There is no doubt that I did everything that I'm accused of. And the list doesn't matter. There are multiple capital crimes in there. Mutiny. Rebellion. Attacking senior officers. Junior officers. Any officer that was handy, really. I did it. I'm guilty of it."

"Do you express remorse, Commander?" Marianne asked.

"Of course not. I'm proud of what I did. I did it for the Empire. For us, here on Delta. These are trying times. We need strength, discipline, and the Empire. You are not the right people to be leading us. Colonel Savard was correct in that."

"You think Colonel Savard would have done better?" Dashi asked.

Roi shrugged. "We'll never know. Take care of your business and be done with me."

Edmunds smiled. "Good enough. Death." He looked down at the council. "Who agrees?"

Each of the others signaled agreement. "The Imperial Council sentences you to death," Edmunds said. "To be carried out by firing squad, forthwith."

The crowd shifted. It wasn't a murmur or a rustle but the tightening of postures and glances. Roi wasn't the only case on the list that day, just the first and most prominent one. The admiral heard the noise. "Death to mutineers. It's in the regs.

"You had a firing squad standing by?" Marianne asked.

"Yes."

"Are you going to shoot all of the Militia involved in the uprising?" Marianne asked. "We captured a lot of them."

"Then, we'll have a lot of firing squads. Anyone who rebelled will be shot." He looked at his notes. "Next case. Lieutenant Perlins."

Perlins stepped forward with her advocate from a line on the side. Roi stood and looked at the council for a moment as the bailiff took his arm. "I appeal," he yelled. "I appeal my sentence."

"There is no appeal from this council," Marianne said. "We are the senior judicial body on Delta."

"I appeal to the Emperor. He's right there." Roi pointed at Dashi. "You claim to be Emperor Dashi III. Very well, I appeal for Imperial clemency."

The crowd stirred. The admiral looked at Roi. "You can't—"

"He can." Marianne said. "He has that right."

Edmunds looked to the side, where Shutt was standing. He nodded, and she put her hand on her revolver. Several of the Militia caught the gesture and put their hands on their weapons. The Free Trader Legionnaires present caught that movement and put their hands on their weapons. Nobody drew, but everybody watched.

Dashi cleared his throat. All eyes swung to him. "State your case, Commander."

"I neither rebelled nor mutinied," Roi said. "I did what I thought best for the Empire, in consultation with the properly appointed officers over me."

"They rebelled against the Empire," Dashi said. "And its appointed agents."

"Which appointed agents?" Roi asked.

"Myself. By virtue of my position, I was in charge," Dashi said.

"Not true. You were neither appointed, nor elected, or, for that matter, acclaimed when this happened," Roi said. "You were not the Emperor then."

"And now? What am I now?"

Roi stared at him for a moment, then gave the crossed arm salute. "The Empire. What are your orders, sir?"

"What if I uphold the sentence of death?" Dashi asked.

"Then, I go willingly. But if you are to be Emperor, you must undertake your responsibilities. All of them. This sentence must come from you."

"You're that willing to die?" Dashi asked.

"I've always been willing to die," Roi said. "Nothing has changed. I serve the Empire. Whoever leads it."

He waited. And waited. Dashi stared out into space and bit his lip. Then he turned to Roi. "Exile. Your sentence is commuted. You are exiled."

The crowd murmured. "Where?" Roi asked.

"Take that boat, the ..." Dashi consulted his notes. "The Gaspar. It has been repaired. Sail it away onto the world ocean. Take the rest of these with you." Dashi pointed to the group of accused officers standing behind Roi. "You may go anywhere you wish on the world ocean or to south continent. I understand you have some knowledge in nautical charting and surveying?"

Roi nodded.

"Then, we will give you supplies as needed, provided you return with charts and maps of the other continents and oceans. You may not return north except to leave the charts you build and collect supplies. Leave now. You have one shift to provision your boat and depart with the rest of them. After that, if you are found north or in orbit, you'll be shot. Any of the officers behind you may go with you under the same conditions. If they choose not to go, then their trials will proceed. Probably with the results the admiral wants."

Roi flicked the bailiff's hand from him, then turned to Dashi and saluted. "The Empire." He turned to the line of rebel officers behind him. "I go directly to the dock. We load food and water and leave within the hour. Whoever comes, come now." Roi walked toward the door.

Perlins stepped immediately into the aisle and followed him. Some stepped in behind her, while a few others had whispered arguments with their advocates.

"I'll be coming with you, sir," Perlins said.

"Outstanding," Roi said. He looked down at Perlins. "Do you like poetry, Lieutenant?"

***

Dashi grunted as he pushed his office door open and entered. Jake Stewart hovered behind him, standing 'til Dashi reached his desk.

"Sit down, Mr. Stewart. Don't wait on me," Dashi said. He slumped into his chair, pulled out his pill bottles, and shoved one in his mouth. Jake watched him worriedly. "Your legs, sir?"

"And the surgery," Dashi said. "They say the pain will never stop."

"What if we run out of pills, sir?"

"These are simple to manufacture," Dashi said. "Morphine. Cheap, easy, and abundant." Dashi stretched and grimaced. "There are other issues, but that is not your concern. In your report you spoke of zombies?"

"I had a misunderstanding at 61 Cygni, sir. There are no zombies."

Dashi waited for Jake to elaborate, but Jake kept his mouth shut. Dashi steepled his hands. "Indeed. You left those rogue Militia officers behind?"

"Insisted on it, sir. Exiled them, in fact. They had no choice."

"Yes, I noticed that. Excellent solution. Remove a problem. Make them grateful for you keeping them alive so that they could be useful in the future. In fact, you were the inspiration for my exile of the others. We've had enough killing. The time of warfare has passed. Now it's the time of rebuilding. It's time to come together under one ruler."

"Which would be you, sir?"

"You sound somewhat cynical about that, Mr. Stewart. Are you a cynic now?"

"Perhaps just older and with a broader perspective, and a better understanding of necessary amplifications, sir."

"Necessary amplifications? Good deflection, Mr. Stewart. I'm pleased to see that you are developing some political instincts."

"Yes, sir."

"I also see you appointed yourself admiral of the Militia."

"Technically, you did, sir. I just made your notification public. I uh ... I would like that rescinded, sir."

"And why is that, Mr. Stewart?"

"Admiral Edmunds is very angry about that, sir."

"And you're afraid of the admiral?"

"I'm afraid of a lot of people, sir. But this is a direct challenge to his authority. And I'm not a direct sort of fellow. I prefer to work with people, rather than against them."

"I can't remove a commission, Mr. Stewart."

"You can remove an appointment, sir. If you wish."

"And if I don't wish?"

"He might shoot me."

"The Free Traders, at the least, would react violently to that. As a group, they grant you a surprising amount of leeway in your actions. They seem to regard you as some sort of fascinating pet, one that is both inherently dangerous and naïve enough to need protection, but fascinating at the same time. They enjoy it when you frustrate the Militia's activities, and they chuckle when you confound their actions. Like a trained dog who can dance and sing but still pees on the floor from time to time."

"Pee on the floor? That's what they think of me?" Jake said. "Should I be proud or upset?"

"A metaphor," Dashi said. "They do not grant the Militia that same freedom. If the Militia harmed you, they would fight back, because it's the Militia doing it."

Jake sat silent before finally speaking. "This is part of your plan, isn't it, sir? You gave me that appointment so that I could do things that would offend the Militia, but not have it traced to you. If I'm shot, you'll just wring your hands and complain about the admiral."

"He's not my enemy, Mr. Stewart.

"If he shoots me, you have justification for removing him, one that even the other Militia people will accept?"

Dashi just smiled.

Jake took a breath. "If you don't rescind the appointment, I'll publicly resign my commission, sir. I looked it up. I can do that. You might get a political victory out of this, but I'd still be dead."

Dashi smiled again. "I'll issue a proclamation."

"Jose said you were the most ruthless man," Jake said. He looked at Dashi. "Where is Jose, sir? He usually attends these briefings."

"Jose is at dinner with the lovely Ms. Marianne. They see a lot of each other."

"Because they are attracted to each other or for political reasons?" Jake asked.

"Would you like to discuss your relationship with Ms. Nadine, Mr. Stewart? Is it personal or political?"

"Personal. Political? On my side. Hers?" Jake thought hard. "You always confuse me, sir, but some things are becoming clear. Your power base is TGI, and the Free Traders support you because you have taken care of their issues. They cannot usurp you, even if they wanted, because you have legitimacy through the loyal Militia winning the coup. The admiral has gained much support, but even if he ignores the legitimacy of your office, he would have to face the Free Traders if he tried to take over. One of your main advisers, Jose, is dating the head of the Free Traders, and any attempt by him to seize power would be viewed by the Militia as the Free Traders taking over, preventing him from usurping your spot. And that's why you placed me and Ms. Nadine together—to put up the same duality. "

"You have achieved some notoriety yourself, Mr. Stewart. Some of the Militia are pleased with the way you handled that exile. The Free Traders admire your problem-solving skills. They find you down-to-earth and hard working. You are the hero of the hour. People would listen to you as well."

"Except I'm dating the admiral's daughter. Well, was

dating."

"Was?" Dashi asked.

"She shot me, sir."

"By your own admission, she shoots lots of people. She's shot you before. She'll get over it." Dashi grimaced and stretched his leg. "This is all very complicated, Mr. Stewart. Is it true?"

"I don't know, sir. I think so. Could a coalition of the Free Traders, the Militia, Jose's contacts with TGI, Nadine, and my ... friends, overthrow you?"

"Probably. But that won't happen," Dashi said.

"Why do you say that, sir?"

"You and Jose are already split apart. You are both competing for the future."

"Competing for what, sir?"

"Mr. Stewart, if it has not already come to your notice, I have no children. Nor will I. Too much radiation, I'm afraid. I will live many more years, but I will die without an heir. At least one of my body."

"Sir?" Jake said. "You have family. I met someone who said he was your cousin on 61 Cygni."

"You did? That wasn't in your report? Who was it?"

"Named Derbi, sir."

Dashi was silent for a moment and held out his hands. "On my mother's aunt's side, I think. More like a third cousin twice removed. Too distant to influence things."

"He said you grew up there, sir."

"I did. My earliest memories are of the ranch."

"How old are you, sir?"

"Much older than you would think. I have years ahead of me but not many."

"Was that really a secret base for the Empire? Was your father really an Imperial Duke?"

"Grandfather. And yes. Sent away because he was more interested in botany than politics. Something my father and I didn't share. In any event, if I die without issue, at that point, traditionally, the Imperial Council appoints an

Emperor, if the reigning one has not already adopted an heir."

"Appoints, sir?"

"You and Jose are both young men, Mr. Stewart. Think of that."

Jake's eyes widened. "Sir?"

"Who knows what the future holds, Mr. Stewart. Now to other business. I have a job for your Jump ship."

"Sir," Jake said. He looked at Dashi. "One final question. You have plans you're not sharing, but I will ask this. What could foil them?"

Dashi leaned back, then heaved himself to his feet with the help of his cane. He walked over to a viewport and looked out. "People who put themselves before the Empire. People without honor."

***

"The Emperor's rusty gonads," Admiral Edmunds said.

"Rusty, sir?" Major Shutt said.

"Rusty gonads. His hairy anus. Imperial nostril. Never mind." Edmunds threw himself in his chair. "He's always one step ahead of me. He's clever. I'll give Dashi that. Or I should say, I'll give the Emperor that," Edmunds said.

"Sir?"

"Never mind. Good job on that trip to 61 Cygni and bringing those parts back."

"I failed, sir," Shutt said. "I didn't take control."

"You tried. But the great Jake Stewart galactic luck took over. Or the Free Trader ramshackle running of things. Or cosmic rays. I don't know." He blew out a breath. "I do see now what my granddaughter sees in this Stewart fellow. There is more to him than meets the eyes."

"He seems so ... ordinary," Shutt said. "You think that you have things sorted out. Then he drops some sort of casual fact on your lap that messes everything up."

"It's a skill. It's his only skill," Edmunds said. "And I can't do anything to him. My own granddaughter would stab me if I did."

"Sir? That's horrible," Shutt said.

"Oh, she'd feel very bad about it afterward, but I'd still be stabbed. I don't want to be stabbed. She's just like her mother."

"Sir?"

"A story for another day," Edmunds said. "At least we're back in Militia HQ. This is quite an office."

"Didn't you occupy it before, sir?"

"Mine was on a different floor and not as elaborate as this. I will say, these Empire-rising people know how to make an office." Edmunds gestured. The room was huge, probably twenty meters a side. It rose a full two stories. The wooden desk was at least three meters wide and occupied a raised area on one side. Visitors would have to march across the floor and stand below the occupant when they arrived. The guest chairs were elaborately carved, rare wood from south continent. The sigil of Polaris occupied an entire wall. Display screens occupied a third wall. "Well, I don't need this much luxury for now. Major, can you set up your presentation? I'm going to the caf to get some food. I haven't eaten all day. I'll be back in ten minutes. We can continue, then."

Shutt saluted. "Sir."

Edmunds walked the twenty paces to the far door, muttering the whole time, and slammed it behind him as he left.

Shutt waited 'til he had left, then walked across the room and swung the office door open. She peeked into the outer office and saw it was empty. She turned, walked back to the desk, and stood in front of it for a moment. She stared at it, looked around, then scuttled back behind it and sat in the admiral's chair. She pulled it in tight to the desk and ran her hands on the carved armrests, then ran them along the smooth wood grain on the top of the desk.

She pushed herself clear, tipped her chair back, looked at the room, then focused on the Polaris design on the far wall. Polaris, the symbol of the Empire, the Imperial forces, and the Emperor. She tipped the chair back farther, put her legs up on the desk, stared at the symbol, and dreamed.

GET A FREE EBOOK

Thanks for reading. I hope you enjoyed it. Word-of-mouth reviews are critical to independent authors. Please consider leaving a review on Amazon or Goodreads or wherever you purchased this book.

If you'd like to be notified of future releases, please join my mailing list. I send a few updates a year, and if you subscribe you get a free ebook copy of Sigma Draconis IV, a short novella in the Jake Stewart universe. You can also follow me on Amazon, or follow me on BookBub.

Andrew Moriarty

ABOUT THE AUTHOR

Andrew Moriarty has been reading science fiction his whole life, and he always wondered about the stories he read. How did they ever pay the mortgage for that spaceship? Why doesn't it ever need to be refueled? What would happen if it broke, but the parts were backordered for weeks? And why doesn't anybody ever have to charge sales tax? Despairing on finding the answers to these questions, he decided to write a book about how spaceships would function in the real world. Ships need fuel, fuel costs money, and the accountants run everything.

He was born in Canada, and has lived in Toronto, Vancouver, Los Angeles, Germany, Park City, and Maastricht. Previously he worked as a telephone newspaper subscriptions salesman, a pizza delivery driver, a wedding disc jockey, and a technology trainer. Unfortunately, he also spent a great deal of time in the IT industry, designing networks and configuring routers and switches. Along the way, he picked up an ex-spy with a predilection for French Champagne, and a whippet with a murderous possessiveness for tennis balls. They live together in Brooklyn.

Please buy his books. Tennis balls are expensive.

BOOKS BY ANDREW MORIARTY

Adventures of a Jump Space Accountant

1.   Trans Galactic Insurance

2.   Orbital Claims Adjustor

3.   Third Moon Chemicals

4.   A Corporate Coup

5.   The Jump Ship.

Decline and Fall of the Galactic Empire

1.   Imperial Deserter

2.   Imperial Smuggler

Made in United States
Orlando, FL
29 May 2024

47302685R00257